Rita's Itch

Art Wiederhold

 www.trafford.com
North America & international
toll-free: 1 888 232 4444 (USA & Canada)
fax: 812 355 4082

Chapter One

Bart Tillman was a predator.

He hung out in the casino every Tuesday night looking for women he could easily seduce. They were usually younger, sexually promiscuous women that were more than willing to fuck him after a few drinks.

His athletic built, cobalt blue eyes and dark wavy hair, combined with his contagious smile and quick wit enabled him to get into the panties of just about every woman he went after.

On this particular night, he sat at a slot machine near the entrance to the casino and watched as the women walked past him. Most were the typical airheaded blondes.

Easy prey.

Tonight, he wanted something different. He was about to give up for the night when he spotted them. Two women who stood out. One was a pretty and sexy exotic with dark brown hair and hazel eyes and a great figure. The one with her was a drop-dead cute and sexy Asian with a nice, tight ass and killer legs. Both wore loose fitting shorts that showed their legs off and Bart got an erection just from watching them walk by.

"Damn!" he thought. "Now those two are hot!"

He watched as they walked to the middle of the casino and parted ways. The Asian went over to the penny slots and sat down at the Deal or No Deal machine. The other woman went to the other side to play the dollar machines.

"Her," he decided as he eyed the Asian.

Her friend had settled down at a machine about 100 feet away. He watched as she slid onto the chair and decided that she also had a very fine ass.

"Maybe later," he thought. "Tonight, I'll scale Mt. Everest."

He watched the Asian insert her card into the machine and hit the play button. He then ordered two mai tais. When the hostess brought them over, he tipped her and took the drinks from her tray. He walked over toward the Asian with the drinks in hand.

The Asian was Rita.

She was five feet two inches tall with jet black hair, a tan complexion and deep, dark eyes. She had, what most men considered to be, a perfect body. She was around 50 years old but looked half her age and she's been happily married to Art for over 20 years.

She'd been a virgin when she married Art and considered herself to be a loyal, faithful wife and she adored Art very much. She was the type of woman who would never cheat on her husband.

Her friend's name was Zoe. She was an Asian-Latina mix. She was the same age, height and weight as Rita and when then the two of them were together, they stopped traffic. They'd been best friends for 20 years and they went just about everywhere together. They met when Art brought Rita home from the Philippines after they got married. Their personalities meshed immediately and they became best friends.

Zoe had been married, but her husband left her for another woman, which shocked the Hell out of her. It also shocked Art and Rita. They couldn't even imagine why anyone would leave Zoe for any other woman. Art just figured that her ex-husband was crazy.

After Zoe's husband left her, she let herself run a little wild. She, too, had been a virgin when she got married and had no idea that her husband had been cheating on her for years. So, she reasoned, since he put his dick into a lot of different pussies, it was her turn to have a lot of different dicks go into her pussy.

And she did.

Tuesday was the girls' casino night. They each had their favorite machines, so they usually separated and met up again around 11 p.m. to go home. Sometimes, Zoe would let a man pick her up and they'd go somewhere to fuck. When she did, she often described her experiences to Rita who teased her by calling her a slut.

But in the back of her mind, she envied Zoe for being such a free spirit and sometimes wondered what it would be like to sleep with other men.

The two also liked to watch porno videos together while drinking wine. When they did, they made fun of the action on the screen and talked about different ways they'd tried sex with men. Zoe was more experienced, having been married and divorced. Since her divorce, she'd had sex with a few different men she'd met at the casino.

"I was a virgin when I got married and I stayed loyal to him for 15 years. Then he walked out on me. Since I love sex, I don't see any reason why I shouldn't sleep with other men. If I really like a guy and feel comfortable with him, I'll fuck him," she said. "I have a hungry pussy and it needs to be fed often."

Rita understood where she was coming from. After all, she was single now and she could have sex with whomever she wanted. What she didn't know was that Zoe had a huge crush on her husband, Art.

Art was well aware of her crush because Zoe had told him several times that if he wasn't married to Rita, she'd fuck his brains out.

"I just want you to know this, Art," she said. "I know you like me because I see the way you look at my legs. I know you'd like to get at what is between them and if I ever get the chance, I'm going to let you."

Rita was different. Her experiences were only with her husband. And that was just fine with her.

"Have you ever thought about having sex with another man?' Eva asked her. "I mean, even once, just to see what it would feel like?"

After some prodding, Rita admitted that she had, indeed, thought about it, especially after watching porn.

"I see those men with those great, big dicks and I wonder if they'd fit inside my pussy. The women in those movies always look like they love it, so I sometimes wonder what it would feel like to let another man fuck me," she said. "How does it feel?"

"It feels exciting. Each guy fucks a little different and each dick feels different. But I tell you this; the one dick I really want to feel inside my pussy is Art's! I'd give anything to fuck him but he's too crazy loyal to you, so I doubt that will ever happen," Zoe said.

Bart didn't know any of this. Even if he had, it wouldn't matter. He saw Rita as a super-sexy woman and he wanted to have sex with her.

He walked up and stood behind her.

"Hello," he said.

When she turned, he handed her a drink. She looked at it and squinted at him.

"Hello," she said.

"My name's Bart. What's yours?" he asked.

"That's none of your business," she replied.

"I brought you a drink. You can at least tell me your name," he said.

"I don't drink so you've wasted your time," she said.

"Really?" he asked.

"Really. Now go away," she said.

"At least taste the drink. It's a mai tai. You might like it," he suggested.

She sipped it and smiled.

"This is good," she said as he sat next to her.

"I'm glad you like it. What's your name?" he asked again.

"I'm not telling you," she said. "If I do, you'll stay here and bother me all night."

"I might do that anyway. I like you and I want to get to know you," he said.

"Forget it. I don't want to know you. Besides, I get bothered by men a lot and you're just another man," she said.

He smiled.

"But I'm different," he said.

"Yeah. Right. Look, I'm married. My husband is very jealous. If he finds out you're bothering me, he'll kill you. So if you value your life, be somewhere else," she said.

He laughed at the sci-fi reference.

"Is he here now?" he asked.

"No," she said.

"Then how would he find out? Are you going to tell him?" he asked.

"I won't if you leave me alone," she said.

"Okay. I'll leave you alone—this time," he said as he left.

She watched him go and sighed in relief.

"What a jerk! I thought he'd never leave!" she said as she returned to her machine.

Bart chuckled to himself.

He really didn't expect her to warm up to him immediately. He knew right from the start that she would be a challenge. That was fine with him. The harder he had to work to get into her panties, the more he wanted her.

And she was far too pretty to ignore.

He also liked her friend and decided he'd try to nail her, too. Even with eyeglasses, she was drop-dead gorgeous. He also liked the fact that neither woman wore makeup. That meant they were comfortable in their own skins.

"Perfect packages," he thought.

As Rita continued to play, she thought about her encounter with Bart. He wasn't the first man to hit on her and she figured he wouldn't be the last. She was just grateful that he gave up easily. The last guy hung around for at least an hour trying to convince her to have sex with him. He proved to be so annoying that she had the security guard escort him out of the casino. She was afraid he would try something.

Zoe also attracted a lot of male hopefuls, but they usually backed off when she lied and said she was married. A couple did try to talk her into having sex anyway, but she didn't like them so she firmly rebuffed them.

For every guy she fucked, there were at least five others she turned away. Most were okay with that and just left quietly. Some kept trying until she got up and left.

In fact, she and Rita often joked about their encounters, especially the rather odd one Rita had had a couple of week s earlier. This was with a woman who was determined to get into her panties.

It started when Rita went to get a cup of coffee. As she filled her cup, a pretty red haired woman walked up and smiled. Rita smiled back, finished filling her cup, and walked back to her slot machine. The woman followed and sat down next to her.

"You're very beautiful," the woman said.

"Thanks," Rita replied. She didn't usually get compliments from women and thought this was a bit strange.

"My name's Madison. What's yours?" the woman asked.

"Rita," she replied.

"You're the most beautiful woman I've ever met. Are you a Filipina?" Madison asked.

Rita nodded.

"Is it true what they say about woman from your country?" she asked.

"What do they say?" Rita asked.

"They say that Filipinas are really good at sex. Men call you little brown fucking machines. Are you one of them?" Madison asked.

Rita laughed.

"Why do you want to know?" she asked.

"Because I want to find out if it's true," Madison said as she put her hand on Rita's knee.

Rita stared at her.

"What?" she asked.

"I want to have sex with you," Madison replied. "I'm not usually this direct or pushy, but you really turn me on. The moment I saw you, I knew that I wanted to have sex with you. Lots of sex!"

"I'm not like that!" Rita said as she studied Madison.

She was around five foot four with a tight, athletic figure and long, smooth legs. Madison's direct approach was so unexpected that Rita wondered what it would be like to have sex with her.

"Really? Have you ever tried it?" Madison asked as she slid her hand along Rita's inner thigh.

For some reason, Rita's just sat still and let her touch her. Her touches were light and titillating and her heart started beating faster and faster. She made eye contact with Madison. They both smiled at each other.

"Have you?" Madison asked again.

"No," Rita said.

"Then how do you know you're not like that? Maybe if you tried it, you'd really like it," Madison said softly as she moved her hand along Rita's thigh and under the leg of her shorts.

Rita said nothing.

She almost felt hypnotized by Madison. As Madison's fingertips reached her panties, Rita parted her legs automatically. This was the first sexual contact she'd had with anyone other than her husband and she was excited beyond words.

"That's it, Rita. Relax and let me take you," Madison whispered. "Give yourself to me."

Madison was making her super horny now. She sat and looked into her eyes as Madison gently ran her fingertips over her pussy.

Madison was very pretty and oh-so sexy. Her hair was flaming red and she had the deepest green eyes. Rita looked down at her legs and wondered what they felt like.

Madison smiled at her and pushed two fingers into now soaked cunt. Rita moaned and trembled slightly as Madison gently "fucked" her. Madison was thrilled she'd gotten this far with her. She was even more thrilled when she realized that Rita had shaved her pussy. She moved her fingers in and out a faster and faster.

Rita quivered.

"That's it, Rita. Let yourself go," Madison whispered. "Your pussy feels so warm and soft. Do you like this, Rita? Do you like what I'm doing to you?"

Rita barely heard her as she was on the verge of coming. She opened her legs wider and nodded at Madison. She smiled and "fucked" her faster and faster.

Then she came.

Hard.

Her head fell back and she shook all over as Madison sent waves of intense pleasure surging through her body. At that point, she would have been willing to do anything Madison wanted. It was her first Lesbian experience and it was a good one.

She kept doing this for another few minutes. Rita came again and again.

"Do you like it?" Madison asked.

"Yes!" Rita gasped.

"Then come home with me. Let me make love to you," Madison said. "Let me take you places you've never been before."

Madison's short dress had crept up her thighs. She noticed that Rita was looking at them so she pulled her skirt up even more to reveal her red satin panties. Rita slid her hand along Madison's thigh and gently fondled her cunt. She could hardly believe that she was doing this.

Madison quivered.

"Let's do it, Rita. Let's go to my place and make love all night long. I'll do things to you that you'll absolutely love!" she said.

Rita was just about to give in when she heard Zoe call her name. She looked at Madison and shook her head. Madison smiled. Nodded and pulled her fingers out of Rita's cunt.

"Maybe next time?" she asked.

"Maybe," Rita said as she caught her breath.

Madison got up and left. Rita watched her behind wiggle and smiled. Then she told Zoe what happened.

"Ooh, I'm jealous!" Zoe joked.

"Why? You want to play with my pussy?' Rita asked.

Zoe simply smiled and said nothing. But in the car on the way home, she pressed Rita for more and more details and asked how it felt to be almost seduced by a woman.

"It was exciting," Rita admitted. "She made me come fast, too."

"Would you have gone with her if I didn't show up?" Zoe asked.

"I think so. She made me so horny that I wanted to go further with her," Rita admitted.

"Wow," Zoe said as she looked into Rita's eyes in a deep, dreamy sort of way, as if she were trying to imagine what it would be like to have sex with Rita.

Rita was accustomed to Zoe. Ever since they'd met. The two had grown closer and closer. They went everywhere together and were nearly inseparable. And both realized that they had a strong and growing physical attraction to each other.

But until now, neither had said anything. But Rita's description of what Madison had done had turned Zoe on beyond belief. Rita realized that she was staring at her crotch as if she were trying to see through her clothes.

Zoe looked into her eyes and smiled.

"You're really beautiful," she said.

Rita smiled.

"So are you," she replied.

They stopped at a light. Zoe leaned close and whispered.

"You're so very beautiful. That's why that woman was attracted to you. That's why she wanted to get into your panties."

Rita turned to look at her. Zoe was very close now. So close that Rita felt her warm breath on her face. She looked into Zoe's eyes and saw something in them she'd never seen before. She became lost in them.

"You're so very sexy, too," Zoe said softly.

She leaned closer and placed her lips on Rita's. The move surprised Rita. Zoe's lips were warm and soft. Erotic. Rita sat still and let her kiss her. The kiss made her heart race faster and faster. She felt Zoe's tongue push past her lips and opened her mouth to accept it.

She was stunned. She was French kissing her best friend and she loved it.

Their kiss was soft and passionate. It was a lover's kiss.

Rita felt her pussy grow warmer and warmer.

A driver in a car behind them hit his horn. They snapped out of it, laughed and Zoe hit the gas and headed home.

"Wow," Rita said softly. "Why did you do that?"

"I don't know," Zoe hedged. "We were so close that I felt like doing it. I've never kissed a woman before but I just had to kiss you."

"That felt nice," Rita said. "Real nice."

"Oh yes," Zoe agreed. "It made my pussy wet!"

Rita giggled.

"Mine, too!" she said

When they stopped in front of Rita's house, Zoe leaned over and kissed her again. Rita responded by sucking Zoe's tongue. The kiss had made her feel horny. So horny that she actually came a minute later. When she did, she almost sucked Zoe's tongue out of her mouth. Zoe realized that Rita was coming. She never expected such a reaction from her friend. In fact, she was as surprised as Rita that this was happening.

Rita was now trembling slightly. Gentle waves of pleasure were wafting through her entire body as they continued to kiss. She expected Zoe to do what Madison had done earlier but she never did.

Zoe kissed her even more passionately. Rita held her close as she came again as feelings she never felt before raced through her body. Seconds later, she felt Zoe quiver all over and realized that she, too, had come!

And just from a kiss!!

They slowly broke off the kiss. Rita sat back and caught her breath as she smiled at Zoe. Her pussy throbbed from her orgasm and she felt warm all over.

"My God!" they both said at once.

Then they giggled like love struck teenagers.

"You made me come!" they both said at once, and then they giggled more.

When they calmed down, they held each other tight and kissed again. After several passionate minutes, they came again. This time, it was even more powerful and neither of them had even touched the other's pussy!

"This is amazing!" Zoe said. "I come whenever we kiss. That's never happened before. Ever!"

"My pussy is still throbbing, Zoe! That was wonderful!" Rita said as she squeezed her hand. "Now what?"

"I don't know. I've never done anything like this before," Zoe said softly.

That had been two weeks ago.

The girls talked about it several times and they even French kissed to see if it would happen again. When it did, they realized their friendship had gone up several notches but both were still too chicken to go further.

Bart hadn't actually gone very far. He stood in the shadows and watched was Zoe walked over to Rita. He heard her call her name and smiled.

"Rita. It fits her," he smiled.

He watched as they left. He heard Rita laugh and grinned at the sound. Her laugh, he decided, was very cute. That made her even more attractive. In fact, everything about her fit her perfectly and made him want her more.

She was a challenge, too.

That intrigued him. Usually, he didn't run into challenges. Women normally gave in to him, married or not. But he knew that American woman were easy, especially if they'd had a few drinks. Rita wasn't an American woman. Her standards were different.

Higher.

"Yeah. She's a real challenge!" he said.

When Rita got home, she complained about some creep hitting on her at the casino again. Art listened and smiled.

"Anyone as beautiful and sexy as you are has to expect to get attention," he said. "Most men would find you irresistible---like I do. Just be firm about turning them down and you know how to handle anyone who gets too aggressive."

She smiled.

"Should I dress differently?" she asked.

"That's up to you. Dress comfortably but try not to show too much skin," he advised. "But even if you do, I'm sure men will still approach you. That's the curse of being so sexy."

She laughed.

She didn't tell him about Madison or what happened between her and Zoe. Hell, she wasn't sure what really happened or why and didn't know how to explain it. She did know that she wanted to be with Zoe again real soon.

Zoe was just as confused as Rita right now and was wondering about her sexuality. She did know that she was sexually attracted to Rita and Rita seemed to feel the same about her.

Neither woman was sure if they should pursue this in any way or, if they did, how far they should take it.

The following Tuesday, they went to casino again. Bart saw them walk in and smiled. He was hoping they'd show up again. He waited until Rita settled down at her usual slot machine and then ordered two drinks. When the hostess brought them over, he grabbed them and walked over to Rita.

She heard footsteps behind and glanced over her shoulder. She saw Bart standing behind her with two drinks and tried to ignore him.

"Hi. Remember me?" he asked as he sat down.

"No," she snapped.

"I talked with you last week. I brought you a mai tai," he reminded her.

"Oh, yes. I remember. I told you to go away. So go away," she said.

"Come on, Rita. At least let me talk to you a little while," he pled.

"How did you know my name?" she asked.

"I heard your friend call out to you last week. I like your name. It fits you very well," he said.

She laughed.

"I love your laugh, too," he said. "Mind if I sit here?"

"I'd like it better if you sat way over there so you can't bother me," she said as she pointed across the room.

He laughed.

"You're funny and cute. You're sexy, too. I love your eyes," he said.

"Er, thanks," she said.

He handed her a drink. She looked at it.

"It's a mai tai. You said you liked it last week," he explained.

"Thanks," she said as she sipped.

She started to relax a little. They spent the next half hour chatting idly. He was surprised when she told him how old she was and said she looked only half that. When he told her his age, she was surprised that he would even bother with someone like her. He laughed and replied that he thought she was only about 25 or 30 years old.

"Disappointed?" she asked.

"Not at all. Your husband must feel like he's the luckiest man alive," he said.

"He always says that I seem to be getting younger each year and that I'm more beautiful now than I was when we got married. I think he needs glasses or something," she joked, secretly pleased by Bart's compliments.

He noticed that her glass was empty and signaled to the hostess. She hustled over with another drink and he tipped her. He handed the drink to Rita.

They sat and talked for another hour. The more they talked, the more Rita felt comfortable with him. As the second drink took hold, she became chattier and giggled a lot. And her way of saying strange things made Bart laugh.

"I really like you, Rita," he said. "If you weren't married, I'd try to get you to have sex with me. I still might."

Rita giggled.

"And you wouldn't get anywhere at all," she said.

"Maybe not, but I might try anyway," he replied.

"Forget it Bart. Don't' even try it," she warned.

He smiled.

"Why are you smiling at me like that?" she asked.

"You called me Bart. At least now we're on a first name basis so we're no longer strangers. That's a start," he said.

She sipped her drink and looked straight at him. They made eye contact and she smiled. He smiled back.

"You're really cute when you smile," he said.

He noticed that her glass was empty and signaled to a hostess to bring two more. When she brought them over, he tossed a ten dollar bill on her tray.

"I thought the drinks are free," Rita said.

"They are. That was a tip," he said as he watched her sip.

"Why so much?" she asked.

"A good tip guarantees good service. I always tip big here. It's only money and it means more to them than it does to me," he said.

"Oh? So you're rich?" she joked.

"Let's just say that I'm comfortable. Why? You interested in money?" he replied.

"I just asked," she said.

"Since you did ask, I now know you like money. What would you say if I offered to pay you?" he said.

"For what?" she asked as she felt the booze start to take over.

"To have sex with me, of course," he replied.

She stared at him. Her stare made his blood turn cold and he realized he'd insulted her big time.

"I should slap your face off for saying that! I'm not a prostitute!" she said.

"I didn't say you were. That was just a fun question. I wasn't going to offer you money because I know you're a nice, decent woman who doesn't fool around on her husband. I'm sorry if I offended you," he said.

"Okay. Apology accepted," she said with a smile. "You're right. I don't fool around."

"You mean not yet," he teased.

She laughed.

"I mean never," she said.

"We'll see," he joked. "You're a real challenge, Rita. I like that. It makes me want you even more."

"You'll never get me, Bart. So give up," she said as she took another sip.

"I can't. You're the sexiest woman I've ever met. I'm going to keep trying. I'm very patient. When I really want something, I'll keep after it no matter how long it takes. And I really want you," he said.

She laughed.

She was a little drunk now and feeling very relaxed. She studied his features and liked what she saw. He was handsome and the fact that he was much younger than her and found her to be attractive sort of flattered her. She told herself that she'd never have sex with anyone but her husband but that tiny voice in her head kept saying to let Bart try.

"I'm too old for you anyway," she said.

"I don't think so," he said. "You look less than half your age and I know you're not too old for sex. Are you?"

"No. But only my husband can have me. No one else. Not even you," she replied.

She looked at her watch.

"I have to go home now," she said.

"Can I see you next week?" he asked.

"Maybe—unless you go blind or something," she joked.

She smiled as she looked for Zoe. Bart fascinated her a little. He was funny and honest and confident enough to tell her what he wanted up front. She sort of admired that because it reminded her of her husband, Art.

She saw Zoe standing at the coffee bar talking to a man. He said something to her. She laughed hysterically and shook her head. He shrugged and walked away. Rita walked over to her.

"Who was that?" she asked.

"Just some guy who wanted to get me into bed with him. He even offered to pay me, so I laughed at him. I think he got the message," she said.

"A lot of men come on to me. Most of them, like that guy, are real creeps. Some are nice, so I talk with them awhile. Sometimes, I tell them I'm married and they leave me alone. I've noticed that men bother you a lot, too," she added.

"Sometimes. They usually go away when they see I'm not interested or they know I'm married. Let's go home," Rita said.

"Okay. I've lost enough money for one week," Zoe said.

Bart watched them leave and smiled.

He had made a little bit more progress with Rita. She didn't rebuff him like she did the last week. He even got her to laugh.

"One step at a time," he thought.

On the way home, Zoe quizzed Rita about Bart. When Rita explained that nothing was going on, Zoe seemed to relax. She noticed that Zoe was acting more than a little bit curious and thought back to the kisses they'd exchanged.

"Does she want me for herself?" Rita thought as she looked at her.

Zoe turned and smiled at her. It was kind of dreamy smile, too.

When they reached the house, they looked at each other before Rita got out. Zoe's expression was soft and sweet. She leaned toward Rita and pressed her lips on hers. Rita kissed her back. The kiss grew more and more exciting. When their tongues met, Zoe held onto Rita tightly. Rita grew hornier and hornier as they kissed.

Her pussy was on fire now.

Moments later, she came. When she did, she sucked Zoe's tongue harder and trembled all over.

Then she heard Zoe moan and realized that she, too, hard orgasmed.

They sat back to regroup. Then they both laughed.

"That was incredible! You made me come again," Rita said. "You're the only one who can do that to me just by kissing me."

"My God. I came, too!" Zoe admitted.

They kissed again. This time, they did it softer. Rita felt her cunt tingling again and sucked Zoe's tongue harder. Zoe responded in kind. Both of them trembled as their passions rose and rose. Moments later, they both orgasmed again. They clung to each other as they kept kissing and coming a while longer. When they stopped, they were both exhausted.

"My God! That was wonderful!" Zoe said as she caught her breath.

Rita nodded.

She expected Zoe to tell her she loved her or something, but Zoe stayed quiet and looked as if she was miles away mentally. Rita decided to stay quiet, too.

They didn't say another word for a few seconds. Then they exchanged one short, soft kiss and Rita went into the house.

Rita wondered why Zoe always asked so many questions when she saw her talking with men. They weren't just casual questions. They wore more prying and sort of possessive sounding.

"Zoe is starting to act like she's jealous or something," she told Art. "She seems to get a little mad at me when I talk to anyone at the casino. I don't get it."

"I think I know the reason," Art said with a grin.

"Oh? What?" Rita asked.

"I think Zoe has a crush on you. She acts the way she does because she feels other people are a threat to her. She wants you all to herself," he said.

Rita laughed.

"Think about it, Rita. The two of you are nearly inseparable. You go everywhere together and she stays real close to you. She says she wants to keep you out of trouble but she really wants an exclusive relationship with you," he said.

"You think so?" Rita asked as she let this sink in.

"I know so. Zoe is in love with you. If you don't believe me, ask her," he said. "She probably wants to get into your panties, too."

Rita smiled.

"It's weird, but I kind of like the idea," she said.

He laughed.

She didn't tell him about their explosive kisses. She was almost dumbstruck by it all and was unsure of where to go next.

Art hit the nail right on the head.

Zoe did have a crush on Rita. A big one and she couldn't hide her jealousy when she saw her talking with anyone else. Although she admitted this to herself, she did her best to conceal it from Rita because she didn't know how she'd react.

She also realized that Art had figured this out.

A couple of weeks earlier, while she was in the living room waiting for Rita to dress for their night out, Art walked up to her.

"I know how you feel about Rita. I can see it when you look at her. If you take your time and play your cards right, you just might be able to get at that pussy you desire so much," he said.

She just stared at him. She had no idea she was that obvious.

"I would much rather fuck you," she said. "And if you play your cards right, you can have this—"

He watched as she undid her shorts and pulled them down along with her panties to reveal her soft, brown muff. Of course, he got an erection. Of course she watched the bulge in his jeans get bigger and bigger.

"I am yours whenever you want me," she whispered.

Before he could say anything, they heard Rita on the stairs. Zoe quickly pulled her shorts back up and smiled at him.

"I mean that," she assured him.

When Rita got down, Zoe smiled at her.

"Can I fuck your husband?" she asked.

"No!" Rita said with a laugh. "He's mine. Get your own husband!"

"Oh, well. I just thought I'd ask," Zoe said.

They all laughed but Art knew that Zoe was serious.

As they drove to the casino Rita questioned Zoe about her remarks.

"Did you mean that? Do you really want to have sex with Art?" she asked.

"Yes I do. I get horny whenever I'm around him. I always have," Zoe admitted.

"You can't have him. He's mine and I'm not letting him go," Rita said.

"I know. Besides, he'd never cheat on you. He adores you too much. But if you ever do anything to hurt him, look out!" Zoe said.

"I love him too much. I'd never cheat on him. Ever!" Rita said.

"Oh? You seem to be getting real cozy with that Bart guy," Zoe said.

"He's just someone I talk to. He knows he has no chance with me," Rita said.

"Really? Then why does he hang around you?" Zoe asked.

"We just talk. Really. There's nothing more to it," Rita protested.

"We'll see. Just in case, I'm gonna try to keep you out of trouble. I don't trust that guy and we both know what he wants from you so I'm going to make sure he never gets it," Zoe promised.

"So you're my guardian angel?" Rita joked.

"Something like that," Zoe smiled. "I don't want to see you get hurt and I sure as Hell don't want you to hurt Art."

"Why are you so worried about Art?" Rita asked.

"Guess!" Zoe said with a grin.

"Oh. Hands off. He's mine!" Rita smiled.

"I know," Zoe said.

They went back to the casino. Bart saw them enter and smiled. He watched as they said something to each other and laughed before going their separate ways. He signaled to the hostess for two drinks. When she brought them over, he tipped her and walked toward Rita.

Zoe was a few feet away when she turned to look back at Rita. She saw Bart approach her with two drinks. He handed her one and she smiled as he sat next to her. She saw them chat for a while and they both laughed. She couldn't hear what they said because she was several feet away, but they seemed to like each other.

A lot.

"She's taking a big chance with that guy," she thought. "I know his type. Oh, well. I did warn her, so she's on her own right now."

She shrugged and went off in search of her favorite slot machine.

Rita didn't feel annoyed with Bart any more. In fact, she kind of liked his company. He was bold, though. He was honest about his intentions and, for some reason, she kind of liked that. But all he did was sit with her and talk and joke. He'd never tried anything with her and he even seemed a little bit awed with her.

Bart got her a second mai tai. And a third.

She was feeling very tipsy and loose now. And very talkative. Bart listened as she prattled on about her family and switched gears in the conversation several times. When she was tipsy, he realized she rambled and said things that confused him and made him laugh.

"You know what I want," he said.

"Uh-huh. But you're never gonna get that. That's only for my husband," Rita said.

"Right now it is. What can I do to change your mind?" he asked.

"Nothing. I'm never gonna change my mind. You have no chance with me. So you might as well forget it," she said with a smile.

"I can't do that," he said.

"Yes you can," she said. "I'll talk with you but that's as far as I'll go."

"You mean right now?" he teased.

"I mean forever," she said. "I won't cheat on my husband."

"We'll see," he smiled.

"Why me?" she asked.

"Because you're the most beautiful and sexy woman I've ever met. I wanted you the moment I saw you and I'm determined to get you no matter how long that takes," he replied.

"Then you'll be waiting until Hell freezes over," she said. "I like your honesty, Bart. I think that's a big plus, but I'm not going to have sex with you."

He smiled.

"We'll see," he repeated.

He excused himself to go to the men's room. A few seconds later, a fairly drunk, middle-aged man stumbled over to Rita and offered her a drink. When she refused, he became pushy. She was just about to call the security guard over when Bart returned. He immediately sized up the situation and grabbed the man by the shoulder.

The man turned and glared at him.

"Can't you see I'm busy here?" he asked.

"Get busy somewhere else. She's with me," Bart said.

The man looked at him and realized he was in over his head. He shrugged and stumbled away. Bart sat down and Rita smiled at him.

"Thanks," she said. "He was a real asshole."

"Like I was last week?" Bart joked.

"No. You weren't really an asshole. I just didn't want to be bothered," she said. "I was gonna call security over to get rid of him but you came to my rescue."

"So I'm like a knight in shining armor?" he joked.

"Kind of," she smiled. "I don't see any armor, though."

"I don't wear armor but I do have a really big lance," he joked.

She let it sink in and laughed.

She was really starting to like him now. She realized there was more to him than she thought. And she liked the fact that he didn't try to bullshit her.

Zoe happened to walk past on the way to ladies room when she saw them chatting. She watched for few seconds and saw that they appeared to be friends. She also realized that Rita was drinking which was very unusual for her.

She wondered what was going on.

At that moment, the only thing going on was a light and funny conversation. The more time Bart spent with Rita, the more enchanted with her he became.

"When I first saw you, I just looked at you like a sexual conquest. Now that I'm getting to know you, I realize that there's something very special about you. I really enjoy sitting here and talking with you like this. Of course, the more time I spend with you, the more I want you," he said.

"That's nice, but you're still not getting anything," she said.

"That won't keep me from trying," he warned.

"I know," she said with a smile as she sipped her mai tai. "You can try all you want, but you're wasting your time."

"If I'm with you, it's not wasted," he said.

She laughed.

"Look, Rita. There are dozens of women here I could easily get into bed with me. But you're different. You're very special and that's why I want you," he said.

She was actually feeling flattered now.

"You'll never get me, Bart. But you can talk to me any time you like," she said. "I kind of like you now."

"You have no idea how happy it makes me to hear you say that," he beamed.

They kept talking for another hour and he made her laugh several times. She also made him laugh. At eleven, she looked at her watch.

"It's time to go now," she said. "Thanks again for rescuing me."

"My pleasure. Will you be here next week?" he asked.

"Maybe," she smiled.

"Then maybe I'll see you then," he said.

She smiled to herself.

"The harder to get I play, the more he wants me. He's very persistent. If I break down and eventually give myself to him, he'll treat me like gold," she thought. Then she laughed at what seemed to be an irrational thought.

She told herself that she'd never break down and sleep with another man, even someone as handsome and persistent as Bart. Still, she realized that she was warming up to him more than she should.

When Zoe and Rita left the casino, Zoe noticed that Rita was fairly drunk and giggly.

"Who was that guy you were talking to?" she asked.

"His name's Bart. He comes here a lot. We met last week. We talk while we play," Rita explained.

"Does he always get you drinks?" she asked.

"Sometimes. He always says he's going to get me drunk and take advantage of me. I think he's joking," Rita said.

"You better be careful. I don't think he's joking," Zoe said.

"You worry too much," Rita said with a giggle.

"Has he tried anything yet?" Zoe asked.

"Not yet. So far, he's only talked about it," Rita said.

"Do you want him to?" Zoe asked.

"I don't know. I'm not sure what I'd do if he did try something," Rita admitted.

She didn't tell her that her pussy got wet and hot when he was near her.

"I don't think you worry enough," Zoe replied.

When they got into the car, Zoe put her hands on Rita's shoulders and looked into her eyes. Rita smiled and they were soon locked into another, deep, long passionate kiss. This time, Zoe slid her hand down Rita's chest and gently caressed her breast through her t-shirt. Rita moaned and came. It was a good, sudden orgasm that made her shake all over.

Zoe was so thrilled that she had made Rita come that she came, too. They just kept French kissing and coming for what felt like forever. When they stopped, they both felt exhausted. Zoe smiled at Rita and caressed her thigh.

"You're so beautiful," she said as she ran her hand over her inner thigh.

"If you want me, I'm yours," Rita whispered as she parted her knees.

They kissed again. This time, it was softer and more like a lovers' kiss. Rita's cunt was still throbbing from her orgasm and she soon felt another one building. So did Zoe, so she sucked Rita's tongue more passionately as she caressed her thigh. Rita reached up and gently fondled Zoe's breast.

Zoe sucked her tongue harder and slid her hand along Rita's thigh and under her shorts. The moment Rita felt Zoe's fingers touch her panties, she came again. So did Zoe. They kept kissing until they came back to Earth a few minutes later.

"Oh my God!" Zoe sighed.

"Wow! That was awesome!" Rita agreed.

Her legs were still apart and Zoe's fingers were still touching her panties. Zoe smiled at her and moved her hand away. Rita sighed softly and leaned back.

"I'm all yours," she whispered, hoping that Zoe would take it further.

But Zoe chickened out. She'd never been attracted to a woman like she was attracted to Rita and wasn't sure what to do. She started the car and drove Rita back home. Just before Rita got out of the car, they kissed again. This time, it was short, gentle one.

Rita told Art what happened.

He laughed.

"Looks like you're about to become lovers," he said. "How does that make you feel?"

"Excited and curious and happy. Eva is very sexy and I've always felt attracted to her, too. But I think we're both kind of chicken right now to go further. I'm going to let Zoe make all of the moves. She might not do anything more, but I can hope," Rita said.

Art hugged her.

"Whatever you decide is okay with me," he assured her.

Chapter Two

Zoe's head was spinning. She realized that she was now very much in love with Rita and had been for years. It was also obvious now that Rita felt the same way about her and had been holding back for years. Both had been sexually attracted to each other from the moment they'd met but were too chicken to do anything about it.

Zoe decided to make sure that Rita knew exactly how she felt the very next time they were together.

The next afternoon, they had lunch in the Boathouse in the park. Afterwards, they decided to take a walk around the lake.

"You've been acting kind of crazy lately," Rita said.

"In what way?" Zoe asked.

"Well, when I'm with Bart you seem to get mad and you try to break things up. What's with that? Are you jealous or something?" Rita asked.

Zoe said nothing.

Rita stopped and looked her in the eyes.

"How do you really feel about me?" Rita asked.

"I love you, Rita," Zoe replied softly.

"As a friend? Or something more?" Rita asked.

"What are you asking me, Rita?" Zoe hedged.

"I'm not sure. You've told me that I'm pretty and sexy and you seem to act differently when someone else tries to get too close to me," Rita said.

"How do I act?" Zoe asked.

"Like you're jealous and possessive," Rita said.

Zoe sat quietly as she maintained eye contact with Rita. Her gaze was soft, almost romantic.

"I didn't realize I was acting that way. I'm sorry," Zoe said.

Rita smiled.

"That's okay. I was curious about why you act that way. That's why I asked how you really feel about me," she said.

"I love you, Rita," Zoe said. "I really love you."

"In what way?" Rita asked.

"In exactly the way you think I do. In fact, I've been steadily falling more and more in love with you. I'm not sure why because I've never had romantic feelings for any other woman. I'm not sure what to say or how to act or anything. I just want you to know that I love you," Zoe replied as she took hold of Rita's hand.

Rita smiled and held her hand as they continued walking. Zoe leaned closer. Rita felt nervous and excited. She and Zoe were about to venture into strange new territory and she wondered how far they should take it and where it might lead them.

"How do you feel about me?" Zoe asked.

"I think I love you, too. I know that what I feel for you is much stronger than just friendship. You know, this is crazy, don't you?" Rita said.

"I know. Now what?" Zoe asked.

"I don't know. I'm not sure. Do we start dating? Do we kiss? Do we make love?" Rita asked.

"I think we've been kind of dating for years, Rita. We go everywhere together and tell each other everything. See how we are now? This is a date and it's kind of romantic because we're holding hands now," Zoe said.

Rita giggled.

"You're right. But I love men. And I love having sex with my husband," she said.

"I love having sex with men, too. But with you, I feel really different. I feel warmer. I like being with you and I miss you when we're apart," Zoe replied.

"Wow. What about Art? How do you feel about him?" Rita asked.

"I think you already know," Zoe smiled.

When they got into the car, they kissed again. By then, Rita was moist between her thighs and she so much wanted to go further with Zoe. Zoe was still a bit unsure of herself so she held back. But as their kiss grew more passionate, Zoe stroked Rita's inner thigh.

Rita sucked her tongue harder as Zoe's hand crept under her shorts. As soon as Rita felt Zoe's fingertips dance over her pussy, she came. Her legs were wide apart now and she just about bit Zoe's tongue off when she stroked her trembling clit. She shook each time Zoe's fingertips moved across her clit. Each touch was almost magical and it sent shivers through Rita's body. She just kept kissing Zoe and coming and coming like never before.

Zoe was so excited that Rita was letting her touch her cunt that she came, too. Soon the car was filled with happy moans. Rita slid her hand under Zoe's T-shirt and fondled her nipple through her light bra.

"Yesss!" Zoe moaned as she came again.

She slid her fingers past Rita's soaked panties and ran them along her quivering labia. Rita shook all over and came again. Rita shook all over and let out a deep, happy moan as the orgasm rippled through her body. He knees were wide apart now and Zoe's fingertips were dancing on her trembling clit. She felt wetter than she'd ever felt before and sucked Zoe's tongue faster and harder. She pushed Zoe's bra upward and teased her nipple.

Zoe groaned.

Rita moved her hand down ward and unbuttoned Zoe's shorts. Zoe almost screamed as Rita slid her hand down into her panties to play with her clit. As soon as Rita touched Zoe's cunt for the first time, Rita came.

So did Zoe.

They kept kissing and playing with each other until they came again and again. They stopped a few moments later. Rita sighed deeply as her pussy throbbed. She looked into Zoe's eyes and smiled.

"I love you," she said softly as they kissed again

"I love you, too," Zoe whispered.

They stopped, smiled at each other and headed back home. They had taken their attraction up a notch and they realized there was no going back now. They kissed again when they reached the house. Zoe waved as Rita went inside. Her knees were still wobbly and she was flushed with excitement.

Art noticed she seemed lost in the clouds. More so than usual. He asked what was on her mind.

"It's Zoe," she said.

"What about her?" he asked.

"She told me that she loves me. You know, in a romantic way," Rita said.

"I figured that out a long time. I see the way she looks and acts around you. I could tell that she had deep, special feelings for you but was too chicken to let them out," he said.

"You knew?' Rita asked.

"Sure. It's so obvious that I'm surprised you didn't catch it," he said. "Are you gonna do anything about it now that you know?"

"I don't know. This never happened to me before. I'm not sure how to handle it. What should I do?" she asked.

"Follow your instincts and your heart. See where they lead. I imagine that Zoe feels just as nervous about it as you do right now," he advised.

She nodded.

"So you think she and I should become lovers?" she asked.

"That is entirely up to the both of you," he said with a smile.

Just before Zoe stepped into the shower later that day, she stopped to look at her reflection in the full length mirror on the bathroom door. Her pussy still throbbed nicely from her series of intense orgasms Rita had given her. She ran her fingers over her cunt and smiled.

"Yes, we are lovers now. We'll always be lovers," she said. "I am deeply in love with you Rita and I am going to make you mine forever."

Rita was lying on her bed staring up at the ceiling as similar thoughts raced through her mind. She had never before imagined that she'd fall in love with a woman or that she'd want to have sex with her. But she was head-over-heels crazy about Zoe and knew that she'd always felt this way.

She also kept thinking about Bart.

Maybe too much.

The only man she'd ever had sex with in her entire life was Art and she was curious how it would feel to have sex with other men. She also knew that once she slipped, Zoe would be all over Art and she was far too beautiful for him to resist.

And she sure as Hell didn't want to lose him to Zoe or anyone else!

But Zoe still wanted to have an affair with Art. In fact, she wanted it more than anything else on Earth and was making plans to get it to happen. She thought that Rita would probably end up fucking Bart sooner or later and once that happened, she was going after Art.

The next morning, Art got an unexpected call at work.

"Hi, Art," she said.

"Oh, hi, Zoe. What can I do for you?" he asked.

"Remember what I showed you the other day?" she asked.

"How could I forget!" he almost laughed.

"Well, I'm free for lunch today. Maybe we can meet somewhere and I'll let you see it again?" she suggested.

"And then what?" he asked.

"Then maybe I'll suck your dick and you can fuck me," she replied. "You can put your nice hard dick in my tight, hot pussy and fuck me as much as you want. How does that sound?"

"Are you joking?" he asked as he felt his dick get hard.

"No. I'm serious. I want to fuck you," she replied.

"I appreciate the offer, Zoe, but I'm married and I will never cheat on Rita with you or anyone else," he said. "Now, if circumstances ever change, I'll be more than happy to fuck the daylights out of you."

"Okay. Can we have lunch anyway?" she asked.

"Not today. I have to meet a client at noon. It might become an all-day thing," he said. "Maybe some other day?"

"How about tomorrow then?" she teased.

"I'm not sure. Call me," he suggested.

"Okay," she said in resignation.

She hung up and almost screamed.

Art was fiercely loyal to Rita. While she knew other men would jump at the chance to fuck her, he actually turned her down and he sounded annoyed with her for asking.

"And I even showed him my pussy! I can't believe he said 'no' to me!" she said as she looked at herself in the mirror. "No matter what or how long it takes, I'm going to fuck you, Art. And once I do, you'll never let me go!"

When Art got home, Rita greeted him with a big hug and kiss as always. He smiled and laughed.

"What's so funny?" she asked.

"I'd rather not say because you might get upset," he said as they sat down on the sofa.

"I promise I won't. The way you just laughed, I've got to know," she pressed.

"Are you sure?" he asked.

"Tell me! Tell me!" she said as she squeezed his arm.

"Alright. Just don't get ballistic on me," he said. "Zoe called me at work today."

"Oh? What did she want?" Rita asked.

"She tried to get me to go to lunch with her," he said. "But it was more than just lunch."

Rita looked at him. She knew what was coming.

"She said that after we had lunch, I could have her," he added. "Of course, I turned her down. You're the only woman in my life and I want to keep it that way and I told her that. I think she was shocked when I turned her down, too."

"Zoe really said that?" she asked.

"To be more precise, she said she wanted to fuck me," he said.

"So the other day, she really meant it when she asked me if she could fuck you?" Rita asked.

"Uh-huh. Now don't get pissed at her. You know how she can be at times. Just forget I said anything," he urged.

She nodded.

"I wish I could have seen her face when you told her no," she giggled.

"Me, too," he said.

They sat down at the kitchen table and Rita served the meal she'd cooked. Rita was an excellent cook and Art really loved it when she got busy in the kitchen on her days off. He looked at her and smiled. She smiled back.

"Oh, you remember Judy? You know your friend who works at the casino?" he asked.

"Uh-huh. What about her?" she asked.

"I ran into her at the downtown deli this afternoon. She said she was kind of worried about the company you've been keeping at the casino lately. She said you've been talking a lot with this guy named Bart and she said to tell you to be careful. He's some sort of Casanova and has quite a reputation down there," he said.

"Oh. I know all about Bart. We just talk while we play. That's all. He hasn't tried anything with me because I told him I was happily married and that you'd beat him to a pulp if you caught him," Rita said.

Art laughed.

"And he still talks to you?" he asked.

"Yes. We make each other laugh a lot," she said. "You don't need to worry about me."

"Okay. If he does try anything, get away from him fast," Art advised.

"I will," she promised.

She had forgotten about Judy. She worked as a cashier at the casino. She was middle aged and kind of plain looking, but she had a good personality. They'd met a few months ago. She had no idea that Judy knew about Bart or that she had been talking with him.

Rita and Zoe went to the casino again the following Tuesday. She had told Zoe about Judy. This made Zoe laugh.

"Now you know you have more than one person keeping an eye on you. So you'd better be good," she teased. "No hanky-panky or Art will hear about it. Even if I don't tell him, someone else might."

"I'll be okay," Rita smiled as she sort of looked around for Bart.

They parted ways as usual and she settled down at her machine. She'd been playing for almost 20 minutes before she saw Bart approaching with two drinks. She smiled as he said hello and handed her one. She said hello back and sipped.

"Miss me?" he asked.

"Sort of," she said. "You're late tonight."

"No I'm not. You got here earlier," he smiled as he sat down.

She smiled as he ogled her legs again.

"Are you showing your legs off for me?" he asked.

"No. But you can look if want," she replied.

"Can I do more than look?" he asked.

"Maybe," she smiled.

Rita had normally rebuffed men who tried to hit on her. Sometimes, she was quite rude about it when she did that and the men got the message and walked away. When she did it nicely, like just telling them that she was happily married, some of them men stayed to chat with her.

Bart fell into the second category.

He was younger. He was handsome and he had an infectious smile and a way of carrying himself that she found appealing. So when he decided to hang around, she really didn't mind.

It had now become a weekly thing with them. He always showed up and always brought her a mai tai and sat down next to her and they chatted for a fairly long time.

Bart was drawn to her more than he'd been drawn to any other woman before. She had a certain quality that attracted him. He loved her smile and laugh and she had that crazy Gracie Allen-like way of saying things that made him laugh. This made him even more determined to get into her panties which he decided to do no matter how long it took. He said she was a real challenge for him and he was up for it.

The fact that he had always stated his intentions at once intrigued and amused her. So she didn't mind when he hung around. In fact, each time they met, she minded it less and less.

Rita didn't normally drink, but when she said she like mai tais, he kept bringing them to her. He soon figured out that one drink made her feel more relaxed and chatty. A second one made her relax her guard and talk even more.

As she sipped the second mai tai, Bart told her how sexy she was and how she made his heart beat faster when they talked like this.

"I like those shorts. They really show off your sexy legs," he said.

"You think my legs are sexy?" she asked.

"Yes. And I bet what's between them is even sexier," he said.

Rita blushed and giggled. He sometimes said things like that and she was starting to like it. Bart smiled.

"I bet you have the sexiest pussy on Earth because you're the sexiest woman on Earth," he said.

"My husband thinks so, too," she said to remind him of her status.

He slid his chair closer and smiled as she sipped her drink.

"He's a very lucky man," he said.

"He says the same thing," she smiled.

"Do you have a lot of sex?" he asked.

"Boy. You're real nosy tonight!" she said.

"Do you?" he asked again.

"Of course we do," she said.

"Have you ever had sex with other men?" he asked.

"No. He's the only man I've ever had sex with or ever will have sex with," she said emphatically.

Bart smiled.

"Have you ever thought about it?" he asked.

"Sometimes when I watch bold movies. I wonder what it would be like to have sex with some of the men—especially if they're very handsome," she replied.

"What do you think about me?" he asked.

"I think you're funny, annoying and kind of good-looking," she said.

"How about sexy?" he asked with a grin.

She laughed.

"Uh, maybe," she said as he put his hand on her knee.

She was surprised he did that and even more surprised that she was letting him do it.

"How sexy?" he asked.

She giggled.

"I'm not sure. Just kind of sexy," she said as she felt his hand creep up her thigh.

Her knees were close together so he couldn't get very far.

"Am I sexy enough to have sex with?" he asked.

"No!" she laughed.

"Not even a little bit?" he pressed.

He gently stroked her leg as they talked. She kept her legs closed but didn't push him away. She was a little bit drunk now and sort of horny.

"Well, maybe a little bit," she teased.

"At least that's a start," he said.

She knew what he wanted and knew he would keep after her. Most of her mind told her to get rid of him before she did something she'd be sorry for. But a small part of her felt attracted to him. She was also feeling the effects of the mai tais she'd ingested and her filters weren't functioning at full strength. She was kind of horny, too.

Bart slid his hand along her inner thigh. Rita smiled and parted her legs as she watched his bulge grow larger and larger. She glanced around and saw that there was no one else around. Bart stroked her crotch then eased his fingers under her shorts. Rita quivered as he touched her through her panties.

Bart leaned very close and kissed her. To his delight, she kissed him back. As their tongues merged, he slid two fingers into her very wet slit. She just about bit his tongue when he found her g-spot and gently rubbed it.

She glanced at his bulge and ran her fingers over it. She felt it "dance" as it got even harder. She was nearly blind with lust now and quivered as his fingers teased her g-spot. She was incredibly wet, too.

She squeezed his bulge several times. Bart sighed, delighted that they were going this far.

"Let's make love, Rita. Come upstairs with me," he urged.

Instead of answering, she stuck her tongue into his mouth again. Bart frigged her faster and she squirmed and came. She reached down and unzipped his pants. She slid her hand into the opening and grabbed his dick

She looked around to make sure no one was watching then pulled it out. It was much longer than she imagined and she was amazed that she was actually touching him like this. She slowly jerked him off as they kissed again.

Bart quivered as her hand moved up and down. Rita varied the pressure as she pumped him. At the same time, he still had his fingers buried in her cunt. They jerked each other off nice and easy. Then Rita came again.

She trembled all over as she climaxed.

"Oooh yes!" she moaned as he kept working her cunt. "Yes!"

She pumped his dick faster and faster. Then Bart came. He shot his first load all over her shirt and shorts. She watched as it jetted out of his knob and splattered her. She gripped him tighter and massaged his knob with her thumb. Bart moaned and shot another line of cum onto her shorts. She ran her fingers through his cum and lubricated his shaft then jerked him off faster and faster. He shot line after line of thick, white goo all over her.

She never imagined anyone could come so much and she was fascinated with the way it shot out of his prick with almost every pump of her hand. Eventually, it slowed to a dribble and ran down over her fingers.

When he went flaccid, she stopped. She sat back and smiled at him then looked at the cum all over her fingers. She was almost in shock that they had gone so far, but glad they had. She looked down at his dick. Even flaccid, it still looked big.

"I guess we're friends now, huh?" he said.

She laughed.

"Yes," she replied.

"That was great!" they both said at once.

They kissed again. It was a nice, soft kiss, too.

"I think I'm falling I love with you, Rita," Bart whispered. "I feel things for you that I've never felt for anyone else and I don't know what to do."

She smiled.

She was starting to feel deeply about him, too, but didn't say anything. She realized that Bart didn't just want to fuck her. He wanted to make love to her. This kind of excited and scared her at the same time. He handed her a handkerchief and watched as she wiped his cum from her fingers and clothes.

Since his dick was still sticking out, she reached over and played with his knob. He sighed as she rolled his foreskin back and forth several times. She felt it getting harder and jerked him off.

"You bounce back fast. I like that," she said.

"You like playing with me, don't you?" he asked as he slid his hand under her shorts again. She parted her legs and smiled as he fingered her cunt.

"Yes I do," she said as she jerked him faster and faster.

"I can't believe this is happening," he said as he played with g-spot.

"Me neither," she said as she kept her eyes on his glistening knob.

She felt him spasm and smiled as cum ran out of his slit and down his shaft. Bart was shaking now and he leaned over and kissed her. He frigged her faster and faster. She moaned into his mouth and came.

This time, it was a good, long and deep orgasm. She kept pumping him until he went totally limp and his dick slipped from her sticky fingers.

She looked at the white goo then smiled at him and wiped it off with the hanky. He laughed.

Again, Bart tried to talk her into going up to his suite. Again, she refused but this time, she left the door open for future possibilities.

To her relief, Bart didn't press the matter.

"I'll see you again next week," he said as he kissed her.

She sighed when he walked away. When she found Zoe, she was obviously pissed off.

"What's wrong?" she asked.

"Some strange guy just tried to feel me up, so I slapped him as hard as I could. What a creep! He didn't even bother to talk to me first. He just walked up and groped me!" Zoe said.

"That's really rude," Rita agreed. "No wonder you slapped him."

"He really asked for it, too," Zoe said. "Hey, I didn't see your friend tonight."

"He was here. He left a few minutes ago," Rita said. "We talked and had a couple of drinks. So I'm kind of drunk now."

"You're not kind of drunk, you're drunk. I'd better get you home before you pass out or something," Zoe said.

When they got into the car, the still-horny Rita stuck her tongue into Zoe's mouth. Zoe immediately sucked it as her heart raced out of control. Their kiss grew hotter and hotter and Rita began to moan softly as she felt herself about to come. Zoe reached up and fondled her breast. Rita kissed her harder and began to shake. She reached down and stroked Zoe's thigh. Now Zoe quivered. She slid her hand under Rita's T-shirt and squeezed her breast.

That's when Rita moaned loudly and came. Somehow, Rita's hand found its way under Zoe's shorts to her panties. As soon as she felt Rita's fingers dance along her slit, Zoe came. They kept kissing and touching each other for a little while longer. Before it was over, Rita's middle finger had found its way into Zoe's pussy and Zoe's was gently sucking Rita's right nipple.

They stopped after they both came again. Rita looked at Zoe and smiled then quickly fell asleep. Zoe laughed and took her home.

When they got back to Rita's house, Zoe helped her inside. Art laughed at her condition and the way she was talking. She sat down on the sofa and promptly fell asleep.

"She's been drinking at the casino lot lately," Art observed.

"It's that Bart guy. He's always giving her mai tais. I think she had two or three tonight," Zoe said.

"That's not good. Rita gets horny when she drinks," he said.

"I think Bart knows that by now. She better be more careful with him," Zoe said.

"Is he good-looking?" Art asked.

"Very," Zoe said.

"Would you fuck him?" he asked.

"Sure. But I'd much rather fuck you," Zoe said as she tried to kiss him.

Art blocked her and smiled.

"You're playing hard to get with me," she smiled. "That just makes me want you more."

"You need to stop this, Zoe, and find yourself another husband. I'm taken and I intend to stay taken,' he said.

"Don't you think I'm pretty?" she asked.

"I think you're gorgeous, really," he said. "I'm married. I don't want to have an affair with you or anyone else. Understand?"

"You're serious?" she asked as she started to undo her belt.

"I'm very serious," he said.

"You're going to pass this up?" she asked as she dropped her shorts and pulled her panties down to show off her muff.

He stared at her as his dick grew harder and harder. She smiled at his bulge.

"I know you want me, Art. I want you, too," she said as she stepped closer.

Before he could react, she massaged his bulge. He looked into her eyes as she played with him. She reached down with her other hand and pried open her cuntlips. He stared at the hot pink interior and her swollen clit while she played with him.

"I'm all yours, Art. You can have me any time you want and as many times as you want," she said softly.

"I can't, Zoe. I won't betray Rita for you or any woman on Earth," he said as he stepped away.

She smiled and pulled up her pants.

"We shall see about that," she said.

Rita stirred. They watched as she opened her eyes, yawned and stretched. She smiled at them.

"Did I miss anything?" she asked.

"No," Art said.

"But I did," Zoe remarked as she left.

Rita laughed.

"I saw what she just did. I'm very surprised and very happy that you turned her down. She's not going to give up, you know," she said.

"I'm not going to give in," he assured her. "The only woman I need in my life is you."

"And you're the only man I need in my life," she said.

"What about Bart?" he teased. "Are you thinking about having sex with him?"

She smiled and said nothing.

"You are, aren't you?" he asked.

"Um, maybe," she replied. "Are you thinking about having sex with Zoe?"

"Maybe," he said after a pause.

Then they laughed.

That week, Zoe went out of town for a vacation. She had tried to get Rita to go with her, But Rita said she had some other things to do.

As usual, she went to the YMCA to work out. The usual crowd of middle aged people were there doing their best to beat Father Time. As she worked out on the treadmill, she noticed a rather handsome young man on the treadmill just behind her. She smiled and nodded at him. He did the same. As she exercised, she realized that he was ogling her legs and behind.

Secretly flattered by his attention, she stepped up her workout. He kept watching her the entire time. When she moved to the stationary bikes, he did, too. She smiled and leaned forward to give him a better view of her ass as she pedaled. His eyes stayed glued to her the entire time.

When she got off the bike 20 minutes later and headed for the Stair Masters, she glanced back and saw that he had a very obvious erection. She figured he was about half her age and the fact that she had aroused him like that turned her on, too.

Again, he followed her. Again he used the machine directly behind her so he could look at her legs and ass while she worked out. Again, she did it in such a way that she showed off all of her curves. After a while, her pussy grew warm and moist.

"My God! He's making me horny!" she thought.

She leaned forward and pedaled faster. This caused her shorts to ride up her ass a bit. The men behind her caught sight of her bikini panties and just about came all over himself. She heard him say "What an ass!" under his breath and smiled.

She reached behind her as if to adjust her shorts and "accidentally" let him see her entire crack for a few seconds.

"Wow!" he said.

She smiled to herself and kept working out. When she looked behind her, he was gone. She laughed. She left about an hour later.

Two days later, she went to the Y again. She didn't see him at first. About 16 minutes into her workout, she saw him enter the room. He looked around, spotted her and took his place on the machine directly behind her again.

She repeated what she did the last time. So did he.

And she secretly watched the bulge in his shorts get bigger and bigger. After her workout, she made it a point to pass close by him. As she did, she glanced down at what appeared to be a massive erection in the front of his shorts.

She made eye contact with him and smiled.

"Hi!" she said.

He blushed.

"Uh, hello," he replied a little nervously. "Uh, sorry about this! I can't help it."

"That's okay. I don't mind," she said.

Rita chuckled to herself as she walked out of the gym and headed to her car.

Just before she got inside, another man approached her. She recognized him as one of the patrons. His name was Greg.

They exchanged greetings.

"That young guy who follows you around isn't the only one who gets hard watching you work out," Greg joked. "I think just about every man who sees you gets an erection. You're the prettiest and sexiest woman who comes here and just about all of us would love to get into your panties." She laughed.

"So you get an erection, too?" she joked back.

"I sure as Hell do, Rita. Whenever I see you in those shorts, I get hard as a rock," Greg said.

"Oh? Do you have one now?" she teased.

"Yes I do," he replied as he made the bulge in his shorts dance. "See?"

She giggled and blushed.

"It looks big!" she said as she watched it move.

"It is pretty big. I think it's about nine inches," he said softly as he took a step closer.

She just kept watching it dance as she realized Greg was coming on to her. She smiled at him.

Greg was a couple of years younger than she was and very handsome and she secretly liked the attention. It was then she realized that she had subconsciously been doing several things to attract the attentions of other men just to see their reactions. Now, she had gotten Greg's attention—big time!

"Nine inches?" she asked as he made it dance more and more.

"Around you, I think it gets longer and harder," he said.

The front of his shorts stood straight out by several inches and what was beneath them looked rock hard. She felt her pussy grow moist.

He leaned closer and lowered his voice. She felt his warm breath on her cheek but didn't back away.

"I think you're the sexiest woman I've ever seen and when I see you in those tiny shorts, I almost have an orgasm," he said. "You make me horny, Rita. Very horny."

They were standing very close to each other now. She kept her eyes on his bulge as he made it dance more and more. Right now, she was horny, too.

"You do know that I'm married, right?" she asked.

He stepped closer.

"Are you trying to seduce me?" she smiled.

"You bet I am, Rita," he said as he gently ran his fingers over her crotch.

This caught her by surprise. But she didn't back away. She just smiled at him and let him fondle her pussy as she grew hotter and hotter. She reached down and felt his bulge. Greg smiled and moved closer.

"I know you're married but I'm not ashamed to say that you gave me a huge hard-on. In fact, I think I've never been harder in my entire life and I'd love to put my good, hard dick inside your pussy," he whispered.

She almost blushed at his bluntness but maintained eye contact. Before she realized it, they were kissing and Greg was still rubbing her pussy and she wanted him to go even further. She was leaning against the side of her car now and Greg's bulge was gently pressing right against her cunt. She felt her hear beat faster and faster as they made eye contact. Greg made his prick dance again. This time, it danced against her crotch. Since she was already hot and wet, she just stood with her legs slightly parted and trembled at the erotic contact.

She glanced around and was glad that the parking lot was empty. Greg pressed his prick against her cunt and started humping her nice and easy. She opened her legs wider and quivered as his prick massaged her pussy.

This was the closest she'd ever come to fucking another man. His prick felt rock hard and oh-so wickedly delicious as it rubbed against her clit. He leaned forward and put his hands on the roof of the car. She put her hands on his hips and quivered as he humped her faster and faster. She soon moved with him. Greg sighed as they "fucked". She dug her fingers into his body and fucked him back as her pussy took control.

"Yes!" she moaned.

He grunted and humped her harder. Each time his prick moved across her swollen clit, she moaned and fucked him back. Her legs were wide apart now and her cunt throbbed deliciously. They moved faster and faster. She gripped him tighter and shook all over.

"My God!" she shouted as she came.

She fucked him as hard as she could as another orgasm rippled through her. Greg had her now. She expected him to pull out his huge dick and slide it into her pussy. But before she could totally lose her self-control, they saw another car pull into the lot and stopped.

"That's my wife," he said as they watched her park. "She's here to pick me up."

He stepped back and ran his fingers over her cunt.

"Maybe next time?" he asked.

She nodded and laughed as she got into the car. She realized that if Greg's wife hadn't shown up, they have fucked for real and his big, hard dick would have been inside her hungry pussy and they would have fucked like mad.

"It still might be," she smiled/

When she got home, Art was working on the kitchen sink. She walked over and smiled. He stopped working.

"I know that look," he said. "You're horny. Really horny. What got you started today?"

She laughed.

"You know me too well," she said.

She told him about her encounter with Greg. He listened and laughed as his dick grew hard. She noticed the bulge and squeezed it.

"So the idea of me almost fucking another man turns you on?" she teased.

"For some reason, yes," he said. "Would you really have fucked him if his wife hadn't shown up?"

"Maybe," she said. "I've never fucked any man but you and I was tempted to see how his dick would feel inside my pussy. That sort of worries me, too. I haven't had such thoughts until lately."

He smiled.

"It sounds like you've gotten the itch. Lots of people get it. Most of them get over it. Some of them end up cheating for a while or joining swingers clubs. The trick is to not let it ruin your marriage," he said.

"The itch is getting stronger. What if I decide to scratch it?" she asked.

"There's nothing much I can do about it if you do. Just remember who you're married to and who really loves you more than anything else on Earth. If you can do that, we'll get through this," he said.

"Do you have the itch?" she asked.

"Sort of," he said honestly.

"Are you going to scratch it?" she asked.

"Only if you scratch yours, too," he admitted. "As long as you let me know what's going on, you won't be cheating. I'll do the same for you."

She took his hand and they went up to the bedroom…

Zoe called the following afternoon and they chatted for nearly an hour. Zoe said she was bored so she decided to cut her trip short.

"I'll be home later tonight. To be honest, I miss you too much and I keep wishing that we were together," she said.

"I miss you, too," Rita replied. "I can hardly wait to see you again."

The next morning, Rita and Zoe met for breakfast at the local café. By now, the locals were accustomed to seeing them walk in holding hands.

As soon as they met outside the door, they kissed. They kissed again after they sat down at their usual table. It was now quite natural for them to kiss passionately when they were together. The café had several customers at the time and most of them watched in amusement. They were seated at booth next to a window. The waitress winked at them as she handed them menus.

They both smiled at her. They didn't bother to conceal their love for each other.

"I always see the two of you together and I always teased you about being lovers. I guess my jokes were pretty accurate," she said.

"I think we fell in love with each other at first sight but we were too chicken to do anything," Zoe said. "Now, we know what we want."

"So I see," the waitress said as she took their orders.

As they ate, Rita told Zoe about her almost fuck with Greg and Art's reaction when she told him.

Zoe laughed.

"Wow, Rita! Would you have really fucked him?" she asked.

"I think so. When he made me come, all I could think about was having him put that huge dick in my pussy. I guess I got saved by the bell," Rita said as she gripped her hand.

"I love being with you," Zoe said. "I think I love you more than I've ever loved any man."

"How many different guys have you fucked since you got divorced?" Rita asked.

"Beats me. I've never counted. Maybe about 20 or 30," Zoe said. "I love sex and I love to feel a nice hard dick moving inside my pussy."

"I didn't know it was that many!" Rita said.

"My pussy is made for fucking---just like yours. So after nearly 20 years of fucking one man, I decided to let myself run wild. It's a lot of fun to try different men. They all like to do different things and that makes it exciting. You should try it," Zoe said.

She smiled at Rita as she stroked her thigh under the table.

"But I never expected that I'd fall in love with you," she said.

After breakfast, they walked hand-in-hand through a nearby park. Since it was still early, the park was deserted. They walked until they found a shaded area beneath an old stone foot bridge and kissed again. This time, they allowed their passions to soar. Within moments, both had their hands down the front of each other's pants and they fingered each other to a powerful climax.

And another.

Rita started fucking Zoe's finger as they kept kissing. At the same time, she was moving her middle finger in and out of Zoe's slit as fast as she could. Waves of pleasure rippled through them and Rita began to feel ecstatic.

She "fucked" Zoe faster and faster. Zoe cried out and shook all over as she came again. This time, she had trouble standing and gripped Rita's shoulders to keep from falling.

"I love you, Rita!" she almost screamed.

They held each other close as they came back to Earth. They kissed again and walked back to the car. It was nearly 8:30 and both of them had to go to work at nine.

Later that morning, Zoe phoned Art at work.

"Did Rita tell you what's happening between us?" she asked.

"Yes. But I already knew that the two of you were in love with each other. You've been acting like teenagers out on a date for years. If it makes you feel better, I don't mind it at all," he said.

She giggled.

"We are that obvious?" she asked.

"You sure are. So if the two of you want to make love, I say go for it. You make a good couple," he said.

"I'm glad you're not upset. You know that I still want to have sex with you, right?" she asked.

"I'm thinking about it," he said. "I really liked what I saw the last time. I have to admit that I've always been attracted to you. Rita's told me that she's gotten the itch, so if she decides to scratch it, you and I are on—big time."

"Good. I think Rita will scratch her itch very soon, too," Zoe said.

"I expect her to," he said.

Rita went to the YMCA after work to do her usual workout. Neither Greg or her other obvious admirer were around, so she got through her routine in peace. As she worked out, she thought about Zoe. The more she thought about her, the hornier she became.

She was on the stationary bike pedaling at a nice, easy rate and thinking about Zoe's pussy. Without realizing it, she slid her hand down into her shorts and started to masturbate. At first, she just flicked her fingertips over her swollen clit. This made her hornier and wetter. Before long, she was moving her middle finger in and out of her cunt. She shut her eyes and emitted a deep, soft moan as she pedaled.

This caught the attention of a tall, dark haired middle aged man who was on the bike next to hers. He watched her hand moving in her shorts and got harder and harder. He was so hard that he had trouble pedaling and he felt like his prick was about to explode.

Rita began breathing harder. Still oblivious to the man next to her, she did herself faster and faster.

"Damn!" she heard him say.

She glanced to the side, saw him watching, and winked at him. Then she closed her eyes and kept at it until she brought herself to a nice, easy orgasm. Since they were the only ones in the room at the time, she allowed herself to moan loudly as she shook all over. She kept "fucking" herself with her finger until she came again. She took her hand out of her shorts and stayed on the bike until it subsided then dismounted.

As she walked past him, she smiled to let him know she didn't mind that he'd watched her. She was still hot and sweaty but not from exercise. He dismounted and followed her to the juice bar and offered to pay for her drink. She accepted and introduced herself.

"Hi, Rita. My name's Joe," he said as they shook hands. "If you don't mind my saying so, that was some nice show you put on."

She laughed.

"I didn't know anyone was there, but when I saw you, I was too far along to stop," she said. "Once I knew you were there and watching like that, I got even hornier and I just had to come. I'm glad you liked the show!"

"I sure as Hell did!" he said as he let her see the still obvious erection he had. "I haven't been this damned hard in years!"

She looked at his bulge and wondered just how hard and big his dick was. She even thought about letting him fuck her. They sat down at a table and chatted for a while to get to know each other better. Joe learned she was married and he told her he was, too. He also told her that he'd never seen anyone as pretty or as sexy as she was.

"I think you're handsome, too," she said

"You ever think about fucking other men?" he asked.

"Sometimes," she admitted as he slid his chair closer.

She glanced down at his bulge and smiled when he made it "dance". To her surprise, it seemed to get even bigger. The sight made her pussy throb.

"You seem to like looking at my dick," he pointed out.

"It's so big," she whispered as she watched it dance.

"Want to do more than just look?" he half teased.

"Maybe," she smiled. "What do you have in mind?"

"All sorts of things," he said as he slid his hand along her inner thigh. "your legs are so incredibly sexy. Can I touch what's between them?"

She nodded and parted her legs. He gently stroked her thigh. The sensations made her pussy wet. She reached over and ran her fingertips along his dick, then squeezed the knob. Joe caught her signals and slid his hand under her shorts. He almost came when he realized she wasn't wearing panties and his fingers danced over her warm, bare flesh.

"You shave your pussy?" he asked.

"My husband does. He just did it last night," she said as she squeezed his knob.

She shivered slightly as he eased two fingers into her warm, moist slit and moved them in and out. She opened her legs further and sighed as he "fucked" her nice and easy. When he located her g-spot, she just about jumped off the chair.

"Oooh, yes!" she sighed as wonderful waves of pleasure rippled through her entire body.

She reached into his shorts and wrapped her fingers around what appeared to be a very long, hard dick. She was surprised she had actually done that, too. It was just the second prick she'd ever touched. She squeezed it, then gave it several slow, easy pulls.

Joe was amazed.

He had never expected to get this far with Rita, since they'd just met. He slid his fingers into her pussy even deeper and moved them around. When he touched her g-spot again, she shook all over and pumped him a little faster as she actually thought about fucking him. The fact that she was doing anything like this with a man she'd just met a few minutes ago, made her heart race. She was letting her libido take over and she at once liked and feared what was about to happen next.

"Oh Lord!" Joe moaned as she squeezed his dick harder.

He rubbed her g-spot faster and faster. She trembled and came—hard. She came so hard that she had trouble jerking him off. Her pulls were erratic and Joe also began to shake with each pump of her hand.

Rita came again and almost cried out. She pumped him as fast as she could now. That's when Joe erupted and fired a huge spurt of cum upward. It struck the underside of the table and splattered downward. She pumped him harder and he fired another stream of cum and another and another.

Since her fingers were around his knob, they became coated with cum. It ran over her fingers and the back of her hand. Each pump of her hand made him cum again and again. It ran down his knob and over her fingers until his dick and her fingers were sticky with it.

He stifled a moan as she jerked him faster and faster. He moved his fingers in and out her cunt until she came again, too.

They stopped and laughed.

She looked down at the dick in her hand and gave him a few more easy jerks. Then she swirled her fingertips all over his knob. Joe smiled at her but didn't get hard again. She had managed to drain him.

"I guess this means that you fool around?" he asked.

"Not yet, but I'm thinking about it," she admitted. "And you caught me at a time when I was really horny."

"I'd really love to fuck you, Rita, but you drained me. Maybe next time?" he asked.

"We'll see," she smiled as she raked her fingers over his flaccid prick, which seemed to still be quite big. She played with his foreskin for a little while to see if he'd get hard again. When he didn't she shook her head and smiled at him.

"Can I see your pussy?" he asked.

"Okay," she said.

She stood and pulled aside the crotch of her shorts to show him her cunt. He leaned over and slowly ran his tongue along her slit and flicked it over her clit several times. She quivered and stroked his hair. Joe slid his tongue into her slit and licked away. She shook harder and fucked his tongue as she came again.

He smiled at her.

"You taste as good as you look," he said.

"Next time," she said.

"You can count on that!" he said as he walked her to her car.

Just before she got in, she turned and slid her hand down into his shorts again. He closed his eyes and sighed as she played with his prick. He leaned into her and fingered her cunt. Before she realized it, he had his tongue in her mouth and they were locked into a deep, passionate kiss.

Moments later, she came again. This time, she nearly bit his tongue off.

Although she kept playing with him, she simply couldn't make him hard again. She pulled his dick out, looked at the glistening knob and swirled her tongue all over it. Joe moaned as she proceeded to suck it. The more she sucked it, the more she liked the taste. But she simply could not get him hard again. She sucked him and jerked him off at the same time. In the back of her mind, she could hardly believe she was actually sucking his dick like some sort of common whore. The idea also excited her to no end and she kept at it.

Joe moaned,

Rita squeezed and massaged his balls. Joe moaned louder and emitted a gasp. To her surprise, he came. She felt his prick jerk a few times and a thick, warm liquid oozed out of his knob and coated her tongue. She licked up every drop of it and kept sucking until he almost begged her to stop.

She wiped her lips with the back of her hand and smiled at him. She studied the dark, pink knob in front of her and gave it a few easy pumps.

"Now I must have you!" he said.

"Next time for sure," she promised. "And I'll fuck your brains out!"

She smiled as she drove home. Playing with his prick had made her so damned horny! So horny that she would have fucked him if she could have gotten him up again. She felt slutty and excited.

That was two sexual encounters she'd had at the gym in one week. She was pleased that so many still found her sexy and wanted to fuck her. And the more they came on to her, the more she was willing to fuck them.

"I'm becoming a slut!" she said as she drove home.

When she told this to Art, he laughed.

"You came really close, didn't you?" he asked.

"I did. When I knew he was looking at me, I started playing with my pussy and I made sure that he could see what I was doing. If I could have made him hard again, I know I would have fucked him, but he's not like you. I couldn't get him hard so I gave up. You get hard fast and you last long," she said with a smile.

He looked at her.

"I'm still horny," she said.

"And I'm really hard!" he said as they rushed to the bedroom...

The next morning, she got up ahead of him and rushed down to the kitchen to cook breakfast. He came down a few minutes later and they talked about various things while they ate. When they were finished, she knelt down in front of him and pulled his dick out of his pants then proceeded to give him a nice, long blowjob. He soon flooded her mouth with cum and she swallowed every bit of it then licked his knob clean.

He smiled.

"You always know the best way to send me off to work," he said as he kissed her good-bye.

She watched him get into the car and waved at him as he drove off. She washed the dishes and went up to shower. She had to be at work at noon. This was her late day at the store and she was in no hurry to get ready.

When she stepped out of the shower, the phone rang. She picked it up and smiled when she heard Zoe's voice.

"What are you up to today?" Zoe asked.

"I have to be at work at noon. Why?" Rita replied.

"That's three hours from now. Wanna get together?" Zoe asked.

"Not this morning, Zoe. I'd really love to but Art wore me out last night. I get off at five. Why don't you meet me at the store then?" Rita suggested.

"Perfect! We should both be good and horny by then!" Zoe giggled

Chapter Three

Zoe was waiting outside the store when Rita got off. She smiled and gave her a hug and kiss on the lips. A few weeks ago, such public displays would have felt weird to them both. Now, it was so natural.

They walked around the corner hand-in-hand and entered a small café. The waitress had seen them many times before but this time, she realized that things were different.

She greeted them as usual and showed them to a small, semi-private booth. As she handed them menus she looked into their eyes and smiled.

"How long have you two been lovers?" she asked.

"We're that obvious?" Zoe asked.

"Oh yes," the waitress said. "It's written all over your faces."

"This started a couple of weeks ago," Rita said. "We've been best friends for years but we finally realized that we've always been in love with each other."

"I fell in love with Rita the first day we met but I was always too chicken to say it. One thing led to another and now here we are."

"Aren't you married?" the waitress asked.

"Yes I am," Rita said.

"Does he know?" the waitress asked.

"He knew it before we did," Rita said. "He said it's been very obvious to him for a long time and he was surprised that we waited so long to let our feelings out. He's okay with it, too. He thinks it's kind of cute and sexy."

The waitress laughed.

"If I did anything like that, my husband would kill me," she said.

"So you've thought about it?" Zoe asked.

"Sure. In fact, there's this woman I met about a month ago. The first time I saw her, I got weak in my knees and I just couldn't take my eyes off her. We started talking and now we're friends. But I'd like to be more than just friends. I think she does, too, because she's been dropping lots of sexy hints lately. What's it like when you make love with each other?" the waitress said.

"It's wonderful!" both Zoe and Rita said.

They ordered their meal and watched the waitress' behind as she walked away.

"She has a very sexy ass," Zoe observed. "And great legs."

"Your legs are much nicer," Rita said as she slid her hand along Zoe's thigh and between her legs.

Zoe parted her legs and smiled as Rita felt her. As usual, she hadn't worn panties and Rita wasted no time in locating and massaging her already swollen clit. The waitress watched from a few feet way. Even though the area around their booth was dimly lit, she could plainly see that Rita's hand was between Zoe's thighs.

A few minutes later, she brought them their drinks. Rita smiled at her but kept feeling Zoe's cunt beneath the table. Zoe now had a dreamy expression on her face.

"You're really sexy," she told the waitress.

"Um, thanks," the waitress replied as she blushed.

She left and stood a few feet away. She saw them kiss several times as they sipped their wine and was glad the place was almost empty. When she brought them their dinner, she saw that Zoe's face was flushed and she had this satisfied grin.

"I just came," Zoe said as she placed the plate in front of her.

"I can see that it was good one, too," the waitress giggled.

"Oh yes!" Zoe sighed. "The first of many tonight!"

"Zoe!" Rita said as she playfully elbowed her.

"That's alright. I enjoyed watching you," the waitress said.

"You have very sexy legs," Zoe said as she ran her hand up the back of her thigh.

The waitress froze in place, unsure of what to do. Zoe's hand moved upward and under her skirt. They stood there making eye contact as

Zoe gently caressed her behind. She ran her fingers up and down the waitress' crack a few times. Each pass made her hornier and hornier.

Rita sipped her drink and watched the show.

"Very sexy legs. I bet what's between them is also very sexy," Zoe whispered as she moved her fingers down to caress her cunt from behind. The waitress shivered as Zoe's fingers danced lightly on her cunt, scared and delighted that she was being felt.

Zoe hooked her finger through the waistband of her panties and slowly tugged them down. The waitress stood still and maintained eye contact as she felt her panties move off her hips and slide down her thighs.

Zoe stopped when the panties were halfway down and caressed her cunt again. She felt her clit for a little while then gently eased her middle finger into the waitress' cunt and moved it in and out. The waitress stifled a moan, shook all over, and came. Zoe kept "fucking" her until she'd come twice more, then removed her finger.

She smiled at the waitress.

"That's what it's like," she said as she licked the juices from her finger. "We do a lot of other things, too. Exciting and wonderful things. I'm sorry that we waited so long to become lovers, but there's no stopping us now. If you want to have sex with a woman, do it and you don't have to tell your husband," Zoe said.

"Wow!" the waitress said.

"Can we see your pussy?" Rita asked.

The waitress grinned. Once she made sure that no one else was watching, she faced them and raised her skirt to show them the tiny blonde triangle between her thighs. Rita leaned over and caressed it.

"I'd love to eat you!" she said.

"And fuck you," Zoe added. "A lot!"

"Maybe some other time? I don't get off until ten tonight," the waitress said.

"I though you already got off," Zoe joked.

"You got me off at work, but not from work!" the waitress said as they all laughed.

She gave them one more good look at her cunt before she pulled her panties off altogether. For the next hour, both Rita and Zoe felt her up whenever she returned to their booth to check on them. The poor woman was so horny that she could barely think straight. During the course of the evening, Rita had also managed to finger-fuck her through two more good comes that left her with wobbly knees.

When they left, they tipped her handsomely. She smiled and walked them outside.

"Thanks, ladies," she said. "That's the most I've come in one night in my entire life! This was great."

She stood with her legs apart so both Zoe and Rita could touch her cunt again. They pulled her into the shadows next to the building. Zoe was behind her and she raised the waitress' skirt above her hips. To her delight, Rita knelt in front of her and licked her cunt. It felt so exquisitely erotic that she came within seconds. Before she realized it, Rita was holding her from behind while Zoe went down on her until she came again.

"No more! Please! I can't take it! Wow!" she cried as she shook and shook.

When Zoe stopped, she stood and stuck her tongue into the waitress' mouth for a good, long kiss while Rita fondled her ass crack.

They stopped and stayed with her until she calmed down. She was breathing very had and she was obviously flushed from all of the orgasms she'd had.

"That was incredible! You both are great!" she said after a few minutes. "My pussy is still throbbing! Wow!"

"So are you gonna go after that woman you're attracted to?" Zoe asked.

"I'd rather make it with you two again," the waitress replied. "A lot!"

They exchanged names and phone numbers and promised to get together real soon. The waitress watched as they walked off hand-in-hand and waved as she wished she were going with them to Zoe's place...

"I am horny today. Very horny!" Zoe said as they immediately headed upstairs to the bedroom and undressed each other.

Rita leaned over and swirled her tongue over Zoe's nipples. Zoe sighed appreciatively.

"What would you like to do today?" Rita asked as they slid into the large bed.

"Everything!" Zoe said as they kissed.

As their tongue merged into one, knowing fingers gently explored their bodies. Rita concentrated on the space between Zoe's thighs until it was very moist while Zoe playfully tongued her dark nipples until they tingled. Then Zoe's fingers moved to the soft, damp folds of Rita's cunt and the two lovers masturbated each other to their first orgasm.

Rita then moved between Zoe's legs so that their pussies touched, then reached behind her pillow. She pulled out a large, flesh colored dildo that had two heads and inserted one of them into her cunt. Zoe grabbed the other end and pushed it up into her cunt and they began a nice, rhythmic fuck.

Before long, Zoe was writhing and moaning on the bed. Rita changed position so that she could do Zoe missionary style, and kept up the steady beat. Zoe soon began moving her hips to match Rita's thrusts and they soared toward sexual oblivion once again.

Rita felt Zoe trembling beneath and knew she was about to come again. She slowed down her thrusts to prolong Zoe's pleasure and so that she could try to come at the same time. Usually this didn't work.

But today was different.

Both women exploded at the exact same instant and filled the air with moans and gasps and the aroma of sex. They hugged each other tight and kissed as yet another, more powerful orgasm rocked them and forced them to rest to recover their breath.

"That was incredible!" Rita gasped after a few seconds.

"Beautiful! One of the best I ever had," Zoe agreed. "If you were a man, I'd marry you."

They followed this up with a long, hot kiss. The kiss quickly led to an even hotter "69", during which the women tried to devour each other. Ten minutes later, the air was once more filled with happy, satisfied moans.

They rested for a while then Zoe inserted Rita's dildo into her snatch and mounted her. Now, it was her turn to be the "man". Rita wrapped her legs around Zoe's hips and clung to her arms as she enjoyed the good, deep fuck she was getting. Soon, she began fucking Zoe back and they matched each other stroke for stroke the rest of the way.

They again erupted at the exact same moment. It was explosive. It was mind numbing. And it was incredibly magical.

They held each other tight and kept humping away. Several more orgasm wracked their bodies and their muscles ached from the strain before they stopped. Zoe slid out of Rita, pulled the dildo from her cunt, and tossed it onto the floor. Rita smiled contentedly at her.

"Sex with you gets better each time," she said. "I should have started this years ago."

"I wish you had," Zoe said as she stoked Rita's inner thighs. "My God, you have such a smooth, sexy body. I would love to go away for the weekend with you, so we can make love all day and night."

"I'll think about it," Rita said as Zoe slowly brought her to a gentle climax.

And she did.

A lot.

Especially when Zoe slid the dildo into her cunt and proceeded to fuck her with it. As Rita fucked her back with passion, she imagined she was being fucked by Art and the images grew more and more vivid with each thrust of the dildo. She threw her legs wide open and fucked Zoe back as hard as she could. As she neared orgasm, the images of Art faded and she made passionate, crazy love with Zoe.

"That's it, Rita! Fuck me! I love you! I really love you!" Zoe cried as she neared her orgasm.

"Love me, Zoe! Love me forever!" Rita gasped as they fucked faster and faster.

As always, both women erupted at the same instant. Zoe fucked her until she started shaking all over, then pulled out and fell beside her. Both were bathed in sweat.

"God, I love you, Zoe. I really love you," Rita said softly as she caressed her cheek.

They kissed a long, long time then lay side-by-side to catch their breath.

Before long, they were kissing and running their hands all over each other. When Rita began moaning softly, Zoe got between Rita's thighs and gently pressed her cunt against hers. Rita positioned herself so their clits and nipples touched, then smiled up at Zoe. After a quick kiss, Zoe began moving against Rita's body nice and easy. Each up and down movement caused their cunts to massage each other and made their nipples tingle deliciously. Zoe really loved to fuck her this way. It was gentler, sexier and far more intimate than using a dildo. And it was incredibly sensual. As they fucked, their cunts grew hotter and wetter. Rita opened her legs wider and moved with her.

Rita sighed and moaned with each wonderful kiss of their cunts.

"I'm nearly there, Zoe," she said. "Oh, God! I love you!"

It didn't seem strange to hear Rita say that now. Nothing about their relationship seemed strange now. They were making love in a very true sense. Zoe began to tremble all over. Rita realized she was coming and fucked her faster. Seconds later, they both erupted and their cuntlips convulsed against each other as if they were actually kissing.

Zoe let out a deep moan and shook all over. Rita opened her legs as wide as she could and sighed as she felt Zoe's warm love juices enter her cunt. She was coming in her again. Rita held her close so she could take in ever squirt and it felt so magical.

"Yes! That's it! Come inside me, Zoe! Fill my pussy! I'm yours, Darling! I'm yours forever!" she said as she came again and again.

Zoe kept fucking her faster and faster as she came and came. Their cunts made wet, slurping noises as they fucked and Zoe's cum ran out of Rita's cunt and slid between her cheeks. It was the longest, most incredibly delicious fuck they'd had so far and by the time it ended, they were shaking all over and covered with sweat.

"I love you!" they both said at once.

Rita got home well after midnight looking happy and tired. Art laughed as she plopped down on the bed next to him. He caressed her shoulders.

"I figured you were with Zoe tonight, so I didn't wait up," he said.

She giggled.

"The more we make love, the deeper in love we fall," she said. "It's crazy but I'm head-over-heels in love with Zoe."

"What about those men who have been trying to get into your panties?" he asked.

"I'm thinking about letting some of them into them," she replied. "I've come very close to fucking a couple of them, so I might go all the way soon. Is that okay?"

"There's nothing I can do to stop you, right?" he asked.

"I guess not. I'm a little bit afraid of letting my inner slut out. I might not be able to stop," she said. "I'm also worried that Zoe will go all out to steal you from me. She really wants you, Art."

"If you fuck other men, I'll certainly fuck Zoe," he said. "Hell, I get an erection whenever I see her so I might as well put it to good use."

She laughed.

"I get horny around her, too," she said. "So we have an understanding?"

"Yes. I admit this is something I never once thought about when I married you. So who are you gonna fuck first?" he asked.

She smiled at him.

"You!" she said.

Two days later, while Art was at work, Zoe paid Rita a surprise visit. As soon as Rita opened the door, Zoe threw her arms around her neck and deep kissed her.

They retreated to Rita's bedroom and slowly removed each other's clothes as they exchanged several slow, deep kisses. After a nice, long easy "69" that left them both panting, Rita slid the dildo up into her cunt and moved between Zoe's open thighs. Zoe bent her knees and moaned as Rita plunged it into her. Then they settled into a good, long, hard fuck.

Zoe came first.

Rita pumped her a few more times, then eased the prick out of her cunt. To Zoe's surprise, Rita slid the dildo up into her ass and began to fuck her again. Zoe wrapped her knees around Rita's waist and groaned and sighed as she fucked her. After a few good thrusts, Zoe began to move with her.

"That's it, Rita! Fuck me! Fuck my ass. Make it yours!" Zoe moaned as waves of intense pleasure raced through her.

Zoe began quivering as she fucked her back. Her orgasm was powerful.

Deep.

"Oooh, yeah! I'm all yours now!" she cried.

Rita soon felt her own orgasm building deep within her cunt and began thrusting in and out of Zoe's ass faster and faster. Seconds later, Rita screamed and came. As she did, she fell forward and drove the dildo way up into Zoe's channel. The sudden thrust caused Zoe to come again and the two women just clung to each other until the waves of pleasure subsided.

"My God! That was incredible!" Zoe said after a while. "Just incredible!"

"It sure was," Rita agreed.

"I don't know why you decided to fuck me in my ass, but I'm glad you did. If I weren't used to that, I'd be sore for a few days," Zoe said as they dressed and headed down to kitchen. "Why *did* you do that?"

"Well, you said that you liked getting fucked in your ass. I want to make you happy, so I decided to try it," Rita replied as she poured them glasses of wine. "And you stuck that vibrator in my ass twice. I wanted to return the favor."

Zoe laughed.

"Now it's your turn!" she said as she picked up the dildo.

Rita lay on her back with her legs wide apart and moaned as Zoe fucked her with the dildo. She realized that Zoe liked to be the "man" most of the time and, since she had become very good at fucking, Rita was more than content to let her take charge. After a few good thrusts, Rita began fucking her back. Rita moaned and fucked faster. Zoe matched her. They steadily increased their tempo until Rita began to shake all over. Zoe realized she was about to come and fucked her faster and faster.

Then she exploded.

So did Rita.

The two fucked wildly for a few seconds. Then Zoe rolled off and lay beside her.

"Wow! That was great," Zoe said.

"Yes. It was," Rita agreed. "We're getting good at this. Maybe too damned good."

Zoe laughed.

"If this keeps up, we won't need any men to satisfy us," she joked.

They stopped around one and went out for lunch. As soon as they got back to the house, they headed upstairs and quickly undressed.

"Lay on your stomach," Zoe said as she turned on the vibrator.

Rita sighed as she slowly ran it along her spine and down between her legs. Zoe had it on "LOW" and she took her time moving it along Rita's swollen, quivering cuntlips. She moved it upward again and along

her ass crack. This time, she stopped at the back door and teased Rita
with it. Rita giggled at the sensations.

"I love your ass, Rita. It's so nice and sexy," Zoe said softly.

Rita felt something ease into her asshole and quivered as the
delicious vibrations surged through her body. She relaxed and sighed.
Zoe eased the vibrator into her about halfway and turned up the
voltage. Rita shook and groaned.

"Oh, my god!" she cried.

Zoe smiled and moved it in and out several times. As before, she
pushed it in a little bit deeper each time.

"I really love your ass. If I had a dick, I'd fuck you there every
chance I got," she said as she gently fucked her.

Rita quivered out of control now. The vibrations were making her
cunt tingle and she wanted to scream as it went in deeper and deeper.
Zoe turned up the power a bit and sent more delicious vibrations
through Rita's ass.

She moaned and buried her face in the pillow.

The vibrations were reaching parts of her body she didn't know she
had and on each inward thrust, she gripped the pillow and emitted a
loud moan. Zoe gradually fucked her faster and faster.

Zoe also loved every second of it. Fucking Rita like this was sending
erotic thrills through her body. Rita's ass was smooth and flawless and
oh-so-sexy.

"I love your ass, Rita! I really love it!" she panted.

"It's yours, Zoe! It's yours! Make me your bitch!" Rita screamed.

Zoe turned up the power and slid it in deeper and moved it around.
Rita cried and moaned and sighed. She began to see stars with each
inward thrust and trembled as waves of pleasure surged through her.

Then she came.

It was a very intense, very powerful orgasm that made her writhe
on the bed and scream for Zoe to stop. Zoe turned off the vibrator and
eased it out of Rita's ass.

Rita turned over and smiled at Zoe mounted her and pressed her
cunt against hers. She looked into Rita's deep, dark eyes and smiled.

"I love you," she whispered as they fucked.

The following Tuesday, Rita and Zoe returned to the casino. Bart
saw them walk in and watched as they parted ways again. He saw

Rita sit down at her usual slot and waited for her to settle in. Then he signaled to the hostess.

She brought him two mai tais. He tipped her, picked up the glasses and headed for Rita. He walked up to her and handed her one. She took it and smiled at him

"Hello, again," she said.

"I'm glad you came tonight," he said. "I've missed you. I was here last Tuesday but you didn't show. So I came again hoping I'd see you."

"You came here to see me?" she asked.

"Uh-huh," he said as he sat next to her. "In fact, I've been thinking about you every day."

She laughed.

"You got a little fresh with me last time. Nosy, too," she said.

"I apologize. But you're so sexy that I just couldn't resist you—and you didn't push me away. I've never met anyone as pretty and sexy as you. I'm sorry that you're married," he said.

"I'm not," she said.

"I know. Who's that lady you always come here with?" he asked.

"That's Zoe. We're best friends. Do you think she's sexy?" she said.

"Yes. But she's nowhere near as sexy as you are. Your legs are incredible," he replied.

She smiled.

"In fact, they're perfect," he said.

She sat still as he again put his hand on her knee. The alcohol was already starting to hit her, so she didn't bother to push his hand away. She just kept her knees shut. Bart leaned closer and whispered in her ear.

"I'd really love to see what you have between them."

"That's only for my husband to see. No one else," she said.

He slowly moved his hand upward and along her inner thigh. Her knees parted a little this time and she sat and looked at him as he gently stroked her thigh.

"He's one lucky guy," Bart said.

"He thinks so," she said.

"Maybe you'll let me get lucky, too?" he asked as he continued to touch her.

"No," she said without stopping him.

"Are you sure?" he asked.

"Yes," she said.

He moved his hand upward and gently rubbed her crotch through her shorts. It felt kind of exciting so she parted her knees a bit more and looked him in the eyes. Bart moved their chat to even more personal areas.

"Do you shave your pussy?" he asked.

For some reason, she actually answered him.

"My husband shaves me once in a while," she said as he rubbed her a little harder. She felt her pussy get warmer and warmer.

"Are you shaved now?" he asked.

"Sort of. Damn! You're really nosy tonight!" she said.

"But you answered me," he pointed out.

"I shouldn't have!" she said as she removed his hand and clamped her legs shut.

She got up and walked away. He smiled and watched her behind.

When she didn't find Zoe, Rita decided to sit down at another slot machine and continue playing. A few minutes later, Bart showed up with two more mai tais. He sat next to her and handed her one of the drinks. She took it and squinted at him.

"How'd you find me?" she asked.

"I followed you. I figured you were looking for your friend, but I knew she wasn't around," he said.

"How'd you know that?" she asked as she sipped her drink.

"I saw her leave here with a guy about an hour ago," he said.

"You're kidding!" Rita said.

"I am not. I guess she let him pick her up. They're probably in his room now fucking like crazy," he said.

She sipped her drink as she processed this. She didn't know that Zoe would do anything like that. But she did know that Zoe liked sex--a lot.

"You said that your pussy was sort of shaved. What did you mean?" he asked.

She laughed.

"My husband shaved me a few days ago so it's kind of fuzzy right now," she said as she let her guard down.

"Can I see it?" he asked.

"No!" she laughed.

"Please?" he asked as he slid his hand up her thigh.

"No way!" she said without pushing his hand away. "You're really rude tonight."

"I can't help it. I get horny whenever I see you. I bet your husband is horny all of the time," he said as he stroked her.

She laughed.

"He is," she said as her knees again parted.

"I can see why. I can barely keep my hands off you," he said as he moved to her crotch.

She sipped her drink and let him touch her again. Her heart beat faster and faster as she vaguely wondered why she was letting him do that. She was feeling pretty horny right now.

"You shouldn't do that," she said.

"Then why are you letting me?" he asked as he rubbed a little harder.

She felt the heat rise between her legs and parted them a bit more. Bart smiled and kept doing it.

"You like this, don't you?" he asked.

"Yes. It feels nice," she said as he made her warmer and warmer.

She snapped out of her fog and pushed his hand away. She was very hot and horny now but she was determined to keep Bart at bay. He signaled to the hostess who brought two more mai tais. Rita took it and smiled.

"I think you're trying to get me drunk," she said.

"You're right," he said as he put his hand on her thigh. "I want to get you drunk enough and horny enough to have sex with me."

"That's never gonna happen," she said with a grin.

They sat and talked while she played. Every so often, he ran his hand up and down her inner thigh. She just giggled and parted her legs more. For some reason, she let him touch her and the more she drank, the less harm she saw in letting him do it.

"We can go upstairs and do what your friend is doing right now," he urged.

"No," she responded.

"Yes we can. No one will know but us," he whispered as he moved his hand even higher.

Her pussy was still warm and moist. And his caresses were making her crazy.

"Let's do it, Rita," he said as he reached the edge of her panties.

"Never!" she said without pushing his hand away.

She looked across the room and saw Zoe at one of the machines. She smiled. Bart tried to slip his fingers under the leg of her shorts. She parted her knees more and shivered as he caressed her slit through her panties. She smiled at him as he gently teased her clit.

"That's it, Rita. Relax and let me take you," he said as he rubbed it.

She trembled and emitted a low, soft sigh. He could feel her wetness through her panties and his prick grew harder and harder. She just looked at him and smiled dreamily as she felt her juices flow. She was now on the verge of coming and she needed release.

Bart seemed to sense this and rubbed her faster and faster. Rita let out a deep, low moan as she trembled all over and came. It was a good, deep come, too. Bart kept playing with her clit. She came more and more.

She knew this was very wrong, but she couldn't stop. She needed him to keep making her come. He smiled at her.

"Let's do it, Rita," he urged.

She was lost in a deep alcohol-orgasmic induced fog now. She was aware that her knees were wide apart and that Bart was rubbing her pussy and that she was oh-so horny. He frigged her faster and faster. She looked at the bulge in his jeans and unzipped them. When she reached inside and wrapped her fingers around his prick, he moaned softly. As she jerked him off slowly, she watched his foreskin roll back and forth over his knob and decided that she liked what she saw.

"Let's make love, Rita! You know you want to," he urged as he fingered her a little faster. She was incredibly wet now and oh-so horny.

She pumped him a little faster as precum coated his knob and ran down over her fingers. He leaned close and pressed his lips against hers. They kissed. It was a good, deep kiss, too. Like the ones they'd shared before. She kept jerking him off nice and easy and he massaged her g-spot.

"Oh yeah!" she moaned. "Make me come, Bart!"

She exploded seconds later. As she came, she beat him off faster and faster. He soon spurted a line of thick, warm goo across her thighs and shorts. She smiled and did it faster and faster. Each pump of her hand sent another spurt of cum soaring upward. She kept at it until he went soft and he made her come again.

"That was wonderful!" she gasped. "My God! My pussy is still tingling!"

They kissed again as they came down from their sexual highs. Rita's fingers and thighs were covered with cum and her cunt throbbed.

They sat back and smiled at each other.

"Come up to my suite with me, Rita. Let's make love," he whispered.

"I'd love to, Bart, and maybe we'll do that soon. But I can't tonight because I have to get home soon," she said.

"How soon?" he asked as he slid his fingers into her cunt again.

"Right after you make me come again," she said as she grabbed his dick and rolled his foreskin up and down his knob.

Ten minutes later, she was gasping for air as another, stronger orgasm surged through her. Bart had already shot another load onto her shorts, so he was quite flaccid now. They laughed as they straightened up.

"What can I do to make you mine, Rita?" he asked.

"You'll never make me yours, Bart, but I'll let you try," she teased.

"That's all I can ask for," he smiled as they kissed again.

"There's my friend. I'm leaving now," she said.

"Will you be here next week?" he asked.

"Maybe," she said.

"Then maybe I'll see you again," he said.

She smiled and walked away. He watched her wiggle her behind and licked his lips.

On the ride home, Zoe noticed that something was on Rita's mind. She looked flushed and a bit tired.

"What's wrong?" she asked.

"Nothing," Rita said.

"Don't give me that. I've known you too long and I can tell when something's bothering you. What happened tonight?" Zoe pursued.

"I just had one too many mai tais. That's all," Rita said.

"Uh-huh. Did you do something you didn't want to?" Zoe asked.

"No. I saw you leave with some guy earlier. Did you get laid tonight?" Rita asked as she switched topics.

Zoe laughed.

"I sure did!" she said. "Did you?"

"Of course not!" Rita said.

"Did Bart get you drunk?" Zoe pressed.

"Yes. He got me four mai tais. I'm pretty drunk right now," she admitted.

"Did you let him do anything that you regret?" Zoe asked.

"No," Rita replied.

"No he didn't do anything or no you don't regret it?" Zoe pushed.

"Just no," Rita said with a laugh.

Zoe frowned.

Rita's laugh said more than she wanted to reveal. She knew that Bart had gotten somewhere with her. It was enough to make Rita feel ashamed. She smiled.

"I had a lot of fun tonight. I came here to get laid and I did. Jessie is younger than me and he can last a long time. He was good, too. He made me come twice. How many times did you come?" she asked.

"I don't know—" Rita said as she realized that Zoe had tricked her.

Zoe laughed.

"I knew it! Want to tell me about it now?" she asked.

"Not really. I think I already told you too much. He didn't fuck me if that's what you're getting at," Rita said as she got annoyed.

Zoe giggled.

"I warned you about this," she said. "Now that you started it, he won't give up until he fucks you. Sooner or later, you're gonna do it, too. And you'll really hate yourself afterward. Once it happens., you can't take it back. You'd better stay away from him."

Rita nodded.

She had gotten so drunk that she had let her guard all the way down. She barely noticed what he was doing until it was too late to stop. And she didn't want to stop, either. She wanted him to make her come.

Now that it happened, she was getting a little scared. She loved Art and did not want to cheat on him with anyone. And tonight, she almost did!

She felt kind of ashamed of herself. She had allowed Bart to get intimate with her. What's more was she was thinking about letting him get even further. She also knew that Zoe was throwing herself at Art.

As sexy as Zoe was, Rita figured that there was no way that he'd be able to keep resisting her. Sooner or later, Art and Zoe would have sex.

And when that happens, she'd let Bart take her all the way. But Art would have to cheat first.

Bart was at once happy and sorry.

He had nearly gotten what he wanted from Rita, but he felt ashamed of himself. He realized that he actually liked her very much and that getting her drunk so she'd have sex with him wasn't the rout he wanted to take with her.

He wanted her sober and in her right mind.

If and when it happened, he wanted it to be because she wanted to do it. She had to be willing and alert. He didn't want to force her to do it.

"I've been a rat most of my life. I don't want to be a rat with Rita. She's different and special. I need to treat her that way," he said.

He looked at himself in the rear view mirror and shook his head.

"Look at you, Bart! You're acting like you're in love with Rita! You finally met a woman who is everything you ever wanted and she's married! You want her so damned bad that you're willing to do anything to get into her panties—even if it means breaking up her marriage. You fucking skunk!" he said.

He laughed.

"Fine time for me to have an attack of conscience!" he said.

When Rita and Zoe got into the car, they spent a few seconds looking into each other's eyes. They soon found themselves locked into another deep French kiss. This time, they held each other tight and Rita shivered as Zoe's hands caressed her back. She reached over and slid her hand along Zoe's bare thigh. Zoe parted her knees and trembled as Rita slid her hand under her shorts to her pantries. They kissed more and more passionately.

Rita slid her middle finger into Zoe's cunt and moved it in and out. Zoe responded by doing the same to her. This time, when they came, it was so explosive that they both nearly screamed. They spent the next several minutes exchanging kisses and fingering each other through a series of smaller, pleasant orgasms.

There was no need for words now.

"Maybe there never was?" Rita thought as she stuck her fingers deeper into Zoe's cunt.

Zoe rolled up Rita's shirt and unclasped her bra. Rita groaned as Zoe started to lick and suck her right nipple while she kept moving her finger in and out of Rita's cunt.

"Oh God! Yes! Yes!" Rita moaned as she came again. "I'm yours, Zoe! I'm yours forever!"

Zoe was too busy enjoying an orgasm of her own to hear her. All she could think about was the fact she was making love with her best friend. It was her dream come true.

When they stopped, they looked at each other and smiled. Zoe caressed Rita's cheek as they maintained eye contact. Rita laughed as she readjusted her clothes. They kissed again and Zoe drove Rita home.

Art saw the expression on Rita's face.

"I think Zoe and I just made love," she said as she sat down on couch.

Then she told him what happened. He laughed and hugged her.

"I think you've fallen in love with Zoe and she's crazy about you, too," he said. "How does it feel?"

"Different. Exciting. And wonderful!" Rita replied. "It's unreal. I feel like I'm in some sort of movie or something. I'm not sure how to act. I do know that I want to keep doing this. Does that bother you?"

"No. I kind of expected it," he said.

"Is this cheating?" she asked nervously.

"No. It's only cheating if you try to hide it from me," he said.

Chapter Four

The next afternoon, the girls met at IHOP for lunch. After they ordered, their conversation centered on the night before.

"You look much better today," Zoe observed.

"I'm okay now. I was really drunk last night. Probably too drunk," Rita smiled.

"So you really let Bart give you an orgasm?" Zoe asked.

Rita smiled.

"Uh, yes. He gave me several—I think," she said. "I let him touch me through my panties and he made me come. It felt so good that I let him keep doing it. I feel pretty guilty about it now because I almost cheated on Art."

"So he jerked you off?" Zoe teased.

Rita giggled.

"Once he got started, I didn't want him to stop. I don't know if it was the booze or if something inside of me wanted him to do it. All I know is, I was really horny!" she said.

"So it felt good, huh?" Zoe asked.

"I think it felt too good and that scares me. Bart will probably try it again and I might let him do it again," Rita said.

"What if he wants to fuck you?" Zoe asked.

"I won't let that happen. I won't give in to him," Rita said.

"What if you do? Then what?" Zoe asked. "Will it be a one-time fling or will you start an affair with him? If he gets into your panties, he'll want you more and more."

"I never thought of that!" Rita said.

"You'd better stay away from the casino for a couple of months. If he doesn't see you there, he might give up and go away," Zoe suggested.

"I don't think that would work. The hostess told me that he's a regular there and he's always on the prowl for women," Rita said. "But I might try it to see if it works."

"Do you want him to leave you alone? I mean, really?" Zoe asked.

"I'm not sure," Rita replied.

"In that case, I think you will end up fucking him," Zoe said with a grin. "If that happens, I'm going after your husband."

"I'd better make sure that never happens. I don't want you to steal Art from me," Rita said. "Not that you could."

"We'll see," Zoe smiled.

"What we did last night was really wonderful," Rita said as she put her hand on Zoe's knee.

"It really was. I didn't expect things to get this far but I'd love to take it further," Zoe said as she looked her in the eyes.

"I'm willing to take it as far as you want to go. I'm yours, Zoe. I'll always be yours," Rita assured her.

They held hands as they left the restaurant. It felt so natural, too.

"Yes," Rita thought. "We are in love with each other."

What neither of them knew was that Judy had witnessed the actions between Rita and Bart and had called Art to tell him what was going on. Art trusted Rita when she was sober but when she was drunk, she was wild and loose. He thanked Judy for keeping an eye on Rita and hung up.

Zoe had also warned him about Bart, but she had an ulterior motive. She wanted Rita to get caught cheating so she could have a clear shot at Art.

Art also knew that Zoe was kind of promiscuous since her divorce. She went to the casino to not only to gamble but also to get laid. As sexy as she was, she could be choosy about who she wanted to have sex with. And Zoe was real choosy!

Art wasn't sure what Judy's motives were. They'd become friends because Art used to accompany Rita to the casino. They'd have dinner and she'd play the slots while he watched. Judy usually served them drinks while Rita played.

Judy was about 30 years old with an hourglass body. She had ash blonde hair, blue eyes and a nice, warm personality.

She knew exactly what Bart was like because he had managed to get her into bed a few months earlier. Judy was also married, but Bart was so smooth that she fell for his lines and ended up fucking him. In fact, she fucked him three different times.

Then he dropped her to go after some redhead.

Judy had to laugh at herself, too.

She should have known better, but sex with her husband had been kind of blah. Bart had spiced things up for her and she used what she'd learned from him on her husband. So now, everyone was happy.

She knew that Rita was kind of naïve so decided to warn Art about what was happening.

But Rita actually knew about Bart because he had told her what he was like and what he wanted. Most men who tried to hit on her also tried to bullshit her. Bart was direct, honest and fun to be with. Because of this, she actually liked him.

Maybe she liked him more than she should and that's why she'd let him get that far. She even contemplated going further and that kind of scared her a little. If she fucked Bart, it would mean that she cheated on her husband. That was the last thing she wanted to do.

But right at that moment, she was walking hand-in-hand with Zoe and the longer she held her hand, the faster her heart raced.

Instead of going to the car, they went into Tower Grove Victorian Park. The park had a dozen restored gazebos and bandstands, narrow paths and secluded shady areas between massive oaks. They walked quietly along a path that wound off towards the back of the park. They crossed a footbridge over a narrow stream and entered a very cool, shady area.

They stopped behind a large a tree and faced each other. Then they kissed. It was a warm, deep, gentle kiss that soon included their tongues. As it became more passionate, Zoe undid the belt of Rita's shorts, popped open the buttons and slid her hand down into her panties.

Rita sucked Zoe's tongue harder as she slid her middle finger into her already moist cunt. After a few seconds of this, Rita managed to get her hand down into Zoe's panties. The two women kept French kissing and fingering each other until they both came. When they did, they held each other tightly and kept going and going.

This felt magical now.

Oh so very magical!

"Oooh, yes! I love you, Zoe! I love you!" Rita moaned as she humped her finger.

Zoe was coming like crazy now, too. She saw stars and trembled uncontrollably as one orgasm after another after another raced through her body.

"I love you, Rita!" she gasped. "I truly love you!"

They stopped a few minutes later to catch their breath. Zoe looked around to be sure no one had seen them, then they kissed again. Rita's shorts had slid down a few inches along with her panties. Zoe stopped to admire it. She'd never seen Rita's pussy before and the sight of her recently shaven cunt and swollen labia almost made her come again.

"You have a beautiful pussy," Zoe said as she ran her fingertips over it.

"And it's yours whenever you want it," Rita said as she eased her hand down into Zoe's panties.

They kissed and frigged each other through another good, strong orgasm. As Zoe fingered her, Rita's panties slid down further, exposing her entire cunt. Zoe's shorts also slid down a few inches. When they stopped coming, they took a few seconds to admire each other before pulling their shorts up.

"Yes, I really love you," Rita said as they walked out of the park holding hands.

"And I really love you," Zoe whispered.

The next Tuesday rolled around and, as usual, Rita and Zoe headed to the casino. Bart was seated at a poker table facing the entrance. He smiled when he saw them come in and finished playing his hand. He watched as they split up again and again got two mai tais.

Then he took them to where Rita sat and handed her one. She took it and smiled at him.

"Hello, Bart," she said as she sipped.

"Hi, Rita. It's good to see you again," he said. "Miss me?"

"Not really," she said.

He sat next to her and smiled.

"I want to apologize for what I did last time. You were too drunk to know what you were doing and I tried to take advantage of you. I feel like such a louse. I got you drunk so I could have sex with you," he said.

She looked at him.

"Isn't that what you normally do to women?" she asked.

"To other women. You're not like them. You're different. You're prettier and sexier and so much nicer. I shouldn't have done that to you. I'm really sorry," he said.

She sat and just looked at him for few seconds.

"Apology accepted," she smiled. "It was partly my fault, too. I should have known better than to drink that much."

"In a way, it was partly your fault," he said. "That's because you're so damned beautiful that I couldn't keep my hands off you."

She giggled.

"Friends?" he asked.

"Friends," she said.

He got her a mai tai. She took it and sort of scowled at him. He smiled.

"I promise I won't try anything—unless, of course, you really want me to," he joked.

She laughed and sipped the drink. They sat and talked while she played. As usual, they made each other laugh. She was hallway through her second mai tai and she felt a little silly and loose. She noticed that he was ogling her legs.

She smiled at him and parted her knees.

"Maybe I will let you," she said.

He put his hand on her leg and slowly stroked her inner thigh. His caresses titillated her and she opened her legs more.

"I'd really love to get at what's between your legs," he said softly as he stroked her.

"Like you did last time?" she asked.

"Yes. And maybe do a little more," he said as he moved his hand upward.

She parted her legs further as if she was inviting him in. He slid his hand under the leg of her shorts. When she felt his fingers on her pussy, she quivered slightly and smiled.

"Are you sure about this? Are you sure it's not the alcohol talking again?" he asked.

She nodded and sipped her drink. She was only a little bit tipsy but a lot horny. His touches were making her hornier. He moved his fingers over her labia and sent delicious tingles through her body.

Bart was thrilled.

Rita was letting him touch her again. This time, she did so willingly. She was sort of drunk but knew what she was doing. She was fully aware of what he was doing and she wanted him to do it.

She sighed.

His touches were exciting and she parted her legs even more. He located her swollen clit and gently teased it. She looked at him and nodded. He massaged her faster and she trembled all over.

"I want to have sex with you," he whispered.

"I know," she said as she felt herself starting to come.

"Do I have a chance?" he asked.

"No. But you can keep doing this," she said.

He rubbed her faster and faster. She let out a deep sigh and came. As she did, she gripped her chair. He did her faster and she came again. She was almost reeling now and her legs were wide apart. He slid his fingers past her panties and ran them along her quivering slit. She was still coming. When he played with her clit again, she came even harder.

She looked at him and forced herself to think straight as she realized he was actually touching her cunt. Bart eased a finger into her slit and moved it in and out. She bit her lower lip as she came again. Bart stopped and withdrew his finger.

Rita caught her breath and smiled at him.

"That was nice," she said.

"Why'd you let me do it again?" he asked.

"I liked what you did the last time so I decided to let you do it again," she replied. "That was way better!"

He laughed.

"Are you ever going to let me do more than just touch you?" he asked.

She giggled.

"Maybe," she teased.

"So you're saying that I do have a chance?" he asked hopefully.

"I'm not sure. We'll see," she replied as she reached over and ran her fingers along his bulge. "You're nice and hard."

"I always get hard when I'm with you," he said, surprised that she was touching him.

She felt him from his balls up to his knob. Her touched made him harder. Yes, she thought. I will fuck him one day.

Bart was already on the verge of coming and Rita's touches were driving him crazy. She swirled her fingertips over the head of his prick and felt it swell even more as she wondered what it would feel like inside her pussy. When she squeezed his knob a few times, he just couldn't hold back and he came in his pants. She smiled at him and kept at it. The more she played with his dick, the more he came. His underwear was now sticky with cum.

Rita was surprised with herself and the more she touched Bart's dick, the hornier she became. In fact, her pussy was still throbbing and her pulse was through the roof. She was also surprised that he stayed so hard, even after he'd obviously come.

They French kissed again. He slid his hand under her shorts and played with her cunt again. Her legs were wide apart now and she just about sucked his tongue off when he fingered fucked her again. She unzipped his pants and pulled out his sticky, cum-coated dick and proceeded to jerk him off nice and easy. She glanced around to be sure no one could see them and smiled at Bart.

She bent over and licked his knob. Bart was so shocked she did it that he spurted almost immediately. His first shot landed on Rita's chin. He expected her to back off. Instead, she slid as much of his dick into her mouth as she could and sucked it. He spurted again and again and again. Rita swallowed every bit of cum she could. Bart was astounded. He realized that this was far more than just a blowjob. Rita was making love to him with her mouth!

She sucked until he was totally spent then stopped and smiled at him.

"I've wanted to do that for a couple of weeks. I love the way your cum tastes, too," she said.

"I can't believe you did that! You're incredible, Rita! Let's you and me have an affair—something long and wonderful," he said.

"We'll see," she said with a grin. "We've already gone much further than I ever thought we would, so anything is possible."

"Let's exchange phone numbers," he suggested.

"Okay," she agreed as she gave him hers.

Then he gave her his number. She smiled.

"You can call me any time but evenings and all day during weekends," she said. "And don't ever text me. I don't want my husband to see it and ask a lot of questions."

"Got it," he said.

She watched as he got up to leave and admired the obvious bulge in the front of his pants. It was a good-sized bulge, too. As he walked away, she smiled because she had let him touch her again and knew that she'd really end up going further.

Bart smiled as he headed for his car.

He was finally making headway with Rita. He would let her moods call the shots from now on. If they ended up fucking, it would be with her consent and mostly her idea. This would be the first time that he ever let a woman take the lead.

"But I know she's worth it," he said as he got in his car and drove away.

While Rita was with Bart, Zoe was up in a hotel suite with the same guy she'd met the week before. He'd spotted her at one of the slots and walked over to talk to her. She knew what he wanted and she certainly wanted the same thing.

Zoe loved to fuck and he was good at it. He'd even hinted at making this a weekly thing. And she agreed.

"My pussy is made to be fucked and I really love to fuck you, Mark," she told him as she bounced up and down on his prick.

They fucked three times that night. Each time, they tried a different position and Zoe put everything she had into it. In between fucks, she sucked his dick to get him hard again and he ate her pussy-which was filled with his cum. Each time he ate her, he made her orgasm and she ended up begging him to fuck her again.

Around midnight, a well-fucked and tired Zoe staggered out of the suite and went in search of Rita. Mark was on the bed in what was nearly a coma and smiling like the Cheshire Cat.

When Zoe found Rita, Brad was nowhere in sight. She saw the two empty glasses on the console next to her.

"I see that you've been drinking again," she said.

Rita giggled.

"I see that you've been fucking again," she replied.

"We'd better get home," Zoe said as she gave her a playful poke.

"Is it time to leave already?" Rita asked.

"Yes. It's nearly midnight," Zoe said. "Where's Bart?"

"He left about an hour ago. He apologized for what he did last week and I said it was okay," Rita replied as they walked to the exit.

"Did he do anything that you didn't want him to do?" Zoe asked.

"No," Rita smiled. "He didn't do anything that I didn't want him to do."

Zoe thought about for a moment and shook her head.

"Be careful, Rita. You'll end up fucking him," she said.

"No I won't," Rita said.

"We'll see," Zoe said.

"I envy you sometimes," Rita said.

"Why would you envy me?" Zoe asked as they got into the back seat of her car.

"You fuck whoever you like and you don't have to worry what anyone else thinks about you. You've had a lot of hard dicks in your pussy since your divorce and you seem to enjoy fucking different men,' Rita said.

Zoe laughed.

"And I envy you because you've only had one man all this time who is very loyal to you," she said.

"Oh," Rita said as it sunk in.

"I would trade all the other men I've had for a man like Art," Zoe said. "You and Art make love. I just have sex. It's good sex, but there are no romantic attachments. No commitments. Nothing, really. I want what you have. I want love, Rita."

Zoe's words hit home.

Since Rita already had Art, why risk losing him?

"If I had your husband, I wouldn't open my legs for anyone else but him. I would be his and his alone. You'd better think about what you're doing," Zoe warned.

Rita nodded.

She smiled at Zoe and they kissed. It was a deep, passionate kiss again. Zoe undid Rita's shorts and tugged them down a little bit. Rita raised her hips off the seat and trembled as Zoe slid her shorts and panties down past her knees to her ankles. Rita sat down and kicked them off then did the same to Zoe. The car was dark and they hoped no one would see them as they frigged each other through two, long and deep orgasms.

Rita gasped and fell back on the seat. Zoe reached over and pulled up her T-shirt and bra. Rita moaned as Zoe leaned over and sucked her nipples. Again, their fingers found their ways into each other's cunts and they "fucked" until they both came. Rita's fingers were now coated with a combination of Zoe's juices and her lover's cum but she didn't care. She just wanted to feel Zoe's cunt suck at her fingers and to make her come and come.

They came again. This time, Zoe fell on top of her. Rita realized that their cunts were resting on each other. She looked up at Zoe and smiled.

"Fuck me," she whispered.

Zoe realized what she meant and positioned herself better so that their labia were actually "kissing". Then she moved back and forth nice and easy so their labia rubbed together. The movements sent incredibly warm and erotic sensations surging through them both. Once Zoe got the hang of it, she began moving faster and faster. Rita held her tight and tried to match her. The sensations were intensely erotic. Each time their clits massaged each other, it sent delicious quivers through their bodies.

"Yes! That's it! Fuck me, darling!" Rita moaned.

They kept going faster and faster. Their sensations mounted and mounted. When they came, it was sudden, simultaneous and explosive.

Magnificent!

That's when Rita felt something warm and sticky ooze into her cunt. She realized that Zoe was actually ejaculating and that her cum was entering her pussy. She gripped her arms and fucked her nice and easy. Zoe came harder and added more cum to the pool inside of Rita.

"I love you! I love you!" Rita screamed.

So did Zoe.

They lay there for a little while, then sat up and kissed. They had taken their romance to a new, exciting level and both knew there'd be no holding back any more.

"My God! I came! I actually came in your pussy! I never did that before!" Zoe smiled.

"It was awesome!" Rita said as they watched the liquid ooze from her open lips. "You came a lot, too! Like a man!"

"I never felt anything like this in my life! God, how I love you, Rita!" Zoe said as they kissed.

They jumped into the front seat and drove home. When Zoe let Rita off at her house, she laughed when she realized that neither of them had bothered to dress. She watched as Rita grabbed her clothes and rushed into the house half naked.

She heard Art laugh like crazy when he let her in.

"What a great night!" she thought as she headed home.

Rita was way up in the clouds. She tossed her shorts and panties on the coffee table and down on the sofa. Art sat next to her and stroked her thigh as they kissed.

"Zoe and I finally did it," she said. "We actually fucked."

He listened as she described it. By the time she was finished, he was rock-hard. She unzipped his jeans, grabbed his prick and led him up to the bedroom...

The next day, Zoe called Art.

"What's up?" he asked.

"I think you need to come up with reasons to keep Rita from going to the casino for a while," she said.

"Bart?" he asked.

"Yes. She's getting much too friendly with him now. I'm afraid that she might get into trouble—and you know what kind I mean," she said.

"I have thought about that. I've already gotten tickets to a show this Tuesday. That should keep her out of the casino," he said.

"Good. Maybe if he doesn't see her there for a few weeks, he'll give up. I don't want Rita—or you—to get hurt," Zoe said.

"Thanks for the heads up, Zoe," he said. "But if she really wants to see this guy, there's not too much that either of us can do to stop her."

"If she does have sex with him, remember that I am available. I'm yours whenever you want me," Zoe said. "I love you, Art."

When she said that, she hung up. He stood there staring at his phone wondering if she really said what he thought she said. He also knew that since she had started the affair with Rita that she wanted her all to herself. Zoe got jealous and sort of possessive whenever she saw Rita with Bart. Maybe she was afraid that she would lose her to him?

He had to laugh.

The situation was becoming stranger by the day.

At that same time, Rita received a call from Bart while she was at work.

"How are you today?" he asked.

"I'm fine. You?" she said.

"I'm great. Yesterday was nice. I'm still surprised that you let me do that," he said.

She giggled.

"Me, too," she said.

"Well, you've always known what I want. Now that I've gotten that far, I plan to go further—but only if you really want me to. We can take this nice and easy. I'm willing to go at your pace and I won't try to force myself on you," he said softly.

"You're still not getting that. But you can try if you want," she said.

"Is that a challenge?" he asked.

"Maybe," she giggled.

"Will I see you next Tuesday?" he asked.

"No. My husband has tickets to a show that night," she said.

"Sounds like fun. How about the week after?" he asked.

"Probably," she said.

"Can I do more than just touch you?" he asked.

She laughed.

"Maybe," she replied. "We'll see."

Chapter Five

The next afternoon, Rita went back to the YMCA for her usual workout. As she entered the room to use the stationary bike, she happened to see Greg pedaling away on one of them. She mounted the one next to him and smiled.

"Hi," she said. "Long time, no see."

"I've been on vacation. We just got back from St. Croix last night," he said as he ogled her. "I figured it's time to work off all those pounds I put on down there."

She laughed.

"You look fine to me," she commented.

"About the last time..." he began.

"I kind of enjoyed that," she said with a smile. "It was different."

"Oh?" he asked in surprise.

"It's true. I never did anything like that before. That was really good," she said.

They continued to talk as they worked out. As they did, she noticed that Greg had gotten a nice-sized boner and he kept ogling her legs and ass. To let him know she approved, she wiggled her behind as she pedaled. She glanced over at him and saw him make his now-obvious bulge "dance".

She smiled and nodded to let him know she was his for the taking today. When they finished, he walked her out to her car.

"You almost got me to cheat on my husband last time," she said.

"How close did we get?" he asked.

"Very close," she said as she turned to face him. "Very, very close."

His prick was fully erect and the sight of his bulge made her feel horny all over. He leaned close and stuck his tongue in her mouth. She leaned back and sucked it as he ran his fingers over her crotch. She responded by caressing his bulge. To her delight, she felt it get harder and longer.

"How close are we now?" he whispered.

She parted her legs and pulled him toward her until his bulge rested against her cunt. He got the message and started dry humping her again. She quivered and moved with him, reveling in the delicious sensations he was sending though her entire body.

She came seconds later. As she did, she humped him faster. He stopped humping her and reached down to free his prick. She grabbed it and jerked him off while he fingered her slit. She shook hard and came again. She fell back onto the hood of the car with her legs apart. Greg was between them with his massive prick bobbing from his shorts.

Rita reached down and pulled aside her shorts to reveal her throbbing cunt. Greg smiled and slid the head of prick along her labia several times. She moaned and trembled all over as it moved across her clit. He did it twice more then eased his prick into her cunt. She felt it enter her nice and slowly. It went deeper than anything else ever had. When she knew he was fully inside, she wrapped her legs around his hips.

Greg fucked her with long, deep and powerful strokes that massaged every part of her pussy each time. She gripped his shoulders and moved with him. It proved to be a nice, long and easy fuck. Her very first time with someone other than her husband.

She moaned with each thrust as he brought her closer and closer to orgasm. He moved faster and faster as if he sensed she was on the edge. She fucked him back with everything she had as she realized that she loved every deep, wonderful stroke of his dick.

"I'm coming!" she cried.

He fucked her faster. She dug her fingers into his arms and arched her back as she erupted. It was one of the most intense orgasms of her entire life, too. She moaned loudly and shook all over as waves of pleasure tore through her. Her orgasm was heightened by the fact she was fucking another man and that it felt so damned good!

Greg grunted and shoved his prick into her as deeply as he could. She used her inner muscles to squeeze his shaft as he proceeded to empty what felt like a quart of cum into her pussy. They kept fucking until she drained him and he eased his semi-hard prick out of her cunt.

"That close!" she smiled as she watched his cum run out of her cunt.

"That was the best fuck of my entire life!" he said after he caught his breath. "The very best!"

She slid down from the hood and giggled at the sensation of his cum running down her thigh. She grabbed his prick and gave it several pulls. To her delight, it became rock-hard again. She let him go and sat on the hood of her car with her legs wide apart. Greg grabbed her thighs and pull3ed her to the edge. She smiled and sighed deeply as he entered her again. This time, they slow-fucked and she savored each good, deep thrust of his prick and he savored the way her cunt hugged his shaft.

They kept at it for several minutes. Rita shook all over and started coming again. At the same time, she felt Greg's cum spurt into her cunt. They fucked until Greg's prick grew flaccid and slid out of her. She smiled as she watched the river of white goo ease fall her cunt.

"That was great," she said as they kissed again.

"My God, you're the best I ever had, Rita. The very best!" Greg said softly.

Before anything else could happen, Greg spotted his wife driving onto the lot. He stuffed his dick back into his shorts and gave Rita a quick kiss on the lips.

"Next time?" he asked.

"Anytime!" she replied.

On the way home, she was a jumble of emotions. She felt exhilarated, satisfied, happy, sad, ashamed and guilty all at once. She had finally crossed that line she never thought she would and had sex with another man.

Now she knew that she would have sex with Bart, but not right away. She was starting to really care about him and she knew he was more than just "attracted" to her now. She decided that she wouldn't play that hard to get, but do it just enough to keep his interest.

She was also glad that Art would still be at work when she got home. She was debating whether or not to tell him about this. Since he said she could try it as long as she told him about it, she decided to tell him.

When he got home, she greeted him in her skimpiest panties and T-shirt and just about sucked the tongue out of his head...

The next day over lunch, she told Zoe what happened. Zoe seemed shocked that she had strayed and warned her to be more careful.

"Just remember that you have two people who truly love you and that neither of us wants to see anything bad happen to you," she said. "How was it?"

Rita giggled.

"It was great! That's the biggest thing I ever had inside my pussy. His dick touched places that had never been touched before. He was good, smooth and gentle and knew what he was doing. I loved it!" she said.

"Are you gonna fuck him again?" Zoe asked.

"Oh yes!" Rita replied with a smile. "And often."

"So I guess that means I can go after Art now, huh?" Zoe teased.

"Sure. Why not? Now that he knows I fucked another guy, I told him he could fuck you as much as he wants," Rita said as she slid her hand along Zoe's leg.

"Let's go to the living room," Zoe whispered.

They went in and sat down on the sofa. Rita took Zoe in her arms and they kissed. After a while, she pulled up Zoe's T-shirt and sucked her nipples. Zoe gasped and let her head fall back as Rita sent delicious sensations racing through her body. While she sucked her nipples, Rita unbuttoned Zoe's shorts and eased her hand into her panties.

"Oooh!" Zoe quivered as Rita stroked her clit.

She stroked her faster and faster until Zoe came. When she did, she shoved her tongue into Rita's mouth and sucked it as hard as she could. Rita made her come a second time. This time Zoe fell back against the armrest and shook all over.

As she lay there panting, Rita slid her shorts down past her knees and kissed Zoe's cunt.

"You smell so wonderful," Rita whispered. "So very sexy."

She tugged Zoe's shorts off entirely then knelt in front of her. Zoe smiled as she spread her thighs. She knew what Rita wanted and she was only too happy to let her have it.

Rita rained kisses on her swollen clit then gently sucked it. Zoe moaned and opened her legs as far as she could as her friend's tongue explored her swollen labia and clit. When Rita finally slid her tongue into Zoe's cunt, Zoe gasped and shook all over.

She came seconds later.

As she came, she seized Rita's hair and fucked her tongue as hard as she could. At the same time, Rita slid two fingers into her cunt and "fucked" her. Zoe let out a loud moan and collapsed into the sofa as she came yet again.

"I love you, Rita! I love you!" she sighed. "I'm all yours now. I'm all yours forever!"

"I love you, too," Rita said softly as they kissed again.

As this kiss grew as passionate as the last, Rita again played with her clit. Zoe sucked her tongue harder and parted her knees as Rita gently stroked her swollen clit. Zoe was so still on the edge after her last orgasm, so she came after a few strokes. When she did, she threw her arms around Rita's neck and sucked her tongue with as much passion as she could summon. Rita kept playing with her clit until she came again. Zoe fell back and trembled as she emitted several deep moans.

After a few seconds, she beamed at Rita.

"I'm all yours now," she whispered. "Do whatever you like with me."

Rita knelt between her legs and kissed her way slowly up her inner thighs. When she reached Zoe's partially open cunt, she stopped to savor her sexual aroma awhile before sliding her tongue along her slit. Zoe's labia were large like rose petals and her clit was swollen and obvious. It was even more beautiful than Rita had imagined. She leaned closer and swirled her tongue over her clit.

Zoe groaned.

She groaned even louder when Rita sucked it.

She arched her back and emitted several gasps as Rita slid her tongue into cunt and lapped at her soft, inner walls.

"Ooh yes! I'm yours! All yours!" she sighed as Rita went down on her in earnest. "Eat me, darling! I love you!"

Rita reached up and played with Zoe's nipples. This heightened her sensations so much, she erupted. She seized Rita's hair and wildly humped her face as she came and came and came again.

"It's wonderful! Fantastic! I love it! I love it! I love you, Rita! I really love you!" she cried.

While her head was still reeling, Zoe shifted so that she was kneeling on the floor between Rita's wide open thighs. She started by raining soft kisses on Rita's cunt then eased her tongue into her juicy slit and licked away. Rita was so wound up that she came within a few seconds. Zoe reached up and tweaked her nipples as she kept licking. Rita shouted and came again and again.

"I love you, Zoe! I love you! Oh, God! How I love you!"

Zoe was totally lost in the taste of her friend's cunt. She was salty, sweet, bitter and everything else at the same time. She kept licking and licking as Rita lay sighing, moaning and trembling through orgasms after orgasm.

When it was over, they sat on the sofa and held each other close as they exchanged several soft, deep kisses. Zoe smiled at her lover. She had finally gotten to live out one of her fantasies.

"I love you, Rita," she whispered.

"I love you, too," Rita replied as she stroked her inner thigh. "I've wanted to have sex with you for a long time. I just never had the nerve to try this before."

"And I've always wanted to have sex with you. Now that we've done this, I'd like to keep doing it," Zoe said.

"Me, too. I want us to stay lovers---forever," Rita agreed as she stroked Zoe's damp bush. "Forever and ever."

Rita took Zoe by the hand and led her up to the bedroom.

"We have all day," Rita said. "And I want to make love with you until neither of us can come anymore."

Zoe watched as Rita undid her shirt, one button at a time, then took it off. Rita's breasts jiggled nicely as she tossed the garment into a corner of the bedroom. She smiled as Zoe studied her.

Rita's breasts were large, perky and firm with large aureoles and pert nipples. Zoe watched as Rita fondled herself until the nipples stood hard and proud from the mounds of her breasts.

She had to admit that the woman was sexy.

Very sexy.

Rita smiled at Zoe's expression.

Zoe's eyes went immediately to the dark, fluffy triangle between Rita's thighs and stayed there.

She had seen nude women before. She had seven sisters. But this was different. This was a nude woman she was about to have sex with.

And she was a beautiful, sexy woman.

Zoe's heart raced as Rita approached her. Since Zoe was seated on the bed, Rita's cunt was at eye level. She could see that it was moist and ready. Zoe looked into Rita's eyes. She smiled at her and nodded. Zoe's right hand moved slowly toward Rita's cunt, then hesitated a moment before continuing. As soon as Zoe's long, sexy fingers touched her, Rita closed her eyes and sighed deeply.

Zoe explored her slowly. She had resisted Rita's advances for days, not wanting any part of girl-on-girl sex. Now, all of her fears melted away as soon as she touched Rita's cunt.

Her soft, beautiful cunt.

Her sexy cunt.

Rita let Zoe feel her for several minutes and nearly came when she slid two fingers inside her. There was no doubt now. Zoe wanted her as much as she wanted Zoe.

Afraid of coming too soon, Rita moved away and told Zoe to stand. She knelt before her.

"What beautiful legs you have," Rita said as she caressed them over and over.

Her touches made Zoe's heart pound harder. It pounded harder still when Rita undid her shorts and tugged them—along with her panties—to the floor. Rita sat back on her haunches and stared. Zoe's cunt was magnificent. It was neatly furred, with large flowery labia and an obviously erect clit.

"Oh yes," Zoe gasped as Rita touched her.

Seconds later, they were on the bed, locked in a hot embrace as they fingered each other to another deep, juicy come,

She climbed on top of Zoe and pressed her cunt against hers. Zoe reached up and gripped Rita's ass as they started to move against each other nice and slow for what proved to be a long, delicious fuck. Whenever Rita sensed that Zoe was about to come, she stopped for a few seconds, then fucked her again. She did this several times and the near orgasms were driving Zoe wild. When they finally did come, it was simultaneous and explosive. They kept fucking and fucking as waves of intense pleasure surged through their sweaty bodies and they both screamed out their love for each other.

After a short break, Rita introduced Zoe to her favorite vibrator and some of her favorite sexual positions. It was an 18 inch long and two inch thick double headed latex dick with a vibrator. She fucked Zoe Missionary style, doggie style and several other ways they could imagine. Each time, Rita turned the vibrator on full just before they came to make each orgasm that much more intense.

Their lovemaking lasted for hours and hours.

They came again and again.

Zoe came more times than she could count. Time and again, she shoved her tongue deep into Rita's quivering snatch or did her with the vibrator. And Rita did the same to Zoe. They kept at it until both women were too tired to move. They fell asleep in each other's arms for a good two hours.

When Zoe woke, she looked at the beautiful woman lying next to her and smiled. Rita smiled back and they made love again....

Chapter Six

The next day at work one of the regular customers at the store showed up. As always, he joked with Rita and she joked back. His name was Steve and he was tall, dark and ruggedly good-looking.

And Rita was definitely attracted to him and she often wondered what it would be like to have sex with him. She'd known him for years and he always made "passes" at her. Their banter was always good-natured and never went beyond talk. He knew she was married but he also wanted to get into her panties.

Today, he seemed a little bolder than usual. Since no one else was at the check-out line, he lowered his voice and smiled at her like usual.

"When are you going to let me do it?" he asked.

"Do what?" she asked, knowing what he meant.

"You know what. I've been coming on to you for years now. You know what I want," he said.

"No I don't," she joked. "Tell me!"

He leaned closer.

"Fuck you," he said. "When are you gonna let me fuck you?"

She blushed. He'd never been that blunt!

"Never!" she said.

"I think you will one day," he smiled.

"No I won't!" she said.

"We'll see," he said.

He paid for his beer and left.

Or so she thought he did. She went down the middle aisle to finish stocking. A few seconds later, she felt a light pat on her behind. She turned to see Steve standing behind her.

"What are you doing here?" she asked.

"I forgot something," he said as he leaned closer.

She turned around to finish stocking.

"What did you forget?" she asked over her shoulder.

"This," he said softly as he squeezed her ass cheek.

This caught Rita by total surprise. Steve had never done anything like this before but today, he decided to take a gamble. She stood still as he felt her behind.

"I want you, Rita. I want you more than anything else I can think of," he whispered as he ran his fingers along her crack. "I want to put my dick in your pussy and fuck you all day and night. I know you want it as much as I do."

He slid his fingers up and down her crack. She quivered slightly and realized that his touches were exciting her. She liked him a lot, too. There had always been an obvious physical attraction between them. She looked around. No one else was in the store at the moment so she sort of relaxed. Steve was amazed that she was allowing him to touch her.

He leaned closer. She felt his warm breath on her neck and his rock-hard erection press against her crack. He ran both hands up her sides and fondled her breasts through her T-shirt. Rita quivered even more as her inner fires ignited.

"I want you, Rita! I must have you!" he whispered as he squeezed her nipples.

Rita moaned.

Since she'd already fucked Greg, why not give Steve a try?

She reached behind her and ran her fingers over his erection. It seemed really thick. She turned and smiled at him and fondled his balls.

"Okay," she said much to his astonishment. "Let's do it."

"You really mean that?" he asked.

She reached down and groped his prick. He nearly came when she tweaked his knob, too.

"I'm off tomorrow and my husband will be at work until five. Come to my house at noon and we'll fuck all day if you like," she said. "I'll show you what Filipinas are called little brown fucking machines."

"You have yourself a date!" he agreed.

Much to Rita's delight, Steve showed up at her house with a bottle of wine. She led him to the sofa and got two glasses from the kitchen. Steve uncorked the bottle and filled the glasses. After a few rounds, she led him upstairs to the bedroom to give him what he came there for.

After a nice, long kiss, they fell onto the bed. Steve undid her blouse then unclasped her bra. He then gently played with her breasts while Rita smiled at him. When he leaned over and started licking and sucking her nipples, she let out several low moans. She liked it when he sucked her nipples and had no qualms about letting him do it as much as he liked. By now, her cunt was on fire. She needed release and she needed it fast.

She didn't object at all when he unbuttoned her shorts and slid his hand into her panties. The second he touched her clit, she parted her legs and moaned louder. Steve slid his middle finger into her slit and "fucked" her nice and fast. Rita groaned and raised her hips. Then she came.

"Ooohhh, yes! More! Do it more!" she moaned.

Steve kept fingering her as she writhed on the bed and cried out. Rita shook harder as she came again. As she lay there in a sexual fog, Steve pulled off her shorts and panties.

He sat back and whistled at her beautiful, shiny black triangle and told her she had the most gorgeous pussy he'd ever seen or touched. He spent the next several minutes fondling it and sucking her nipples again while he slowly brought her to another good, strong orgasm. While she was still quaking, he got on top of her and started kissing her. At the same time, he massaged her clit. Then, much to her delight, he slid his tongue along her slit and into her cunt.

"Oooh, yes! That's it!" she sighed as he licked her clit. "I'm all yours now. Take me where you want."

Steve licked harder and harder.

Rita moaned and sighed then screamed as she came again. Her head was reeling from all of her orgasms now and her thighs were wide open. She was so far gone, she was barely aware of the fact that he was between her open thighs or that he had his prick out. Steve massaged her labia with the knob of his prick. The sensations caused Rita to quiver and open her legs even more. Steve eased his prick into her wet, hot channel. Rita shivered and bent her knees. Then she felt something long, hard and oh-so delicious moving in and out of her cunt. The movements were slow and exciting. She lay there and let him continue.

She moaned and moved with him. It was then she realized that Steve was fucking her and it felt so damned good! Rita moaned and fucked him back. His prick felt so good inside her. Better than anything. She continued to move with him as he thrust harder.

Rita moaned louder and moved with him faster.

"Fuck me!" she said. "Fuck me good!"

"Your wish is my command!" he replied as he slid his massive prick deep into her eager cunt.

"Oooh, yes!" Rita sighed as his knob struck bottom. He felt bigger than usual today.

Much bigger.

Steve then began moving in and out of Rita's cunt. Rita quivered with each delicious down stroke, then moved with him.

Again and again and again.

Rita fucked him faster and faster.

Harder and harder.

"Oooh yes! Yes! I love it! It's wonderful! Fuck me harder! Give it to me good!" she moaned.

They fucked harder and harder.

"Fuck me! Fuck me! Fuck me! More! More! Make me come!" she screamed as she fucked him with everything she had.

Then she came.

It was a strong, deep orgasm that sent her mind reeling. She moaned and cried and continued to drive her hips upward. Steve fucked her faster and faster. Rita groaned loudly, quivered all over and came second time.

"Oh God! That feels so good!" she moaned.

Rita lay there moaning and gasping for breath as she slowly returned to Earth. When she opened her eyes, Steve was still very hard and kept fucking her for a while longer. He bent her legs back a little ways and fucked her deeper. She screamed and came again. Rita heard him grunt as he slammed his prick into her cunt as deeply as he could and came inside her. When he pulled out, a river a snow white liquid oozed from her throbbing cuntlips.

"Your pussy is tighter than I remembered. Wow! You're one really great fuck!" Steve said.

Rita grabbed his prick and stroked him until he was rock hard again. Then she laid down and opened her legs.

"Make me yours," she said.

This time, she wrapped her legs around his waist and gripped his arms as he fucked her. She matched him stroke for stroke right from the start and sighed and moaned as they moved faster and faster.

"Give me all you can now! Make me your slut! Make me all yours!" she cried.

Steve fucked her harder and harder. Rita moved with him eagerly and squeezed his prick with her cunt muscles. Steve gasped at the unexpected pleasure.

"Ooooh, yeah! I love it! This is the best fuck! A great fuck! A wonderful fuck! Give it to me! Make me yours!" she cried as she fucked him faster and faster.

Then she came again.

This time, she came harder than she ever came before. As she did, she fucked him wildly and begged for more and more of his massive prick. Steve was only too happy to oblige.

"Make my pussy yours now! It's all yours! Do what you want with me!" Rita gasped as she came again.

As she came, she fucked him faster. Steve groaned, drove his prick as deeply into her cunt as he could, and emptied his balls inside of her. Rita shuddered as she felt his cum splash into her cunt walls.

And she came again.

"Oooh yes! That's what I want! Fill me! Fill my pussy!" she moaned.

Steve gave her a few more deep thrusts, then slid his prick out of her cunt. A river of cum followed and ran down between Rita's cheeks. Rita recovered and swallowed most of Steve's prick and give him a good blow job. She sucked his prick until he was rock hard again, then laid down and spread her legs. They fucked like maniacs for a good ten minutes. Then Rita came again and shook all over. Steve kept fucking her as hard as he could, then he grunted and emptied another load of cum deep inside her cunt. He fell on the bed next to her. Rita stroked his prick. To her delight, it quickly rose to full salute again.

"How do you do that?" she asked.

"Trade secret," Steve said.

Rita laid back and opened her legs. She sighed happily as the huge prick went into her cunt again. This time, they fucked nice and easy for a few minutes. Then Rita began fucking him faster and faster. Steve matched her thrust for thrust. Then both of them came at the exact same moment. Steve pulled out and a river of cum oozed from Rita's still pulsing cunt.

"Happy?" she joked.

"You have no idea! You are even better than I thought you'd be! Can we do this again one day?" he said.

She laughed.

"Maybe. We'll see," she said.

When Steve left, she ran upstairs to shower. As the hot water cascaded down her body, she smiled. She'd had sex with two different men in one week. Good, hard, all-out sex. She also knew that she'd probably fuck a few more men.

"My pussy is taking over the rest of me now. I'm becoming a slut!" she said.

Two days later, Steve called Rita on her cell phone.

"What do you want—as if I didn't know?" she teased.

"I'd like to see you today. I've missed you," he said.

"I've missed you, too. I'm shopping right now. I'll be home around one. Why don't you stop by then?" she suggested.

"You have a date," he said. "I'll see you then. Make sure Art's not around."

"I'll call you if he's home," Rita promised.

Much to her relief, Art had gone to the office. She sat down and waited for Steve to arrive. When he did, she greeted him at the door dressed in her very sheer robe. As soon as he walked in and shut the door behind him, Rita let the robe slide to the floor and stood before him completely naked. He gawked at her smooth, lovely body as his prick hardened. She walked up to him and groped him. Within seconds, he, too was naked and Rita was kneeling before him stroking his cock. She had a hungry look in her eyes. Sort of like a cat ogling a canary.

Steve led her to the dining room and had her lean forward on the table with her legs apart. Then he knelt behind her and lovingly licked her puckered anus for a few seconds before sliding his tongue up into her cunt. Rita gasped as he explored her soft, flowery lips and nibbled at her clit. It was a very pleasant and exciting sensation that made her fidget. At the same time, Steve reached up and massaged her nipples. That really made Rita squirm.

Now that she was good and wet, Steve stood up and eased his prick into her channel. She sighed as his knob pushed past her labia and sunk deep into her pussy. She felt him moving in and out. He did her slowly at first, trying to find his balance. When he did, he began fucking her faster and faster. Rita sighed and trembled all over. Steve grabbed her behind and humped her even faster. This caused her to shriek with delight as his knob raked across her g-spot several times.

Steve loved the way her cunt convulsed around his prick each time he thrust into her. She felt so good, too. So tight. So silky smooth. In fact, this was one of the best fucks he'd had in weeks.

And Rita had one of the best cunts.

Each time Steve's prick moved inside her pussy, Rita sighed happily and trembled with lust. She felt herself growing wetter and hotter as they fucked and she began thrusting her hips back at him to match his rhythm.

Each time, he pushed into her all the way to his balls. Each time, he thrust harder. And each thrust caused her to moan.

Rita felt herself coming. It was a good one, too. From deep inside her cunt. Steve realized what she was going through and picked up the pace of his thrusting. Rita moaned and threw her head back.

"Oohh! That's it! Fuck me, Steve! That feels so good! So fucking good!" she moaned.

Steve fucked her even faster. He soon felt his balls spasm a few times and held onto her even tighter as he hammered away at her sopping cunt. Rita shook wildly and sighed. Then she fell across the table and lay trembling while he continued to fuck her like a madman. After several more deep thrusts, Steve pushed his prick as deep into Rita's cunt as he could and released a flood of cum. The sensations caused by the hot cum slamming into her cunt walls triggered another orgasm in Rita and she began groaning loudly. Spurt after spurt jetted into her. She felt each and every one of them, too.

And they felt delicious.

So wonderfully delicious.

Steve kept humping away until his prick slid out of Rita's cunt. As it did, a shower of cum dripped from her open slit and splattered onto the carpet. He fingered her slit while she slowly fell back to Earth. Rita turned and wrapped her fingers around his half-hard shaft. To her delight, it began to get hard again.

"Let's finish this upstairs," she said.

Once in bed Steve pushed Rita onto her back. She immediately opened her thighs so he could mount her. Since her cunt was still lined with cum, Steve's long prick slid into her with ease and they began a slow, easy fuck. After a few Seconds, Rita gripped his behind and began thrusting her pelvis upward with a wild abandon. Steve stopped in mid-thrust and allowed her to do most of the work for a few seconds before he joined in with a vengeance.

They moved faster and faster now. Steve felt her cunt convulse around his prick as she came and came hard. He fucked her as fast as he could until, Seconds later, he emptied another large load of cum deep inside her pussy. But this time, he remained hard and he kept going at her with all of his energy. Rita fell back with her arms and legs akimbo as he deep fucked her until he fell across her chest. She felt his knob slam into her cervix. The impact was followed by yet another gusher of warm cum that blended with his earlier deposits.

They rested for a few minutes. Then Rita wrapped her fingers around Steve's prick and jerked him off. He leaned over and licked her nipples as he fingered her slit. When Steve was fully erect once more, Rita straddled him and impaled herself on his cock. She rode him nice and slow this time as she savored the feeling of his meat moving in and out of her cunt. Steve grabbed her behind and fucked her back. They soon got into a nice, steady rhythm. It took several minutes for them to come this time. Steve did first. He drove his prick straight up Rita's snatch and drained his cum inside of her. He shot wad after wad into her. So much, in fact, that it leaked out of her cunt and coated his balls.

By then, she was riding him very hard. Her head was back and she emitted load, happy moans as she bounced up and down on his prick. When she came, she fell on top of him and sighed deeply.

She slid off him and grabbed his cum-coated prick. When it didn't respond after a few good pulls, she slipped the head into her mouth and sucked away until Steve's balls ached and he had to beg her to stop.

She gave up and lay next to him.

"I guess we've reached your limit," she said. There was a definite tone of disappointment in her voice.

"I need to rest for a while. Then we can try it again if you like," Steve offered.

"I like," she replied.

They did it one more time that day. This time, they did it laying on their side, facing each other so that Steve could suck on her nipples while they fucked. This time, they did it until they could barely move and Steve had added yet another shot of heavy cream to the lake of cum inside of Rita's cunt.

Steve dressed and staggered out to car. Rita threw on her robe and watched as he drove away. Her cunt still tingled from all of the sex they'd had. She could hardly believe his staying power or how quickly he was able to get it up again after coming.

"My God! That man can fuck!" she said as she went up to shower. "He makes my pussy purr!"

Zoe got a chance to be alone with Art the next afternoon. Now that she knew Rita had already fucked other men, she decided to go after Art in a very big way. She put on her sheerest blouse and skimpiest shorts and headed right for his house.

"Did you know that Rita's been fucking this guy named Steve?" she asked as she flashed her seductive smile.

"Of course. She bragged about it last night," he said as he gripped her shoulders. Damn! You're so very sexy!"

"Am I sexy enough to fuck?" she asked.

"Definitely!" he assured her as she moved closer.

They kissed. It was a kiss that sent an electric shock surging through them. A very powerful one!

He smelled the aroma of her perfume. It was very light and sexy. He looked into her hazel eyes deeply.

"I think I love you, Zoe. I think I've always loved you," he said softly.

"Let's make this special, Art. Let's make love!" she said.

He felt his prick hardening and wondered if he should try to hide it. Zoe's blouse was low cut this day and he could plainly see her hard nipples straining at the light material. He realized that she wasn't wearing a bra and fought down an urge to rip her blouse off.

Art was at full mast now. Zoe noticed the obvious bulge in his jeans and smiled. It was all she needed to know. She ran her fingertips along his prick from balls to tip, then stopped and squeezed the head lightly. As she did, she felt his prick get harder—and bigger.

"I bet your great big dick would feel so good inside my tight little pussy, don't you think so?" she whispered as she repeated what she'd done twice more. She looked him in the eyes and smiled.

"Let's make love, Art. Real love!" she said softly.

She could tell that her closeness was making him a little bit nervous—and a lot horny. Zoe took it up a notch. She reached down and slowly unzipped her shorts to reveal the top of her soft, brown triangle. Now that she had his attention, she slid the zipper down a little more to show that she wasn't wearing panties. The sight almost made Art cum on the spot.

"You like my pussy, Art? I'm yours, Art. All yours!" she whispered as seductively as possible as she again ran her fingers along the huge bulge in his jeans.

She felt him shudder. She smiled and tweaked the head of his shaft several times as she lowered her zipper all the way so he could now see her entire bush.

"My pussy is soft, warm and very wet now. Don't you want to put your nice, hard dick inside it? Don't you want to fuck me?" she whispered as she tweaked his knob again and again.

Unable to hold back, Art began to come in his pants. Zoe felt the warm sticky goo spurting from his prick and worked him faster and faster. The more she tweaked his knob, the more he came and the more Zoe played with his prick. She kept at this until she could no longer grip the end of his prick. By then, her entire hand was sticky and he had huge, dark stain in his jeans. Despite this, she kept tweaking away until Art began to shudder all over.

He couldn't believe she was doing this, but if she wanted to play with his prick that badly, who was he to stop her? Besides, it felt fantastic. To her surprise, he began to get rigid again—just enough to enable her to grip the tip better. She tweaked him faster and faster. To her surprise—and his—he came gain. Again, she continued to milk him until she was sure he'd shot his entire load into his pants.

By then, her shorts had slid down a few more inches. Unable to resist, Art gently stroked her soft brown muff. His touches send wild sensations all through her body. She nearly jumped out of her clothes altogether when he massaged her swollen clit and ran his fingers along her moist, warm labia.

"I'm almost there, Art. Finish me," she whispered. "Take me all the way."

Art responded by flicking her clit until she came. When she did, she fell against him and dug her nails into his arms. He kept flicking her through two more good, long orgasms, then stopped. They were both sweating profusely and the room had taken on a decided sexual aroma.

"I'm all yours," she whispered. "Fuck me."

Zoe unzipped his jeans and grabbed his prick. She started off with a few good pulls to try and get him hard. At the same time, she let her shorts slide down her legs and stepped clear of them. Still gripping his prick, she led him to the sofa. He was still only half-erect. Determined to get laid, she sat down and slid his member into her mouth.

That did it.

Art's prick became hard and long again.

Zoe smiled, leaned back on the sofa, put her feet on the cushions and spread her thighs.

"Fuck me!" she said.

He got between her legs and slowly penetrated her. She felt him go in all the way to his balls, then she used her inner muscles to massage his shaft.

"Wow!" Art gasped as he had never felt anything like that before.

Zoe grinned and squeezed his prick with her pussy walls, then she began to hum him nice and easy. Art let her do this for a little while, then began to fuck her back. Zoe moaned softly and gripped his arms. This was good.

Better than she had expected.

Better than anything.

They picked up the pace. It was a nice, easy rhythm that radiated pleasure throughout Zoe's body. She felt herself nearing liftoff and fucked him faster. He caught her signal and moved with her, this time, his thrusts became a little harder and deeper. They fucked for a long, long time.

It was the longest fuck Zoe had ever had.

And she was tingling all over.

Especially between her legs.

She felt the pressure building inside her pussy and fucked him harder. Art understood and matched her move for move. He, too, was on the edge of coming. But he wanted to hold back so they could come together.

He wanted this to be the most perfect fuck Zoe ever had.

Zoe suddenly tensed, convulsed and emitted a long, low moan as she came. Art exploded at the same instant and began pumping load after load of cum into her sucking pussy. They kept at this until their bodies ached and Art's prick shriveled and popped out of Zoe's pussy.

He sat back on his heels and smiled at the river of cum that was now oozing from Zoe's slit. She smiled happily back at him.

"That was magnifico!" she sighed. "You left me up in the clouds. I've never been fucked that good before."

That was the first time they'd actually fucked and to her, it was by far the best. It was at that moment she decided that she would do everything she could to make him hers. Art had no complaints either. They kissed several times, then Zoe dressed. He walked her out to her car and waved as she drove off.

Art told Rita what happened.

"So she finally got you, huh? How was she?" Rita teased.

"Amazing!" he replied.

"Are you gonna keep seeing her?" Rita asked.

"Definitely! There's no turning back now. We're going to make love every chance we get," he said.

"Love? Not fuck?" Rita teased. "You love Zoe?"

"I think I've always loved her. Not as much as I love you, but there's more between us than just sex," he admitted.

"I think that from now on, you'll have two wives. Just remember who is you real wife," Rita said.

"I will if you remember who you're married to," he replied. "I think Bart wants you all to himself."

"That's what scares me about him," she said. "He's very open, honest and very attractive. I'm really starting to like him a lot, too. I think that's why I keep putting him off. I'm scared that I'll like it too much to stop."

He laughed.

"Every time you fuck another man, I'll make love with Zoe. The more you fuck, the more we'll fuck," he said.

"I know. I don't mind that, either. Do you have anything left for me tonight?" she asked.

He took her by the hand and led her upstairs...

Zoe was elated.

She could hardly contain herself as she showered.

"We did it! We did it! We really did it! And it was wonderful!" she shouted. "I'm never letting you go, Art! Never! You're mine now! Mine forever! And I'm yours!"

To prove it, she paid him a visit the next afternoon.

"I've been thinking about you," he said.

"And I've been thinking about you," she said as she undid her shorts and pulled them and her panties off. "I want to suck your dick. I also need you to eat my pussy and a lot of other nice things."

Art smiled as they finished undressing and climbed onto the bed. As soon as he lay down, Zoe grabbed his prick and slid it into her mouth. Art let her suck it for a little while, then he grabbed her ass and stuck his tongue into her pussy.

Zoe came first and began fucking his tongue while she sucked his prick harder. Art popped moments later and emptied a good sized load of cum into her mouth. Zoe hungrily lapped up most of it.

That's when she felt Art's tongue slide into her asshole.

"Ooohhh! That's nice," she cooed. "Nobody but you ever licked me there. I never knew it could be so exciting."

Art slid his tongue in deeper. Zoe shivered, then returned to sucking his prick. When she made it hard again, she slid off his face and went into an all-fours position.

"Fuck my ass, Art! I need it!" she said.

Art got behind her and eased his prick into her rear channel until his balls touched her cheeks. Zoe gasped.

"That feels just about perfect," she said.

Art grabbed her cheeks and started to fuck her nice and easy. Zoe moaned and gasped with each in-thrust then began to move with him. Seconds later, she felt his prick spasm inside of her and squeezed him tight with her ass muscles. Art kept fucking her until he'd pumped every last drop of cum he had into her fine, smooth ass. When he was finished, Zoe rolled onto her back with her legs open wide.

Art smiled and went down on her again. This time, he licked her clit as fast as he could until she erupted and rocked from side-to-side.

He laid still and watched her nipples bob up and down as she caught her breath. When she came back down, she smiled and kissed him.

"I'm so glad you came to see me today," she said.

After a short rest, Zoe rolled onto her back and spread her legs wide. As tired as Art was, the sight of her soft brown muff caused his cock to stir. Zoe gave him a come hither look and walked into the bedroom with Art right behind her.

There, they kissed passionately as Zoe wrapped her fingers around Art's prick and gave it a few easy strokes. Then she sat down on the edge of the bed with her thighs apart. Unable to resist, Art fell to his knees and slowly licked her already juicy slit. Zoe sighed as his tongue danced in and out of her cunt and fell back on the bed. Art cupped her cheeks and pulled her to him as he ate her.

"Oh, yes!" she sighed as Art's tongue sent shivers up her back.

She loved the way he ate her. No one else, she decided, could do the things he did with his tongue. She was always happy and eager to feel it dancing between her legs.

As for Art, he adored her bitter-sweet-salty flavor and delightful scent. Zoe tasted and smelled so different.

So delightfully sexy.

Now, he was as hard as could be. He stood up, pushed Zoe's legs as far apart as possible and slid his prick into cunt all the way to his balls. Zoe gasped. She wrapped her legs around his hips and closed her eyes as they began that slow, deep-penetrating fuck they both loved. It was the most incredible sex they could have. It was exhilarating, wonderful sex. But it was far more than that. What they had now went far beyond the mere physical union of two people. It was an incredible melding of two into one—a perfect union of body and spirit.

Art took his time with Zoe. He always went as slow and as deep as possible, not only to give her the utmost pleasure but also to savor the feel of her silky-smooth cunt as he moved in and out of her. The way Art made love to her made Zoe feel especially wonderful.

Wanted.

Sexy.

Each time they made love, they added more cement to their blossoming relationship. Each time, the bond between them grew stronger and stronger.

Soon, Zoe felt herself coming and began humping Art faster. He caught her signal and tried to hold back as long as possible. He wanted to time their orgasms perfectly. To make this one really special.

He did.

Both he and Zoe erupted at the same moment and became suspended in time for a few seconds. They clung to each other like there was no tomorrow and humped until their bodies ached and sweat covered them. At the height of ecstasy, Zoe cried out.

"I love you, Art! I love you!"

To her delight, he echoed her words. They rested now. Art was still on top of her, his semi-hard prick still buried inside Zoe's pulsing cunt, their lips fused together in a long, hot kiss. When they broke off, Zoe looked into Art's eyes and saw the love in them.

Zoe used her inner muscles to squeeze Art's prick. The delicious sensations caused him to harden once again. Instead of doing her, Art slid to the floor and used his fingers to pry apart Zoe's pussy lips. The center was dark pink now and very moist. He leaned forward, sniffed her heady perfume, and then licked her thighs near her slit.

Zoe shivered with anticipation as she waited for his tongue to work its magic. She didn't have to wait long. Art slipped it into the bottom of her cunt then moved it slowly up toward her swollen clit. Zoe gasped and emitted a deep "ah!" as his tongue swirled around her love button.

It felt so good.

So very very good.

Art ate her for a long, long time. Each time he sensed her about to come, he eased up, then did it all again. Several times, he brought her to the brink or orgasm and stopped short of making her come. Soon, Zoe was begging him to finish her off. When he did, she blew like a volcano and just about rolled off the bed. Then Art did the unexpected.

While she was in mid-come, he climbed on top of her and rammed his prick into her cunt hard. Zoe screamed with joy. She wrapped her arms and legs around him and they gave each other a nice, steady—and somewhat harder—love. The movement of his hard-on inside her convulsing cunt caused Zoe to come again and again. Each orgasm was stronger than the last and she soared ever skyward and became lost in the clouds.

"Yes! Yes! Fuck me, Art! Fuck me good!" she screamed as her body trembled uncontrollably with each hard thrust of his prick.

She was getting the best sex of her entire life now and she didn't want it to end any time soon. Art humped her harder. Zoe clung to him, unable to move, unable to love him back. All she could do now was to take it, to enjoy the glorious ride he was giving her. Then her quivering, quaking body became too much for him. He rammed his prick into her as deep as he could and groaned as streams of white good jetted into her pussy.

He stayed motionless as Zoe milked him until her pussy was flooded with his cum. Then he leaned over. They kissed passionately. Zoe tasted her cunt on his tongue. The taste excited her again and she began humping his half-hard prick. Art trembled as she humped him. He was nearly exhausted now. He just hovered over her and let Zoe do the work. He was so numb, he barely noticed he was still coming like crazy inside her wonderful cunt.

Then Art pulled Zoe to him and squeezed her behind. Zoe giggled and slipped free. Zoe's body was nearly perfect and her legs were gorgeous. He played with her nipples as she jerked him off. When he was ready, she ran her tongue over the knob and along his shaft several times. Art groaned as she eased it into her mouth and sucked it gently. She soon felt his balls spasm. She stopped and smiled up at him.

"Not yet," she said. "I want this to last."

She spread her legs as Art sunk his tongue into her cunt. Now it was his turn to tease her and he kept nibbling and licking at her swollen clit until he senses that she was ready to come.

Zoe pushed him onto his back, then straddled him and slowly impaled herself on his erection. She lowered her hips until their pubic hairs merged, then proceeded to bounce up and down slowly. Art grabbed her behind and began humping her back harder and harder. Soon Zoe's head fell back and she emitted a deep, satisfied moan as she came. Art kept driving in and out of her until he came, too. Then he pulled her down on top of his cock and emptied his cum into her pussy until it ran out of her and coated his balls and stained the sheets. Still not finished, Art rolled Zoe onto her side and kept hammering away at her. Zoe screamed and moaned with each hard, deep thrust of his cock. Then she felt him spasm again as he added yet another good load of cream to his earlier deposit. They rested for a few minutes, then Art began to get hard again. Zoe eyed his growing cock and smiled.

She laid on her back.

"Want to try something different?" asked Art.

"Okay. What?" she asked.

"You'll see," he said. "It's a little strange but I think you'll like it."

He then sat on her chest and placed his erection between her breasts. Zoe stared at the swollen glans which was just an inch or two from her chin as Art used his hands to push the sides of her breasts against his cock. When it felt nice and snug, he began moving his hips back and forth. Zoe was totally surprised—and somewhat mesmerized—with the sight of his cock moving in and out between her breasts. She'd seen this in porno movies before but never once thought of doing it.

As Art humped her, he played with her swollen—and sensitive—nipples. That sent delicious tingles racing all through Zoe's body and she began to writhe in pleasure. Art was also enchanted. He'd always wanted to try this with her. She had the greatest breasts her ever saw. Now that he was doing it, he realized how good this was. Laying her breasts was nearly as good as laying her pussy and it was an incredible turn-on. Zoe felt Art's balls jerk suddenly. She saw his knob expand and watched as the first of several long streams of cum rocketed from his cock. This one splattered the underside of her chin and neck. The second landed from her chin to her hairline and the third across her lips and nose. As Art kept humping, Zoe opened her mouth. She caught most of the next few spurts on her tongue, then bent her head and allowed his cock to move in and out of her open mouth. As it did, she licked the knob several times, which caused Art to ejaculate even harder.

She gripped his behind and pulled him forward until he was laying her mouth. Art groaned and heaved one last load straight down her throat. Zoe swallowed every last bit of it, too. Then Art rolled off. Still horny, Zoe straddled his face. Art gripped her behind and licked away until she came several times. Then both lay still to catch their breath.

"That was incredible! Awesome," Art said after several minutes.

"Yes," Zoe agreed.

The next morning, Rita got up early. Art was already gone. As she brushed her teeth, she saw the tube of "pussy warming gel", as she called it, on the shelf in the cabinet. She smiled and decided to give it another try.

She took it into the bedroom, squeezed some onto her fingertip and gently massaged it into her clit. A few minutes later, she was so wet and horny that she couldn't stand it. She picked up the phone. Instead of calling Art, she dialed Steve's number.

"My pussy is on fire. Can you come over today and help me put it out?" she asked.

Steve arrived at Art's house around 10:15 and was greeted at the door by Rita, who was dressed in nothing but a short robe, which she dropped to the floor immediately. The sight of her slender nude body gave Steve an obvious erection.

"Today I am your slut," she announced as she took his hand and led him to the bedroom.

Once there, Steve disrobed. Rita stared at his huge, bobbing member. It looked bigger than she remembered. The sight made her pussy wet.

She walked over and gave it a few pulls as Steve gently sucked her left nipple and rubbed her pussy. Rita didn't seem to notice. Her eyes were riveted to the ever-growing prick in her hand.

"Damn, you're wet," Steve said as he eased his middle finger into her cunt.

"You make me wet. Wow! Your dick is so big!" she replied as she continued to pump away on it.

"And it's all yours," Steve said.

She smiled and pulled him to the bed by his prick. Then she climbed on and pulled him with her. She pushed him onto his back, twisted around so that her cunt was close to his face, and proceeded to go down on his prick with a hunger that surprised him. He massaged her bush for a little while, then reached over and pulled her toward him so that her cunt rested on his mouth. When his tongue entered her pussy, Rita trembled and sucked even harder at his prick.

Steve ate her for a several minutes then licked his way up into the crack of her behind and eased it into her puckered anus. At the same time, he massaged her g-spot with his fingers. Rita emitted a deep moan and came very hard. Even so, she kept sucking at his member. When she tasted the first bit of his cum spurting into her mouth, she sucked harder and beat him off with her hand. He fired so much cum into Rita's mouth that she had trouble swallowing all of it. A lot dribbled out of her mouth

After several more minutes of this, they fell next to each other and tried to catch their breath. She reached over and stroked Steve's prick until it became good and hard again. She opened her legs wide and smiled at him.

"My little Asian pussy needs to be fed," she said.

Steve got between her thighs and slid his prick home. Rita wrapped her legs around his hips and they jumped right into a good, hard, steady fuck. Steve grabbed her ankles and pushed her legs back toward her breasts. Then he began fucking her harder and harder. Rita groaned and sighed with each deep thrust.

She was Steve's slut. She would always be his slut.

His little brown fucking machine.

She should have been ashamed of doing this. Good girls never did such things. But now she didn't care. All she cared about was the good hard prick in her pussy and the ferocious fuck she was getting.

The sensations felt intense.

Powerful.

Wicked.

Delicious.

His prick filled every part of her pussy. It stretched her to the limit and she could feel his heavy knob knocking at her womb. Each push sent shockwaves of intense pleasure coursing through her sweaty body.

Her orgasm was sudden and explosive.

"Yes! Fuck me, Steve! Fuck harder!" she cried as she clawed at the bed.

He did as she asked. The harder he fucked her, the harder she came. Then she felt Steve's prick expand suddenly inside her cunt and knew he was about to blow.

"Fuck me harder, Steve! Fuck me! Come inside me. I want to feel it. Fill my pussy!" she ranted as several more orgasms washed through her.

Steve hammered at her with a vengeance, then shoved his prick all the way into her pussy as he emptied every last drop of cum he could produce into her. There was so much that it oozed out of her slit and ran down between her cheeks to the bed.

But he wasn't through.

Not yet.

He released her legs and humped her missionary style. Rita wrapped her arms and legs around his body and tried to fuck him back. All the while, he kept pumping lots and lots of sticky cum into her happy pussy.

When it was over, Steve slid his half-erect member out of her still pulsing cunt. Rita saw the long string of cum that followed it out of her and laughed. She reached over and gently squeezed it. Steve smiled at the river of white liquid running out of her cunt.

It had been the single most intense fuck that Rita'd ever had. So intense that she still tingled all over and was completely exhausted.

"That felt good. Real good," she said. It's good to feel a different dick inside my pussy once in a while."

"Thanks Rita," Steve said. "I needed this more than you could imagine."

"So did I," Rita thought as she smiled blissfully.

Steve got up and dressed. Rita watched for a little while, then got up and threw on her robe. She walked him down to the front door.

"When would you like to do this again?" Steve asked as he fondled her cunt.

"I don't know. Let's not plan anything. Let's just let things happen naturally," she said. "If you keep doing that, I'm going to drag you back upstairs."

Steve laughed and kissed her on the cheek.

"I'd better leave before you kill me," he joked.

Rita watched him get into the car and drive away. As he vanished around the corner, she wondered why in Hell she didn't call Art to come home and fuck her. She shook her head and laughed.

Chapter Seven

Bart decided to prowl the casino on Tuesday anyway. Since Rita wasn't available, he figured he'd pick up someone easy for the night.

He watched as Zoe entered alone. She wore a sleeveless blouse and dark red miniskirt. He looked around but didn't see Rita, so he decided to ask Zoe where she was.

She recognized him right away and sort of smiled when he walked over.

"Rita's in Las Vegas with her husband this week," Zoe explained.

"That lucky guy! You know that I've been talking with Rita for the last few weeks, right?" he asked.

"Yes. I've seen the two of you sitting together a few times. She kind of likes you," Zoe said.

"Then you probably know that I've been trying to get into her panties, but she's playing real hard to get," he said.

"That's because she's married and very happy," Zoe said.

"Are you married?" he asked.

"I'm divorced," she said as she smiled at him.

"I saw you leave with a man last week. Is he a good friend of yours?" he asked.

"We're friends now," she laughed. "Real close friends, too."

He laughed.

"Then maybe I should go after you instead?" Bart joked.

"You can try," she smiled.

"What's your name?" he asked.

"Zoe. You're Bart," she said.

"How about I buy you dinner?" he asked.

"Okay," she agreed.

Bart told her to order whatever she wanted. When she ordered the surf and turf, he didn't bat an eye. He ordered the same and a bottle of wine. She found him to be very pleasant company and she liked being with him.

"I know that you have the hots for Rita, so why did you invite me to have dinner with you tonight?" she asked.

He smiled and placed his hand on her knee.

"I just thought that since you're single, you might be open to having sex with me," he said.

"Maybe you figured wrong. I don't jump into bed with every man I meet," she replied. "I also think you should leave Rita alone. If her husband finds out about you, he'll beat you to a pulp."

"How would he know? Are you going to tell him?" Bart asked.

"Maybe," she said.

"Rita already knows what I want because I told her up front. She hasn't slapped me or anything yet, so I guess she likes the attention. Even if she did slap me, I'd still try for her because she's beautiful and poses a challenge. You're very beautiful, too," he said.

"I'm not interested," she said as he eased his hand upward.

"We'll see," he smiled. "What are you, ethnically?"

"I'm half Chinese and half Puerto Rican and a few other things," she said.

"No wonder you're so beautiful!" he said.

"Flattery won't get you anything," she smiled as she ate.

"What would I have to do to get you to like me?" he asked.

"Maybe you could die? That might help," she giggled.

He laughed.

"Rita suggested the exact same thing," he said. "You two think alike."

"That's because we've been friends for a long time. We go everywhere together. Rita's husband says we're joined at the hip," Zoe smiled.

"Like lovers?" he teased.

She smiled and nodded.

"I thought so," he said. "I wondered about that. Then when I saw the two of you enter the casino holding hands, I knew it for sure. How long have you been lovers?"

"It's a recent thing," Zoe said. "We fell in love with each other at first sight but we were too chicken to admit it. We were also worried what other people might think. Now, we don't care."

She looked into his eyes.

"Why did you go after Rita?" she asked.

"I'm not sure—or I wasn't at first. To be honest, I'm crazy in love with her," he replied as he stroked her inner thigh. "I don't want to just fuck her. I want to make love to her."

"What about me?" she asked.

"I think you already know," he said.

They kept eating and drinking. Zoe was feeling quite tipsy now and very horny. So when Bart slid his hand up her leg, she parted her knees to let him know she was willing. He moved it to her crotch and gently stroked her through her panties. Zoe had gone to the casino to get laid and she thought that Bart would be the perfect one for the job.

"I have a suite upstairs," he said.

"Let's go," she said.

When they entered the suite, they headed straight to the bedroom. Zoe undid her skirt and let it fall to the floor. She bent over to pick it up and placed it on a nearby chair. As she did, she made sure to give Bart at good long view of her ass.

They were standing close to each other. Zoe was partially seated on the edge of the dresser. Bart put his hand on her thigh and stroked her. Zoe giggled and parted her knees as he lightly raked her panties with his fingertips. Zoe shivered.

"You're so damned sexy, Zoe," he said softly as he fondled her crotch.

"How sexy?" she asked as she became hornier and hornier.

"This sexy," he replied as he grabbed her by the shoulders and stuck his tongue into her mouth.

Zoe responded by sucking on it with unexpected passion. Emboldened, Bart slid his hands down into her panties and massaged her cheeks. She kissed him harder. He slid his fingers up and down her crack. Zoe quivered.

He slowly led Zoe to the bed. She seemed to be too horny to resist now. As he pushed her down, she smiled. He sat next to her and slid his hand to her crotch. She parted her thighs and sighed deeply as he eased his finger into her wet slit and moved it around. Zoe opened her legs wider. Bart kissed her again. She kissed him back like she did earlier and put her arms around his neck. That's when he dragged her down.

They lay there kissing for quite some time. Bart also fondled her breasts and played with her nipples until she began to writhe with excitement. He slid his hand back down into her panties. Zoe felt his finger enter her pussy and opened her legs wider. Then she gasped and moaned as he fingered her through her first good orgasm.

"Yes! Yes!" she screamed as she came hard. "Oh, yes!"

She lay on her back panting. She was so far gone, she barely noticed that he was peeling her soaked panties off. Her thighs were still wide open. Through clouded eyes she though she saw Bart remove his jeans and underwear. She saw his prick bobbing dangerously from his crotch as he climbed back onto the bed and suck his tongue into her mouth again. As they kissed, she began to realize that Bart was now between her open thighs and his prick was resting on her pubic hair.

Their kiss grew more exciting. Bart moved his mouth to her right nipple and gently sucked. Zoe moaned and shivered. He then did the same to her left nipple then again stuck his tongue into her mouth. At the same time, he moved his hips so the head of his prick gently massaged Zoe's labia.

She could feel it teasing her.

Feel it knocking at her door.

The sensations caused her to quiver and she began to *like* it.

So much that she parted her legs even further.

She felt his knob stop in the center of her labia. Then Bart began to press inward.

Zoe quivered with excitement as she felt his prick enter her pussy. When he was all the way in, she bent her knees and moaned.

Her pussy felt so damned good, too, as he moved his prick in and out. Zoe gasped on the first thrust.

And moaned on the second.

And the third.

Bart fucked her a little faster.

Zoe opened her legs wider and moved with him. His prick, she decided, felt so good inside her cunt. She dug her fingers into his arms and fucked him back a little faster. Bart matched her, then did it harder. Zoe moaned and shook with each hard thrust. And she drove her hips upward to take him in even deeper.

"Ooooh! That's it, Bart! Give it to me good now. Use my pussy!" she moaned.

She wanted it now and she fucked him as hard as she could to prove it. Bart stuck his tongue into her mouth and fucked her harder. Zoe quivered, arched her back, and came. As she did, she fucked him faster.

"Fuck me, Bart! I love it! Make me yours now!" she cried as she wrapped her legs around him.

They fucked for what seemed like a long, long time. Then Zoe erupted again. This time, her orgasms was so strong, she rocked from side-to-side. Somehow, Bart stayed in her. When she settled down, he began fucking her again.

Zoe moaned and gasped as he used her. His strokes were slow and very deep now. She could feel his knob massage the entrance to her womb each time he plunged in and felt a delicious tingle when his prick raked across her g-spot She arched her back, wrapped her thighs around him and moved with him. Bart was delighted with her responses. When Zoe fucked, she held nothing back and her warm, tight cunt massaged his prick perfectly with each thrust. He steadily picked up the pace. Zoe moaned and matched him.

Again and again and again.

Faster and faster.

Zoe began thrusting harder and dug her fingers into his arms. Bart let her go for a little while then fucked her back just as hard. He leaned over and sucked her nipple. Zoe cried out, trembled all over and erupted. As she did, she fucked him as fast and as hard as she could. Seconds later, he slammed his prick into her all the way and flooded her cunt with cum. They kept fucking until both were spent.

As they lay next to each other, Bart propped himself up on his elbow and smiled at her.

"So you and Rita are really lovers?" he asked.

She laughed.

"Oh. Yes. Are we that obvious?" she asked.

"Well, the way you always act when she and I are together kind of sent me signals," he said.

"Is there anything else I should know about either of you?" he asked.

"Maybe. If I tell you, you have to promise not to tell Rita I said anything—okay?" she said.

"I won't," he assured her as he stroked her cunt.

"I'm fucking her husband and she knows about it," Zoe said.

"Isn't she upset with you or him about that?" he asked.

"She doesn't dare get upset," Zoe replied.

"Why not?" he asked.

"She's fucked a couple of other guys. After she did that, she told him he could fuck me if he wanted to. Naturally, we both jumped at the chance!" Zoe said. "Now that I've started fucking him, I'm never letting him go. Ever!"

"So she's already cheated?" he asked.

"Yes," Zoe said.

"Then why does he play so hard to get with me?" he asked.

"She's kind of afraid to get involved with you because she knows you really like her—a lot—and she feels the same way about you. She's afraid you'll end up in an affair or something. Does that make sense?" Zoe said.

"Yeah. It does actually. I told you that I'm absolutely crazy about Rita. I've never wanted anyone as much as I want her," he said. "Of course, you're in the same league as Rita and now that we've done this, I'd like to do it again with you."

She smiled and put her hands around his shoulders.

"We still have the whole night ahead of us," she said…

Rita and Art returned from Vegas the following morning. She called Zoe to tell her they were back and the two agreed to meet for lunch the next day. Then Zoe caught her up on what happened.

"I fucked your friend Bart last night," Zoe said. "We started talking and drinking and ended up in bed together. I hope you don't mind."

"Why would I mind? He's not my boyfriend or anything like that. Was he any good?" Rita asked.

"He was, actually. He was nice and caring and he has a real big, hard dick," Zoe said with a grin.

"How long did you stay with him?" Rita asked.

"All night. I just home two hours ago," Zoe almost bragged.

"You really fucked him?" Rita asked.

"Oh yes!" Zoe smiled.

"Do you think I should try him?" Rita asked.

"No way! I can fuck anybody I want because I'm single. You're married to a terrific guy who makes you happy. You don't need to try anyone else—ever! I know I sure as Hell wouldn't screw with other men if I had a husband like yours," Zoe said.

"How good was he, really?" Rita asked.

"He's so good that if you ever fuck him, you'll want to do it again and again. That's why you need to stay away from him," Zoe said.

"I guess you're right, Zoe," Rita said. "Are you gonna fuck him again?"

"Maybe. I sure as Hell want to," Zoe admitted. "But you need to steer clear of him before you do something you'll regret later. Don't ruin what you have."

Rita nodded.

But Zoe had piqued her curiosity now.

"Yes, I will fuck him," she told herself.

They met at their favorite café the next day and had a nice long, giggle-filled lunch. During the meal, they felt each other up several times. By the time they were finished, both were so horny that they could barely see straight.

After lunch, they retreated to Rita's bedroom and slowly removed each other's clothes as they exchanged several slow, deep kisses. After a nice, long easy "69" that left them both panting, Rita slid the dildo up into her cunt and moved between Zoe's open thighs. Zoe bent her knees and moaned as Rita plunged it into her. Then they settled into a good, long, hard fuck.

Zoe came first.

Rita pumped her a few more times, then eased the prick out of her cunt. To Zoe's surprise, Rita slid the dildo up into her ass and began to fuck her again. Zoe wrapped her knees around Rita's waist and groaned and sighed as she fucked her. After a few good thrusts, Zoe began to move with her.

Faster and faster.

"That's it, Rita! Fuck me! Fuck my ass. Make me yours!" Zoe moaned as waves of intense pleasure raced through her.

Zoe began quivering as she fucked her back.

"Oooh, yeah! I'm all yours now!" she cried.

Rita soon felt her own orgasm building deep within her cunt and began thrusting in and out of Zoe's ass faster and faster. Seconds later, Rita screamed and came. As she did, she fell forward and drove the dildo way up into Zoe's channel. The sudden thrust caused Zoe to come again and the two women just clung to each other until the waves of pleasure subsided.

"My God! That was incredible!" Zoe said after a while. "Just incredible!"

"It sure was," Rita agreed.

"I don't know why you decided to fuck me in my ass, but I'm glad you did. If I weren't used to that, I'd be sore for a few days," Zoe said as they dressed and headed down to kitchen. "Why *did* you do that?"

"Well, you said that you liked getting fucked in your ass. I want to make you happy, so I decided to try it," Rita replied as she poured them glasses of wine. "And you stuck that vibrator in my ass twice. I wanted to return the favor."

Zoe laughed.

"Now it's your turn!" she said as she picked up the dildo.

Rita lay on her back with her legs wide apart and moaned as Zoe fucked her with the dildo. She realized that Zoe liked to be the "man" most of the time and, since she had become very good at fucking, Rita was more than content to let her take charge. After a few good thrusts, Rita began fucking her back.

Again and again and again.

Rita moaned and fucked faster. Zoe matched her. They steadily increased their tempo until Rita began to shake all over. Zoe realized she was about to come and fucked her faster and faster. Then she exploded.

So did Rita.

The two fucked wildly for a few seconds. Then Zoe rolled off and lay beside her.

"Wow! That was great," Zoe said.

"Yes. It was," Rita agreed. "We're getting good at this. Maybe too damned good."

Zoe laughed.

"If this keeps up, we won't need any men to satisfy us," she joked.

"The rubber dick is nice, but I still prefer a real one," Rita said. "What shall we do next?"

"Roll onto your stomach," Zoe said as she slid the dildo back into her cunt.

Rita did as she said. She heard her turn on the vibrator. Zoe moved it along her ass crack several times. Each time, she stopped at the back door and teased Rita with it. Rita giggled at the sensations.

"I love your ass, Rita. It's so nice and sexy," Zoe said softly.

Rita felt something ease into her asshole and quivered as the delicious vibrations surged through her body. She relaxed and sighed. Zoe eased the vibrator into her about halfway and turned up the voltage. Rita shook and groaned.

"Oh, my god!" she cried.

Zoe a smiled and moved it in and out several times. As before, she pushed it in a little bit deeper each time.

"I really love your ass. If I had a dick, I'd fuck you there every chance I got," she said as she moved it in and out gently.

Rita quivered out of control now. The vibrations were making her cunt tingle and she wanted to scream. The vibrator went in deeper and deeper.

Rita moaned.

The vibrations were reaching parts of her body she didn't know she had and on each inward thrust, she gripped the pillow and emitted a loud moan. Zoe gradually fucked her faster and faster.

Zoe was also loving every second of it. Fucking Rita like this was sending erotic thrills through her body. Rita's ass was smooth and flawless and oh-so-sexy.

"I love your ass, Rita! I really love it!" she panted.

"It's yours, Zoe! It's yours! Make me your bitch!" Rita screamed.

Zoe fucker her harder and faster.

Rita cried and moaned and sighed. She began to see stars with each inward thrust and trembled as waves of pleasure surged through her.

Then came.

It was a very intense, very powerful orgasm that made her writhe on the bed and scream for Zoe to stop. Zoe turned off the vibrator and eased it out of Rita's ass.

Rita emitted a deep, happy sigh. She rolled over and smiled up at Zoe.

"That was the most awesome sex of my life!" she said.

After exchanging several deep kisses, they found themselves locked into a nice, long and gentle "69".

The next morning, Art called Zoe to see what she was up to. She laughed.

"I'm just waiting for a big handsome man to come over and fuck the daylights out of me. Until one shows up, maybe you could come over and keep me company?" she teased.

Art went straight to her house at noon. When Zoe opened the door, she pulled him inside and stuck her tongue in his mouth. They kissed for a long, long time. As they did, Zoe felt Art's prick grow harder and harder.

"Looks like it's just you and me," Zoe said with a smile.

She unbuttoned her shorts and let them fall to the floor. Art watched them slide down her pretty legs, then fixed his gaze on the prize between them. He was already rock hard as he slid to the floor and pressed his lips against her fleecy cunt. As his tongue entered, Zoe sighed deeply. Usually, Art licked her pussy just long enough to get her ready for his cock. This time, he tongued her labia and clit until she came.

Zoe groaned, then convulsed as her nectar gushed into Art's open mouth. He lapped up every drop, then stood up. Now, Zoe knelt. She pulled down his jeans and stared as his throbbing cock. She gave it a few strokes with her hand then twirled her tongue around and over the knob. Art moaned.

Zoe was good.

So very good.

She licked him to the balls then back several times before slipping the swollen head into her mouth. Moments later, Art grunted and Zoe drank his first load of cum as it jetted down her throat.

"No one does that better than you, Zoe. You're the best," Art said.

She smiled, then grabbed hold of his prick and led him to the bedroom. Seconds later, they were completely nude and locked in a hot embrace. Zoe kept hold of his prick and pumped it until he was hard again. She spread her thighs, laid back and guided him into her open cunt.

He slid into her nice and slow. Her cunt felt tight, hot and comfortable as they began to fuck in their usual style. Both liked it slow, deep and easy.

Zoe wrapped her arms and legs around his body and pressed her lips to his. As their tongues merged, the tempo of their union increased. Art used deeper thrusts now. Penetrating strokes that made Zoe sigh with pleasure each time he moved inward. She let her body take control and began driving her hips upward to meet him each and every time, taking his cock deeper and deeper into her hungry cunt. It was a hunger only Art could feed now.

Zoe quivered.

"I love you, Art! I love you!" she sighed.

Art moved his arms so Zoe's legs draped over them. He leaned forward then, almost pressing her thighs to her chest, and drove his cock into her as hard as he could. Zoe gasped and dug her nails into Art's shoulders. This was something new for her. Something exciting.

Art ground his cock into her and she shivered as magical sensations emanated from deep within her cunt and tentacled through her entire body. She was soon speeding uncontrollably toward orgasm.

Art shivered, too. Zoe's cunt felt warm, tight and incredibly delicious as it clutched his prick. They humped good and hard now, sweat beading up on their naked bodies.

Zoe came first. It was deep, hard come that rocked her to her very soul. She drove her hips up and down on Art's prick and cried out in Spanish as her pussy took complete control of her. She fucked Art like she'd never fucked before and begged him to come inside her. At the same time, she tightened her cunt muscles to increase the friction—as well as Art's pleasure—as much as she could.

That did it.

Art exploded—no erupted—and kept filling her cunt with what seemed like gallons of thick, hot cum. Before he could finish, Zoe rolled him over and straddled his cock. He was still hard. She was still horny. And the day was young.

As she bounced up and down on his prick, Art played with her dark nipples. He was still coming, too, and his cum oozed out of Zoe's cunt and covered his balls. Zoe kept fucking. she seemed insatiable now. She lived only for the feel of Art's prick inside her cunt.

Art caught his second wind. He gripped her thighs and drove his prick upward into her cunt. This was, by far, the longest, most sensational love he ever had—that either of them ever had. They were as one now. Two halves of a whole that lived only to please each other. They fucked until both ached from the strain. Just when Art thought he was about to collapse, Zoe came.

She threw her head back, screamed with delight, shook violently on his prick, then fell on top of him. She lay in his arms, her eyes closed, emitting soft cooing sounds as she basked in the afterglow of their lovemaking.

"My god! That was wonderful!" she managed to say after a while. "Wonderful! I'm all yours now, Art. Forever and ever."

Art smiled and stroked her hair.

Chapter Eight

When Rita saw them get out of the car in front of the house later that evening, she studied the happy expression on Zoe's face and knew exactly what they'd been doing all day. She laughed as they walked in.

Zoe grinned at her.

"We just spent the afternoon fucking," she announced. "And it was better than I expected."

Rita looked at Art. He was obviously worn out.

"So she fucked the daylights out of you?" she asked.

"And then some!" he said as he sat down at the kitchen table.

Rita poured them each a glass of iced tea and sat with them. This was inevitable. Zoe had finally gotten what she wanted and Rita couldn't say anything because she'd fucked Greg and was about to fuck Bart. Plus, she and Zoe were lovers in every sense of the word.

"I told Art that I'm all his now," Zoe said. "Just like I am all yours."

"You now have two wives, Art. Can you handle it?" Rita joked. "We both have tight, hungry pussies that need to be fed often. We might kill you with sex."

He laughed.

"That's a risk I'm willing to take," he said.

"Whenever you're off fucking another guy, I'm gonna be here fucking Art," Zoe said.

"So how many other men have you fucked so far?" Art asked.

"Just three," Rita said.

"Three? Who're the other guys?" he asked.

"Oh! I forgot to tell you about him! His name is Carl and I met him about a week ago. We've fucked twice since then," Rita said. "Then there's Steve."

She then told them of her encounters. And she was very, very descriptive about it!

She was eating breakfast at a local café when he walked up and smiled at her. He was very handsome, so she smiled back. To her surprise, he sat down at her table and introduced himself. She laughed at the way he did it and they shook hands.

They sat and talked.

Before they realized it, almost two hours had lapsed.

Even though he knew she was married, he asked her to join him for lunch that afternoon. She really enjoyed his company, so she agreed to meet him at a nice, cozy and pretty romantic place a few blocks away.

They ended up having several glasses of wine and she was so loose and horny that she allowed him to get his hand between her legs. After several minutes of him feeling her cunt, she was on fire.

So when he suggested they go to his place and have sex, she was more than willing to give her new friend a try. He took her to his apartment and they sat on the bed and kissed and felt each other as they undressed.

That's when she realized that Carl had one of the longest, thickest pricks she'd ever seen. She grabbed it and beat him off. As soon as she saw a bead of precum appear on his knob, she swirled her tongue all over it. He gasped as she slid as much of his prick as she could into her mouth and proceeded to suck away.

She stopped after a few second sand looked up at him.

"Now," she said as she laid back and parted her legs.

Carl got between her thighs and slid his prick home. Rita wrapped her legs around his hips and they jumped right into a good, hard, steady fuck. Carl grabbed her ankles and pushed her legs back toward her breasts. Then he began fucking her harder and harder. Rita groaned and sighed with each deep thrust.

She was Carl's slut. His little brown fucking machine.

She should have been ashamed of doing this. Good girls never did such things. But now she didn't care. All she cared about was the good hard prick in her pussy and the ferocious fuck she was getting.

The sensations felt intense.

Powerful.

Wicked.

Delicious.

His prick filled every part of her pussy. It stretched her to the limit and she could feel his heavy knob knocking at her womb. Each push sent shockwaves of intense pleasure coursing through her sweaty body.

Her orgasm was sudden and explosive.

"Yes! Fuck me, Carl! Fuck harder!" she cried as she clawed at the bed.

He did as she asked. The harder he fucked her, the harder she came. Then she felt Carl's prick expand suddenly inside her cunt and knew he was about to blow.

"Fuck me harder, Carl! Fuck me! Come inside me. I want to feel it. Fill my pussy!" she ranted as several more orgasms washed through her.

Carl hammered at her with a vengeance, then shoved his prick all the way into her pussy as he emptied every last drop of cum he could produce into her. There was so much that it oozed out of her slit and ran down between her cheeks to the bed.

But he wasn't through.

Not yet.

He released her legs and humped her missionary style. Rita wrapped her arms and legs around his body and tried to fuck him back. All the while, he kept pumping lots and lots of sticky cum into her happy pussy.

When it was over, Carl slid his half-erect member out of her still pulsing cunt. Rita saw the long string of cum that followed it out of her and laughed. She reached over and gently squeezed it. Carl smiled at the river of white liquid running out of her cunt.

It had been the single most intense fuck that Rita'd ever had. So intense that she still tingled all over and was completely exhausted.

They exchanged cell phone numbers and Carl drove her home.

"I'd like to see you again," he said.

"Call me whenever you want, Carl," she said. "I really enjoyed today and I'd like to do this again."

"When does your husband leave for work?" he asked.

"Around seven. He's usually gone until four," she replied.

"Okay. I'll see you tomorrow then," he said as they exchanged a short kiss.

Much to Rita's surprise (and delight), Carl showed up her house around nine the next morning. Rita had just gotten out of bed. All she had on was her plaid pajama shirt and light blue panties.

When she saw Carl, she scowled playfully.

"What do you want?" she asked as she let him in and shut the door.

"Guess," he replied as he smiled at her.

She looked at him and smiled back. When he stepped toward her, she stood still and let him kiss her. As he did, he fondled her crotch. Rita kissed him back harder to show she was interested and groped his prick.

"Let's go upstairs," she said.

As soon as they reached the bedroom, Rita unbuttoned her shirt and let it drop to the floor. While Carl quickly undressed, she peeled off her panties and laid down on the bed with her thighs apart. Carl, she observed, was nearly erect. As he slid in next to her, she grabbed his prick and slowly jerked him off. Carl sucked her nipples and moved his middle finger in and out her already wet cunt.

When a bead of precum appeared on his knob, Rita leaned over and licked it off. Then she slid half his prick into her mouth and sucked away. As she did, she almost smiled. She liked the taste of Carl's prick now. As she sucked, she pumped him gently.

Carl slid his fingers deeper into her cunt and massaged her g-spot. Rita moaned and pumped him a little faster. After she decided he was hard enough, she let him go and laid back with her legs wide apart.

"I'm yours now. You can do whatever you like," she said.

"Even fuck you in your ass?" he asked as he fingered her faster.

"You can fuck me anywhere you like!" she sighed.

She quivered with excitement as she licked his way down her belly to her cunt. He stopped to suck her clit awhile. This caused her to writhe and gasp and pump his prick faster and faster. When he dipped his tongue into her slit, she groaned and let go of his prick so she could use both her hands to push his face into her cunt while she fucked his tongue.

"Oh, God! Yes! Eat me, Carl! Eat me good!" she cried as she came.

As she began to come back down, she saw Carl move between her open thighs. She opened them wider and bent her knees. Then she smiled and nodded at him.

"Do it, Carl! Fuck me. Make me yours again," she said.

Then she groaned as he entered her.

"Oh, yes! Yes!" she moaned as they fucked.

This time, she moved with him from the first thrust. She even wrapped her legs around his waist and gripped his arms as she thrust her hips up to meet every down thrust of his prick. They kept at this for a few more deep thrusts.

"Fuck me harder! I love it! I love your great big dick! Oooh yes! I love it! I'm your little brown fucking machine and I want all of your dick!" she cried as she drove her hips up as hard as she could. "My pussy's all yours now! Take it!"

Carl grunted and fucked her as fast as he could as he emptied his balls into her cunt. As soon as the first stream of cum slammed into her, Rita came, too. It was a good, deep and hard orgasm that shook her from head to toe.

"Fill my pussy, Carl! Fill it with your cum!" she moaned as they kept going.

After a few good hard thrusts, Carl pulled out. When he saw the cum ooze between her cheeks, he reached down and massaged it into her asshole. Rita rolled over, grabbed his cum-soaked prick and stuck it into her mouth. Carl moaned as she worked it with her tongue and fingers. When she got him up again, she got onto her hands and knees.

"Do it, Carl! Fuck me in my ass—but go easy," she said.

Since Carl was fully erect, he only slid his prick in about two thirds of the way. When he heard her groan, he stopped to let her get used to the feel of it. Then he fucked nice, slow and easy. Rita shivered on each inward thrust but didn't complain. Once she grew accustomed to the size, Carl's prick didn't feel all that different from Art's. Carl saw that she was able to take it and fucked her a little faster.

Rita quivered and began to move with him. The more he fucked her, the more she liked it and soon, her entire body began to tingle. It was a delicious kind of tingle.

Carl knew he was about to come again. As he got closer to erupting, he slid his finger into Rita's cunt and played with her clit and g-spot.

Rita gasped and came. As she did, she clenched her ass cheeks. This caused Carl to tremble and shoot his load deep into her ass. Rita fell face down. Carl fell on top of her with his prick still buried in her ass. He was in deep, too. Rita used her inner muscles to squeeze his prick several times just to see how he'd react. He groaned.

"Damn! That feels great!" he said.

"Fuck me again, Carl," she said as she felt his prick stiffen.

They moved together from the start this time. It was a nice, deep, easy rhythm. One that caused Rita to sigh and shudder on every inward plunge of his prick. It felt good, too. Better than she wanted it to feel. She began fucking him back harder and faster.

"Oooh, yeah! Fuck me, Carl! Fuck me!" she moaned.

Carl gave her a few more good thrusts. Rita groaned and matched each of them. Then she stopped and smiled at him.

"Fuck me in my pussy now," she said.

Carl pulled out. Rita rolled over and spread her legs. She sighed when he buried his prick in her cunt all the way to his balls. Rita sighed and bent her knees. After a couple of good strokes, she began thrusting her hips to take him deeper.

"Ahhh! That's it! Fuck me! Fuck me!" she moaned.

They began moving faster and faster. Rita dug her fingers into Carl's arms and fucked him as hard as she could. He stopped momentarily and let her ride him. After a few strokes, he began fucking her as hard as he could.

Rita arched her back and moaned.

"Ohhhh, yes! I love it! Fuck me!" she cried.

Then, all of a sudden, she slowed her thrusts and began shivering all over. Carl realized she was coming and tried to quicken his pace. Rita wrapped her legs around his waist and moved faster. Carl kept pace.

"I'm yours! All yours! Use me! Fuck me good!" she screamed as she came. "I love, love, love, love it!"

Carl came right afterward and shot what little cum he had left into her cunt.

"My God! My God!" she said as she slowly came back to Earth. "I never felt anything like *that* before!"

"That was great! The best yet!" Carl said.

Rita sat up and looked at him. She was totally wiped out now.
What's more, she felt good.

Too damned good.

So good, it scared the Hell out of her.

She reached over and played with his prick for a while. When it
didn't respond, she laughed.

"I think you'd better leave now," she said softly.

Carl kissed her and got up. She watched him dress and shook her
head. She was getting too easy now. Much too easy.

She threw on a robe and walked him to the front door. He kissed
her on the cheek, then walked out to his car. She watched him drive
away and shut the door.

"My life is turning inside-out," she said. "It's like my pukki is in
control of me now."

"So we've noticed," Art and Zoe said with smiles.

"When I fucked the first guy, I didn't see any reason not to fuck
other men, too," Rita said. "Like you once told me, Art, my body was
made for sex. Until lately, I've been only yours. Now that I'm fucking
other men, I want to keep doing it. This works out for the both of you
because now you and Zoe can fuck each other as much as you like."

"And we will, too," Zoe smiled. "Be careful, Rita. I might decide to
steal Art from you!"

"If you do, we'll still be lovers, Zoe—forever," Rita said as she
stepped closer and kissed her on the lips.

"What about Bart?" Zoe asked.

"Oh, I'll fuck him eventually. Since he's really crazy about me, I'll
make him work for my pussy. That way, it will be even more special for
him," Rita said. "Besides, I really like him."

"I think that maybe you like him too much!" Art said.

She laughed.

"But not as much as I love you," she assured him.

Things were really heating up between Zoe and Rita now. Before
they'd started making love, Lesbian sex was something Zoe had only
seen in porno movies and sometimes fantasized about.

Now, having sex with Rita is all she could think about. When she
woke the next morning, she was bathed in sweat and incredibly horny.
She showered, splashed a very light perfume on her cunt, and threw on

a t-shirt and jeans—with no underwear. Then she drove over to Rita's house and rang the doorbell.

Rita beamed when she saw her standing on the step.

"Zoe! I'm glad you came. Please come in," she said.

That's when Zoe realized that Rita was wearing a knee length T-shirt that clearly highlighted her erect nipples. Zoe caught herself staring at them.

"I just finished showering," Rita explained as she pulled back the covers on the bed.

"I've been thinking of you all night, about what we did the last time," Zoe said as she unbuttoned her blouse.

Rita stared at her nice, firm breasts and pert, brown nipples. She smiled.

"Me too. That was very nice," Rita said as she helped Zoe out of her jeans.

Her eyes went straight to the soft, brown triangle between Zoe's thighs. That's when Zoe realized Rita had no panties on. Rita pulled off her T-shirt.

Naked, they fell into each other's arms and kissed passionately as they virtually melted into the bed. Hesitant at first, Zoe cast away all doubts and threw herself into the affair with wild abandon. It soon became a wonderful, wild ride. Lips met lips, then graced necks, chests, nipples and navels. As their tongues played across their bodies, excited fingers explored their moist, warm folds and danced deliciously within eager slits.

Zoe let Rita do as she pleased with her at first, then followed her lead until both women were burning with lust.

Incredible lust.

Neither woman could recall being so horny before. They were both very wet and their sexual perfume hung heavy in the humid afternoon air of the bedroom.

Zoe's cunt enchanted Rita. Her labia were like tender flower petals. Soft and pliant, they quivered noticeably when Rita caressed them. Her slit was long, moist and deep pink in color. It glimmered in the sunlight and her wonderfully swollen clit peeked at her invitingly from beneath its fleshy cover. This marvelous cunt was covered with a rich, brown carpet of silken pubic hair.

"You're so beautiful," Rita said.

Rita inserted two fingers into Zoe's cunt and moved them in and out. Zoe groaned with passion as Rita kissed her navel and licked her way slowly downward.

"Do it, Rita! Eat me!" Zoe whispered.

When Rita's soft, warm tongue touched her swollen clit, Zoe nearly jumped off the bed. She grabbed Rita's head and opened her legs wide as that wonderful, knowing tongue played and danced between her thighs.

"Aiee! Aiee—yes!" Zoe yelled.

No one had ever eaten her like this.

Rita used her fingers to pull Zoe's labia open so she could suck on her clit. This caused Zoe to cry out with pleasure. She felt her orgasm mounting from deep within her cunt and clawed at the mattress.

Rita understood what was happening. She responded by dipping her tongue deep into Zoe's cunt. Then she slowly moved one of her fingers into her and teased her g-spot.

That did it.

Zoe came.

It was an explosive, deep-from-inside come that rocked her sweat-covered body from head to toe. Zoe grabbed Rita hair and pulled her face hard against her vulva. She humped Rita's face wildly now as orgasm after orgasm surged through her body. At the same time, Rita slid another finger deep inside Zoe's cunt and massaged her g-spot even harder.

This increased the intensity of Zoe's orgasm and she shook all over as the stars exploded in front of her eyes. She let go of Rita's hair and fell, arms akimbo, back onto the bed. Rita moved upward so her cunt was merely inches from Zoe's lips. The delightful aroma of Rita's open pussy enticed Zoe. She reached up, gripped Rita's behind and pulled her down onto her tongue.

Then Zoe ate her.

Rita tasted sweet.

Inviting.

Intoxicating.

Zoe felt wicked. She was eating her best friend's pussy—and she loved it. She loved the smell, the feel and especially the flavor. She explored Rita from cunt to asshole several times, then settled down and concentrated on her pretty little clit. She was so enraptured by what she was doing that she barely noticed that Rita was eating her again.

Rita came.

Zoe felt her bittersweet juices jet into her mouth and hungrily lapped them up. The taste was sensationally erotic. It blew Zoe's mind so much, she came again and they both held on to ride the waves that surged through them.

"Th-that was unbelievable!" Zoe gasped. "My head is spinning like crazy!"

"Mine, too. You are a good lover, Zoe. You eat me almost as good as Art does," Rita replied as she came down from the clouds.

Zoe smiled at her lovely sex partner, then reached out and ran her fingers over her soft, black pubic hair. It felt so natural to be with Rita like this. Zoe told her this, too.

Rita smiled.

"If you want me, Zoe, you can have me anytime you like," she said. "I am all yours."

She was feeling Zoe's pussy now. As she inserted two fingers into it, Zoe moaned.

She was surprised how easily she gave herself to Rita. She never had any real lesbian inclinations before, even though she often fantasized trying it just once to see what it was like.

As she lay naked on the bed, she looked down at the pretty Filipina lovingly licking her pussy and smiled. It seemed and felt so natural now.

And so very, very good.

She closed her eyes and enjoyed the ride. Soon, she would sink her tongue into Rita's delicious cunt. She sighed as Rita nibbled her clit.

God, she was good at this.

"The best," Zoe thought.

A sudden surge of pleasure roared through her. She arched her back to take Rita's tongue deeper into her cunt, then came seconds later. As she did, she humped Rita's tongue and cried out in Spanish.

Sex with Rita was intense.

Very intense.

Zoe groaned and fell back to the mattress. Rita stopped licking and sat back to watch Zoe's petal-like labia throb visibly as her orgasm subsided.

"You're very beautiful, Zoe," she said.

"You are, too. Let's fuck," Zoe replied.

Wordlessly, Rita got on top of her and began rubbing her pussy against Zoe's nice and easy. Zoe's eyes went wide. Rita was actually fucking her! It was the most incredible thing she'd ever felt. She moaned softly and dug her fingers into the bed as her body took control and loved her back.

"Yes!" Rita gasped. "Yes! YES!!!"

Zoe didn't hear her cry out. She was completely lost in the sex they were having. All she cared about was the way her cunt felt as it ground into Rita's and the fact that she was coming...and coming...and coming...

She couldn't recall ever coming so much, so many times. Sweat covered her—and Rita—from head to foot as they continued to make love all through the warm afternoon. The bedroom was filled with their sexual aromas now. The scent only served to heighten their lovemaking.

They soon switched positions. Now, Zoe was on top and the two women fucked away in the scissors position until their bodies literally ached. They were tired, sweaty and almost unconscious by the time they'd each come for the last time that afternoon.

As Zoe lay next to Rita, she smiled. She felt good all over now. Rita looked content, too.

"Fuck me again," she whispered.

She never imagined that she'd say that to a *woman*.

When Art came home two hours later, the ladies were seated at the kitchen table looking well-fucked. He laughed and sat with them.

"Good day?" he asked.

"A great day!" they both said.

Three days later, Rita went to the DMV to renew her driver's license. To her dismay, the place was packed and the lines were moving slowly. She picked up the forms and sat down to fill them out. A younger and very handsome man sat next to her. She glanced at him and they smiled at each other.

"My name's Dave," he said.

"Rita," she replied.

As they chatted, she noticed that he was ogling her legs. He also made eye contact several times which told her he was confident. Dave got called up front a half hour later. She watched him get his photo taken. Instead of leaving, he returned and sat beside her again.

She smiled.

"Why didn't you leave?" she asked.

"I like it right where I am just fine. That's because you're still here. When you leave, I'll leave," he said.

She laughed.

"Are you coming on to me?" she joked.

"Definitely," he said. "Does it show?"

"Yes," she said with a grin.

"Good. You're very pretty. In fact, you're prettier than any other woman I've ever met. It's too bad you're married," he said.

"Why?" she asked.

"If you weren't, I'd ask you to have lunch with me," he said.

"Okay. Where?" she asked.

Caught by surprise, he hesitated. He smiled at her.

"How about I make it a surprise?" he suggested.

"That sounds interesting. Okay," she agreed.

"What's your address? I'll pick you up at noon and we'll go have a nice meal and get to know each other better," he said.

"Then what?" she said.

"That's entirely up to you, Rita," he replied. "Whatever happens, happens."

Noon.

Dave arrived right on time. Rita saw him drive up and walked out to the car. As she got in she smiled.

"Where are we going?" she asked.

"Café Mochi. It's sushi bar," he said.

"I like that place," she said.

The place wasn't very crowded when they arrived. They sat at a corner table. When the waitress came over, Dave ordered two bottles of warm sake. Rita smiled at him.

"You like sake?" he asked.

"My husband drinks it all the time. I've never really tried it," she said.

"Well, I've got you your own little bottle. If you don't like it, I'll finish it for you," he promised.

The waitress brought the sake and they gave her their order. As they ate, they talked and joked and laughed. Dave kept telling her how pretty she looked and how he wished she weren't married. And they drank the sake.

All of it.

The Sake was stronger than she expected. She began to grow more talkative and animated. Dave noticed this and decided to go for it. He ordered them each a glass of plum wine—which she really liked. So he bought her another...

After lunch, he helped her back to the car and took her home. Since her knees were a little wobbly, she asked him to help her into the house. He did and got her safely to the sofa. She felt loose, very relaxed and somewhat horny.

"Thanks for the nice lunch—and the drinks," she said. "Art says I talk too much when I'm drunk and I say a lot of weird things. He said I'm really funny when I'm a drunk, too."

"Yes, you are. What else do you do when you get drunk?" Dave asked.

"I get horny—Oh! I'm so ashamed. I shouldn't have told you that!" she exclaimed as she covered her mouth with her hand.

He laughed.

"That'll be our secret," he assured her. "How horny do you usually get?"

"I'm not saying another word about that!" she laughed. "Thank you again for the lunch. It was very nice. So are you."

"Am I nice enough to kiss again?" he teased as he leaned closer and looked into her eyes

She smiled at him as she tried to clear her brain. Before she could answer, he pressed his lips against hers. Again, it felt nice and warm and easy. After a few seconds, she moved her face away.

"I like that," she said as she moved closer to him.

He put his arms around her and pulled her closer for another, long, easy kiss. This time, he decided to go a little further. He ran his free hand over her shoulder then down to her left breast. When she didn't move away, he gently squeezed it as he put his hand on her thigh.

She grabbed it and pushed it away.

"I think you'd better leave now. I need to get some sleep," she lied.

She escorted him to the door on still-wobbly legs. To steady herself, she leaned against the frame. Dave leaned over and kissed her again. As they kissed, he eased his hand up her body to her right breast. This time, she let him touch her for a while. He felt her heart beat faster and faster and realized he'd aroused her. He eased his other hand up to her left breast. Rita emitted a muffled moan as he played with her nipples.

She felt him undo her shorts and quivered when he reached into her panties and stroked her clit. She moaned and sucked his tongue even harder. Dave eased her shorts and panties down to her knees.

They continued to kiss. After a few seconds, she felt something hard and stiff pressing against her crotch. As the hard knob slid across her labia, Rita opened her stance. Dave slid his prick deep into her cunt and fucked her again. As his prick massaged every part of her cunt, she sucked his tongue a little harder. After a few seconds, she began moving with him. As she did, she became more and more excited. She moved faster and faster.

Her cunt grew warmer and wetter as her body went onto autopilot. He moved his hands to her hips and thrust faster and faster. She felt him quiver and moved her body against his as fast as she could.

"Yes! Yes! Yes!" she moaned.

They moved faster and faster. She felt herself shake all over and fucked him as hard as she could.

She came first.

When she did, she leaned into him and sucked his tongue harder. She soon came again. As she did, she moved against him and cried out as she used her muscles to work his prick.

"Oooh yes! Yes!" she moaned as he fucked her.

After a few thrusts, she fucked him back. They quickly settled into a nice, long energetic rhythm that took their passions higher and higher. She sighed and moaned on each inward plunge of his hard prick. She clung to him and fucked him back just as hard as she savored their illicit tryst.

"Yes! I love it! Fuck me, Dave! Fuck me good!" she ranted.

She could hardly believe she had let him get this far again but now that he was fucking her, she wanted to make the best of it. His prick felt so good to her. So very good. When they came, they came together in one long, powerful super nova of an orgasm that left them gasping and sweating. She moaned and quivered as he spurted several lines of cum into her cunt. When he finally pulled out, she watched some of it drip to the floor. She caught her breath and smiled weakly at him.

"Wow." she sighed.

"So are we friends yet?" he joked.

She slid her tongue into his mouth for another good, deep kiss.

"I guess we are!" he laughed. "When can I see you again?"

"When would you like?" she asked.

"Tomorrow?" he suggested.

"Okay. Call me first," she said as she escorted him to his car on very wobbly knees.

He arrived at eleven bearing a bottle of red wine. She got two glasses from the kitchen and they sat on the sofa. Dave had noticed that booze made Rita loose and horny. He told her this as they drank the first glass.

Dave poured her another glass of wine. She smiled and sipped. As they chatted, he switched gears and told her how very beautiful she was and how much he wished she wasn't married and how much he wished she was his girlfriend. During the course of this, Rita blushed and told him he was crazy, but she secretly liked hearing him say it.

She had another glass of wine.

And another.

She was fairly drunk now. As she attempted to think straight, he leaned closer and kissed her on the lips. She tried to say something but he kissed her again. This time, he managed to slip his tongue into her mouth. The second it touched hers, she felt as if lightning had flashed. She leaned back and looked at him.

"What was that?" she asked almost breathless.

"Let's find out," he said.

He leaned over and kissed her again. And lightning flashed again. She allowed this kiss to continue and her passion slowly ignited. As it lingered, she realized that she enjoyed this.

Maybe too much.

Dave was on fire, too. By now, he had an erection and the tent in the front of his jeans was obvious to Rita. She broke off the kiss and looked at him.

"Wow!" she gasped.

Dave refilled her glass. Her head was still foggy but she drank anyway.

"That was nice," she said.

"Want to do it again?" he asked.

"Well, since we've already done it, another kiss won't hurt," she said.

This time, he pulled her close. Again, their tongues merged and sparks ignited. Rita was getting horny.

Very horny.

Her heart began racing inside her chest as Dave stroked her thigh nice and easy. His touches made her even hornier and she sucked his tongue with passion. He moved his hand between her legs and massaged her through her shorts. His touch sent slight, pleasant tingles through her body and she trembled.

And her cunt was growing hotter.

He rubbed her crotch a little harder. She squirmed and sucked his tongue harder as the fire in her cunt spread. Before Rita could respond, they were again locked into a deep, passionate kiss. This time, she threw her arms around his neck and sucked his tongue like there was no tomorrow. After a few seconds, she felt him tug her zipper open. She trembled all over as he eased his hand down into her panties and oh-so-gently fondled her now hot, wet slit. She just about sucked the tongue out of his mouth when he began playing with her clit. She was so damned horny now. She craved release. She was now sopping wet between her legs and quivering all over with lust. Dave realized this and kept playing with her clit faster and faster.

Then it happened.

Rita's head fell back and she emitted a long, loud moan as she came. It was a nice, almost electrifying orgasm that made every muscle in her body twitch. She fell against him and gripped his arms as he eased his middle finger into her convulsing slit. Rita gasped as she came again.

And again.

"You're bad," she said.

"I'd like to get even badder," he said.

"How bad?" she smiled.

"This bad," he said as he slowly pulled her shorts and panties down.

She let him undress her and lay there with her legs parted. Dave stood up and removed his jeans. His prick was straight, long and hard. She reached up and gave it several strokes, then let him go. He moved between her thighs and slid his prick into her all the way to his balls. She moaned and wrapped her arms and legs around him. She moaned louder as he fucked her.

They began moving together. Dave stuck his tongue into her mouth. She moved faster as they kissed. His prick felt so good now. So wonderfully good as it massaged every part of her cunt.

They fucked faster and faster. She thrust her hips up at him and screamed for more. Each time, she felt the knob of his prick slam into her walls. Each time it did, she shuddered with passion.

"Fuck me, Dave! Fuck me good!" she gasped as she started to come.

He sensed she was coming and fucked her faster and faster. She groaned and went over the top. She groaned louder when she felt his cum jet into her.

"I'm yours. I'm yours. Fuck me harder!" she begged as she continued coming.

They kept at it until Dave went limp and slipped out. She looked down at the river of cum oozing from her pulsing cunt and smiled.

"You're good at this," she said. "Real good."

"That's because you inspire me," he replied as he stroked her thigh. "I can't seem to get enough of you. Now that we've started this, I want to keep doing it."

"So do I. Whenever you want me, you know where to find me— and my pussy," she joked. "I can't believe we did this again. I guess I'm drunker than I thought I was. Hornier, too," she said. "And it was fun. Maybe too much fun."

He pulled her to him and they kissed again. She opened her legs wider and let him touch her again. She felt her body shake all over as she held on tight. He stroked her clit faster and faster.

She came again and fell back with her thighs wide open. She saw that his prick was hard once again and smiled at him as he rammed it home.

"Aaahh, yes!" she sighed as her body shook with pleasure. "Ohhh, yes! Yes!"

They began moving together in a nice, steady rhythm again. She felt waves of pleasure surge through as they fucked and fucked and fucked. This time, they erupted together and he emptied a second good load into her cunt.

She beamed at him as she sat up. She felt incredibly well-fucked now.

"That was even better," she said.

"Are we done for today?" he asked.

"Can you get it up again?" she asked.

"Sure," he replied.

"In that case, we aren't done yet," she smiled as she ran her fingers over his wet prick.

To her delight, it sprang back to life. She worked it with her hand until he was rock hard again and lay back down with her legs apart. She felt him enter her cunt and shivered slightly. He held her tight and began to fuck her again. She sighed and moved with him as she savored the way his prick moved in and out of cunt, which was still throbbing from her previous orgasm.

"Oooh, yes!" she sighed as she moved with him. "Fuck me!"

They fucked faster and faster. She matched his every thrust as she clung to him.

"More! Do it harder! Ohhh, yes!" she sighed.

Then she came again. As she did, she gripped his arms to steady herself. She gasped and moaned as she came and he kept fucking her and fucking her until he finally shot his final load into her hot, wet cunt. He eased out of her and sat back to catch his breath.

"Are you always like this?" he asked.

"Not all the time. You got lucky today," she smiled. "I was really horny."

"You're going to be hard to keep up with," he said as he dressed. "But I'll do my best."

Before he could zip his jeans up, she reached over and grabbed his prick.

"Your dick feels so big," she whispered as she ran her fingers along the shaft and tweaked his knob. "And so thick!"

He smiled at her as she gave it several pulls.

"That's all yours whenever you want it," he offered.

"I'm going to make this really good for you," she said.

She knelt down and slid it into her mouth, then bobbed her head back and forth while she pumped it. He gasped and sighed as she sucked it. Seconds later, he began firing lines of cum into her mouth. She kept sucking and pumping and swallowing until he was totally drained. When she knew she had it all, she stood and wiped the cum from her lips with the back of her hand.

She looked down. Even when it was flaccid, it looked large.

Her cunt was still throbbing and wet. He looked down and smiled at her patch of shiny black fur and partially open labia. She let him run his fingers over it a few times while she played with his prick. When she couldn't make it respond, she tried sucking it again. After a few seconds, she gave up.

"That was the best blowjob I ever had in my life. I can't wait to fuck you again," he said as he zipped his jeans up.

"You're fresh!" she said as she pulled on her shorts and escorted him to the door.

Just before he left, he pulled her close for another, long, deep kiss. Rita pushed him away and shoved him out the door. She watched him walk away and sighed.

Art was also very busy that afternoon. Instead of going to work, he called Zoe and set up a date at. She threw her arms around his neck the moment she saw him and they locked into a long, deep and passionate kiss. She took his hand and led him into her bedroom.

"You can't imagine how much I missed you," she said. "I've been so miserable these last few days."

They sat on the bed. Art kissed her on the lips softly, then slowly undid her blouse and helped her off with it. Her nipples were still erect and he leaned over to tease them with his tongue.

"Ah, that's nice," she sighed.

Art sat up as she helped him out of his shirt, then she leaned forward and sucked each of his nipples until he felt his balls tingle. While she was doing that, she unzipped his jeans and pulled out his now fully erect prick. It felt even bigger now.

Harder, too.

She gave it a few slow pulls. Art stood up and she undressed him altogether. She then leaned forward and played with his balls, then turned her attentions to his prick.

Art sighed happily as she jerked him off.

She took her time now. There was no need to hurry.

She stuck her tongue out and ran it all over his swollen knob a few times. Art moaned and put his hand on her shoulder. She kept licking for a moment, then pushed half of his cock into her mouth.

She never really liked to suck cock. But Art's was different. She loved the way he tasted. She loved to suck it. She especially loved it when he came in her mouth and the way his cum felt as it slid down her throat.

Art really loved what she was doing, too. What man wouldn't? She wasn't just sucking his prick. She was actually making love to him with her mouth. And no one, he decided, could do that any better than her. She stopped and lay down on the bed with her legs dangling over the side. Art knelt and undid her shorts, then slowly pulled them off. Naked, she looked gorgeous. He kissed and licked his way up her inner thighs to the soft, brown patch between them. She was already quivering with anticipation. Her labia and clit were wet and swollen and her sexual perfume permeated the room.

She smiled lovingly at him.

"Eat me, darling," she whispered. "Make love to me."

Then she sighed deeply as Art's tongue entered her more-than-willing cunt. He was marvelous with his tongue. He knew when and where to lick and how to fire all of her sexual triggers.

She was so excited that she came within seconds. She threw her legs over Art's shoulders, gripped his hair and began humping his tongue with a wild abandon. She came again and again. So many times that she could barely breathe or speak.

She didn't have to. Her body did all the talking for her and it was screaming for more. Art got the signal loud and clear and kept licking her quivering, dripping snatch until his tongue began to ache.

"Enough! That's enough," Zoe gasped as she pushed his face away from her cunt. "Fuck me, Art. Please fuck me."

Her body was still trembling when Art took his place above her. He pressed his glans to her soft, moist labia then moved it up and down several times before easing into her. He went in slowly in order to get the feel of her tight, hot channel as it caressed his prick. She spread her legs as far apart as she could, then bent her knees. She gripped Art's shoulders and drove her hips upward until she felt the head of his prick touch the opening to her womb.

"Oh yes!" she sighed as Art began to move his hips in a circular motion.

At the same time, he thrust in and out of her cunt nice and slow. He felt her inner flesh hug his shaft tightly as he pulled out, then part again as he slid back in. Each time, she moved with him in perfect unison.

Art had fucked many women in his life, but no one's cunt felt as exquisitely sexy as hers. She was warm, tight and silky smooth and she could really use her inner muscles. He often felt as if her were making love with an angel. They were a perfect match.

That's why he was taking his time. This wasn't just sex. It was lovemaking at its best, with all of the emotional ties that went with the word. They made love gently, slowly and with a lot of passion. They matched each other stroke for stroke, thrust for thrust. Their lips met again. Art reached beneath her and put her right leg over his shoulder, then drove into her a little bit harder and faster. She emitted a loud moan and dug her nails into his back as his cock massaged her secret g-spot perfectly. She felt herself spinning out of control.

"Faster, Art! Do it faster," she begged. "Make me come!"

She closed her eyes and allowed the movements of Art's prick inside her cunt carry her away. She began crying out and gasping for air. She clawed at his back like a mad woman as an explosive series of orgasms raced through her body. She felt his prick jerk a few times, and then relaxed as Art emptied his seed into her sucking pussy. Like earlier, he pumped a large amount of cum into her love tunnel. Her body, which seemed to be suspended in time, eagerly accepted his seed, greedily making it one with her.

She always let Art come inside her. She always would.

After a few more deep thrusts, Art eased his half hard member out of her and rolled onto his back. His prick glistened with their combined love juices. She rolled on top of him and they kissed once again. It was a long, deep kiss that spoke volumes of their feelings for each other.

"I love you," she whispered. "I wish I could have your baby."

"I love you," Art said.

Chapter Nine

The next morning, Rita and Zoe went out to breakfast. Afterward, they returned to Rita's house and sat down on the sofa to talk—and other things. Their chat was broken here and there when they exchanged kisses a few times. Each successive kiss was more passionate than the one before it.

"I love you, Zoe. I want to make love with you again," Rita said softly. She moved closer and slid her hand slowly along the inside of Zoe's thigh.

Zoe smiled and parted her legs as she looked into Rita's beautiful dark eyes.

"I'm all yours," she whispered.

Rita looked into Zoe's eyes and leaned forward, her lips pursed. Zoe closed her eyes as they lips touched and felt a surge of electricity race through her body. She opened her mouth and merged her tongue with Rita's. It mingled deliciously with hers. It felt so good, so delightfully wicked. Zoe's heart pounded harder with each passing second.

Rita's soft hand moved to Zoe's crotch. Delicate fingers pushed aside her panties and slowly entered her garden. The soft, moist flesh of her cunt parted eagerly and accepted Rita's gentle fingers as they massaged her g-spot. At the same time, Zoe used her inner muscles to squeeze those fingers.

"My God. You're so tight. Like a virgin " Rita said. "I wish I had a prick so I could feel what it's really like to fuck you."

Zoe's legs were wide open now. She was lost in the sensations of the fingers moving in and out of her steamy cunt. Rita, she decided, was good at this.

Very good.

Zoe wasn't idle either. She managed to undo Rita's shorts and pulled them halfway down her silken thighs. Before long, Zoe's long, sexy fingers were "fucking:" Rita's gorgeous cunt and sending shivers of delight through the pretty Filipina.

They kept fingering each other for several minutes. Zoe's head spun wildly. She shook and moaned as her orgasm approached and put her feet up on the sofa so Rita could finger her deeper.

Then it happened. Rita slid two fingers into Zoe's cunt all the way to the knuckles and wriggled them around. The fingers found her g-spot. It sent Zoe flying over the edge and into a delightful abyss of hard, multiple comes. She was still aware of where her own fingers were and began fingering Rita hard and fast. Moments later, she joined Zoe in the abyss.

Rita stood up and pulled off her clothes. Zoe eyed her wet pubic patch, then went to her knees. Rita's aroma titillated Zoe. She licked her inner thighs and stopped just short of Rita's cunt each time.

"Don't tease me, Zoe. Eat me. Let me feel your tongue in my pussy," Rita begged.

Zoe gripped her behind and pulled her forward until her cunt rested against her lips. Rita's scent was strong and erotic. Rita reached between her thighs and pulled her labia open, exposing the hot pink center of her cunt.

It was all Zoe needed. She buried her tongue between those soft lips and lovingly tasted her cunt. God, she was delicious.

Zoe licked, nibbled and sucked at Rita's clit and inner cunt until the woman came and flooded her mouth with her bittersweet nectar. Rita moaned and fell onto the sofa. She watched Zoe undress except for her bikini panties.

Rita slid off the sofa and knelt in front of Zoe. She slowly pulled off her panties, eager to see the most fabulously sexy cunt of her life again.

What she saw literally enthralled her. Zoe's cunt was the most erotic, most perfect cunt ever. she had large, pliant flower-like lips and a delightful pink clit that protruded from an enticing fleshy hood. A light cover of dark brown hair that was just enough to make her irresistible surrounded it.

Rita became horny all over again. She pushed Zoe down onto the sofa and moved her face between her sexy, smooth thighs. As soon as Zoe felt Rita's soft tongue touch her labia, she put her hands on her shoulders and closed her eyes.

"Yes! Yes! That's it. Eat me, Rita. Make me yours. Make me all yours," she gasped as Rita's experienced, eager tongue danced and played between her thighs.

Rita was enchanted with Zoe's magnificent cunt. She had a wonderful clean scent and a fabulous sweet-salty flavor that served to heighten Rita's pleasure as she hungrily devoured Zoe.

Zoe came first. She shook and rolled from side-to-side and humped Rita's face frantically. She'd been eaten before, but no one tongued her as good as Rita. She arched her back and groaned as orgasm after explosive orgasm wracked her body.

When it was over, they kissed and kissed. Rita smiled at her.

"I love you, Zoe," she whispered as they held each other tight.

Carl called early the next morning and told her he'd be there around noon. Rita said that would be perfect as her husband would be at work until five or six.

When Carl arrived, she met him at the door naked and just about dragged him up to the bedroom. They spent the first hour exploring each other orally, during which Rita sucked Carl's prick almost to orgasm twice. But just before he came, she squeezed the base of his prick hard to cut it off. Carl played the same game with her by licking her clit until he felt she was about to come. Then he backed off until she settled down and began anew.

Rita got onto her hands and knees. Carl got behind her and eased his prick deep into her cunt. She gasped as he filled every bit of her then sighed when he moved in and out. As he fucked her, he grabbed her thighs. She let him go for a few thrusts, then tried to move with him. They soon got into a good, hard rhythm and each had inward thrust of his prick made Rita's teeth chatter.

Rita gasped and moaned. Then she came. It was a good, deep come that shook her entire body. She fell forward with her ass up in the air and moaned as Carl continued to fuck her. She soon her him gasp.

Then came that familiar deep thrust followed by a satisfied grunt as he fired his cum into her cunt. Rita rolled onto her back with her legs wide apart. Carl's prick was still half erect. She wrapped her fingers around and gave it several slow, easy pumps until he was at full salute.

"Fuck me again," she said.

Carl smiled as he entered her. This time, they moved together from the first thrust. They fucked each other as hard and as fast as they could.

"That's it, Carl! You have me now! I'm all yours!" she panted as they fucked faster and faster. "Fuck me!"

This time, they orgasmed together.

And it was a beaut!

Carl grunted and shook all over as he emptied every last drop of cum deep into Rita's hungry cunt. She gripped his shoulders and kept fucking him as hard as she could as waves of intense pleasure rippled through her. When she finally stopped, she just laid on the bed bathed in sweat. Carl fell next to her. Both were so spent they slept for a good two hours.

She told Art about it when he got home.

"So Carl's your favorite?" he asked.

"No. You are," she said. "He's just become my friend with benefits," she said as she hugged him.

"And Bart?" Art asked.

"He scares me a little. I think he wants something permanent," she replied. "And I really do like him."

Later that night, she got a text from Bart.

"I miss you," it read.

"I miss you, too," she replied.

"Will you be at the casino tomorrow?" he asked.

"Yes. See you then," she texted.

"I love you," he texted back.

That surprised her, too. It was something she never expected to see from him. Her mind reeled as she wondered if he really meant that. He liked to play the field and he probably used that line to get what he wanted from lots of women. Saying it to get laid is one thing. Most women expect a man like him to say that. But putting the words into writing was another. It was more permanent.

"What if he does love me?" she thought as she erased the messages.

The next evening, she went to the casino. She wore a short skirt and bikini panties to make things easier for Bart. She sat down at her favorite machine and played while she waited. Bart showed up with two mai tais five minutes later. He handed her one and they kissed. It was a long, pleasant one, too.

"I'm glad you came tonight. I've been thinking about you all week long," he said.

"You missed me that much?" she teased.

"Yes. I'm nuts about you, Rita," he said as he slid his hand along her thigh.

She smiled and parted her knees. When he reached her panties, he got an almost instant erection. He looked into her eyes as he slid a finger into her cunt. She quivered as he moved it in and out nice and easy. He was very gentle with her all the time and she liked the way he handled her. She leaned back on the chair and shut her eyes as he took her higher and higher. Seconds later, she came.

It was a nice, long and easy orgasm. The kind he always gave her. She opened her legs wide and quivered as he kept fingering her. She came again. As she did, she leaned forward and stuck her tongue into his mouth.

She was glad the casino was virtually empty at that moment and that their little corner was out of view of everyone else. She unzipped his pants and pulled out his prick. Bart trembled as she ran her fingers over his knob. He was really hard now, too.

She jerked him off for a little while, then leaned over and slid his prick into her mouth. Bart moaned as she licked his knob. He moaned louder when she sucked it. He sat back and smiled as she bobbed her head up and down. It felt so exciting that he spurted seconds later. Rita swallowed it reflexively and kept sucking. Bart spurted several more times and she managed to swallow every bit of cum he produced.

She kept sucking and beating him off until he felt his balls spasm and ache. When he grew flaccid, she sat up and smiled at him.

"Let's go get dinner," he said.

They went to the steakhouse in the casino and feasted on prime rib and sweet red wine. Rita was soon very drunk and horny again as Bart kept playing with her pussy the entire time. She also played with his prick and he was soon good and hard again.

They left the steakhouse two hours later. Rita checked her watch.

"It's almost eleven! Time really flies when you're having fun," she said as she looked at his now obvious bulge.

"I'd really love to fuck you," he whispered.

"I know. But I'm not ready for that yet," she said as she rubbed his prick.

He took her hand and led her to the far side of the casino where it was nice and dark. They found a bunch of unused slot machines and looked around to make sure no one was around. Rita slid onto a stool and they kissed. Bart kissed her neck as he felt her cunt. She parted her legs wide and shivered with excitement as he slid two fingers deep into her cunt.

"Ooohh!" she moaned as he "fucked" her.

She was on fire now. Bart knelt in front of her, reached under her skirt and slid her panties down. He then rolled her skirt up. She opened her legs wide as she kissed her thighs. When she felt his tongue caress her labia, she moaned loudly. Bart sucked her swollen clit, then slid his tongue into her slit. Rita groaned, gripped his head and pulled him into her.

"Yes! I love it!" she sighed as he ate her.

Bart was thrilled. This was the furthest he'd gotten with Rita and he was delighted with the way she smelled and tasted. He licked and licked as she fucked his tongue. Rita came and almost screamed. He kept eating her until she came again and again and again.

When he thought she'd had enough, he stood and unzipped his pants. She eyed his massive erection and beat him off while she massaged his balls. Then she again slid as much of it as she could into her mouth and proceeded to suck away. Bart spurted quickly. She moved her head back and forth as he came again and again. He came so much that some of his cum ran out of the sides of Rita's mouth and dribbled down her chin.

When she was finished, he was still half-hard. She smiled and sat back with her legs wide open. She expected him to try to fuck her and she was more than willing to let him. He got between her legs and teased her labia with his knob a few times. Rita quivered and let out a soft moan s his cock head parted her lips. He was just about to enter her when they heard voices nearby. He stopped and zipped up his pants. She slid her panties back on and they laughed.

Bart escorted her to her car. They kissed again and she got in. He leaned close as she opened the widow.

"I love you, Rita," he said.

She stared at him for a few seconds and smiled.

While she was at the casino, Art and Zoe were in the master bedroom having a night of unfettered sex. Zoe was on her hands and knees moaning and crying out in ecstasy as Art moved his prick in and out of her tight, wet cunt.

Zoe had shown up at the house less than ten minutes after Rita left for the casino. She had on nothing but her bath robe and a smile. When she got inside, she simply let it slide off her shoulders and stood there naked. Art immediately grabbed her and carried her to the sofa. Seconds later, he had his tongue buried in her cunt.

After several orgasms, he led her upstairs where they proceeded to fuck in any position they could think of. They did it missionary style, spooned, 69ed, her on top and now he was fucking her from behind as hard as he could.

Zoe's body was lean, athletic and almost perfect and she had the tightest pussy he'd ever sunk his dick into. While Rita was off fucking another man somewhere, Art and Zoe were living out their mutual fantasies.

Zoe sighed and moaned with each hard, deep thrust of his dick as he brought her closer and closer to yet another orgasm. When she came, she shook all over and screamed. Art came at the same instant and fucked her as hard and as fast as he could. She screamed again and fell onto the bed. Art fell on top of her. As he did, he cried out.

"I love you, Zoe!"

It was what she wanted to hear ever since they'd met.

Rita saw Zoe get into her car and drive away just as she approached the house. She smiled because she knew that Art didn't miss her. How could he when he had a dish like Zoe to play with?

Art greeted her when she came in.

"You look tired," he said.

"So do you," she said as they hugged.

She and Zoe met for lunch later that day and laughed at their experiences.

"I never thought we'd end up doing anything like this," Zoe said. "I've always wanted to fuck Art, but I never thought you'd clear the way for us by fucking other guys. I never thought you'd stray like this."

"Me neither. I always felt that Art would be my only lover forever. But once the idea of cheating got into my mind, I just couldn't let it go. I have to admit that I really enjoy fucking other men, too. But what I really am amazed at is that you and I fell madly in love with each other! It's been a crazy couple of months, hasn't it?" Rita said.

"Yes it has. You'd better be careful, Rita. I still might try to steal Art away from you. Once I get him, I'm never letting him go," Zoe warned half playfully.

That's when she told her what Art had cried out the night before. Rita giggled and told her that Bart had said the same thing to her.

"Do you think they meant it?" Zoe asked.

"I don't know for sure. Since Art has always liked you very much, I think he meant it. I'm not so sure about Bart, but he does treat me nicer each time. He's real good at eating pussy, too!" Rita said.

They both laughed.

That night, Rita stayed home and cooked dinner, then she and Art made love. Zoe just rested up at home and planned to surprise Art again the next day.

Bart sat at his desk and stared into space. He was becoming obsessed with Rita. She was in his thoughts all day and night. In fact, he had even turned down dates from other women he knew, women who would eagerly jump into bed with him.

He thought about what he'd said to her as she drove away. He'd never said that to anyone before. He'd never felt this way about anyone before either. Rita wasn't just another woman. She was someone very, very special. Someone he truly wanted and hoped like Hell that she wanted him, too.

"You're going soft," he said to himself. "You let a woman capture your heart!"

Rita was torn between two great loves. She adored Art more than anyone else on Earth and wanted to be his wife forever. She was also crazy-mad in love with Zoe. She also had become very fond of Bart.

Maybe too fond.

The other guys were just what Art called "fuck buddies". She felt no emotional attachment to either of them. They just had good, hard dicks and were good with them.

And she planned to keep fucking them whenever she could.

The next morning, Carl called Rita.

"Hi, Carl. Ready to get it on again?" she teased.

"Hell yeah. I'd like to see you today. I've missed you," he said.

"I've missed you, too. Why don't you stop by at one?" she suggested.

"You have a date," he said. "I'll see you then."

When Carl arrived, she greeted him at the door dressed in her very sheer robe. As soon as he walked in and shut the door behind him, she let the robe slide to the floor and smiled. She walked up to him and groped his dick. Within seconds, he, too was naked and Rita was kneeling before him sucking his cock and stroking his balls.

She stopped just before he came and stood. He dropped to his knees and buried his tongue in her slit. She gripped his hair and moaned as he tongued her clit faster and faster until she came. While she was still reeling, he led her to the sofa. She knelt on the floor and put her elbows on the sofa. Carl got behind her licked her puckered anus for a few seconds before sliding his tongue up into her cunt again. When she was good and wet, he eased his prick into her rear channel. She sighed as his knob went deep into her ass. He fucked her slowly at first then started doing it faster. Rita sighed and trembled all over. Carl grabbed her behind and humped her even faster.

Carl loved to use her this way and she was more than happy to let him. His prick felt incredible as it massaged her asshole. Carl loved the way her ass convulsed around his prick each time he thrust into her. She felt so good, too. So tight. So silky smooth. In fact, this was one of the best fucks he'd had in weeks.

Each time Carl's prick moved inside her ass, Rita sighed happily and trembled with lust. She felt herself growing wetter and hotter as they fucked and she began thrusting her hips back at him to match his rhythm. Each time, he pushed into her all the way to his balls.

Rita felt herself coming. It was a good one, too. From deep inside her body. Carl realized what she was going through and fucked her faster. Rita moaned.

"Oohh! That's it! Fuck me, Carl! That feels so good! So fucking good!" she moaned.

Carl fucked her even faster. He soon felt his balls spasm a few times and held onto her even tighter as he let himself go. Rita shook wildly and sighed. Then she fell across the sofa and lay trembling while he continued to give her several more deep thrusts. He then shoved his prick as far into her ass as he could and released a flood of cum. The sensations caused by the hot cum slamming into her ass walls triggered another orgasm in Rita and she began groaning loudly. Spurt after spurt jetted into her. She felt each and every one of them, too.

And they felt delicious.

So wonderfully delicious.

Carl kept humping away until his prick slid out. As it did, a shower of cum dripped from her open asshole and splattered the carpet.

"Let's finish this upstairs," she said as she took his hand.

Once in bed Carl pushed Rita onto her back. She immediately opened her thighs so he could mount her. Since her cunt was still wet, his long prick slid into her with ease and they began a slow, easy fuck. After a few Seconds, Rita gripped his behind and began thrusting her pelvis upward with a wild abandon. They moved faster and faster. Carl felt her cunt convulse around his prick as she came again. He fucked her as fast as he could until he emptied a large load of cum deep inside her pussy. But this time, he remained hard and he kept going at her with all of his energy. Rita fell back with her arms and legs akimbo as he deep fucked her until he fell across her chest. She felt his knob slam into her cervix. The impact was followed by yet another gusher of warm cum that blended with his earlier deposits and triggered yet another orgasm for Rita.

After a few minutes Rita wrapped her fingers around Carl's prick and jerked him off. He leaned over and licked her nipples as he fingered her slit. When Carl was fully erect once more, Rita straddled him and impaled herself on his cock. She rode him nice and slow this time as she savored the feeling of his dick moving in and out of her cunt. Carl grabbed her behind and fucked her back. It took longer for them to come this time.

Carl came first and drove his prick straight up Rita's snatch and drained his cum inside of her. He shot wad after wad into her. So much, in fact, that it leaked out of her cunt and coated his balls.

Now, she rode him very hard. Her head was back and she emitted load, happy moans as she bounced up and down on his prick. When she came, she fell on top of him and sighed deeply.

But she wasn't finished by any means. She slid off him and grabbed his cum-coated prick. When it didn't respond after a few good pulls, she slipped the head into her mouth and sucked away until Carl's balls ached.

"Holy shit, Rita! You're insatiable!" he groaned. "I'm done for the night. Hey, look at the time! I'd better get going. I have to pack for a business trip tomorrow. I'll be gone for a couple of weeks. Can I call you when I get back?"

"You'd better!" she said as she squeezed his prick.

Rita went to work early the next morning. This was her late night at the store and she wouldn't be home until almost nine. Knowing this, Zoe phoned Art.

"Are you alone today?" she asked.

"I won't be after you get here," he said.

"I love the way you think! I'll be there in 10 minutes!" she said as she hung up.

Art greeted her at the door with a big hug and prolonged French kiss that nearly took her breath away. As they kissed in the foyer, Art ran his hands up under her shorts and fondled her smooth, round behind while she unzipped his pants and played with his already-erect prick.

After a few minutes of foreplay, Zoe pulled Art into the living room by his prick then dropped to her knees. She rained soft kisses onto his member and licked the knob several times before sliding it into her mouth. Art stood there groaning with pleasure as Zoe proceeded to give him one of the best blow jobs he ever had. Moments later, he found himself coming inside her hungry mouth as she greedily swallowed every last drop of cum he could produce.

Zoe licked her lips and stood up.

"Let's go into the bedroom, Art. We have all day," she said as she looked into his eyes.

Art took Zoe's hand and led her up the stairs. Once inside the bedroom, Zoe pulled off her T-shirt and cupped her breasts. Art licked each nipple until Zoe felt her entire body tingle and her breathing grew heavy. Then he licked his way down her belly. As he dropped to his knees, Art pulled Zoe's shorts to her ankles. She stepped free of them and spread her legs, then closed her eyes. She trembled deliciously as Art's soft, knowing tongue adored her aching, eager cunt.

"Yes. Oh God, yes!" she sighed.

Art was in Heaven now. Zoe's cunt tasted like slightly salted honey and her aroma made his dick harder than ever. He kneaded her behind as he ate her, savoring the flavor of her womanhood. It was, by far, the sweetest pussy he'd ever tasted.

He pushed his tongue up into her as far as it would go and swirled it around. Zoe's knees almost buckled. She gripped Art's shoulders and began humping his tongue as her passion soared higher and higher.

Art was good at eating pussy.

Very good.

Her head soon rolled back as waves of intense pleasure tentacled outward from her cunt and touched every nerve ending of her quivering body. When she came, she felt as if every volcano on earth was centered in her cunt and they had all erupted at the same time. Unable to maintain her balance any longer, Zoe fell backward onto the bed. Her momentum carried Art with her.

He never missed a beat. His tongue remained buried inside Zoe's quivering muff as he continued to work his magic on her swollen clit.

Zoe thrashed around on the bed, screaming his name as several white hot orgasms tore through her. Art stopped. He stood up and removed his clothes.

Zoe stared at his swollen prick and eagerly opened her thighs. Art climbed atop her and slowly slid his prick into her expectant cunt until their pubic hairs touched. Zoe shivered.

"That feels so good. Fuck me, Art! Make me all yours today," she whispered.

Then came that slow, deep, gentle in and out movement that massaged every part of her cunt. That warm, happy fuck that made her feel so damned good inside. She let him use her for a few minutes, then matched him thrust for thrust.

Their rhythm was perfect. They soon became as one. Zoe couldn't tell where she left off and Art began anymore. She didn't care either. All she cared about was the intense pleasure she now felt as she oh so willingly gave herself to Art body and soul.

She felt herself coming and increased the speed of their fuck. This time, she wanted him to come inside her. She wanted him to fill her pussy with his love cream until it ran down her trembling thighs.

They came together in one, huge, prolonged flash of bright, white light. Then they rested and kissed several times.

"Turn over," Art said.

Zoe lay on her stomach with her legs wide open behind her. Her cunt was hot and wet from their earlier fuck and it still tingled. It was a delicious prelude to what was to come next. She felt the bed move, then felt Art's breath on the back of her neck as he kissed it gently. She sighed happily as his prick slid into her. Then he began fucking her nice and easy.

"Oh yes! Yes! Yes!" Zoe moaned as he rammed his cock deeper and deeper on each thrust. She used her cunt muscles to squeeze his prick, and increased the intensity of the pleasure they both felt. Art's tongue tickled her ear. Zoe trembled and gripped the pillow as he fucked her harder and harder. Her cunt felt velvety and warm around his prick. In fact, it felt sexier each and every time they made love. When they came, it was together. So perfect. So very perfect.

Art fucked her even faster now, emptying himself deep inside Zoe's hungry channel. She kept moaning with pleasure as each good, hard thrust made her orgasm even more intense, more satisfying than ever.

They rested a few minutes. Then Zoe stroked Art's prick until he was good and hard again. When she thought he was hard enough, she got onto her elbows with her behind up in the air. Her thighs were spread wide as she offered her back door to him.

Art stared at her near perfect ass, then leaned over and gave her sphincter a few easy licks. Zoe laughed. Art got out of bed and walked to the dresser. He returned with a bottle of baby oil which he massaged into Zoe's crack and anus. He then slid two fingers into her ass and wriggled them around gently. Zoe bit her lower lip at the strange mixture of pain and pleasure felt. She'd never had anything up there before. It felt very strange.

Art coated his prick with oil and put the bottle down. He spread Zoe's cheeks apart and teased her ass with the head of his cock. Zoe felt his knob moving up and down between her cheeks a few times before stopping at her back door. She held her breath as Art slowly entered her an inch at a time.

"Ahhh!" she screamed.

She bit her lip harder now as Art's meat missile penetrated her, working its way deep into her channel until Zoe thought she would crazy with the pain—and lust she now felt.

"Yes!" she cried.

Art straightened up a bit, put his hands on her ass, and began a nice, slow, easy fuck. After a few good, rhythmic thrusts of Art's prick, she let herself relax.

"This isn't so bad," she thought. "In fact, I kind of like it."

Art could hardly believe he was fucking Zoe in her behind. Her ass felt exquisitely tight and warm. He moved slowly in and out so he could enjoy every second and to give her as much pleasure as he could.

"I'm coming, Zoe," he gasped. "It's gonna be a big one, too!"

"I can feel it, too, Art! Come inside me! Fill me ass with your cum!" Zoe almost shouted. She never knew anyone could come from being ass fucked, but here she was, on the verge of a real good come. A very deep come.

Art moaned. She felt him tremble. His weight pressed forward against her ass as his cock drove into her even deeper. As he emptied his balls inside Zoe's throbbing ass, he reached around and rubbed her clit.

That was all it took.

Zoe erupted. This orgasm was so intense, she virtually milked Art's prick with her sphincter muscles until he had nothing left to give.

They held each other close for a few minutes. Art smiled lovingly at her.

"That was magnifico!" she sighed as they kissed.

The next afternoon, the girls met for lunch. As they chatted over their meal, Zoe slid her hand under Rita's skirt and fingered her cunt. Rita smiled and parted her thighs as Zoe slowly too her into a pleasant orgasmic fog.

"I want you again," Zoe said softly.

"I want you, too," Rita replied.

They headed to Zoe's house this time. When they reached the bedroom, they spent several minutes slowly undressing each other and kissing softly and deeply. When they were totally nude, Rita pulled Zoe down onto the bed and caressed her cunt. There was no need to rush. Rita kissed her way to Zoe's cunt then slowly licked her until she came. After Zoe came twice, they switched positions. Rita was so horny that she erupted within seconds. After a short rest, Zoe opened her thighs.

Rita climbed on top of her and slowly ground her cunt against Zoe's. Zoe moaned and opened her thighs further. Rita gently fucked her. Zoe quivered then matched her movements. She came first this time and lay trembling and sighing while Rita fucked her faster and faster until she also came.

Zoe expected Rita to stop for a while. Instead, she kept going. Faster and faster. Zoe moaned and held her tight as she tried to match her. Their movements became erratic and more intense.

"I love you, Rita! I love you! Fuck me harder! I'm all yours!" Zoe groaned as she came again and again.

Rita kept fucking her and coming—and coming—and coming again. When they'd had enough, Rita collapsed on top of her and stuck her tongue into Zoe's willing mouth. When they calmed back down, Zoe giggled.

"What's so funny?" asked Rita.

"I never thought I would tell another woman that I loved her and mean it. I also never thought I'd beg that woman to fuck me. Sex with you is fun and very exciting," Zoe replied.

Rita smiled.

"I love you, too," she said softly.

They got up and dressed. Both were very happy and exhausted. They poured themselves a glass of iced tea and sat down at the kitchen table.

"This is Tuesday," Zoe said. "Casino night."

"I know. I told Bart I'd see him there tonight," Rita said.

"How far are you gonna let him get this time?" Zoe asked.

"I'm not sure. What if your guy shows up?" Rita asked.

"If he does, I'll fuck him again," Zoe said with a giggle. "I like the way he does it. So maybe we'll both be really busy tonight?"

Rita grinned.

"Maybe," she said.

When they got to the casino, the place was busy. They were having some sort of special tournament and several of the older players had shown up to get in on the action. They looked around at their usual spots. Rita's favorite place was still unoccupied so she walked over and sat down.

Zoe waited to see if Bart would show up.

He did.

Zoe watched as he brought Rita a drink. They played, laughed and he got her another one. She saw him lean closer and whisper in her ear.

"Is your pussy still fuzzy?" he teased.

She blushed and laughed and gave him a playful shove.

"That's none of your business!" she said.

"Ever since you told me that, I've been trying to imagine what it looks like. Let me see it, Rita," he said as he put his hand on her knee. "The last time was magical. I'd love to eat you again. In fact, I want to make love to you all night long."

She sipped her drink and laughed.

Zoe watched as Bart obviously slid his hand up Rita's thigh. When she didn't push him away, Zoe giggled. She moved closer and saw Rita smile and nod at him.

"My God! She's letting him touch her!" Zoe thought.

Rita was!

Bart had managed to get his hand between her thighs again. Since she was wearing jeans, she just let him rub her crotch while she shivered dreamily. She didn't mind this now. The drinks had made her horny again anyway.

"Can I see your pussy?" Bart asked.

She smiled at him as she continued to sip her mai tai. Bart undid her belt. When she didn't object, he popped her top snap open and slowly eased down her zipper. She smiled as he moved his seat closer, very aware of what he was doing and so freaking horny that she didn't mind it.

Zoe moved closer to get a better view.

"She's actually gonna let him touch her there!" she thought. "She thinking of cheating!"

She moved closer and watched as he eased his hand into Rita's jeans. She saw her head go back and watched as Rita shut her eyes and sighed as Bart's fingers gently massaged her swollen clit. She thought about interrupting them but a light tough on her elbow diverted her attention. She smiled when she saw Greg.

"I have a nice, hard dick that's looking for a soft warm pussy to play in," he said.

"And I have a soft, warm pussy," she said as they headed for the hotel elevators.

"I really enjoyed what we did last time," Bart said as he stroked Rita's clit.

"So did I," she said softly as she watched his bulge get larger. "I was sort of surprised at myself for doing that."

"You can do that anytime you want," he said. "Let's do it, Rita," he said. "You know you want to. No one will ever know about it but us."

Rita sat there and quivered as she felt his middle finger enter her slit. She felt him move it in and out nice and slowly. Her head was in the clouds now. She reached over and ran her hand over his bulge.

Bart smiled and moved a little closer. While she caressed his dick, he fingered her faster and faster. She located his knob and played with it through his pants.

"Let's do it, Rita," he urged. "Let's make love."

That's when she came. It was another long, deep orgasm, too. He kept fingering her faster and faster until she became lost in a long series of orgasms. At the same time, she kept working his knob. Bart moaned and came all over his pants again. Rita kept at this until she felt his cum seep through his pants and make her fingers sticky.

They smiled at each other.

"That was fun," she said.

"Let's have even more fun," he said.

"No. I'm not ready for that yet," she said.

"Will you ever be?" he asked as he stroked her leg.

"Maybe," she smiled as she sipped her drink. "To be honest, Bart, the more we do this, the more I want to have sex with you. But I'm happily married to a great guy and I still don't feel right about cheating on him."

"Oh? Is there anything that would make this right for you?" he asked.

"Well maybe if he cheated I'd do the same," she said. "But I don't think he'll ever do that."

"You know that I'm going to keep after you," he said. "Now that we've gone this far, I want you even more."

She nodded.

He signaled to the hostess. She brought over two more drinks and he tipped her. Rita leaned back. Her jeans were still undone. Bart looked at her and she nodded as he slid his hand down into her soaked panties. Since the place was crowded, she decided not to suck his dick again. As his finger slowly worked her slit, she hoped that no one was watching. But she was incredibly horny and getting more so by the second.

"Let's go for a walk," Bart suggested.

She smiled and took his hand. She knew where he was taking her and hoped like Hell that no one would be around. They crossed the crowded floor and went to the darkest area again. To Rita's relief, no one was around as these machines were still out of service. She slid onto one of the chairs and smiled. Bart moved close and they kissed. As she sucked his tongue, she groped his bulge and the slowly freed his hard prick from his jeans. She gave it several easy pulls, then leaned over and licked the pre-cum from his knob.

Bart gasped as she slid his prick into her mouth and bobbed her head back and forth as she sucked it. The sensations were awesome. So awesome that he fired his first load straight down her throat within a minute. She kept pumping and sucking. Each pump sent a spurt of thick, warm cum into her mouth which she happily swallowed. He gripped her head and slowly fucked her mouth. Rita managed to take more and more of his prick into her mouth. Bart kept coming the entire time, too. He came a lot. More than she thought any man could.

She kept sucking his prick until he went limp and it slipped out of her mouth. She sat back and smiled at him as she wiped his cum from her lips. Bart undid her jeans. Rita stood and allowed him to pull them down to her ankles then she stepped out of them. He whistled when he saw her cunt. She sat down and parted her legs.

Bart knelt between her thighs and slid his tongue up and down her quivering slit several times before plunging it into her. Rita closed her eyes and leaned back as he ate her. She was so horny that she came right away and began fucking his tongue. Bart made her come again and again and again. She felt limp, like a rag doll now. She sat there and smiled up at him with her legs open wide. His prick was almost fully erect once again.

He stepped forward and slid his knob up and down her slit. She quivered and put her feet up on the seat. Bart smiled and eased his prick into her cunt. She moaned and wrapped her legs around his hips as he went deeper and deeper.

Bart was amazed!

After weeks of trying, he finally got his prick into Rita's pussy. He stopped to savor the way it hugged him. She smiled and tightened her inner muscles around him. He moaned and started to move nice and slow. Each thrust was gentle, deep and easy. She felt his prick massage every bit of her cunt each time and shivered with passion. Bart wasn't just fucking her. He was making love to her. They moved together slowly to enjoy every second.

Rita had never felt anything like this before. Each move was exciting and passionate. It felt like they'd been made for each other. They moved a little bit faster. Rita felt herself nearing orgasm and fucked him faster. Bart understood her signal and fucked her harder and harder. When Rita came, she trembled all over and emitted a long, low moan.

Bart also exploded.

She felt his cum jet into her cunt and fucked him harder. He did the same and they kept fucking and fucking until they both came again. This one shook Rita to her core and she had to bite her lip to keep from screaming.

When Bart pulled out, she grabbed him and stuck her tongue into his mouth.

"I love you!" they both said at once.

Rita dressed.

"This was wonderful," she said as she hugged him tight. "The best ever!"

"We finally did it, Rita. We made love! It was even more fantastic that I'd ever imagined it would be. You're the best! The very best," he said.

"And I'm all yours whenever you want me, Bart," she assured him.

They kissed for a long time, then went back into the main part of the casino. Bart ordered two more mai tais and they sat and chatted. They maintained eye contact the entire time.

"I want to make love to you forever, Rita," Bart said as he held her hand.

She smiled.

"I'm yours for as long as you want me. If that becomes forever, I'm okay with that," she said.

When Zoe finished fucking Greg, she went down to the casino. She'd been with Greg almost two hours and, like before, he'd fucked the daylights out of her and she had left him for dead.

When she got to the casino, she looked for Rita. She saw her seated at her usual machine. Bart was seated very close to her and, from the happy expression on Rita's face, Zoe realized that Bart was playing with her pussy.

She moved to get a better view and saw that he had his hand down the front of Rita's jeans. For some reason, that made Zoe angry and she decided to intervene. She called Rita's name and watched as she snapped out of her sexual trance. She saw her approach and greeted her.

"It's almost midnight," Zoe said. "We'd better get home before Art gets mad."

"Oh. Alright," Rita said.

She smiled at Bart. He shrugged.

"I have to leave now. See you next time, Bart," she said

"Sure thing. Good night, ladies," he smiled.

On the way to the car, Zoe quizzed Rita.

"Well, did you do it/?" Zoe asked.

"Oh, yes. And it was wonderful!" Rita sighed. "Truly wonderful."

"Is that why your jeans are still open?" Zoe asked as they got into the car.

Rita looked down and laughed as she zipped back up.

"I didn't realize that," she lied.

"In that case, you're too drunk to notice," Zoe said. "From the expression on your face, I could tell that he had his hand on your pussy and you liked what he was doing. If I hadn't stopped him, you'd have ended up in bed with him and you'd fuck all night."

Rita giggled.

"Maybe you're right," she said. "That's sounds like a great idea, too!"

"What I don't understand about you is that you're married to a great guy who's terrific in bed. Yet you want to fuck other guys and possibly ruin that," Zoe said. "I think you're getting too involved with Bart. He wants something more permanent from you because he's nuts about you. I think you're also nuts about him."

Rita nodded.

"I thought so! You know what this means, right?" Zoe smiled.

"You're going after Art with everything you've got!" Rita said.

"Damned right I am. And I'm telling you right now that I will try to steal him from you if you keep fucking other men. I'll make him mine," Zoe warned. "Don't forget that!"

"I won't," Rita said.

She knew that Zoe had a crush on Art and expected to hear her say that. She was right, of course. She had been very aware of Bart was doing the entire time and that it was wrong. But she liked Bart. Maybe too much and she was at once fascinated by and scared of him. She knew exactly what he wanted because he'd always been up front about it.

And yes. She let him fuck her.

And yes, she'd let him do it again.

She sighed.

It was both a sigh of relief and frustration.

What Zoe didn't know was that she and Bart had exchanged cell phone numbers. She had also told when the best times were to contact her. That's how he knew when she'd be at the casino.

"Are you thinking of having sex with Bart regularly?" Zoe asked.

"Maybe. I'm not sure right now. I might I'm just have a little fun with him," Rita said.

"Careful. Your fun might mean that you'll end up with his dick in your pussy every night.

Bart wants you, Rita. He won't give up until he gets you all to himself," Zoe warned.

"I won't let him get that far," Rita said.

"From what I saw tonight, I think you've let him get really far. You're encouraging him, Rita. That's dangerous," Zoe said.

"I can handle Bart," Rita said.

"Just don't get so drunk with him that you give him what he wants. Don't throw Art away for him because if you do, I'll gladly catch Art and keep him for myself.!" Zoe said.

"Okay, "mother"," Rita joked.

"I just don't want to see you get into trouble," Zoe said.

"You sound like you're jealous or something," Rita teased.

"I sort of am. I don't want you to overuse your pussy. I want you to save it for me," Zoe said as she leaned closer.

Rita smiled at her then kissed her.

"You can have me whenever you want me," she said softly. "You know that."

When she got home, Art laughed.

"You have that well-fucked look again," he said as she sat down on the sofa. "You finally did it, didn't you?"

She nodded.

"Yes. Before you ask, I'll tell you. He was great. In fact, he was better than ever hoped he'd be," she said.

"So you're gonna keep seeing him?" Art asked.

"Oh yes!" Rita smiled. "I'm sorry." "Don't be. You can have sex with whomever you want as long as I get to have sex with Zoe. That was our deal from the start. When you decide that you've had enough and stop fucking other men, I'll give Zoe up," he said.

"Zoe just told me that she's never giving you up, so that might be impossible. She's crazy in love with you, Art and she said she plans to steal you from me," Rita said.

"That will never happen," he assured her.

She nodded but didn't feel convinced.

Chapter Ten

Neither one of them knew it, but things were about to become even more interesting for Rita.

Rita liked to work out at the YMCA a couple of times a week. She liked to ride the stationary bikes and use the Stair Masters.

On this particular day, there was a younger man on the bike behind her and as they worked out, he got a very nice view of he thought was the best-looking ass he'd ever seen.

The longer he watched, the harder his dick grew. By the time Rita was finished, he had the biggest erection of his life.

He followed her to the Stair Masters and got on the one directly behind her so he could watch her cheeks move up and down. He also admired her killer legs and made up his mind to go after her. By the time the workout ended, he was on the verge of coming all over himself.

Rita retreated to the ladies room. He went to the snack bar and bought two protein drinks and waited for her to come out. When she did, he handed her one. She took it and smiled.

"Thanks," she said.

"I thought you could use one," he said. "My name's Rocco. My friends call me Rocky. What's yours?"

"Rita," she said. "What do I owe you?"

"Nothing. I did this to get acquainted with you. I've seen you here several times and I finally worked up enough courage to talk to you," he said.

"Courage?" she asked as she noticed the very large bulge in his shorts.

In fact, it was the biggest one she'd ever seen and she realized that she was the cause of it.

"Yes. You're so damned beautiful that you leave me speechless. Are you married?" he said.

"Yes. I've been married over 20 years," she said.

"No kidding? I thought you were only 25 or 30 years old. You look very young," he said.

"Asians don't age like American women. Why did you want to get to know me?" she asked.

"To be honest, I fell in love with the second I saw you so I decided to get to know you better," he replied.

"That's really nice. Really. But now that you know I'm married and much older than you thought, you know that you have no chance with me," she said.

"Well, even so, we can still be friends. We can work out together sometimes. There's no harm in that, is there?" he asked hopefully.

"Not really. It might be fun to have somebody to work out with," she smiled.

"Great. I usually come here on Monday and Friday. I notice that you do, too. Want to meet this Friday?" he asked.

"Okay. I'll see you then. Thanks for the drink," she said.

Rocky smiled.

She didn't tell him to get lost. In fact, she was very friendly. He watched her ass as she walked away.

"I have lots of time," he said.

Rita grinned on the way to her car. The idea that she had given someone like Rocky such a huge erection flattered her. From the looks of the bulge, he was at least nine inches and real thick. She also knew that he'd give almost anything to be able to put his massive dick into her pussy. She wondered what Rocky would do if she gave him the chance?

That same night, she and Zoe went to the casino. They got there earlier than usual and the place was almost empty.

"Not much to choose from tonight," Zoe said as she looked at some of the men. "Oh, well. I guess I'll go play the slots. See you later?"

"Sure," Rita said.

She played for a little while and got bored because Bart wasn't around. She decided to look for Zoe and headed in the direction of her favorite machine. The seat was empty so she looked around.

She found Zoe in one of the dark niches along the back wall of the casino. She was on her hands and knees and smiling as the man she'd met only an hour ago fucked her from behind. Rita watched as his long prick moved in out of Zoe's cunt nice and slowly. She'd never seen anyone fuck outside of a porno movie and watching Zoe and her lover was making her hornier.

Zoe looked over her shoulder at Rita and smiled. Then she licked her lips to show her she was enjoying it. Rita watched for another few thrusts then left. She stopped outside to gather her thoughts and went back to her slot machine. When she arrived, she spotted Bart walking toward her with two drinks in hand.

They sat down at the machine and he handed her one. She smiled at him.

"You looked flushed," he observed. "I saw you back there. What were you looking at in that alcove?"

"I was watching Zoe and some guy she just met. They were fucking," Rita said.

"Really? Did that make you horny?" he asked as he slid his hand along her inner thigh.

"Yes," she smiled as she parted her knees.

"Maybe I can help you with that problem?" he suggested as he eased his hand under her shorts.

"Maybe you can," she smiled as he parted her legs more.

He ran his fingers over her panties a few times and realized she was very damp. She smiled as he eased two gingers into her cunt and then shut her eyes and moaned softly as he "fucked" her.

"Yes," she whispered as he frigged her faster.

By now, he was as hard as steel. She reached over and stroked the bulge in his pants then started to play with the tip.

"I'm very horny tonight," she said.

"So I see," he smiled as he teased her g-spot.

She convulse as she came. It was a strong, long-lasting orgasm that made her shake all over. At the same time, she kept playing with his dick and wondering how it would feel inside her cunt. She kept doing it until she knew he had also come.

When he removed his hand from her panties, her cunt was still throbbing deliciously.

"Are you still horny?" he asked.

She unzipped his pants and reached into them. She pushed aside his briefs and started playing with his cum-coated knob. Caught by surprise, Bart came again. This time, she covered his head with the palm of her hand so that his cum ran back down his shaft. Then she ran her fingers up and down his prick to make sure it was covered with his cum.

He again had his hand between her legs. She squirmed and sighed as he massaged her clit until she came again, too. She kept playing with his dick the entire time. Without realizing it, she had pulled it out of his pants. She looked down and stared at it as she pumped him faster and faster.

Afraid of being seen, she stopped and shoved his prick back into his pants but she kept playing with the tip for a while. She was amazed that he had remained hard the entire time.

They stopped and looked at each other.

"Yes," she said.

"Yes what?" he asked.

"I was still horny," she smiled. "How do you stay hard so long?"

"I don't know. I think that has a lot to do with being with you. I can't believe you did that. That was terrific," he said. "Are you ready to go all the way with me?"

She caught her breath and smiled at him.

"I'm not sure. My God! My head is still up in the clouds!" she said.

He got them another drink. They sat and sipped as they talked. She was happy that he didn't try to push her into doing more. And sort of disappointed.

"I'm crazy about you, Rita. You're all I ever think about lately. I'm really glad we did this and if you're not ready to go all the way, I understand. I'm willing to take this one step at a time and we'll go at your pace. I have a feeling that you're really worth waiting for," he said.

She smiled at him.

When she looked down, she saw that the head of his dick was slowly emerging from his open zipper. She reached down, grabbed it with her fingertips and tweaked it. Within seconds, most of erection was standing straight up. She looked around to be sure they were alone, then leaned closer as she jerked him off and it became long, thick and very hard. She watched as the foreskin moved back and forth in her hands.

Bart sat still and sighed happily as she jerked him off. Rita moved closer and closer. Then, to his delight, she opened her mouth and swirled her tongue all over his knob. Bart stifled a moan as she slid his prick into her mouth and proceeded to suck away. It felt so damned good that he came seconds later and shot one last, thick wad of cum into Rita's mouth. She kept sucking and jerking him off until his dick shriveled back to its normal size.

She sat up as she swallowed and wiped her lips.

He stared at her as if he was in awe.

"Wow!" he whispered.

She laughed and sipped her drink. He sat back, put his dick away and patted her on the knee.

"After this, you know that I want to have sex with you more than ever. I'm never going to stop chasing you and I'm going to want you more and more," he said.

"I know," she replied.

"If I thought that no one would see us, I'd pull off your shorts and eat you right here," he said.

"We still have time," she said.

"What about the rest?" he asked.

"Definitely!," she said.

They made their way back to the dark area around the unused slots. They stopped to kiss for a little while, then Bart undid Zoe's shorts and slowly peeled them and her panties down to her ankles. Rita kicked them off and sat down on one of the chairs with her legs open wide. Bart knelt between them and slid his tongue into her cunt. Rita shut her eyes as he took on a wonderful, exciting ride that ended with a terrific orgasm. She gripped his head and fucked his tongue until she came twice more then let him go. By then, his prick was rock hard. She smiled and leaned back.

Bart slid it home and they proceeded to slow fuck. She loved the way her took his time to make sure she enjoyed each and every long, easy thrust of his dick. She wrapped her legs around his hips and held onto his shoulders as she fucked him a little faster.

God! It felt so good!

Bart wasn't just fucking her and she wasn't just fucking him. They were actually making love. She was all his now and she made sure to use her pussy in ways that he knew it. Bart did know it. In fact, he was doing the same thing to Rita.

They moved perfectly together.

Faster and faster and faster.

When they came, it was together. And it was a deep, powerful mutual orgasm that shook Rita to her very core and caused Bart to unleash a torrent of cum deep inside her pussy. They fucked and fucked until they were both completely spent. Just before he slid out, he looked into her eyes.

"I love you, Rita," he whispered.

"I love you too," she replied and she realized that she meant it!

As they walked back onto the casino floor hand-in-hand, they heard Zoe call Rita's name. Bart straightened himself up and smiled as she approached. She looked at them, saw the expressions on their faces, and laughed.

"It looks like we all got what we came here for," she said.

Rita and Bart laughed, too.

As they got into the car, Zoe smiled.

"I saw you watching me earlier. Did you enjoy the show?" she asked.

Rita giggled.

"Yes, I did. Your friend has a real long dick. What's his name?" she said.

"Beats me. I never asked. Did watching us make you horny?" Zoe asked.

"It made me very horny," Rita replied with a giggle.

"So? Did you fuck Bart?" Zoe asked.

"Oh yeah!" Rita said.

"Was it as good as the first time?" Zoe asked.

"Better!" Rita said.

"What else did you do? Tell me what you did," Zoe urged.

"I, er, sucked his dick," Rita admitted as she blushed.

"You did? You really sucked his dick?" Zoe asked.

"Yes. I sucked it," Rita said. "I got the urge to suck it, so I did. Then we fucked him and it was incredible!"

"Wow! That means you officially cheated on your husband. Now that you've gone this far, when are you gonna keep fucking him?" Zoe asked.

"Definitely. That part scares me," Rita said.

"I love this!" Zoe said.

"Why?" asked Rita.

"Now that you're having sex with Bart, I'm going after Art. By cheating—which you are—you made Art fair game. You can't even complain about it because you don't have any moral high ground to stand on. So I am going after him and when I get him, I'm gonna keep him," Zoe said happily.

Rita stayed silent.

Zoe meant every word of what she said and Rita realized that she could lose Art to her.

"I love you, Rita. But I love Art more. I always have. And now, I'm gonna get him," Zoe continued. "So keep fucking Bart and those other men all you want. I'll make sure that Art doesn't miss you at all. Deal?"

Rita laughed at the absurdity of it all.

"Okay. Deal!" she said.

"When you think about, you've already cheated on him with me. Even though we're women, it's still extramarital sex," Zoe said.

"I've never thought of that way, but you're right. Are you still gonna fuck other men?" Rita asked.

"Maybe. But I'd prefer to be Art's only. But I don't mind sharing him with you. After all, you are his wife and I think you will always be his wife. He's crazy in love with you and I think that will never change. But he will end up with two wives. I'll make sure of that," Zoe said.

Bart was on Cloud Nine when he drove home. Rita had gone much further than he expected she would. He didn't ask her to do it. She did it of her own free will.

And she was damned good!

Now, he wanted her even more. But he was still determined to let her take the lead and go at her own pace. He wanted her to be 100% sure so there would be no guilt or regrets later.

What none of them suspected was that Judy had seen Rita go down on Bart. This totally blew her mind because she never thought Rita would do such a thing. She watched her suck his dick until he came and used her cell phone to capture it on video. Then she t then left the area.

A half hour later, she took out her cell phone and called Art to tell him what was happening. As proof, she sent him the video.

Art watched it several times. As he did, he got an erection. It was strangely erotic to watch his wife suck another man's dick.

"There's nothing I can do about it now," he said. "This changes everything, too. The next time Zoe goes after me, I'll let her catch me."

When Rita got home, he didn't say a word. Instead, he turned on his cell phone, located the video Judy had sent to him and placed in front of her. Rita gaped as she realized what she was watching. It was like she watching herself star in a cheap porno movie. She watched it until the end then looked at Art.

"Judy sent me that," he said. "It looks like you and Bart are more than just friends now," he said as she sat down with her.

"I, I—" she stammered.

He smiled.

"I knew this would happen. Once I dug into his past, I knew you'd end up having sex with him," he said. "You can't deny it. That's definitely you sucking his dick. Did you fuck him?"

"Yes" she said. "I told you I was."

"Look, Rita. If you want to fuck another guy or two, I can't make you stop. You'll just sneak around on me anyway. But keep this in mind—Zoe is after me. Now that I know about you and Bart, I see no reason to stay loyal to you," he said. "As long as it's in the open, we're not cheating. We'll just experiment with having an open marriage for a little while."

"I don't know what to say!" she said as she almost cried.

She expected to get yelled at or worse. Instead, he stayed calm and collected and even said it was okay as long as he got to have sex with Zoe. There was nothing she could say. She was trapped.

"Let's go upstairs," he said as he took her by the hand.

The next day, Rita met Zoe for lunch in the park. They talked about their weird lifestyle changes and how things were getting stranger as they all became more sexually adventurous.

"What really surprises me most is that we are in love with each other and I feel that love will only grow stronger as time passes," Rita said. "In fact, whenever I'm near you, I want to make love with you."

"Well, Art's at work, isn't he?" Zoe smiled.

Rita laughed.

They headed back to her house and hurried upstairs to the bedroom.

"I've been thinking of you all night, about what we did the last time," Zoe said as she unbuttoned her blouse.

Rita stared at her nice, firm breasts and pert, brown nipples. She smiled.

"Me too. That was very nice," Rita said as she helped Zoe out of her jeans.

Her eyes went straight to the soft, brown triangle between Zoe's thighs. That's when Zoe realized Rita had no panties on. Rita pulled off her T-shirt.

Naked, they fell into each other's arms and kissed passionately as they virtually melted into the bed. Hesitant at first, Zoe cast away all doubts and threw herself into the affair with wild abandon. It soon became a wonderful, wild ride. Lips met lips, then graced necks, chests, nipples and navels. As their tongues played across their bodies, excited fingers explored their moist, warm folds and danced deliciously within eager slits.

Zoe let Rita do as she pleased with her at first, then followed her lead until both women were burning with lust.

Incredible lust.

Neither woman could recall being so horny before. They were both very wet and their sexual perfume hung heavy in the humid afternoon air of the bedroom.

Zoe's cunt enchanted Rita. Her labia were like tender flower petals. Soft and pliant, they quivered noticeably when Rita caressed them. Her slit was long, moist and deep pink in color. It glimmered in the sunlight and her wonderfully swollen clit peeked at her invitingly from beneath its fleshy cover. This marvelous cunt was covered with a rich, brown carpet of silken pubic hair.

"You're so beautiful," Rita said.

Zoe shivered. and gave herself willingly to Rita. She simply closed her eyes and allowed her more experienced lover to take her wherever she wanted.

Rita inserted two fingers into Zoe's cunt and moved them in and out. Zoe groaned with passion as Rita kissed her navel and licked her way slowly downward.

"Do it, Rita! Eat me!" Zoe whispered.

When Rita's soft, warm tongue touched her swollen clit, Zoe nearly jumped off the bed. She grabbed Rita's head and opened her legs wide as that wonderful, knowing tongue played and danced between her thighs.

"Aiee! Aiee—yes!" Zoe yelled.

No one had ever eaten her like this.

Rita used her fingers to pull Zoe's labia open so she could suck on her clit. This caused Zoe to cry out with pleasure. She felt her orgasm mounting from deep within her cunt and clawed at the mattress.

Rita understood what was happening. She responded by dipping her tongue deep into Zoe's cunt. Then she slowly moved one of her fingers into her and teased her g-spot.

That did it.

Zoe came like she'd never come before.

It was an explosive, deep-from-inside come that rocked her sweat-covered body from head to toe. Zoe grabbed Rita hair and pulled her face hard against her vulva. She humped Rita's face wildly now as orgasm after orgasm surged through her body. At the same time, Rita slid another finger deep inside Zoe's cunt and massaged her g-spot even harder.

This increased the intensity of Zoe's orgasm and she shook all over as the stars exploded in front of her eyes. She let go of Rita's hair and fell, arms akimbo, back onto the bed. Rita moved upward so her cunt was merely inches from Zoe's lips. The delightful aroma of Rita's open pussy enticed Zoe. She reached up, gripped Rita's behind and pulled her down onto her tongue.

Then Zoe ate her.

Rita tasted sweet.

Inviting.

Intoxicating.

Zoe felt wicked. She was eating her best friend's pussy—and she loved it. She loved the smell, the feel and especially the flavor. She explored Rita from cunt to asshole several times, then settled down and concentrated on her pretty little clit. She was so enraptured by what she was doing that she barely noticed that Rita was eating her again.

Rita came.

She actually made Rita come.

Zoe felt her bittersweet juices jet into her mouth and hungrily lapped them up. The taste was sensationally erotic. It blew Zoe's mind so much, she came again and they both held on to ride the waves that surged through them.

"Th-that was unbelievable!" Zoe gasped. "My head is spinning like crazy!"

"Mine, too. You are a good lover, Zoe. You eat me almost as good as Art does," Rita replied as she came down from the clouds.

Zoe smiled at her lovely sex partner, then reached out and ran her fingers over her soft, black pubic hair. It felt so natural to be with Rita like this. Zoe told her this, too.

Rita smiled.

"If you want me, Zoe, you can have me anytime you like," she said. "I am all yours."

She was feeling Zoe's pussy now. As she inserted two fingers into it, Zoe moaned.

She was surprised how easily she gave herself to Rita. She never had any real lesbian inclinations before, even though she often fantasized trying it just once to see what it was like.

As she lay naked on the bed, she looked down at the pretty Filipina lovingly licking her pussy and smiled. It seemed and felt so natural now.

And so very, very good.

She closed her eyes and enjoyed the ride. Soon, she would sink her tongue into Rita's delicious cunt. She sighed as Rita nibbled her clit.

God, she was good at this.

"The best," Zoe thought.

A sudden surge of pleasure roared through her. She arched her back to take Rita's tongue deeper into her cunt, then came seconds later. As she did, she humped Rita's tongue and cried out in Spanish.

Sex with Rita was intense.

Very intense.

Zoe groaned and fell back to the mattress. Rita stopped licking and sat back to watch Zoe's petal-like labia throb visibly as her orgasm subsided.

"You're very beautiful, Zoe," she said.

"You are, too. Let's fuck," Zoe replied.

Wordlessly, Rita got on top of her and began rubbing her pussy against Zoe's nice and easy. Zoe's eyes went wide. Rita was actually fucking her! It was the most incredible thing she'd ever felt. She moaned softly and dug her fingers into the bed as her body took control and loved her back.

"Yes!" Rita gasped. "Yes! YES!!!"

Zoe didn't hear her cry out. She was completely lost in the sex they were having. All she cared about was the way her cunt felt as it ground into Rita's and the fact that she was coming...and coming...and coming...

She couldn't recall ever coming so much, so many times. Sweat covered her—and Rita—from head to foot as they continued to make love all through the warm afternoon. The bedroom was filled with their sexual aromas now. The scent only served to heighten their lovemaking.

They soon switched positions. Now, Zoe was on top and the two women fucked away in the scissors position until their bodies literally ached. They were tired, sweaty and almost unconscious by the time they'd each come for the last time that afternoon.

As Zoe lay next to Rita, she smiled. She felt good all over now. Rita looked content, too.

"Fuck me again," she whispered.

She never imagined that she'd say that to a *woman*.

Rita lay on her back with her legs apart moaning with pleasure as Zoe fucked her with a long, latex prick that protruded from her own soft, brown pussy. Rita's legs were wrapped around Zoe's hips and the two women were matching each other thrust for thrust.

"I love you, Zoe! I love you! Fuck me, darling! Fuck me harder!" Rita ranted as she neared her orgasm.

Zoe's eyes were half shut as she happily pounded away at Rita's delicious cunt. The boys could clearly see the dildo moving in and out their cunts now and the room was now filled with the scent of sex and the slurping sounds of the prick moving in and out of their cunts. Soon both women started moving erratically. Rita begged Zoe to fuck her faster and faster as she dug her fingers into her ass and drove her hips upward.

Then they came. It was a long, powerful and simultaneous explosion that caused them both to shiver uncontrollably for several moments. When the orgasms subsided. Zoe eased out of Rita's cunt and lay next to her, panting hard.

"Wow! You're the best lover I ever had," she said after a few moments. "Everything we do feels so magical. I could make love to you forever!"

Rita smiled and parted her legs again.

"It's only two o'clock!" she said.

This time, Zoe tossed the dildo aside and pressed her cunt against Rita's for another long, easy, slow fuck...

Three days later, Rita and Zoe went to the casino. Zoe smiled at her and headed for her favorite machine. Rita saw Bart and waved to him. Bart smiled and walked over. He gave her a warm hug. She hugged him back and smiled.

"Let's find a machine in a nice, dark corner tonight," he whispered.

She nodded and took his hand. He led her to the far back of the casino floor to where the older penny slots still were. Hardly anyone ever played these machines now. They found one in a dimly-lit area and sat down.

Bart signaled to a hostess.

Seconds later, she hustled over with their drinks.

As she sipped her drink, she turned toward Bart and parted her knees wide. He smiled and slid his hand along her thigh to her panties. As Bart played with her pussy, she watched the bulge rise in his pants and ran her fingers over it.

Bart gently played with her swollen clit. Rita slid forward and opened her legs wider. Bart moved his chair closer and looked into her eyes. That's when they kissed. It was a surprisingly warm, passionate kiss.

A lover's kiss.

Rita reached over and unzipped his pants. She then reached inside, grabbed his already hard dick, and pulled it into the open. He smiled as she ran her fingers all over it for a few seconds as it grew even longer and harder.

He pushed her panties aside and played with her labia. Her skirt was almost at her hips and he was able to see the tiny red bikini panties she was wearing

She wrapped her fingers around his prick and rolled his foreskin back to expose the entire knob. When she did, a few drops of pre-cum oozed from the tip. As wonderful as it felt to have her touch him like this, what happened next was even more so. Rita ran her fingers through his pre-cum and rubbed it all over his knob to make it gleam. Then she used her thumb to massage it into it his head nice and slow.

Bart moaned.

The sensations racing through his knob and prick were intense. She massaged him harder. He gasped as he watched her thumb work its magic.

"You're beautiful," Bart said as she gave him a few east pumps. Watching his foreskin roll back and forth over his dark red knob made her even hornier. God, how she wanted to fuck him!

Bart sat there and shivered with each pump of her hand, turned on beyond belief by the fact this she was jerking him off.

At the same time, he was fingering her cunt faster and faster. Rita's heart raced in her breast as she continued to beat him off. Her thighs were wide open now as she invited him inside. Bart probed her deep and rubbed her g-spot. Rita quivered and pumped his prick a little faster. By now, the pre-cum was oozing down his knob. Rita stopped pumping him and ran her fingers through it. Bart trembled slightly as she rubbed it all over his knob. The more she did this, the more pre-cum he produced.

"This is unreal," she thought. "I'm sitting here playing with his prick and letting him play with my pussy. And I don't want to stop."

She pumped him faster and faster. At the same time, Bart moved his fingers in and out her cunt as fast as he could. Rita shivered uncontrollably. His touches were thrilling her now. She squeezed his prick a little harder as she pumped away. Both his prick and her fingers were sticky with pre-cum now and her heart was racing a mile a second. Bart massaged her clit a little faster then slid it into her deep. She almost squealed when he found her g-spot and quivered all over as he massaged it.

He then withdrew and went back to playing with her clit. Rita moaned and shuddered.

She was almost there now and she jerked him off faster and faster. Bart knew she was on the edge so he slid his fingers into her cunt as deep as he could and wriggled them around. Rita shook all over and came.

It was a nice, hard come, too.

"Oooh, yes! That's nice!" she gasped as she shook all over.

As she came, she beat his prick faster and faster. Bart kept fingering her cunt. Rita came again.

So did Bart.

To keep him from spurting his cum all over the place, she quickly placed the palm of her free hand over his knob while she tightened her grip and pumped his slower. He tried not to moan as he came. His first shot hit the palm of her hand and oozed back down his shaft. The second shot did the same.

Bart came a lot, too. It kept splattering against her palm and running back down over his prick. She smiled as she continued to play with her g-spot as more intense sensations raced through her body.

She looked around.

The immediate area was deserted. She kept pumping away until both of her hands and Bart's prick were slick and sticky with cum. To her astonishment, he was still hard and she was still coming and coming.

She leaned closer and swirled her tongue over his knob then slid his entire dick into her mouth. Bart watched her head move back and forth as she sucked his dick. Then he shut his eyes and sighed as he fired one last, good wad of cum down her throat.

"You're the best," Bart grunted as she kept sucking.

She stopped after he finally went limp and wiped her lips with the back of her hand. She looked at him and smiled. Her pussy still throbbed and she felt sexually drained. This was the second time she'd sucked Bart's dick and she knew this wouldn't be the last.

He caught his breath and ordered them more mai tais.

As Rita sipped, they maintained eye contact. For a long while, they were silent. Then Bart smiled.

"I love you, Rita," he said.

His words surprised and flattered her.

"You really mean that, don't you?" she asked.

"Yes. I do mean it. I've never even said that to a women before. You know how I've always been. I can hardly believe I even said it, but I did and I mean it," he said. "I don't want to have sex with you, Rita. I want to make love with you."

She smiled.

They kissed again. This time, it was even more passionate. She expected him to ask her to fuck like he usually did. But he just held her and continued to kiss her. When they stopped a minute later, she looked down at his half-hard prick and played with his knob and foreskin until he was good and hard again. She leaned back and smiled as he slid her panties off. When she felt his soft, warm tongue enter her pussy, she almost screamed.

Bart ate her and ate her until she came again. While she was still in the throes of one terrific orgasm, he stood and slid his prick into her throbbing cunt. She gripped his arms and moaned softly as he fucked her. Since he'd already come a lot, she knew this would last very long. Bart moved in out of her slowly. She quivered and quivered with each deep, easy thrust. What they were doing no was far beyond just fucking. They were making love in every sense of the term. She moved with him as they kissed. Bart seemed to get even harder now and he moved faster and faster. She matched him and dug her fingers into his arms.

His dick felt awesome.

So damned perfect.

Each time they'd made love, it felt better. More exciting. More erotic.

More real.

They fucked and fucked and fucked. She felt him move faster and erratically and fucked him back just as hard. When she came, she saw stars and nearly screamed. She felt his come jet into her and fucked him even faster.

"All of it," she gasped. "Gimme all of it! Fill my pussy!"

Bart came and came.

His dick made squishing sounds as they kept fucking and he added more and more cum to the pool that was already inside her.

"I love you, Bart! I love you!" she said as she stuck her tongue into his mouth.

When they finally stopped, they held each other tight for a little while. Bart was too overwhelmed to even talk. He just stroked her hair while his dick stayed inside Rita's cunt and she used her inner muscles to tease him and to let him know that she was all his.

They kissed and straightened up.

Rita looked around for Zoe. When she didn't see her, she walked hand-in-hand with Bart back to the steak house where he bought her a nice dinner.

"I would love to make this a permanent arrangement," Bart said. "I'm head over heels in love with you, Rita. If you weren't already married, I'd beg you to be my wife and I never imagined that I'd ever say anything like this to any woman."

"And I never thought I'd tell any other man but my husband that I love him. But I do love you, Bart. I really do and I'm yours whenever you want me. But I'm not ready for any sort of exclusive kind of affair," she said.

"I am, Rita. I can't even think of other women anymore. You've turned me inside-out and I love it. I don't want to destroy your marriage, but if you ever decide to leave your husband, I'm more than willing to take his place," Bart said.

After dinner, they returned to Rita's favorite machine. Just as they sat down, Rita's cell phone went off. It was Zoe.

"Are you and Bart done yet?" she asked.

"For tonight. Where are you?" Rita asked.

"I'm at your house. I'm on your bed with my legs open and Art is eating my pussy. We've been making love all night," Zoe said. "Pick me up in about an hour. Is that okay?"

Rita laughed. She looked at Bart.

"I've been married over 20 years and my husband is the most wonderful man on Earth. I have never had any sort of sexual contact with anyone but him and I never once imagined that I'd do anything like this," she said.

"But you do things to me, Bart. Wonderful things. That's why I'm thinking about fucking the daylights out of you every chance we get."

She got up to leave. He escorted her back to her car. Just before she got in, they kissed again. He stood and watched as she drove away and had to restrain himself from doing a backflip.

When Rita got home, she found Art seated on the sofa. She smiled and sat down next to him. He put his arm around her and pulled her close.

"Judy called a few minutes ago," he said.

"Oh," Rita said flatly. "Did she send you another video?"

"No. She doesn't need to now. What's next?" he asked.

"I don't know. What do you think I should do?" she asked.

He laughed.

"I can't advise you that, Rita. If you're looking for my approval, I'd say that's pretty much been given. It's not like I can stop you. Sooner or later, you're going to cheat. If you don't do it with Bart, then you'll probably do it with someone else. You've got that itch and you need to scratch it. Just keep in mind that while you're out doing that, I'll be fucking Zoe."

She laughed.

"I know. She said she was going to steal you away from me," she said.

"There's no chance of that," he assured her.

Chapter Eleven

The next day, Rita met Rocky at the YMCA and they started their workout. As usual, they began with the stationary bikes. Rita smiled because she knew Rocky was eyeing her ass and getting an erection. That why she put on her smallest running shorts and bikini panties. She wanted to see what he'd do if he saw a lot more of her.

After 30 minutes, they headed for the Stair Masters.

Again Rocky kept his eyes on her legs and ass the entire time. When she stopped, she saw a huge and obvious bulge in his shorts. She looked at him and smiled.

Her smile almost made his knees buckle.

"Is that for me?" she joked.

He looked down and blushed.

"Oh this," he said shyly. "I can't help it, Rita. I get hard the minute I see you. You have the most beautiful body I ever saw and when I see your legs and behind, I automatically get hard."

She smiled at him.

"There's no need to apologize or feel ashamed, Rocky. It's kind of flattering, really," she said. "So you really get this excited around me?"

"Yes. Hell, Rita. I get hard just from thinking about you," he replied.

"Even though you know how old I am?" she asked as she kept looking at his bulge.

"Sure. You are the sexiest woman I ever met. I don't care how old you are. That doesn't matter. I'm still crazy about you," he blurted.

"You're really sweet, Rocky. Handsome, too. To be honest, if I wasn't married, I'd really consider having you as a boyfriend," she said.

"That's good to hear, Rita," he smiled.

"Now, let's finish our workout. Okay?" she said as they headed to the weight room.

Rocky showed her how to use light weights properly and watched as she did the reps. As she worked out, he gave her some pointers and advised her not to go too hard the first few times out.

"You have to ease into weight training so you don't hurt yourself," he said as he helped off the bench.

She watched as he worked out. She decided he had a great build and his muscles were hard—especially the one between his legs. As he worked pout, he kept looking at her legs and wondering what she had between them.

They kept at for another half hour, then Rita said she'd had enough. Rocky bought her another protein drink and they sat at a table to talk while they drank. She liked his sense of humor and the fact that he wasn't egotistical. He reminded her of Art in many ways. He also liked to work out and he rarely let his ego show.

Maybe that's why she felt attracted to Rocky.

"Do you have a girlfriend?" she asked.

"I did but she left me a few weeks ago. She said that I'm not ambitious enough for her because I have this disregard for money. I've never been money driven. I make enough to live comfortably and I don't see a need to try to make more," he said.

"My husband says the same thing," she said. "You two have a lot in common. I think you'd like each other."

"Maybe I could meet him some time? I'm not sure how he'd feel about us working out, though," Rocky smiled.

"I've already told him about that. He said it was smarter to do it that way and you might teach me a few things," she said.

"Have I?" he asked.

"Oh yes. I've learned a lot today. Thanks," she said.

"I just love your smile," he said.

"Thanks," she said as she almost blushed.

"Would you like to join me for lunch? There's a nice place a few streets from here," he offered.

"Well, okay. I am kind of hungry right now. Do I need to change?" she asked.

"It's real casual. I go there after a workout once in a while and I don't bother to change," he said.

"Okay. What's it called?" she asked.

"La Capella," he said. "It's kind of Italian fusion place."

"Let's go. I'll follow you over there," she said.

When they got up, she noticed he was still hard and smiled. He blushed a deep red and it made her laugh. As they walked out, she "accidentally" backed into him and rubbed her ass against his erection.

"Uh, sorry," he apologized.

"I'm not," she smiled.

When they arrived, the only table available was a small one near the back of the restaurant. They sat down and decided to order the antipasto platter. Rocky ordered two glasses of red wine to go with it. They sat and joked with each other for at least two hours.

"The more I get to know you, the crazier I become about you," he said. "I've never met anyone as beautiful and as nice as you. I really wish you weren't married so we could date."

"You're really nice, too, Rocky. I like you a lot," she said as she sipped her wine.

She half expected him to try something but he remained polite the entire time. The fact that he didn't try anything with her made him even more appealing. Considering how he felt toward her, she admired his restraint.

"I'd better get home now," she said. "How much do I owe you?"

"Nothing. This is my treat," he said as he handed the waiter his credit card. "And it really was a treat, too. This is the most fun I've had in a while. You're a real pleasure to be with."

She smiled.

He looked at her and almost felt his knees buckle.

"I'll pay next time," she offered.

"No you won't," he smiled. "When I invite a lady to lunch, I pay. That's what a real man is supposed to do."

"You're a rare kind of person, Rocky. You're special. Don't ever change," she said as they stood to go.

"I won't," he replied as he walked her to her car. "If we were on a date right now, I might try to kiss you."

"And I might just let you," she said. "I'll see you next week."

"You can count on that, Rita. Bye!" he said as she drove off. "Just my luck. I finally found the perfect woman and she's married. That makes her off limits—for now."

When Rita got home, she showered and laughed to herself. Rocky had admitted that she gave him erections and that he'd love to have sex with her. But he also said that he was far too chicken and awed by her to push the matter. In fact, he said he'd gladly settle for being her workout buddy if she didn't mind him looking at her.

Of course she didn't.

She liked him, too.

He was nice and polite and kind of shy.

He was the opposite of Bart who was overly confident and persistent and had finally broken through her defenses--big time! She was also madly in love with Zoë which had added an extra, unexpected dash of sexual spice to her life.

Art was in a quandary now.

While he wasn't nuts about Rita fucking other men, he also realized that there was nothing he could actually do to stop her. He loved her and didn't want a divorce, so he told her to keep it all in the open and that way he'd be able to tolerate it.

Rita's wanderings opened the door for Zoe to go after Art with everything she had—which was plenty. Art found her exotic, cute and oh-so sexy and she was unbeatable in bed. When he was with Zoe, he barely thought about Rita at all. Plus, Zoe had openly announced that she planned to steal him from Rita no matter how long that took.

And she was coming very close to doing just that.

This was now an exciting, sex-charged and weird ride and Art was determined to hand on to the end. He was also aware that both Zoe and Rita were fucking other men, but Zoe vowed to stop having sex with anyone but him—and Rita, of course.

That was yet another strange twist in the crazy road they were now traveling down.

While Art was at work the next day, Zoe decided to drop in on Rita. Twenty minutes later, Zoe was seated on a loveseat with her long lovely legs draped over each arm. Rita knelt between them. Her tongue gently darting in and out of Zoe's petal-like cunt. They had retreated to Zoe's house after breakfast. Without saying a word, Zoe had removed her shorts and positioned herself on the chair. The sight proved to be inspiring for Rita.

Even irresistible.

Rita kept licking away at Zoe's pussy eagerly. She loved its sweet, sweet taste and the softness of her womanly perfume. As Rita ate her, she fingered her own sopping cunt. She was very horny now. Spending time with Zoe always did that to her, always made her hungry for her pussy.

Zoe knew this and was only too happy to give herself to Rita any time she wanted her. She sat on the loveseat with her long lovely legs draped over each arm. Rita knelt between them. Her tongue gently darted in and out of Zoe's petal-like cunt.

"Oh yes, darling. Yes! Make love to me!" Zoe moaned as she came hard.

Rita sat back and wiped the love juices from her face and chin as she watched Joy come. It always took a long time for Zoe to recover from an orgasm and Rita loved to watch the lips of her pussy twitch as she calmed down.

Zoe watched as Rita stood up, her eyes on that shiny black triangle between her legs. Rita held out her hands. Zoe clasped them and sighed as Rita pulled her to her feet, then exchanged places with her.

As she beheld Rita's cunt, she started coming again. She came harder when she leaned over and slipped her tongue between Rita's soft pussy lips and tasted her sweetness.

Rita was so horny that she came almost instantly. She pulled Zoe's face into her cunt and wildly fucked her tongue as she erupted in a series of good, deep orgasms. When she managed to come back to Earth, she saw Zoe standing before her with one end of the double-headed dildo protruding from her cunt. She smiled and opened her legs as wide as she could.

Zoe eased the dildo into her and fucked her with a nice, easy rhythm. Rita sighed and moaned as she matched her every thrust. Zoe was a sweet, gentle lover and she concentrated on satisfying Rita. After about 20 good thrusts, Zoe turned on the vibrating unit. The sudden change caused Rita to convulse and come.

Very hard.

As she did, she fucked her back as fast and as hard as she could. A few seconds later, Zoe also climaxed and her movements and thrusts became wild and erratic. They kept this going until both had come a second time. Now totally spent, Zoe turned off the vibrator and pulled the dildo from her sopping cunt. Rita picked it up and licked her juices from it while Zoe watched and smiled.

"I love you, Rita. If you were a man, I'd marry you," she said. "Sex with you is very exciting."

"That's because I have such a beautiful partner," Rita smiled as she stroked Zoe's thigh.

Zoe sighed as Rita gently played with her bush. As far as she was concerned, Rita could touch her anywhere she liked and as often as she wanted.

"Which do you like more? Having sex with me or having sex with a man?" Rita asked.

"When I'm with you, I enjoy having sex with you. When I'm with a man, I enjoy having sex with him. It all depends on who I'm with at the time," Zoe replied. "How about you?"

"I feel the same," Rita said as she gently massaged Zoe's clit.

"I like the way you touch me, but I'm so worn out, I don't think I can handle any more today," Zoe said softly.

"I just like the way your pussy feels and looks—and tastes. You're so sexy that I can't keep from touching you," Rita said as she leaned over and slid her tongue along Zoe's slit.

Zoe gasped and opened her legs as wide as she could.

"Well—once more couldn't hurt!" she thought as she felt Rita tongue enter her.

They went out to lunch and spent two hours chatting about their situations. During the course of their break, Zoe managed to get her hand between Rita's thighs again. Rita smiled and licked her lips slowly to show she was ready again.

They hurried back home and dashed up to the bedroom where they spent a few minutes kissing deeply and undressing each other. Zoe laid back with her legs wide apart. Rita climbed on top of her and began running her pussy against Zoe's nice and easy. Zoe moaned and gripped her arms as she moved with Rita. This was a nice, gentle and very slow fuck. They slowly moved faster and faster as the sensations grew more and more intense.

"Fuck me, Rita! Fuck me! I love you! Oh, God! How I love you!" Zoe moaned as she came minutes later.

Rita came a few moments later and screamed as her orgasm tore through her quivering body. She fell on top of Zoe and buried her tongue in her mouth as her cum flooded into Zoe's cunt...

When Friday rolled around, she put on her skimpiest running shorts and headed for the YMCA. This time, she decided to omit her panties to see what Rocky might do when he got a glimpse of her cunt which she knew would happen several times during the course of their workout.

In fact, she made sure of that.

Each time she mounted or dismounted one of the devices, she moved in such a way that her shorts would "accidentally" reveal her cunt. In no time at all, Rocky had a huge hard-on and he had a lot of trouble concentrating on their workout.

She even backed into him a couple of times and wiggled her ass against his prick. The second time she did it, he actually moaned.

After the workout, he walked her out to her car. She opened the door to the back seat and slid inside. Once she was in, she parted her knees and pulled aside her shorts.

Rocky got in next to her and they kissed. The sensations were off the charts for Rita. She reached into his shorts and pulled out his massive prick.

He was horny that he came the second she touched him. The spurt sailed at least two feet straight up and landed on his dashboard. She giggled and began to jerk him off nice and easy. Each pump of her fist made him spurt. Some landed on her thighs and t-shirt.

Rocky moaned and gasped as she played with his dick. He was so amazed this was happening that he stayed rock hard. He reached over and slid his hand along her thigh. She parted her legs and smiled as his fingers danced over her cunt. When he slid two of them inside her, she quivered all over. The entire time, she kept pumping his dick and staring at the large, dark pink knob.

It was huge, too.

At least 10 inches long and good and thick. As she continued to jerk him off, she wondered what it would feel like to fuck him or if her pussy could handle something that size. By now, her fingers and his dick were sticky with cum and even more still oozed from his knob. She never thought anyone could come so much.

She smiled at him, then leaned over and licked his knob.

Rocky moaned. He moaned even louder when she slid half his dick into her mouth and sucked it. As she sucked, she bobbed her head up and down. Rocky gasped, gripped her shoulders and came again. This time it was in Rita's mouth and he was amazed that she actually swallowed it all.

When she stopped and sat back, he kissed her. She put her arms around his shoulders and kissed him back with as much passion as she could. His fingers were still moving in and out of her cunt and she came seconds later. As she did, she cried out and bounced around on the car seat. She laid back to catch her breath.

Rocky beamed at her. He reached over and slowly eased her shorts down. Rita raised her hips to enable him to pee them all the way off. When he finished, he stopped to stare at what he said was the most beautiful cunt he'd ever seen. Rita's labia were partially open and her clit was still swollen. The sight caused Rocky's dick to harden again.

Rita watched as it grew longer and harder. When he was fully erect once again she parted her legs as much as she could. Rocky moved between them and slid the head of his dick up and down her labia a few times.

"Fuck me!" she said.

He moved into position and eased his dick into her cunt slowly so he could savor the way it felt as it wrapped its walls around him. When he was all the way in, she squeezed his prick with her inner muscles to see his reaction. He moaned and started fucking her. His thrusts were deep, strong and incredibly gentle.

"That feels nice," she said. "So very nice."

"So do you," he said.

After a few thrusts, she began to move with him. It was a nice, slow and easy fuck that made her feel good all over. After a while, she realized that Ricky wasn't just fucking her. He was making love to her and she was making love to him in return.

"That's so nice. So nice. I love it! I love it!" she sighed.

"You're perfect, Rita! Perfect!" he said as he fucked a little faster.

Nothing had ever filled her cunt so completely or massaged he so deeply. Wave after wave of deep pleasure wafted through her body as she came. Rocky kept fucking her a little faster. She came again and again as she fucked him back.

They kept at it for a long, long time. She couldn't believe that any man could last so long or stay so hard. IT was easy for Rocky. He had his dick in the pussy of whom he considered to be the most sexy and beautiful women on Earth. Just the thought of fucking her kept him hard and he determined to take full advantage of this moment.

Rita lost track of her orgasms. She just kept fucking him back and coming and coming.

"That's it, Rocky! Make love to me! My pussy's yours now. All yours," she moaned as another strong orgasms tore through her.

That's when she heard him moan deeply. She felt him shake all over and his thrusts grew erratic. She felt his cum flood into her and threw her body up to take every inch of his prick inside of her cunt.

"Oooh yes! That's it! Fill my pussy! Come in my pussy!" she moaned.

Rocky stopped thrusting after a few seconds and sat up. He took several deep breaths and smiled at her. She laid there with her legs apart and his cum oozing from her labia.

"That was wonderful," she said. "Now this is what I call a workout!"

They laughed.

She picked up her shorts and slid them on. Rocky watched her every move. She smiled at him and ran her fingertips along his shaft. Even flaccid, it was the biggest dick she'd ever seen.

"Can we do this again soon?" he asked.

"We can do this any time you like, Rocky," she assured him.

"I'm still in the clouds, Rita. I always hoped we'd do this but I never really expected to do. You're the most beautiful and sexiest woman on Earth and, if you don't mind my saying so, you're the best damned lover I ever had," he said.

They kissed again.

"And you're the best I've ever had," she said. "You said you live alone?"

"Yes, I do," he said.

"Then instead of meeting at the YMCA next time, let's meet for lunch instead then go to your place for the rest of the day and fuck," she suggested.

"You have yourself a date!" he replied.

When Art got home, Rita had dinner ready. He kissed her and sat down while she served the meal. She sat across from him and smiled.

She looked at him.

"I fucked Rocky today," she said.

He put down his fork and stared at her. She almost looked ashamed.

"You mean the guy you work out with at the YMCA?" he asked.

"That's him," she said.

"He's less than half your age," he said with a grin.

"Uh-huh. We've been flirting with each other ever since we met. So today, I decided to have sex with him. It was great, too. He has a real big dick and he lasted a long time and made me come a lot," she said.

"I expected that. Are you gonna fuck him again?" he asked.

"I'm going to meet him for lunch next Monday then go to his place for the rest of the day. He scares me a little because he said he's crazy about me. He might want to make this a regular affair," she said.

"Kind of like what Zoe wants with me," he said.

"Are you gonna do it?" she asked.

"I'll make a deal with you, Rita. I won't have an affair with Zoe unless you decide you want to have one with Bart," he said. "Or anyone else."

She laughed.

"Okay. That's fair," she said.

The next afternoon, Zoe arrived at Art's house. Art opened the door and smiled as he let her in.

"Rita told me that she's going to spend the entire night with Rocky, so I thought you'd like some company," she said as she stuck her tongue in his mouth.

They held each other close as they kissed. She felt his dick harden and ran her fingers over the bulge. Now that Rita was openly fucking other men, they had the green light to have sex as often as they wanted. There was no holding back now.

She looked into his eyes.

"I'm going to do everything I can to steal you away from Rita," she said.

"I don't know if you can, but I'm willing to let you try," he replied as they walked upstairs. "You are off to a terrific start."

She giggled.

"Let's try for spectacular today," she said.

Rock called Rita and said he wouldn't be able to meet her for lunch but he gave the address to his apartment.

"Give me an hour to get things ready then come on over," he said. "We can go out for dinner later and breakfast tomorrow if you like."

"I like," she said.

Rita walked up the stairs to the second floor and stopped in front of apartment number eight. She took a deep breath and knocked. Rocky opened the door and smiled as she walked in. He'd lit some incense and had spent the entire night cleaning up so she'd feel more comfortable. He even had a bottle of champagne on ice on the kitchen counter.

She smiled.

"Champagne?" she asked.

"I thought that since this was a special occasion, we'd celebrate," he said. "You want some now or afterward?"

"How about during?" she suggested. "I'm yours for the entire night, Rocky. We can do whatever you like and as many times as you like."

Rocky uncorked the bottle and filled two glasses. They smiled as they clinked them together and sipped. She followed him into the bedroom where they kissed several times as they slowly undressed each other.

She smiled at his erection. He was much longer and thicker than she thought. She grabbed it and led him to the bed and pushed him onto his back. She straddled his face and shivered as he ate her, then she leaned over and sucked his dick. Tonight, she was going to forget she was married and just concentrate on having sex with Rocky.

Lots of sex.

After a few moments of this, Rita twisted her body so that she now sat on Rocky's thighs. She moved her body upward as she grabbed his prick and guided it into her open cunt. Once there, she slowly lowered herself down until his entire length was buried deep of inside her. She stopped to savor the feel of it for a little while, the way it filled her so completely. It felt good, too. Maybe too good.

Wickedly good.

She wiggled her hips a little bit, and then bounced up and down nice and easy. She wanted this to be a nice, slow, deep fuck. One she could control. That's why she got on top. Rocky didn't care about control. All he cared about at that moment was the warm, tight, silky cunt that was wrapped around his erect prick and the pretty woman it was attached to.

As Rita rode him easy, he reached up and played with her nipples. This sent waves of pleasure racing through Rita's body and caused her to ride him a little faster. Rocky moaned and grabbed her behind. Then he thrust upward into her cunt as hard as he could. Rita quivered as his knob slammed into her womb and sent delicious sensations running all through her body...

"Yes!" she cried. "Fuck me, Rocky! Harder!"

They moved faster and faster now, each matching the other's thrusts perfectly.

In and out.

Up and down.

Repeatedly until both were perspiring. Rita's head was back and she began making soft gurgling sounds as she rode his prick as fast as she could. Rocky laid there and took it as she gave him one of the best fucks of his entire life.

"I'm coming!" Rocky gasped after a while.

"Good," said Rita.

She rode him harder now, took his prick into her pussy deeper and deeper. His own thrusts grew erratic as he tried to hold back his orgasm.

It was to no avail.

Rita felt his cum spurting into her and sighed. She kept pumping and pumping as more and more of his seed emptied into her cunt. Rocky grunted and fucked her harder as he continued coming. Rita matched him with equal vigor and a wild abandon that took his breath away.

"Yes! Oh God, yes!" she moaned.

There was no guilt this time. No second thoughts. Just raw, uncontrolled sex. When Rita came, she saw fireworks exploding all around her. She fell atop Rocky's chest and lay still with his half erect member inside her cum-flooded channel. There was no sense moving. She knew that he'd be hard again real soon and she wanted to make sure she was still on top of the situation when he did. Five minutes later, she felt him getting hard inside her cunt and another wild ride ensued. This one lasted for several long, wonderful minutes. When Rocky came again, his entire body shuddered as if every bit of energy he had left was being sucked right out of him and up into Rita's cunt. He seized her behind and rammed his prick into her as deep as he could, then unleashed a torrent of sticky cum which ran out of her cunt and down his prick to his balls.

Rita came at the same instant. She threw her head back and emitted a long, satisfied moan as she stopped in mid stroke to savor the sexual gusher that now overwhelmed her so completely. As the room spun around her, she tumbled off his prick and lay next to Rocky gasping for air.

Rocky propped himself up on his elbows and stared at his prick. It was still half-erect and glistened with both his cum and Rita's juices. He looked at Rita and smiled. She was on her back with her legs parted. He could see a stream of cum oozing from between her partially open labia and that her cunt hairs were sticky.

He nodded off to sleep for a few minutes only to be awakened by the feel of Rita's fingers on his prick as she jerked him off. When he was once again at full salute, Rita lay on her back. She bent her knees and threw her thighs open as she guided his prick into her pussy with one smooth motion.

He fucked her for several minutes, using hard, deep strokes. They fucked for such a long time that their sides ached and sweat covered them from head to foot. They were nearing exhaustion now, but were far too horny to stop. Rocky grabbed her ankles and pushed her legs backward until her thighs touched her breasts. This enabled him to fuck her even deeper. So deep, he swore that he was ramming his prick right into her womb a few times. Rita dug her fingers into his arms and cried out with pleasure. She'd been fucked like this before by Art, but Rocky's longer and thicker prick was reaching places inside her pussy that no other prick ever had before. It was the deepest, hardest and most total fuck she ever had.

"Oooh yes! That's good! That's what I want! Fuck me!" she moaned.

Rocky leaned forward and began fucking her faster. The sudden extra friction triggered something deep inside Rita's cunt. She exploded quickly and fell back with her arms akimbo, sobbing with pleasure.

"Yes! Oh YES! Fuck me, Rocky! Fuck me!" she moaned as she came and came and came.

Rocky quickly followed suit and emptied every last drop of cum his balls could produce deep into her quivering body. When his prick finally went limp, he slid off her and lay panting beside her on the bed.

"That was *unbelievable!*" Rita sighed.

"I could get used to this," Rocky said.

"So could I. Maybe too used to it," Rita agreed.

A few minutes later, Rita lay on her back and sighed as Rocky explored the folds of her cunt with his tongue. Each pass of his tongue across her swollen clit made her quiver and moan. When he knew she was close to coming, he licked her clit faster and faster. Rita gasped and raised her hips off the bed. Then she grabbed his head and fucked his tongue as she came and came.

Rocky got between her thighs. She bent her knees and smiled, then trembled as he slid his prick deep into her cunt. She closed her eyes and relaxed as he began fucking her nice and easy. It felt nice, she decided.

Very nice.

After a few good thrusts, she wrapped her legs around him and began to fuck him back. Rocky increased the tempo. Rita moaned, dug her fingers into his shoulders and moved with him as he fucked her harder and harder. They immediately began moving together. This time, the rhythm was faster and a little bit harder.

"Oooh, yes! Yes! Fuck me, Rocky! Fuck me good!" she moaned

They fucked faster and faster. Rita gasped, arched her back and cried out as she came. It was a good, deep orgasm, too. One that shook her entire body.

"Yes! I love it! Fuck me!" she cried

He leaned into her and fucked her as fast as he could. Rita moaned and gripped his arms as she matched him stroke for stroke. Then she came again.

Rocky did, too.

He filled her cunt with every drop of cum he had. Then they kissed and caressed each other for a long time. Rocky started out with another French kiss while he stroked her cunt and she pumped his prick. He kissed his way down her chest and sucked and licked each nipple. By then, Rita's body was on fire. Rocky eased his middle finger into her slit and "fucked" her nice and fast. Since she was so close to the edge already, she arched her back, emitted a deep moan and came.

Hard.

As she came, she pumped his prick a little faster. As another wave of warm, intense pleasure rippled through her sweaty body, she let go of his prick. Rocky moved and positioned himself between her open thighs. She opened her legs as far as she could and bent her knees. Rocky slid into her all the way. Rita shivered and moaned.

Rocky then began moving in and out.

In and out.

It was a nice, easy rhythm that sent waves of pleasure through Rita's body again. After a few beats, she began to move with him.

Rocky picked up the pace.

Rita matched it with enthusiasm.

"Oooh yes! Yes! Fuck me, Rocky! Fuck me!" she cried.

Rocky slid his prick all the way in. Rita quivered and used her inner muscles to squeeze him several times. Rocky moaned. It felt exquisite. Then he began to move. Rita moaned on each thrust then began to fuck him back. They soon fell into a good, easy rhythm. Rita wrapped her knees around his hips and smiled up at him.

"That's it, Rocky! Fuck me!" she said. "That feels so nice. So nice!" she moaned. "Fuck me harder now!"

Rocky did as she asked. He thrust into her faster and faster. Rita quickly matched him thrust for thrust.

"Oooh yes! Yes! That's the way I like it! Fuck me!" she cried. "Use my pussy! Make it yours!"

They kept at it for a few more good thrusts. Then Rita came.

Hard. As she did, she fucked him faster.

"Yes! Yes! I love it! I love it!" she screamed

Rocky held off as long as he could, then rammed his prick all the way into her and erupted. He came so much and so hard that he nearly passed out. Rita kept milking his prick with her cunt muscles until she could barely move. He fell next to her and gasped for air as he came back down to Earth.

"My God! This is fantastic! I never fucked so much in my life!" he finally said. "Do you fuck Art like this?"

"Most of the time," she said with a smile. "I admit that I'm giving you a little extra. Your dick is like a brand new toy for me. I want to keep playing with it. So, you like this, huh?"

"Do I ever! Do you do this with your girlfriend?" he asked.

"We do different things than this, but our lovemaking can become very exciting and intense," she said as she stroked his prick. "Do you think you can do it again?"

"Well, maybe—if you make me hard again by sucking my dick," he suggested.

She smiled then slid his prick into her mouth...

Art and Zoe wasted little time. They sat on the bed. Art kissed her on the lips softly, then slowly undid her blouse and helped her off with it. Her nipples were still erect and he leaned over to tease them with his tongue.

"Ah, that's nice," she sighed.

Art sat up as she helped him out of his shirt, then she leaned forward and sucked each of his nipples until he felt his balls tingle. While she was doing that, she unzipped his jeans and pulled out his now fully erect prick. It felt even bigger now.

Harder, too.

She gave it a few slow pulls. Art stood up and she undressed him altogether. She then leaned forward and played with his balls, then turned her attentions to his prick.

Art sighed happily as she jerked him off.

She took her time now. There was no need to hurry.

She stuck her tongue out and ran it all over his swollen knob a few times. Art moaned and put his hand on her shoulder. She kept licking for a moment, then pushed half of his cock into her mouth.

She never really liked to suck cock. But Art's was different. She loved the way he tasted. She loved to suck it. She especially loved it when he came in her mouth and the way his cum felt as it slid down her throat.

Art really loved what she was doing, too. What man wouldn't? She wasn't just sucking his prick. She was actually making love to him with her mouth. And no one, he decided, could do that any better than her. She stopped and lay down on the bed with her legs dangling over the side. Art knelt and undid her shorts, then slowly pulled them off. Naked, she looked gorgeous. He kissed and licked his way up her inner thighs to the soft, brown patch between them. She was already quivering with anticipation. Her labia and clit were wet and swollen and her sexual perfume permeated the room.

She smiled lovingly at him.

"Eat me, darling," she whispered. "Make love to me."

Then she sighed deeply as Art's tongue entered her more-than-willing cunt. He was marvelous with his tongue. He knew when and where to lick and how to fire all of her sexual triggers.

She was so excited that she came within seconds. She threw her legs over Art's shoulders, gripped his hair and began humping his tongue with a wild abandon. She came again and again. So many times that she could barely breathe or speak.

She didn't have to. Her body did all the talking for her and it was screaming for more. Art got the signal loud and clear and kept licking her quivering, dripping snatch until his tongue began to ache.

"Enough! That's enough," Zoe gasped as she pushed his face away from her cunt. "Fuck me, Art. Please fuck me."

Her body was still trembling when Art took his place above her. He pressed his glans to her soft, moist labia then moved it up and down several times before easing into her. He went in slowly in order to get the feel of her tight, hot channel as it caressed his prick. She spread her legs as far apart as she could, then bent her knees. She gripped Art's shoulders and drove her hips upward until she felt the head of his prick touch the opening to her womb.

"Oh yes!" she sighed as Art began to move his hips in a circular motion.

At the same time, he thrust in and out of her cunt nice and slow. He felt her inner flesh hug his shaft tightly as he pulled out, then part again as he slid back in. Each time, she moved with him in perfect unison.

Art had fucked many women in his life, but no one's cunt felt as exquisitely sexy as hers. She was warm, tight and silky smooth and she could really use her inner muscles. He often felt as if her were making love with an angel. They were a perfect match.

That's why he was taking his time. This wasn't just sex. It was lovemaking at its best, with all of the emotional ties that went with the word. They made love gently, slowly and with a lot of passion. They matched each other stroke for stroke, thrust for thrust. Their lips met again. Art reached beneath her and put her right leg over his shoulder, then drove into her a little bit harder and faster. She emitted a loud moan and dug her nails into his back as his cock massaged her secret g-spot perfectly. She felt herself spinning out of control.

"Faster, Art! Do it faster," she begged. "Make me come!"

She closed her eyes and allowed the movements of Art's prick inside her cunt carry her away. She began crying out and gasping for air. She clawed at his back like a mad woman as an explosive series of orgasms raced through her body. She felt his prick jerk a few times, and then relaxed as Art emptied his seed into her sucking pussy. Like earlier, he pumped a large amount of cum into her love tunnel. Her body, which seemed to be suspended in time, eagerly accepted his seed, greedily making it one with her.

She always let Art come inside her. She always would.

After a few more deep thrusts, Art eased his half hard member out of her and rolled onto his back. His prick glistened with their combined love juices. She rolled on top of him and they kissed once again. It was a long, deep kiss that spoke volumes of their feelings for each other.

"I love you," she whispered.

"I love you," Art said.

Rita got home around ten the next morning. Rocky had literally fucked her the entire night and she'd lost track of the time and the number of orgasms she'd had. She was pleasantly tired and her pussy still tingled from the near-constant sex.

Zoe opened the door and let her in. Rita smiled when she saw that Zoe was wearing only a T-shirt. She walked up to her and fondled her cunt.

"Where's Art?" she asked as they walked into the kitchen and sat down at the table.

"He's still asleep. I woke him earlier and just about fucked him to death, so he's sleeping it off. We've been making love since yesterday afternoon. How was your date?"" Zoe asked.

Rita smiled.

"Incredible! Rocky can last a very long time and that big dick of his hits all of my buttons. He's also very gentle and likes to do it slowly," she said.

Zoe laughed.

"I never thought I'd hear you talk about fucking anyone but Art. Rocky must be really good," she said.

"Oh yes. He's very good," Rita said. "I never imagined that I'd do anything like this either. But here I am."

"So, are you gonna fuck Bart?" Zoe asked.

"Definitely," Rita said. "I'm gonna fuck the daylights out of him. But he sort of worries me because he said that he's in love with me."

"I feel the same way about Art. I'd steal him from you if I thought I could and you know that. From now on, he's the only man I'll ever make love with," Zoe said.

Rita reached out and squeezed her hand.

"You worry me, too," she said.

Art came down and smiled when he saw them.

"Let's go out for breakfast. I guess we all got what we wanted last night, huh?" he said.

The women smiled and nodded.

"I've always wanted to spend an entire night with you. Now that I did, I want to spend more nights with you—if Rita lets me," Zoe said.

"I think that can be arranged easy enough," Rita said with a giggle. "I'm sure we'll all find something to keep us happy—if you can handle me spending entire nights with other men."

"I think we'll have to play this by ear, Rita. While last night was great, I'm still not sure I like the idea of you fucking a lot of other men. Maybe if you limit yourself to one or two men, we can make this work," Art said.

"So you don't like my sharing my pussy with other men?" she asked.

"No. But as long as you insist on doing it, I'll make love with Zoe as much as possible," he replied.

"Love? Not just fuck?" Rita teased.

Zoe beamed.

"I think Art and I are way past that, aren't we, Art?" she said.

Art pulled Zoe close and slid his middle finger into her cunt. She stuck her tongue in his mouth and gripped his shoulders. Rita watched as Zoe came. She shook all over and let out a deep, happy moan. She then dropped to her knees, grabbed Art's dick and proceeded to suck it. Rita was amazed that they'd do this in front of her, but she knew they were making their point. She watched Zoë's head move back and forth as she jerked Art off.

Just before Art came, Zoe stopped and stood up. She smiled at Rita.

"Your turn!" she said.

Rita smiled and slid Art's prick into her mouth. Moments later, she swallowed a thick load of cum. As soon as she stood up, Zoe stuck her tongue into Rita's mouth. They looked at Art.

"Give us an hour, then come upstairs," Rita said.

"And be ready to fuck us both!" Zoe giggled.

Rita knelt between her legs and kissed her way slowly up her inner thighs. When she reached Zoe's partially open cunt, she stopped to savor her sexual aroma awhile before sliding her tongue along her slit. Zoe's labia were large like rose petals and her clit was swollen and obvious. It was even more beautiful than Rita had imagined. She leaned closer and swirled her tongue over her clit.

Zoe groaned.

She groaned even louder when Rita sucked it.

She arched her back and emitted several gasps as Rita slid her tongue into cunt and lapped at her soft, inner walls.

"Ooh yes! I'm yours! All yours!" she sighed as Rita went down on her in earnest. "Eat me, darling! I love you!"

Rita reached up and played with Zoe's nipples. This heightened her sensations so much, she erupted. She seized Rita's hair and wildly humped her face as she came and came and came again.

"It's wonderful! Fantastic! I love it! I love it! I love you, Rita! I really love you!" she cried.

While her head was still reeling, Zoe shifted so that she was kneeling on the floor between Rita's wide open thighs. She started by raining soft kisses on Rita's cunt then eased her tongue into her juicy slit and licked away. Rita was so wound up that she came within a few seconds. Zoe reached up and tweaked her nipples as she kept licking. Rita shouted and came again and again.

"I love you, Zoe! I love you! Oh, God! How I love you!"

Zoe was totally lost in the taste of her friend's cunt. She was salty, sweet, bitter and everything else at the same time. She kept licking and licking as Rita lay sighing, moaning and trembling through orgasms after orgasm.

When Art went upstairs, they were both on the bed naked with their legs wide apart. He quickly undressed. His prick was harder than he'd ever remembered as he watched the two women stroke their clits.

Rita's cunt was wide open and the inside was dark pink and very wet. He could see that she was really horny, too. He smiled and moved between her thighs and plunged his prick into her. She wrapped her legs around his hips and moaned happily. She was delighted that he chose her first and she fucked him back with everything she had.

Zoe massaged her clit as she watched them. They were making love. Real, intense and honest love. She saw them move together perfectly and felt jealous. But watching them also made her horny so she moved over and straddled Rita with her legs apart and faced Art. She gripped his head and pulled his face into her cunt.

"OOOhhhh yeah!" she moaned as his tongue explored her.

Rita reached up and caressed Zoe's ass crack then slid a finger up into her ass. Zoe shook all over as Rita "fucked" her. She had never felt anything so wonderful. So intense.

She emitted a scream and came.

Rita pushed her forward so Art could keep eating her and she fingered Zoe's asshole faster. Zoe came again and screamed. So did Art and Rita. He began pumping lines of cum into Rita's cunt while both women came and came hard.

Zoe moaned and fell onto the bed with her legs wide apart. Art finished fucking Rita and pulled his dick out her cunt. Zoe saw the line of cum running out Rita's cunt and started licking it up. Rita moaned and thrashed around in ecstasy as she came and came and came.

They rested for a while, then Zoe smiled up at Art.

"It's my turn—if you can handle it!" she challenged.

Art got between her thighs, positioned his cock against her trembling slit, and slowly penetrated her. Zoe groaned and dug her nails into his shoulders as he went in as deep as he could. Just as he thought, she had the tightest most wonderful pussy he'd ever been in. He stood still for a few seconds to savor the way her warm flesh felt around his cock, then he began a slow, in and out movement.

Zoe tightened her cunt muscled around his prick as she thrust back at him. After several minutes, they came again. This time, it felt even better.

"I love you!" she screamed. "I'm all yours forever and ever! I love you!"

It was the first time she had said that to anyone. And she meant every single word. He was in love. It was nothing like she'd ever felt before. She wanted do sing and dance and whirl around—everything. She felt light and happy and excited. Those feelings double when she was with him, too.

She wasn't just fucking him.

She was making love with him and he with her. It felt so right. So wonderfully perfect. And she was all his.

They moved faster and faster until they both came at once. It was a deep, strong, warm and exciting simultaneous orgasm that ended with them collapsing into each other's arms.

Zoe had let him set the rhythm, and then matched him thrust-for-thrust. It was a nice, prolonged and deep fuck. To her, it was the most incredible fuck of her life. When they came, they came together.

His prick was still inside her cunt, so Zoe used her inner walls to massage it. When she felt him getting stiff, she moved her hips up and down slowly. Rita watched as Art grew nice and hard again and they began fucking faster and faster. She knew from experience that this would be a very long fuck, too.

Zoe wrapped her legs around his hips and began fucking him back with everything she had. Art groaned and matched her thrust for delicious thrust. Her pussy was warm and very tight and she knew exactly how to use it.

Zoe felt herself coming and began moving faster and faster. Art felt her body tremble and realized she was about to explode. He leaned forward and fucked her faster as he tried to bring her to a climax.

He did.

And what a climax it was.

Zoe had to bite her lower hard to keep from crying out as a powerful wave of intense pleasure and release rippled through her quivering body. She'd never felly anything like it before. Her cunt muscles convulsed around Art's prick. It felt so exciting, it triggered his orgasm. He held back as long as he could, then thrust his prick into her as hard as he could and let himself go. He came so hard and so much that everything around them turned white. As the intensity of the orgasm subsided, he gave her a few more deep thrusts and slipped out of her pussy. As he did, a long stream of white liquid dripped from between Zoe's labia and onto the couch.

Zoe grinned happily at him.

"That was perfect!" she gasped as they clung to each other.

Chapter Twelve

For the next few days, Rita and Art dated and stayed home with each other. Zoe said she needed a few days to recover anyway and wanted a short break. Two straight days of nearly non-stop sex with Art and Rita had worn her out.

On Tuesday morning, Rita got a call from Bart.

"I'm glad you called. Are we on for today?" she asked.

"Of course. But I have another idea," he said.

"What?" she asked.

"Let's do something different today," Bart said.

"Like what?" she asked.

"Instead of going to the casino, let's meet for lunch this afternoon. I'll buy," he suggested.

"I'm not sure---" she began.

"Come on, Rita. No one will know," he urged.

She thought it over.

"Where?" she asked.

"You pick the place," he said.

"How about the Thai restaurant on Jessica Street?" she suggested.

"Okay. Do they know you there?" he asked.

"Art and I go there every once in a while for dinner. I've never been there for lunch, so no one there should know me," she said.

"It's a date. I'll meet you there at noon," he said.

"Okay. See you then," she said as she hung up.

She smiled.

He said 'date'. To her, they were just two people meeting for a nice lunch. She never thought of it as a date.

She looked at the clock. She had two and a half hours. She decided to shower and wash her hair. For some reason, she took extra time to wash her pussy, too. She dried herself off and looked in a mirror.

"No makeup," she said. "Well, not much anyway."

She also added a short spritz of rose scented perfume to her neck and pubic hair. She laughed because she'd never done that before. She also decided to dress differently. Instead of her usual shorts and T-shirt, she put on a white satin blouse and short, pleated dark red skirt. Underneath the skirt, she wore her gold bikini panties.

She checked herself out in the mirror and smiled.

"I look sexy enough," she said.

Then she stopped to wonder why she even said that or dressed this way. She momentarily thought about changing her clothes but when she checked the clock, she realized she had only 20 minutes before she had to meet Bart.

"I have no time to change!" she said as she hurried out to her car.

When she arrived, Bart was waiting outside. They hugged warmly. He smiled.

"You look stunning as usual," he said. "I thought this would be better than meeting at the casino. Besides, I'm tired of making love in some dark corner. I've gotten us a room at the Rialto if that's okay with you?"

She grinned.

"Are you planning what I think you are?" she joked as they entered the restaurant.

"Only if you want it, too," he said.

The waitress, a pretty young Thai woman, smiled when she saw them.

"Hi, Rita," she said. "Where's Art?"

"He's still at work," Rita said as she showed them to a table.

"Oh?" she said as she looked at Bart. "Can I bring you something to drink?"

"Bring us two mai tais," Bart said.

She glanced at Rita. She knew that she normally didn't drink and decided to make hers fairly weak.

As she mixed the drinks at the bar on the other side of the room, she saw Bart lean close and whisper in Rita's ear. Rita blushed and giggled nervously.

"Something's not quite right," she thought. "Who the Hell is that guy she's with? I've never seen him before, but she seems to like him a lot. I've never seen her dress like that, either. It's like she's dressed for a date."

She decided to keep an eye on them while they ate.

She placed the drinks in front of them and took their order. Bart watched her, then turned his attentions to Rita. The waitress watched as he slid his chair closer. Then she saw his right hand vanish beneath the table.

"Wow. Is she cheating on her husband? I never would have expected that!" she thought.

She also saw them arrive in separate cars so no one could actually see them together. The more she watched, the more annoyed with Rita she became.

Ten minutes later, she brought them their meals.

"Bring us two more mai tais," Bart said.

She looked at Rita. Even though her drink had been fairly light, she looked a little flushed. She decided to put almost no rum in this one so Rita could keep her mind clear.

As she mixed them, she saw him move his hand under the table again. Rita just sat there and smiled at him the entire time.

"Is he feeling her up?" she wondered.

Bart was feeling Rita up. He was running his hand up and down her inner thigh while she sat with her knees part and let him do it. She had dressed like she did for this purpose and his caresses were driving her crazy and making her pussy moist

The waitress brought their drinks out a few minutes later. She could tell by the look on Rita's face that she was becoming aroused. She silently mouthed "don't do it" to her. Then she walked away.

"Did you dress this way for me?" he asked.

"Yes," she said. "Do you like it?"

"You look wonderful and I love the way your skirt shows off your beautiful legs," he said as he placed his hand on her knee.

He leaned closer and whispered.

"What color panties are you wearing?"

"Gold bikinis," she said.

"Are they small?" he asked as he moved his hand upward.

"They're very small," she said.

"Can I see them?" he asked.

She blushed.

"Maybe," she said as his hand crept upward.

"Can I see what's beneath them?" he asked.

"I don't think so," she said as she felt his fingers on her cunt.

"Please?" he said as he rubbed her clit.

She smiled.

"Maybe," she said softly.

"Then maybe you'll have sex with me?" he asked as he gently teased her labia through her panties.

She looked at him and parted her legs. He pushed aside her panties and rubbed her clit. She trembled.

"Yes," she whispered.

"Now what?" he asked as he moved his finger along her moist lips.

"We'll see after we eat," she said.

"I want to make today special for us," he said as he massaged her clit.

"What makes you think it will special?" she asked as she squirmed in her chair.

Her cunt was on fire now.

"Because you're letting me do this and because you dressed this way so that I can do this and because you know you really want to," he said as he slid his fingers into her hot, moist slit.

She stopped drinking and stared at him as she felt his fingers slide deeper into her cunt. She was surprised she was letting him do this and that she wanted him to do it.

"Yes," she said softly.

"I love you," he whispered as he moved his fingers in and out.

She was quivering all over now and when he located her g-spot, she almost jumped out of her chair.

"Really?" she asked.

"Yes," he said as he "fucked" her nice and easy.

She was oh-so wet now.

And oh-so horny.

The waitress walked over and cleared her throat. They stopped and looked up.

"Will that be all, Rita?" she asked.

Rita clamped her knees together tightly and nodded. Bart looked at her and then smiled at the waitress.

"Bring us the check," he said.

The waitress smiled at Rita.

"You know her?" he asked.

"Yes. She's been here forever. She normally works the dinner shift. She knows me and my husband," Rita replied.

"Shit!" Bart said.

The waitress brought him the check. He paid it and gave her a substantial tip in the hope that this wouldn't get back to Rita's husband. As they got up to leave, the waitress smiled at Rita.

"Tell Art I said hello," she said as she collected the money.

Rita saw the expression on Bart's face and laughed. He just shook his head.

"I think she saw everything," he said.

"Of course she did. She was looking at us the entire time," Rita said.

"Do you think she'll say anything to your husband?" he asked.

She shrugged.

"Maybe. But you shouldn't have done that here," she said.

"Well, then you shouldn't have let me do it here," he laughed. "Can I call you later?"

"Why wait?" she asked.

Bart laughed as they walked to his car. They drove to the casino and parked on the roof. They held hands as they got into the elevator. Rita noticed that Bart had an obvious erection and playfully squeezed it. They got off in the casino and walked to the back where the unused machines were.

She turned and stuck her tongue into his mouth. After a long, deep kiss, she slid to her knees and unzipped his pants. She pulled out his prick and gave it several slow pumps before sliding it into her mouth. Bart moaned softly as she sucked it and played with his balls.

"Now, Rita!" he whispered.

She stopped and slid onto the chair behind her. He raised her skirt and pulled off her panties. He smiled when he saw it had just been shaved. She leaned back and grinned at him. He gripped her thighs and pulled her to the very edge of the chair. She opened her legs wide and sighed as he entered her.

It was a nice, deep and easy fuck. The type she loved and only Bart could give her. She gripped his prick with her cunt muscles and fucked him back. She shivered with each delicious thrust, too.

"Yes, Bart! Yes! Make love to me!" she moaned.

And he was making love her. Real, passionate and true love. The kind that she had only experienced from Art before. The more they fucked, the more she desired him. The more she wanted to feel his hard dick moving in and out of her quivering cunt. His dick felt perfect to her and her cunt felt perfect to Bart.

They fucked and fucked and fucked.

Rita began moaning louder and shaking all over. Bart realized she was about to come and fucked her harder and faster. She gripped his shoulders and thrust her body up at him. Bart grunted as they both came at the exact same time. He kept fucking her until he'd emptied every last drop of cum he could into her eager cunt. When they were both satisfied, he eased out and they kissed again.

Bart looked into her eyes and smiled.

"I love you, Rita," he said sincerely.

She got home just as Art got back from work. He smiled as she greeted him with a kiss.

"Bart?" he asked.

She giggled and nodded as they went inside.

"He told me he loved me again," she said as she sat down on the sofa.

"How do you feel about him?" Art asked.

"I'm not 100% sure. To be honest, I love having sex with him. When he does it, it feels like he' making love to me and I'm making love to him. We're perfect together, Art. Kind of like you and me are. If I could, I'd fuck him every other day," she said. He smiled.

"I figured this might happen," he said. "I feel the same way when I'm having sex with Zoe. It's like we're made for each other. She says that she loves me, too. I'm not sure how I feel about he exactly, but it sway beyond just liking her."

"Now what, Art?" Rita asked.

"We stick with our original deal and see where this goes," he said.

Later that night, she got a call from Zoe.

"I heard that you had lunch with Bart today at the Thai restaurant," she said.

"Wow. News gets around fast!" Rita said. "It doesn't matter because Art knows."

"How is it with Bart?" Zoe asked.

"Magical!" Rita admitted.

"That's how it feels for me when I make love with Art. I guess we both have something special going, huh?" Zoe said.

"I think so—and it kind of excites and scares me at the same time," Rita said.

"I'm not scared. I told you that I'm going to steal Art from you and the more we fuck, the more he'll want me. But I also want to keep out relationship going. Now that I've tasted your pussy, I always seem to crave it!" Zoe said.

Rita laughed.

"You can have me any time you like. I love you, Zoe. I mean that," she said.

"And I love you, too, my darling," Zoe said.

Art decided to do a background check on Bart to make sure Rita was in no real danger from him. He'd just gotten the results when she went upstairs to the den to tell him dinner was ready.

"I know about your lunch date," he said.

She turned a deep red.

"I did a background check on Mr. Tillman. He has a totally clean record. He's an Army veteran with an honorable discharge and he doesn't even have a traffic violation. He's also quite wealthy and he dabbles in various businesses.

Judy over at the casino said he has a reputation as a ladies man. He's a fuck 'em and leave 'em type and he definitely wants to get into your panties. Has he?" Art said.

"Yes," Rita said. "He's told me all of these things from the start. So now I know he's honest."

"Oh? He told you he wants to have sex with you?" Art asked.

"Yes," she admitted. "Of course I told him that will never happen. Usually when I tell men that, they go away. He kept coming back and we talked a lot while we played. Yu already know the rest."

"So the waitress at the restaurant was mistaken when she told me had his hand between your legs?" Art asked.

"No. He was feeling my pussy again," Rita said.

"Zoe also told me that he's felt you up a few times and that you let him do it," Art said.

"That's true. We've also fucked a couple of times. Zoe told me she wants to steal you away from me," Rita said.

He laughed.

"Yes. She's told me that a few times," he said. "The next time she throws herself at me, I'm going to catch her. I've always wanted to have sex with her and she doesn't disappoint me. Now that you're going down that road with Bart, I'm going there with Zoe."

"She has a nice pussy. It's nice and tight," Rita said. "But mine is a lot better."

He laughed as he followed her upstairs to the bedroom...

The following morning, Zoe stopped by the house to see Art. She knew that Rita was at work and that it was Art's day off. She also dressed to attract attention. She wore a plain white T-shirt and dark red running shorts that left little to the imagination.

"It's time to make my move," she said.

Of course he noticed.

And of course, he got an erection.

He led her into the parlor and poured her a cup of coffee. As they sat down, she parted her knees to show him that she wasn't wearing panties.

"What do you think of Rita's friend?" she asked.

"I'm not sure. What do you think of him?" he asked.

"I know that he's after Rita and she knows it. I think she enjoys his attentions and company a little too much," she said.

"Do you think they'll have an affair?" he asked as he eyed her cunt.

"Not yet but they're getting real close. She lets him touch her pussy—a lot-- and they fuck, so I think they will sooner or later," she replied.

He nodded.

"He's young. He's handsome and he has a good, hard dick and he knows how to use it. I know that because I've fucked him. We stayed together all night, too. He doesn't wear out easy so if Rita does have an affair with him, she'll have a very good time," she added.

"Maybe we should also have a very good time," she said.

She stood and slowly peeled off her shorts. His eyes went straight to the soft, dark triangle between her thighs as his dick hardened even more.

"I have a pussy, Art. It's warm and tight and you can feel it as much as you like," she said as she stood just inches from him with her feet apart.

She was so close that he could smell her pussy.

"Do it, Art. Touch me," she said as she took his hand and placed it on her cunt.

He gently explored her swollen labia and engorged clit. Her cunt was gorgeous and her sexual aroma made his mouth water. She closed her eyes and trembled while he felt her.

"Yes! Yes! Make me come, Art. Make me yours," she moaned.

He slid his middle finger into her slit and moved it in and out. She felt her knees quake and humped his finger. Then she came.

It was a good, explosive come. She gripped his shoulders and kept trembling as he "fucked" her faster and faster. She came again and screamed.

"I'm yours now! All yours!"

Art was totally enraptured by her cunt now. He loved the way her inner walls convulsed around his finger. Zoe grabbed the back of his head and pulled his face into her crotch. Caught up in the moment, he started licking her.

"Ooohh! Yes! Eat me! I love it!" she screamed as she fucked his tongue.

He held onto her ass and sucked her clit. She felt her knees buckle as she came again. She let him go and fell back onto the sofa with her legs wide apart. She reached up, undid his jeans and grabbed his erect prick.

"I've always wanted to do this," she said as she slid it into her mouth.

That did it for him. He came within seconds and fired lined of cum into Zoe's mouth. She kept sucking and massaging his balls until he was totally spent. When she knew he was finished, she let him go and smiled up at him.

"I have you now, Art. And I am not letting you go," she said.

He sat down next to her and smiled as he stroked her inner thigh. Zoe had seduced him—big time. She reached over and pumped his prick until he grew hard again. Then she led him upstairs.

When they got upstairs, she immediately threw her arms around his neck and French kissed him. He responded by running his hands all over her. She led him to the sofa where they kissed again while he played with her nipples. She laid there sighing as he rolled up her T-shirt and swirled his tongue over each nipple.

"Wait!" she said.

She sat up and peeled off her shirt. Her breasts were firms and perfect. He leaned over and sucked each nipple while he massaged her crotch. She unzipped his pants and pulled out his prick. He almost came when she jerked him off. She let him go and lay down. He kissed his way down her body, lingered at her navel, and slowly pulled her shorts down.

She was naked now.

And he obviously loved what he saw. She closed her eyes as he slid his tongue up and down her slit.

"Yes!" she thought. "He's eating me! This is the day!"

He buried his face in her cunt and licked away. She gasped, moaned and convulsed. Then she came. It was a long, wonderful, deep orgasm that caused her to rock from side-to-side. He made her come twice more. As she lay panting, he stood and removed his clothes.

This was the first time she ever saw him naked.

And she liked what she saw, too.

She sat up, grabbed his prick, and slid it into her mouth. He gasped as she sucked it and bobbed her head back and forth. After a minute or two, she let him go and laid back with her legs wide apart.

"Fuck me!" she said.

There was no stopping him now. He moved between her thighs and eased his prick into her cunt. She pulled him to her and wrapped her legs around his hips. It was the moment she'd been hoping for. She felt him move in and out and quivered with each thrust.

"Yes! Fuck me!" she moaned.

She soon moved with him. It felt better than she hoped it would. In fact, she loved it. They fucked faster and faster. She matched him thrust for thrust. He loved the way she fucked and how tight her cunt was.

Nothing mattered but the intensity of their lovemaking and the pleasure they were giving each other.

He came first. When she felt his cum spurting into her, she also came. They kept fucking as hard as they could until both were totally spent. She smiled up at him and they kissed again. They had done it. They had crossed the line and committed adultery.

Rita didn't care. She'd finally had full out sex with Bart and his half hard prick and pool of cum inside her pussy felt wonderful. She sucked his prick until he was fully erect again and lay back down. He slid his prick into her cunt and they moved together slowly.

"I finally have you all to myself!" she whispered. "I'm all yours now."

They moved together perfectly. It was as if their bodies were made for each other. His thrusts were deep and strong and she quivered with every one of them. The second one lasted longer than their first and felt even more exciting.

"I'm gonna come," he whispered.

"Come in my pussy. Make me yours!" she gasped as she fucked him faster.

The timing was perfect, too.

They both came at the same time and kept fucking until he slipped out of her. She looked down at the stream of white that oozed from her throbbing cunt and smiled.

"I am yours," she said as they kissed.

They fucked twice more that day. Each time, he came inside her cunt. She decided that she would always let him cum inside of her and the consequences be damned. As she beamed up at him after their last fuck, she said: "I love you."

Rita got home just as they came downstairs. She looked at the expression on Zoe's face and smiled. They'd been fucking—no— making love all day.

"Are you two having an affair yet?" she asked as Zoe kissed her on the lips.

'We all are!" Zoe replied. "I'm making love with you and Art and you're fucking Bart and me and Art. When you think about it, that's a lot of sex!"

"Yes it is," Rita giggled. "And it's all great sex!"

Art laughed.

"Are you having an affair with Bart?" he asked.

"Not yet," Rita said.

"Are you thinking about it?" he asked.

"Oh yes!" she said.

Chapter Thirteen

Rita received a call from Bart early the next morning. She beamed when she heard his voice.

"Hello," he said.

"Hello," she replied.

"I'm sorry about the other day," he said.

"Me, too," she said.

"Are you sorry I did that? Or sorry that we got interrupted again?" he asked.

"Maybe a little of both," she admitted. "But it turned out great anyway."

"Let's get together again tomorrow," he said.

"Sure. Where?" she asked as her heart raced.

"How about lunch at the Prime Steakhouse? I'll buy. You can wear what you wore yesterday," he suggested.

"Are you serious?" she asked.

"Very serious. Is it a date?" he asked.

"Okay. What time?" she asked as she was surprised she agreed to meet him again.

"How about one?" he asked.

"Okay. I'll meet you there," she agreed. "What about after?"

"Let's see how it goes," he replied.

He met her outside the restaurant with a kiss and a single rose. She smiled and followed him inside to the dark, cozy table in a corner.

"You look gorgeous!" he said as she sat down.

"Oh, come one!" she smiled.

"No. Really. Is your skirt a bit shorter today?" he asked.

"A little bit," she said.

"Are you wearing the same panties?" he asked.

"Maybe," she smiled.

"Then maybe you'll let me see what's under them?" he teased.

"Maybe. We'll see," she said with a grin.

"I'll be honest with you, Rita. I'm going to do whatever it takes today to get you to make love with me again. I want you, Rita. I want you more than I've ever wanted anyone in my entire life. I don't care how much it costs or how long it takes, but I'm going to get you to fall in love with me," he whispered.

She giggled.

"We'll see," she said.

He laughed.

"At least you didn't say no. That's a good start. I've ordered us a bottle of sweet red wine. I thought you'd like to try something different," he said.

They drank and ate and talked for what seemed like hours. During the course of the evening, Bart had managed to get his hand between her open thighs. She smiled dreamily at him as he gently teased her clit. She also responded by squeezing his dick and running her fingers up and down his bulge.

"I want you," he whispered.

She smiled at him.

Her heart raced faster as she felt him hook his finger through the waistband of her panties. As she slowly slid them downward, she slightly elevated her hips. Bart smiled and eased them down past her hips and along her thighs.

She smiled as her moved them past her knees and down her calves. When they reached her ankles, she lifted her feet to allow him to remove them altogether. He stuffed them into his pocket and slid his hand under her skirt again.

When he reached her cunt, she parted her knees and smiled dreamily at him. He gently ran his fingers over her pussy and teased her clit. When he slid two fingers into her hot, wet slit she quivered.

"Yes!" she sighed as he explored her. "Yes!"

He moved his fingers in and out. She grew hotter and wetter. She was glad the restaurant was dimly lit and that they were in one of darker areas so no one could see what he was doing. He fingered her gently but faster and sent waves of pleasure surging through her body. She quivered harder and came again.

He 'fucked" her faster and faster. She stifled a moan and kept coming and coming. She couldn't tell if she was having multiple orgasms or one terrifically long one. She realized that she was his now. That she wanted to fuck him.

"Let's do it, Rita," he whispered. "Give yourself to me."

Her legs were wide open now and his fingers made low squishing sounds as they continued to move in and out. Her pussy was on fire and she came again and again.

"Let's do it, Rita. Let's make love. You know you want to," he said.

"Yes, Bart! Yes!" she moaned. "Oh, God! You're making me crazy!" she shivered as she came again.

"Are you sure?" he asked.

"Yes! I'm sure," she sighed.

He smiled and withdrew his hand. She closed her thighs and caught her breath as she looked at him. She had just agreed to have sex with Bart. She had agreed to cheat on her husband. She smiled back. She felt exhausted. Sexually spent.

She reached over and unzipped his pants. After she was sure no one was watching, she pulled out his erection and slowly jerked him off. It seemed to get harder with each pump of her hand. He sat still and smiled at her as she did it faster and faster. She felt his pre-cum run onto her fingers and squeezed him tighter. He trembled at the incredible sensations she sent through his body. She pumped him faster and faster. His first shot struck the underside of their table. So did his second and third. His cum ran down the his prick and coated her fingers. She looked at him and kept jerking him off until he felt his balls ache and his prick shrank back to its normal size. She played with his knob and foreskin for a while, then stopped.

He watched her take the napkin and wipe her fingers off.

"You're really good at this," he said. "In fact, you're terrific."

"Thanks. So are you," she said softly as they maintained eye contact.

Bart signaled for the check. The waiter brought it over along with a second bottle of wine. He paid it and gave the man a nice tip.

"I have a suite upstairs," he said.

She smiled and took his hand.

They spent less than a minute undressing each other. Bart sucked each of her nipples while she stroked his prick. He pushed her down onto the bed and licked his way to her cunt.

Rita opened her legs and bent her knees.

"Fuck me!" she said.

"Your wish is my command!" he replied as he slid his prick deep into her eager cunt.

"Oooh, yes!" Rita sighed as his knob struck bottom.

He began moving in and out of Rita's cunt. Rita quivered with each delicious down stroke, then moved with him.

Again and again and again.

Rita fucked him faster and faster.

Harder and harder.

"Oooh yes! Yes! I love it! It's wonderful! Fuck me harder! Give it to me good!" she moaned.

They fucked harder and harder.

"Fuck me! Fuck me! Fuck me! More! More! Make me come!" she screamed as she fucked him with everything she had.

Then she came.

It was a strong, deep orgasm that sent her mind reeling. She moaned and cried and continued to drive her hips upward. Bart fucked her faster and faster. Rita groaned loudly, quivered all over and came second time.

"Oh God! That feels so good!" she moaned.

Bart wasn't finished. He bent her legs back a little ways and fucked her deeper.

"Make me yours," she said. "All yours!"

This time, she wrapped her legs around his waist and gripped his arms as he fucked her. She matched him stroke for stroke right from the start and sighed and moaned as they moved faster and faster.

"Give me all you can now! Make me your slut! Make me all yours!" she cried.

Bart fucked her harder and harder. Rita moved with him eagerly and squeezed his prick with her cunt muscles.

"Ooooh, yeah! I love it! This is the best fuck! A great fuck! A wonderful fuck! Give it to me!" she cried as she fucked him faster and faster.

Then she came again.

This time, she came harder than she ever came before.

As she did, she fucked him wildly and begged for more and more.

"Make my pussy yours now! It's all yours! Do what you want with me!" Rita gasped as she came again.

As she came, she fucked him faster. Bart groaned, drove his prick as deeply into her cunt as he could, and emptied his balls inside of her. Rita shuddered as she felt his cum splash into her cunt walls.

And she came again.

"Oooh yes! That's what I want! Fill me! Fill my pussy!" she moaned.

Bart gave her a few more deep thrusts, then slid his prick out of her cunt. A river of cum followed and ran down between Rita's cheeks.

Rita grabbed Bart's prick and sucked it until he was rock hard again, then she laid down and spread her legs.

"Again!" she said.

Rita laid back and opened her legs. She sighed happily as he entered her cunt again.

This time, they fucked nice and easy for a few minutes. Then Rita began fucking him faster and faster. Bart matched her thrust for thrust. He gave her everything he had left for the next few minutes. When Rita came, he kept going until he fired one last load deep inside her cunt.

They held each other tightly and kissed. It was a long, deep and passionate kiss. Bart's dick was still nested inside Rita's cunt and he was still semi-hard. He felt her muscles squeeze him several times. When it began to grow good and still again, she started moving her hips up and down. His prick grew harder and harder and they soon started fucking again.

Bart was amazed.

He was living out his wildest hopes and dreams. He was in a hotel suite making love to Rita and he never wanted it to stop.

Neither did Rita.

"I love you, Bart! I love you!" she moaned.

"Can you spend the night with me?" he asked.

"Yes!" she said as they fucked faster...

While Rita and Bart were enjoying a night of passion at the hotel, Art and Zoe were also going at it hot and heavy at the house.

Once Zoe learned that Rita planned to spend an entire night with Bart, she made a bee line to Art's house. As soon as he opened the door, she threw her arms around his neck and stuck her tongue into his mouth.

"I am all yours tonight—and forever after!" she said.

They kissed passionately as they undressed. Zoe wrapped her fingers around Art's prick and gave it a few easy strokes. Then she sat down on the edge of the bed with her thighs apart. Unable to resist, Art fell to his knees and slowly licked her already juicy slit. Zoe sighed as his tongue danced in and out of her pussy and fell back on the bed. Art cupped her cheeks and pulled her to him as he ate her.

"Oh, yes!" she sighed as Art's tongue sent shivers up her back.

She loved the way he ate her. No one else, she decided, could do the things he did with his tongue. She was always happy and eager to feel it dancing between her legs.

As for Art, he adored her bitter-sweet-salty flavor and delightful scent. Zoe tasted and smelled so different. So delightfully sexy.

Now, he was as hard as could be. He stood up, pushed Zoe's legs as far apart as possible and slid his prick into pussy all the way to his balls. Zoe gasped. She wrapped her legs around his hips and closed her eyes as they began that slow, deep-penetrating fuck they both loved. It was the most incredible sex they could have. It was exhilarating, wonderful sex. But it was far more than that. What they had now went far beyond the mere physical union of two people. It was an incredible melding of two into one—a perfect union of body and spirit.

Art took his time with Zoe. He always went as slow and as deep as possible, not only to give her the utmost pleasure but also to savor the feel of her silky-smooth pussy as he moved in and out of her. The way Art made love to her made Zoe feel especially wonderful.

Wanted.

Sexy.

Each time they made love, they added more cement to their blossoming relationship. Each time, the bond between them grew stronger and stronger.

Soon, Zoe felt herself coming and began humping Art faster. He caught her signal and tried to hold back as long as possible. He wanted to time their orgasms perfectly. To make this one really special.

He did.

Both he and Zoe erupted at the same moment and became suspended in time for a few seconds. They clung to each other like there was no tomorrow and humped until their bodies ached and sweat covered them. At the height of ecstasy, Zoe cried out.

"I love you, Art! I love you!"

To her delight, he echoed her words. They rested now. Art was still on top of her, his semi-hard prick still buried inside Zoe's pulsing cunt as their lips fused together in a long, hot kiss. When they broke off, Zoe looked into Art's eyes and saw the love in them.

At that moment, they both realized their "affair" had grown into something so much more.

Zoe used her inner muscles to squeeze Art's prick. The delicious sensations caused him to harden once again. Instead of fucking her, Art slid to the floor and used his fingers to pry apart Zoe's pussy lips. The center was dark pink now and very moist. He leaned forward, sniffed her heady perfume, and then licked her thighs near her slit. Zoe shivered with anticipation as she waited for his tongue to work its magic. She didn't have to wait long. Art slipped it into the bottom of her pussy then moved it slowly up toward her swollen clit. Zoe gasped and emitted a deep "ah!" as his tongue swirled around her love button.

It felt so good.

So very very good.

Art ate her for a long, long time. Each time he sensed her about to come, he eased up, then did it all again. Several times, he brought her to the brink or orgasm and stopped short of making her come. Soon, Zoe was begging him to finish her off.

When he did, she blew like a volcano and just about rolled off the bed. Then Art did the unexpected. While she was in mid-come, he climbed on top of her and rammed his prick into her cunt hard. Zoe screamed with joy. She wrapped her arms and legs around him and they gave each other a nice, steady—and somewhat harder fuck. The movement of his hard-on inside her convulsing cunt caused Zoe to come again and again. Each orgasm was stronger than the last and she soared ever skyward and became lost in the clouds.

"Yes! Yes! Love me, Art! Love me good!" she screamed as her body trembled uncontrollably with each hard thrust of his prick.

She was getting the best sex of her entire life now and she didn't want it to end any time soon.

Art fucked her harder. Zoe clung to him, unable to move, unable to fuck him back. All she could do now was to take it, to enjoy the glorious ride he was giving her. Then her quivering, quaking body became too much for him. He rammed his prick into her as deep as he could and groaned as streams of white goo jetted into her cunt. He stayed motionless as Zoe milked him until her cunt was flooded with his cum. Then he leaned over. They kissed passionately. Zoe tasted herself on his tongue. The taste excited her again and she began humping his half-hard prick. Art trembled as she humped him. He was nearly exhausted now. He just hovered over her and let Zoe do the work. He was so numb; he barely noticed he was still coming like crazy inside of her.

"My God! That was wonderful. I love you, Art. I honestly and truly love you. I love you so much that I want to have your baby," she said.

"And I love you deeply," he whispered.

Art grabbed her and pressed his lips to hers. Zoe was taken aback by his sudden move but didn't resist as he slipped his tongue into her mouth. That's when it hit her. A sudden, almost electrifying jolt that seemed to surge throughout her body. She had never felt anything like it before.

She returned his kiss with incredible eagerness after that. As they kissed, Art slid his hand under her t-shirt and gently fondled her breast. Zoe responded by sucking his tongue passionately. His touches were making her crazy now. Art seemed to know exactly what to do to get her started. Before she knew it, her fingers wrapped around his warm, erect prick. She stared at the large pink knob and the way Art's foreskin rolled back and forth over it with each up and motion of her fist. She decided that she liked the way it looked and became fascinated with the clear liquid that soon oozed from the knob. She also liked the way it felt in her hand and was now eager to feel it deep inside her pussy again.

Art dropped to his knees in front of her. Zoe raised her hips to make it easier, and then opened her legs wide. Art ogled the soft, hairless slit for a few moments, then began kissing her inner thighs. He moved slowly upward. When Zoe felt his hot breath on her pussy, she opened her legs as wide as she could and leaned back.

Art slid his hands beneath her cheeks and raised them so that her pussy was tilted up toward his mouth. Then he began licking all around her cunt, moving closer and closer to Zoe's labia on each pass. Zoe was literally shaking with anticipation as Art continued to tease her by moving his tongue slowly along her gash. Each time he reached her swollen clit, he gently sucked it awhile, and then licked his way back down her labia.

Zoe was hot now.

White hot.

And her pussy was wet.

Incredibly wet.

The room became permeated with her sexual scent as Art concentrated on her labia and clit. Each time his tongue touched her clit, Zoe sighed and trembled with excitement. After what seemed like an eternity, he finally inserted his tongue into her quivering snatch. Zoe reached down and pulled her labia open. Art accepted the invitation by sliding his tongue into her as deeply as possible and moving it around. Zoe began bouncing up and down on the sofa as she moaned and moaned. Art slid his finger into her pussy and massaged her g-spot. Zoe saw stars as she came. It was the hardest, most explosive orgasm she ever had. She gripped his head and fucked his tongue like wild woman now as she begged him to keep going.

Art licked her clit and fingered her pussy until Zoe said she couldn't take any more. She fell back to catch her breath. When Art stood, she eyed his boner, then spread her legs again.

"Fuck me, Art! Take me right now!" she whispered.

Art didn't hesitate. He got onto the sofa and slid his prick home. Since Zoe's pussy was still pulsing from her orgasms, her inner walls acted like a soft, wet mouth as they closed eagerly around his flesh pole.

Zoe was tight, too.

Wonderfully tight.

Both he and Zoe then decided that his prick was a perfect fit for her pussy. Then Art began fucking her. Zoe just laid still for the first few thrusts as she grew accustomed to his rhythm. When she knew the pace, she moved with him. They moved slowly.

Gently.

It was a nice, soft, easy fuck.

One that said: I LOVE YOU.

She felt herself drifting away on a wave of pleasure. She felt the pressure building inside her pussy and knew she was about to come again. She warned Art by humping him faster. He understood her signal and sped up the pace. His thrust became deeper and sharper. Zoe emitted moans of pleasure as she climbed toward her climax. Then it happened.

A deep, powerful eruption that had her gasping and clawing at his arms. Art barely noticed. He was too busy pumping streams of cum into Zoe's hungry pussy. By some stroke of fortune, they had triggered simultaneously. Caught up in the passion of the moment, they kept at it until they were totally exhausted. When Art pulled his prick out, it was followed by a river of sticky whiteness that oozed down Zoe's ass crack. After they caught their breath, they kissed several times.

"That was...*magical*," Zoe said after a while.

"Better than sex with a woman?" Art asked.

"Hell yeah. But I doubt that any other man could do this as well as you do," she replied. "That was perfect. In fact, we are perfect together."

Art laughed and held her close.

"It's magical because you make it so," he said.

When Rita got back home late the next morning, she found Art and Zoe seated on the sofa looking very happy and tired. She smiled and sat next to them.

"Looks like we all had a terrific night," she remarked.

They nodded.

"I think we all got exactly what we wanted last night," Zoe said. "Last night was the most wonderful night I ever had. In fact, it was perfect. How was yours?"

"Perfect," Rita replied as she leaned back. "I'm going to see Bart again the day after tomorrow. I'll probably spend the night with him again, so you and Art can make love all night, too."

Art smiled.

Rita had said make love—not fuck. She knew that his relationship with Zoe had gone far beyond just great sex. He also knew that she felt the same way about Bart. Life had gotten a little more complicated and interesting than any of them expected.

"I need to shower," Rita said. "We can go out to breakfast after I'm finished."

Zoe giggled.

They watched her wobble up the stairs.

"She has been very well fucked," Zoe said. "Just like me!"

Art laughed.

"Wanna have an affair?" he asked.

"I thought we already were—and the answer is Hell yes!" Zoe replied. "From now on, you are the only man who will ever put his dick in my pussy—ever!"

They kissed deeply.

As Rita showered, she thought about her situation. She had openly violated their marriage vows by having sex with several other men. She didn't plan on getting romantically entangled with any of them, but Bart had turned her world inside-out. Now, she couldn't get him out of her mind and she found herself missing him after only a few hours. It was the way she also felt about Art. She realized that she was crazy in love with both of them—and Zoe, too. She also realized that she had opened a door of opportunity to allow Zoe to actively seduce and steal Art from her.

"Now what?" she wondered.

Bart was also in turmoil.

What started out as making Rita just another conquest had resulted in his falling madly in love with her. She had become much more than just another woman to fuck and leave to him. He no longer thought about fucking other women. His thoughts were filled only with Rita and how much he truly cared for her.

He didn't want to destroy her marriage, but the way thinks looked he wondered if that was going to happen. He felt happy that she had said that she loved him, too, but he also felt like a lowlife skunk for getting romantically involved with a very married woman.

"Now what happens?" he asked himself. "I could to the honorable thing and break this off, but it's already gone further than I ever expected. Hell, I don't want to stop now. I never want to stop. I just want Rita to be happy."

He had to laugh.

This was the first time in his entire life that he actually cared about someone other than himself. Rita had turned his entire world on its axis!

"God, how I love her!" he said.

Chapter Fourteen

Bart waited at the restaurant for Rita. When she failed to show after an hour, he dialed her phone. To his surprise, she answered.

"I'm sorry, Bart. I have to skip tonight," she said.

"Are you having second thoughts?' he asked.

"Maybe. I'll meet you in the casino tomorrow night if you like," she suggested.

"Fair Lady, I will definitely be there!" he assured her.

She turned off the phone and smiled weakly at Art.

"Is it okay?" she asked.

"It's your life, Rita," he said. "I already called Zoe and told her to come over tomorrow night. So enjoy yourself—but not too much!"

She laughed.

"You, too! As weird as this sounds, I still don't want to lose you to her," she said.

"Don't worry. You won't," he promised.

"We have a strange marriage now," she said. "I never imagined we'd do anything like this. It's crazy."

"Enjoy it while it lasts, Hon," he said.

"What if it lasts forever?" she said.

"Then we'll enjoy it forever," he said.

The next night, Rita put on her miniskirt and headed for the casino. Less than 15 minutes later, Zoe arrived wearing her dark red running shorts and a T-shirt. She also had a small overnight bag with her.

"Let's make a weekend out of this, Art. Let's make love until we pass out then do it all over again!" she said as they kissed.

Bart smiled when he saw Rita enter the casino and walked over with two drinks. She took one and hugged him.

"I'm very glad you came tonight," he said. "You know, when I decided to go after you, the last thing I expected was to fall in love with you. You played hard to get at first and that only increased my desire for you. That desire turned into a deep, warm love for you."

"I'll admit that you annoyed me at first," she said as the drank. "But I really appreciated your honesty. It was no bullshit from the first and I found that refreshing because you remind me of the way my husband is."

"He must be one great guy," Bart said.

"He is. So are you, Bart. I think that's what attracted me to you. I was also amazed that you wanted to make love with someone my age!" she smiled.

"I've never met anyone like you, Rita. I think I fell in love with you that very first night. You're very, very special and so wonderfully sexy," he said as he slid his hand up her thigh.

She parted her knees. He slid his hand under her dress and smiled when he realized she wasn't wearing panties. He ran his fingers along her slit as his dick grew harder and harder.

"You're exactly the kind of woman I know you are. You're a rare gem, Rita. I would love to have you all to myself because I love you. I truly do. But that has to be entirely your decision. You have to do it on your terms and only when you're 100% sure about it," he said as he played with her clit.

He looked her in the eyes.

"I started out viewing as just another easy conquest," he said. "But then something happened that never happened to me before. I fell in love with you."

"Wow!" she said.

"That's something I thought I'd never admit," he laughed. "Be honest with me, Rita. Tell me how you feel about me."

"I'd be lying if I said that I wasn't attracted to you. Part of me wants to scream I love you—and I guess I actually do. Part of me also says that's just wrong. But I love being with you more than I ever imagined I would and I love making love with you. I've fucked a few other guys lately, too. But they don't hold a candle to you or my husband, so I've come to tell that I'm ready to have an affair with you, Bart. I'll be yours for as long as you want me," she said as he slid his fingers into her damp, hot slit.

He laughed.

"It'll be a long one, Rita, because I don't ever intend to let you go. I'll give up all the other women if you say you'll be mine," he said.

"I'm yours whenever you want me, Bart," she said as she squeezed his dick.

"Your friend, Zoe, thinks we're already having an affair. I hope she doesn't stir up any trouble for you," he said. "Rumors can do a lot more harm than good sometimes. I think she's kind of jealous because we hang out together. Are you two girlfriends?"

"Yes.," Rita said with a giggle. "So you'll have to share me with her and my husband. Zoe is also crazy in love with my husband and I think he feels the same way about her. They've been fucking like crazy, too, and as long as they do that, I'm yours. Last night, I stayed home to show her it wouldn't be that easy to steal him from me."

Bart laughed.

She looked into his eyes and smiled as he played with her cunt. He looked at her. She nodded.

"Are you sure?" he asked.

"Yes," she said. "I'm sure."

"I have a suite in the hotel," he said as he rubbed her clit.

"Let's go," she whispered. "I'm all yours, Bart. All yours."

"Can you stay for the entire weekend?" he asked hopefully.

She laughed and squeezed his hand. He smiled happily.

"I'm going to make this as special as I possibly can, Rita. This weekend, I'm going to make you mine," he said.

"Just for this weekend?" she teased.

"We'll see," he said softly.

Minutes later, they were on the bed of his suite stark naked and locked in a heated embrace. As they kissed, he eased his hand up her body to her right breast. This time, she let him touch her for a while. He felt her heart beat faster and faster and realized he'd aroused her.

He eased his other hand up to her left breast. Rita emitted a muffled moan as he played with her nipples.

After a few seconds, she felt something hard and stiff pressing against her crotch. As the hard knob slid across her labia, Rita opened her stance. Bart slid his prick deep into her cunt and fucked her again. As his prick massaged every part of her cunt, she sucked his tongue a little harder. After a few seconds, she began moving with him. As she did, she became more and more excited. She moved faster and faster.

Her cunt grew warmer and wetter as her body went onto autopilot. He moved his hands to her hips and thrust faster and faster. She felt him quiver and moved her body against his as fast as she could.

"Yes! Yes! Yes!" she moaned.

They moved faster and faster. She felt herself shake all over and fucked him as hard as she could.

She came first.

When she did, she leaned into him and sucked his tongue harder. She soon came again. As she did, she moved against him and cried out as she used her muscles to work his prick.

"Oooh yes! Yes!" she moaned as he fucked her.

After a few thrusts, she fucked him back. They quickly settled into a nice, long energetic rhythm that took their passions higher and higher. She sighed and moaned on each inward plunge of his hard prick. She clung to him and fucked him back just as hard as she savored their illicit tryst.

"Yes! I love it! Fuck me, Bart! Fuck me good!" she ranted.

His prick felt so good to her. So very good. When they came, they came together in one long, powerful super nova of an orgasm that left them gasping and sweating. She moaned and quivered as he spurted several lines of cum into her cunt.

"I love you, Bart!" she screamed as she came again.

Back at the house, Zoe sat on the sofa with her feet on the cushions and her thighs wide apart. She smiled up at Art and used her fingers to open her cuntlips.

"Fuck me," she said.

He got between her legs and slid his prick into her cunt. It felt moist and oh-so tight. She sighed happily as he went in deep and moved around inside of her. Then he fucked her with long, deep and easy strokes. Each stroke felt better than the last. She moaned and wrapped her arms around his shoulders as she moved with him.

"I'm yours, Art! I'm yours forever and ever!" she moaned.

They fucked—no made love—for a long time. Each time he felt himself start to come, he stopped to let it subside, then started fucking her again. She loved it, too. She loved the way he was taking his time to make sure she enjoyed it.

"Faster," she sighed. "Do it faster!"

They moved together perfectly now. Harder and harder. Zoe felt herself coming and threw her hips up at him as hard as she could. At the same time, she squeezed his prick with her cunt muscles and fucked him harder.

"Yes!" she cried as they both came at the same time.

They kissed as they kept fucking. Each hard thrust of his prick made her come again and again. It was just as she'd hoped it would be, too. He stayed hard and kept going as he filled her cunt with cum. Zoe had the perfect pussy and the sexiest body he'd ever plunge his dick into and she really knew how to use both.

"I love you, Art! Oh, God! How I love you!" she cried as she erupted again.

This time, she gripped his shoulders and fucked him as hard as she could while her entire body shook with pleasure. He held on for the ride until they were both spent and he fell on top of her.

They spend the next few minutes holding each other tightly and French kissing. She stopped and smiled up at him.

"From now on, I am your second wife," she said.

At the hotel, Rita ran her fingers over Bart's prick and teased the tip. They had finished fucking only a few minutes ago, but she wanted more. He smiled as she played with him. At the same time, he was moving his middle finger in and out of her slit.

"I love you, Rita," she said softly.

"Then take me, Bart! Make love to me!" she whispered.

His prick was straight, long and hard. She reached up and gave it several strokes, then let him go. He moved between her thighs and slid his prick into her all the way to his balls. She moaned and wrapped her arms and legs around him. She moaned louder as he fucked her.

They began moving together. Bart stuck his tongue into her mouth. She moved faster as they kissed. His prick felt so good now. So wonderfully good as it massaged every part of her cunt.

They fucked faster and faster. She thrust her hips up at him and screamed for more. Each time, she felt the knob of his prick slam into her walls. Each time it did, she shuddered with passion.

"Fuck me, Bart! Fuck me good!" she gasped as she started to come.

He sensed she was coming and fucked her faster and faster. She groaned and went over the top. She groaned louder when she felt his cum jet into her.

"I'm yours. I'm yours. Fuck me harder!" she begged as she continued coming.

They kept at it until Bart went limp and slipped out. She looked down at the river of cum oozing from her pulsing cunt and smiled.

"You're good at this," she said. "Real good."

"That's because you inspire me," he replied as he stroked her thigh. "I can't seem to get enough of you. Now that we've started this, I want to keep doing it."

"So do I. Whenever you want me, you know where to find me—and my pussy," she joked.

He pulled her to him and they kissed again. She opened her legs wider and let him touch her again. She felt her body shake all over as she held on tight. He stroked her clit faster and faster.

She came again and fell back with her thighs wide open. She saw that his prick was hard once again and smiled at him as he rammed it home.

"Aaahh, yes!" she sighed as her body shook with pleasure. "Ohhh, yes! Yes!"

They began moving together in a nice, steady rhythm again. She felt waves of pleasure surge through as they fucked and fucked and fucked. This time, they erupted together and he emptied a second good load into her cunt.

She beamed at him as she sat up. She felt incredibly well-fucked now.

"That was even better," she said.

She leaned over and licked his dick from balls to knob several times, then sucked it. Bart moaned. To her delight, it sprang back to life. She worked it with her hand until he was rock hard again and lay back down with her legs apart. She felt him enter her cunt and shivered slightly. He held her tight and began to fuck her again. She sighed and moved with him as she savored the way his prick moved in and out of cunt, which was still throbbing from her previous orgasm.

"Oooh, yes!" she sighed as she moved with him. "Fuck me!"

They fucked faster and faster. She matched his every thrust as she clung to him.

"More! Do it harder! Ohhh, yes!" she sighed.

Then she came again. As she did, she gripped his arms to steady herself. She gasped and moaned as she came and he kept fucking her and fucking her until he finally shot his final load into her hot, wet cunt. He eased out of her and sat back to catch his breath.

Back at the house, Art sighed happily as Zoe jerked him off. She took her time now. There was no need to hurry. She stuck her tongue out and ran it all over his swollen knob a few times. Art moaned and put his hand on her shoulder. She kept licking for a moment, then pushed half of his cock into her mouth.

She never really liked to suck cock. But Art's was different. She loved the way he tasted. She loved to suck it. She especially loved it when he came in her mouth and the way his cum felt as it slid down her throat.

Art really loved what she was doing, too. What man wouldn't? She wasn't just sucking his prick. She was actually making love to him with her mouth. And no one, he decided, could do that any better than her. She stopped and lay down on the bed with her legs dangling over the side. Art knelt and undid her shorts, then slowly pulled them off. Naked, she looked gorgeous. He kissed and licked his way up her inner thighs to the soft, brown patch between them. She was already quivering with anticipation. Her labia and clit were wet and swollen and her sexual perfume permeated the room.

She smiled lovingly at him.

"Eat me, darling," she whispered. "Make love to me."

Then she sighed deeply as Art's tongue entered her more-than-willing cunt. He was marvelous with his tongue. He knew when and where to lick and how to fire all of her sexual triggers.

She was so excited that she came within seconds. She threw her legs over Art's shoulders, gripped his hair and began humping his tongue with a wild abandon. She came again and again. So many times that she could barely breathe or speak.

She didn't have to. Her body did all the talking for her and it was screaming for more. Art got the signal loud and clear and kept licking her quivering, dripping snatch until his tongue began to ache.

"Enough! That's enough," Zoe gasped as she pushed his face away from her cunt. "Fuck me, Art. Please fuck me."

Her body was still trembling when Art took his place above her. He pressed his glans to her soft, moist labia then moved it up and down several times before easing into her. He went in slowly in order to get the feel of her tight, hot channel as it caressed his prick. She spread her legs as far apart as she could, then bent her knees. She gripped Art's shoulders and drove her hips upward until she felt the head of his prick touch the opening to her womb.

"Oh yes!" she sighed as Art began to move his hips in a circular motion.

At the same time, he thrust in and out of her cunt nice and slow. He felt her inner flesh hug his shaft tightly as he pulled out, then part again as he slid back in. Each time, she moved with him in perfect unison.

Art had fucked many women in his life, but no one's cunt felt as exquisitely sexy as hers. She was warm, tight and silky smooth and she could really use her inner muscles. He often felt as if her were making love with an angel. They were a perfect match.

That's why he was taking his time. This wasn't just sex. It was lovemaking at its best, with all of the emotional ties that went with the word. They made love gently, slowly and with a lot of passion. They matched each other stroke for stroke, thrust for thrust. Their lips met again. Art reached beneath her and put her right leg over his shoulder, then drove into her a little bit harder and faster. She emitted a loud moan and dug her nails into his back as his cock massaged her secret g-spot perfectly. She felt herself spinning out of control.

"Faster, Art! Do it faster," she begged. "Make me come!"

She closed her eyes and allowed the movements of Art's prick inside her cunt carry her away. She began crying out and gasping for air. She clawed at his back like a mad woman as an explosive series of orgasms raced through her body. She felt his prick jerk a few times, and then relaxed as Art emptied his seed into her sucking pussy. Like earlier, he pumped a large amount of cum into her love tunnel. Her body, which seemed to be suspended in time, eagerly accepted his seed, greedily making it one with her.

She always let Art come inside her. She always would.

After a few more deep thrusts, Art eased his half hard member out of her and rolled onto his back. His prick glistened with their combined love juices. She rolled on top of him and they kissed once again. It was a long, deep kiss that spoke volumes of their feelings for each other.

"I love you," she whispered.

"I love you," Art said.

Rita straddled Bart's face so he could eat her pussy while she sucked on his prick. After a few moments of this, Rita twisted her body so that she now sat on Bart's thighs. She moved her body upward as she grabbed his prick and guided it into her open cunt. Once there, she slowly lowered herself down until his entire length was buried deep of inside her. She stopped to savor the feel of it for a little while, the way it filled her so completely. It felt good, too. Maybe too good.

Wickedly good.

She wiggled her hips a little bit, and then bounced up and down nice and easy. She wanted this to be a nice, slow, deep fuck. One she could control. That's why she got on top. Bart didn't care about control. All he cared about at that moment was the warm, tight, silky cunt that was wrapped around his erect prick and the pretty woman it was attached to.

As Rita rode him easy, he reached up and played with her nipples. This sent waves of pleasure racing through Rita's body and caused her to ride him a little faster. Bart moaned and grabbed her behind. Then he thrust upward into her cunt as hard as he could. Rita quivered as his knob slammed into her womb and sent delicious sensations running all through her body...

"Yes!" she cried. "Fuck me, Bart! Harder!"

They moved faster and faster now, each matching the other's thrusts perfectly.

In and out.

Up and down.

Repeatedly until both were perspiring. Rita's head was back and she began making soft gurgling sounds as she rode his prick as fast as she could. Bart laid there and took it as she gave him one of the best fucks of his entire life.

"I'm coming!" Bart gasped after a while.

"Good," said Rita.

She rode him harder now, took his prick into her pussy deeper and deeper. His own thrusts grew erratic as he tried to hold back his orgasm.

It was to no avail.

Rita felt his cum spurting into her and sighed. She kept pumping and pumping as more and more of his seed emptied into her cunt. Bart grunted and fucked her harder as he continued coming. Rita matched him with equal vigor and a wild abandon that took his breath away.

"Yes! Oh God, yes!" she moaned.

There was no guilt this time. No second thoughts. Just raw, uncontrolled sex. When Rita came, she saw fireworks exploding all around her. She fell atop Bart's chest and lay still with his half erect member inside her cum-flooded channel. There was no sense moving. She knew that he'd be hard again real soon and she wanted to make sure she was still on top of the situation when he did. Five minutes later, she felt him getting hard inside her cunt and another wild ride ensued. This one lasted for several long, wonderful minutes. When Bart came again, his entire body shuddered as if every bit of energy he had left was being sucked right out of him and up into Rita's cunt. He seized her behind and rammed his prick into her as deep as he could, then unleashed a torrent of sticky cum which ran out of her cunt and down his prick to his balls.

Rita came at the same instant. She threw her head back and emitted a long, satisfied moan as she stopped in mid stroke to savor the sexual gusher that now overwhelmed her so completely. As the room spun around her, she tumbled off his prick and lay next to Bart gasping for air.

Bart propped himself up on his elbows and stared at his prick. It was still half-erect and glistened with both his cum and Rita's juices. He looked at Rita and smiled. She was on her back with her legs parted. He could see a stream of cum oozing from between her partially open labia and that her cunt hairs were sticky.

He nodded off to sleep for a few minutes only to be awakened by the feel of Rita's fingers on his prick as she jerked him off. When he was once again at full salute, Rita lay on her back. She bent her knees and threw her thighs open as she guided his prick into her pussy with one smooth motion.

"Again?" he asked.

"Again—and make it a real good one," she replied.

Bart did.

He fucked her for several minutes, using hard, deep strokes. They fucked for such a long time that their sides ached and sweat covered them from head to foot. They were nearing exhaustion now, but were far too horny to stop. Bart grabbed her ankles and pushed her legs backward until her thighs touched her breasts. This enabled him to fuck her even deeper. So deep, he swore that he was ramming his prick right into her womb a few times. Rita dug her fingers into his arms and cried out with pleasure. She'd been fucked like this before by Art, but Bart's longer and thicker prick was reaching places inside her pussy that no other prick ever had before. It was the deepest, hardest and most total fuck she ever had.

"Oooh yes! That's good! That's what I want! Fuck me!" she moaned.

Bart leaned forward and began fucking her faster. The sudden extra friction triggered something deep inside Rita's cunt. She exploded quickly and fell back with her arms akimbo, sobbing with pleasure.

"Yes! Oh YES! Fuck me, Bart! Fuck me!" she moaned as she came and came and came.

Bart quickly followed suit and emptied every last drop of cum his balls could produce deep into her quivering body. When his prick finally went limp, he slid off her and lay panting beside her on the bed.

"That was *unbelievable!*" Rita sighed.

"I could get used to this," Bart said.

"So could I. Maybe too used to it," Rita agreed. "This makes my pussy happy."

Bart laughed.

"Now what? Do we keep seeing each other?" he asked.

"Yes. I'd like that very much," she said.

"Me, too. For how long?' he asked as he held her tight.

"I don't know. Until we get tired," she suggested.

"What if we never get tired?' he asked. "Do we keep doing this forever?"

"Forever sounds nice right now, Bart," she replied as they kissed.

Zoe looked up at the ceiling fan spinning around and sighed dreamily. She had spent an entire weekend making love with the man she loved. She had given herself to him totally and he also held nothing back.

"This has been the best weekend of my entire life," she said. "In fact, it's perfect!"

"Yes it is," he said as he stroked her thigh. "It was kind of like a honeymoon, wasn't it?"

She giggled.

"This is a honeymoon, Art! I am you second wife now. I am yours now and forever. I wish I was young enough to have your baby. That would make it even more perfect!" she said. "How do you think Rita and Bart are doing?"

"I imagine that Bart's dick is deep inside Rita's pussy right now," he said.

Zoe opened her legs.

"And I want yours deep inside mine," she said softly as he entered her again.

When Rita got home late Monday evening, she was greeted at the door by a tired and barely dressed Zoe. Rita smiled and kissed her on the lips then they went to the sofa and sat down.

"I see you kept Art happy while I was with Bart," Rita said as she studied Zoe's partially open cunt.

"I sure did—and he really made me happy, too. Was it good?" Zoe asked.

"It was incredible! I think we fucked more than 10 times. Bart really knows how to make my pussy purr!" Rita said.

"Is he as good as Art?" Zoe asked. "I've already fucked Bart and I prefer making love with Art. I think that's because I'm crazy mad in love with him and always have been. This weekend felt like our honeymoon."

"So did my time with Bart! I lost count of the times he made me come. The only time we dressed was to go out and eat. It was a wonderful weekend!" Rita said as she leaned back.

Art came down and sat across from them. He smiled at Rita. She laughed and smiled back.

"I'm glad you had such a good time," he said. "I know me and Zoe sure did!"

"I told Bart that I'd like to keep seeing him," Rita said.

"That's good because Art and I are definitely going to keep making love every chance we get," Zoe said. "So we can both keep our affairs going. Are you and I still lovers?"

Rita patted Zoe's cunt.

"Forever," she said. "In fact, why don't you and I go away this weekend?"

"I'd love to!" Zoe said as they hugged.

Art laughed.

"I'm glad because I need to recuperate!" he said.

When Zoe left, Art and Rita showered together.

"Do you love Bart now?" he asked.

"Sort of—but not as much as I love you. Of course, that could change over time. Do you love Zoe?" she asked.

"In the same way as you love Bart," he said. "We can keep this going for as long as you want."

"How about indefinitely?" she asked.

"That works for me," he said.

Chapter Fifteen

Zoe and Rita had breakfast at their favorite diner the next day. Both were still up in the clouds over their weekends with their lovers.

"This is great," Zoe said. "I feel like Art and I are newlyweds now. There's no hiding it anymore. We are lovers and I plan to keep him. What about you and Bart?"

"I have to admit that I'm falling in love with him. I think about him all of the time and I miss him when we're apart.," Rita said.

"What about those other guys you've fucked? Are you gonna give them up and stay exclusively with Bart? Or are you still gonna play the field?" Zoe asked.

"I'm not sure. I really like fucking them, too. What about you?" Rita asked.

"I'm sticking only with Art—and you. That's all the good sex I'll never need. I still plan to steal Art from you so you'd better be careful," Zoe smiled.

Rita slid her hand along Zoe's inner thigh. Zoe parted her knees and smiled at her.

"I love you," she whispered. "I'll always love you."

Twenty minutes later, Zoe was seated on a loveseat with her long lovely legs draped over each arm. Rita knelt between them. Her tongue gently darting in and out of Zoe's petal-like cunt. Right after breakfast, they went to Rita's house. Without saying a word, Zoe had removed her shorts and positioned herself on the chair. The sight proved to be inspiring for Rita.

Even irresistible.

Rita kept licking away at Zoe's pussy eagerly. She loved its sweet, sweet taste and the softness of her womanly perfume. As Rita ate her, she fingered her own sopping cunt. She was very horny now. Spending time with Zoe always did that to her, always made her hungry for her pussy.

Zoe knew this and was only too happy to give herself to Rita any time she wanted her. She sat on the loveseat with her long lovely legs draped over each arm. Rita knelt between them. Her tongue gently darted in and out of Zoe's petal-like cunt.

"Oh yes, darling. Yes! Make love to me!" Zoe moaned as she came hard.

Rita sat back and wiped the love juices from her face and chin as she watched Joy come. It always took a long time for Zoe to recover from an orgasm and Rita loved to watch the lips of her pussy twitch as she calmed down.

Zoe watched as Rita stood up, her eyes on that shiny black triangle between her legs. Rita held out her hands. Zoe clasped them and sighed as Rita pulled her to her feet, then exchanged places with her.

As she beheld Rita's cunt, she started coming again. She came harder when she leaned over and slipped her tongue between Rita's soft pussy lips and tasted her sweetness.

Rita was so horny that she came almost instantly. She pulled Zoe's face into her cunt and wildly fucked her tongue as she erupted in a series of good, deep orgasms. When she managed to come back to Earth, she saw Zoe standing before her with one end of the double-headed dildo protruding from her cunt. She smiled and opened her legs as wide as she could.

Zoe eased the dildo into her and fucked her with a nice, easy rhythm. Rita sighed and moaned as she matched her every thrust. Zoe was a sweet, gentle lover and she concentrated on satisfying Rita. After about 20 good thrusts, Zoe turned on the vibrating unit. The sudden change caused Rita to convulse and come.

Very hard.

As she did, she fucked her back as fast and as hard as she could. A few seconds later, Zoe also climaxed and her movements and thrusts became wild and erratic. They kept this going until both had come a second time. Now totally spent, Zoe turned off the vibrator and pulled the dildo from her sopping cunt. Rita picked it up and licked her juices from it while Zoe watched and smiled.

"I love you, Rita. If you were a man, I'd marry you," she said. "Sex with you is very exciting."

"That's because I have such a beautiful partner," Rita smiled as she stroked Zoe's thigh.

Zoe sighed as Rita gently played with her bush. As far as she was concerned, Rita could touch her anywhere she liked and as often as she wanted.

Again their tongues merged, while Rita eased her fingers into Zoe's more than willing slit. Zoe moaned softly as Rita "fucked" her, then leaned over and swirled her tongue around Rita's left nipple. Each time they made love, it was more passionate, more adventurous.

Zoe slid her finger into Rita cunt and moved it back and forth several times. Rita groaned as they brought each other to the first climax of the day. After a brief rest to catch their breath, Zoe leaned over and slid her tongue into Rita's cunt. Rita threw her legs wide apart and pulled her into as she fucked her tongue. Zoe ate her until she erupted again and again. Rita arched her back and quivered all over as Zoe slid her fingers into her cunt again while she sucked her clit.

"Oooh, yes! I love you!" she cried as she came yet again.

Zoe stopped and laid down with her legs apart. Rita rolled over and returned the favor. As she licked Zoe's cunt, she eased a finger up into her asshole and gently moved it in and out. The combination of sensations threw Zoe over the edge. She bucked around crazily as she gripped Rita's hair. She came so many times, she began to see stars.

Rita stopped and they kissed again. Zoe smiled up at her.

"Fuck me," she whispered. "Make love to me."

Rita positioned herself so that her cunt rested on Zoe's. When she was sure it was right, she moved up and down and massaged Zoe's cuntlips with her own. Zoe sighed then picked up the beat. Before long, both were fucking wildly. When they came, they came together and their juices flowed into each other, making them one. They kept fucking until they had nothing left and slept in each other's arms.

Rita woke. She reached behind her pillow for the double headed dildo. Zoe smiled as Rita slid one end into her cunt, then moved between her thighs. Zoe opened her legs wide and groaned as Rita penetrated her and they soon became locked into a good, deep fuck.

Zoe gripped Rita's ass and fucked her back as hard as she could. This was an intense and powerful fuck. One of the very best she'd ever had.

"I love you! I love you! I love you!" she screamed as she trembled through one of the most powerful comes she'd ever felt.

Rita barely heard her. She was also caught up in her own intense orgasm and was having trouble maintaining her rhythm. She kept fucking Zoe for another minute or two, then fell to the side and lay gasping for air.

"Wow! That was great!" Zoe sighed as she looked up at the ceiling. "You're getting to be as good as Art."

Rita laughed.

"So are you!" she said as they kissed.

Zoe got between Rita's thighs and gently pressed her cunt against hers. Rita positioned herself so their clits and nipples touched, then smiled up at Zoe. After a quick kiss, Zoe began moving against Rita's body nice and easy. Each up and down movement caused their cunts to massage each other and made their nipples tingle deliciously. Zoe really loved to fuck her this way. It was gentler, sexier and far more intimate than using a dildo. And it was incredibly sensual. As they fucked, their cunts grew hotter and wetter. Rita opened her legs wider and moved with her.

Back and forth.

Faster and faster.

Rita sighed and moaned with each wonderful kiss of their cunts.

"I'm nearly there, Zoe," she said. "Oh, God! I love you!"

It didn't seem strange to hear Rita say that now. Nothing about their relationship seemed strange now. They were making love in a very true sense. Zoe began to tremble all over. Rita realized she was coming and fucked her faster. Seconds later, they both erupted and their cuntlips convulsed against each other as if they were actually kissing. As they did, they exchanged juices.

Rita opened her legs wide and moaned happily as she felt Zoe's love juices squirt into her cunt. She loved the way it felt. Zoe was coming in her. She was filling her pussy with cum and Rita was eagerly accepting it like she would do with any male lover. Zoe just kept fucking her nice and easy as she squirted more and more cum into Rita's cunt and wished she could make her pregnant. They kept fucking and coming again and again. Rita's body trembled in ecstasy as their labia caressed slowly and lovingly in what had become the most incredible fuck of their lives.

"I love you!" they both shouted at once.

They held each other and kissed again. Rita looked into Zoe's eyes and smiled.

"I'm yours, Zoe. I'm your forever and ever," she said softly.

"I love you," Zoe replied.

When Art got home late that evening, Rita and Zoe were sitting at the kitchen table drinking wine and giggling. Both were dressed in T-shirts and nothing else. The sight of the two of them gave him an erection. They smiled at him as they stood up.

"We've been waiting for you," they both said as they led him up to the bedroom.

When Zoe left later that night, she had cum deposits in both her ass and her cunt. So did Rita. They had managed to get him up several times and they'd just about fucked him to death.

Rita smiled as he staggered down the stairs and plopped onto the sofa. She sat next to him and he held her close.

"Which of us is better?" she asked.

"That's too close to call, Hon," he said. "You're different and you both know how to use your pussies to provide the most pleasure. Zoe is a bit more intense than you."

"I know. She can get really wild during sex," Rita said. "I'm too tired to cook tonight."

"Let's get dressed and go out for dinner," he said. "Pick a place."

"How about the Thai restaurant?" she suggested.

"That sounds perfect!" he replied.

Bart called Rita two days later.

"You didn't call me for two days," she teased.

"Hell, Rita. After last weekend, I could hardly walk. I needed a couple of days to recover. You are the absolute best lover I've ever had," he said.

She laughed.

"I've missed you," she said softly.

"Want to get together this Friday? I can get us a suite at the Adams Mark and we can make a real weekend out of it," he suggested.

"That sounds wonderful, Bart! I'll meet you in the lobby at five," she agreed.

"I can hardly wait! I'll see you then," he said as he hung up.

Bart grinned.

He could hardly believe this was happening. It had taken several weeks to get her to have sex with him and now, he felt almost empty when they were apart. He had fallen in love with Rita and it seemed like she felt the same way about him.

"You're an asshole, Tillman!" he told himself. "You're having an affair with a married woman and you don't want to stop. And the crazy thing is her husband knows and doesn't mind because he's fucking Zoe!"

Rita told Art about her plans with Bart.

"You're spending the entire weekend with him again? This must be serious," he said with a grin.

"It's as serious as your affair with Zoe. I've already told her and she said to tell you that she'll be here around five on Friday. I know you won't mind," Rita teased as she elbowed him.

"What about the other guys you've been having sex with?" he asked.

"I'm not sure. I really enjoy fucking Steve, so if he calls, I'll probably meet him somewhere. I just can't see myself limited to just you and Bart," she said.

"Whatever floats you boat, Hon," he smiled.

She told Art what she had planned. He laughed and phoned Zoe and asked her to come over that same night.

"Now, we'll both be busy," he said.

"And happy!" she added.

After dinner, Rita raced up to Bart's hotel room with him. He pulled her onto the bed and she fell next to him. He pecked at her earlobe and then licked his way down her neck as he undid the buttons of her blouse. Rita tried to struggle, but Steve batted her hands away and literally tore her light bra from her chest and tossed it onto the floor. As she lay there helpless, he swirled his tongue around each of her nipples. She soon felt her cunt tingling and allowed herself to relax while Bart undid her jeans and peeled them off her. He ran his hands all over her legs and stomach and even her behind until Rita became good and horny. Then he removed her panties.

"I love you, Rita," he said as he quickly undressed.

Rita closed her eyes as he ate her until she came. When she did, she gripped his hair and fucked his tongue until she came again. Bart stopped and moved between her open thighs. She smiled up at him and nodded as he entered her.

Bart did her slowly and his stroked were good and soft and deep. She moaned and sighed with each of them and moved with him. She soon wrapped her arms and legs around him and fucked him back with everything she had.

He leaned into her and fucked as hard as he could. Rita couldn't help herself. Her pussy had taken control once again and eagerly accepted Steve's massive cock. In fact, everything she did after that literally screamed "fuck me!"

Just when she was about to come, Bart fucked her harder. She quivers, moaned and came like she never did before. Her entire body trembled and she kept moving with him until both were bathed with sweat. He grunted and emptied his balls into her cunt. She moaned loudly and fucked him back as hard and as fast as she could. Another orgasm shot through her.

And another.

"Fuck me! Fuck me! Fuck me!" she cried as she threw her hips up at him.

"I'm gonna come again!" he grunted as he fucked her faster.

"Inside! I want to feel you come inside me!" she gasped.

Bart did exactly that. In fact, he came and came and came until it oozed out her cunt with each thrust of his prick. She just kept fucking back as hard as she could until her entire body went numb.

"I love you!" they both cried just before they fell asleep in each other's arms.

Rita was awakened a few hours later by the sensation of Bart's tongue moving over her newly-aroused clit. When he thought she was ready, he moved on top of her and slid his prick into her wet channel. This time, he fucked her nice and easy.

She smiled up at him and wrapped her arms and legs around his body, As before, Rita's libido took command of her body and she began to hump him back. She matched him stroke for delicious stroke, taking him deeper inside her body each time.

Before long, they merged into one warm fucking machine that moved in perfect unison. Rita had never had so much sex within a 24 hour period. Her body responded eagerly now and she soon came so hard, she felt as if her legs had been blown off. She felt Steve's cock jerk suddenly inside her cunt and humped him back hard. Steve groaned with pleasure as she worked his rod like no one ever did before. He pulled out until the head of his cock was only an inch or two from, her open cunt and released a long stream of cum. It splashed inside her quivering pussy and dribbled down between her cheeks.

To her delight, he was still rock hard...

While Rita was with Bart, Art and Zoe had dinner at a nearby bistro. She looked dreamily at him and smiled.

"What's on your mind?" he asked.

"I was just thinking how much I love you, Art. I'd love to steal you away from Rita," Zoe replied.

He smiled.

"Maybe you already have," he said as he took her hand and squeezed it. "You are a beautifully exotic and sexy woman with a great personality. In fact, I like everything about you. I always have. So maybe you've already stolen me."

She just about screamed with delight.

"Right now, Rita is lying on a bed letting another guy fuck her. As long as she keeps doing that, the way is clear for us to have a real romantic affair. I think this is something we've both wanted to do ever since we met," he said.

"I think so, too," she agreed. "You know she plans to spend the entire weekend with Bart again, right?" Zoe said.

"Uh-huh. And this weekend will belong to you and me. I was thinking about taking you for a nice long getaway soon. Maybe for a week? It will be sort of like a honeymoon," he said.

"That sounds wonderful! I'll go anywhere you want and spend as much time with you as you like. I'm yours now, Art. I'll always be yours," she said.

Chapter Sixteen

Rita got home early Monday afternoon looking totally spent but happy. When Art let her into the house, she kissed him on the lips and went into the living room where a half-naked Zoe lounged on the sofa. They both giggled like lovesick schoolgirls.

Rita looked at Art.

"Bart and I are going to spend next weekend at the hotel, too," she announced. "In fact, we'll probably spend at least two weekends each month together and we've talked about going away for a week's vacation. Is that okay?" she asked.

"That's interesting because I've suggested that exact same thing to Zoe," he replied.

"We're going on a honeymoon," Zoe said with a grin. "I told Art that he has two wives from now on—and you have nothing to say about it."

Rita frowned then laughed.

"Looks like we're all getting what we want," she said.

The next Friday evening, Rita arrived at the hotel with a small overnight bag. Bart met her in the lobby with a warm hug and kiss and they headed up to the suite he'd reserved. A bottle of champagne was in a bucket of ice on the table.

Bart smiled.

"I wanted to make this special," he said.

"Let's drink that later," she said as she took his hand and led him into the bedroom.

He watched as she slowly undressed. As she removed each article of her clothing, she did a slightly erotic "dance" that made his dick as hard as an iron rod.

Rita lay on the bed with her legs wide open as she rubbed her cunt. Bart undressed and walked over with his prick bobbing up and down. He smiled at her and climbed onto the bed.

As soon as he lay down, she grabbed his prick and slid it into her mouth. He let her suck it for a little while, and then he grabbed her ass and stuck his tongue into her pussy. She came first and began fucking his tongue while she sucked his prick harder. He popped moments later and emptied a good sized load of cum into her mouth. Rita hungrily lapped up most of it.

That's when she felt his tongue slide into her asshole.

"Ooohhh! That's nice," she cooed as he slid his tongue in deeper.

She shivered, then returned to sucking his prick. When she made it hard again, she slid off his face and went into an all-fours position.

"Fuck my ass, again! I need it!" she said.

He got behind her and eased his prick into her rear channel until his balls touched her cheeks. She gasped.

"That feels just about perfect," she said.

He grabbed her cheeks and started to fuck her nice and easy. She moaned and gasped with each in-thrust then began to move with him. Seconds later, she felt his prick spasm inside of her and squeezed him tight with her ass muscles. He kept fucking her until he'd pumped every last drop of cum he had into her fine, smooth ass. When he was finished, she rolled onto her back with her legs open wide.

He smiled and went down on her again. This time, he licked her clit as fast as he could until she erupted and rocked from side-to-side.

He laid still and watched her nipples bob up and down as she caught her breath. When she came back down, she smiled and kissed him.

Now, he was harder than ever. He pushed her legs as far apart as possible and slid his prick into cunt all the way to his balls. She wrapped her legs around his hips and closed her eyes as they began that slow, deep-penetrating fuck she loved. Now, he was as hard as could be. He pushed her legs as far apart as possible and slid his prick into cunt all the way to his balls. She wrapped her legs around his hips and closed her eyes as they began that slow, deep-penetrating fuck she loved.

When she neared another orgasm, she fucked him back as hard as she could. Bart caught her signals and did the same, determined to make this another deep, simultaneous explosion.

He did.

"I love you, Bart!" she screamed as she came. "I love you!"

"I love you, too," he whispered as he emptied his cum deep inside Rita's cunt.

Zoe arrived wearing her usual mini skirt and T-shirt. As soon as Art let her in, she threw her arms around his neck for a long, hot kiss that gave him an erection. They walked over to the sofa and sat down.

Zoe smiled.

Art grabbed her and stuck his tongue into her mouth. Again their kiss lingered. Again she felt his hand sliding up her thigh. This time, she parted her knees and allowed Art to massage her crotch. After a few seconds, her legs opened even wider. This enabled Art to slip a couple of fingers past her panties and deep into her wet, sucking cunt.

"My God!" she sighed as she fell back against the sofa.

"I'm yours, Art," she said softly. "Fuck me."

He picked her up and carried her upstairs to the bed. This time, he stripped her completely. Then he stripped and climbed in with her. He kissed his way down her body and stopped to admire her cunt once again. He licked her slowly, until Zoe grew half-crazy with lust and begged to get laid. Instead, he grabbed her ass and buried his tongue even deeper in her quivering snatch. At the same time, he eased one of his fingers into her and moved it in and out as fast as he could.

Zoe exploded.

Her orgasm was so powerful; she thought that the lower half of her body was melting away. As she lay there trembling, Art pushed her legs apart and plunged his cock into her deep and hard. This time, Zoe wrapped her arms and legs around him and they proceeded to fuck like two rabbits. All the while, Zoe kept coming and coming. She was completely lost in a sexual fog. All she cared about was that huge prick moving in and out of her eager body.

She was his now.

His personal slut.

She fucked him as hard as she could while begging him for more and more. She loved the way his prick felt inside of her. She loved the way it massaged and stretched her cunt with each delicious stroke. She arched her back and came again. As she did, she gripped his arms and fucked him as fast as she could. Art pulled out at the last second. He took her right hand and wrapped her fingers around his prick. It was slippery with Zoe's juices. Somehow, she managed to jerk him off nice and easy. After a few strokes, he started firing line after sticky line of cum all over her belly, chest and cunt. She worked his cock until it shrunk from her grasp. She looked down at herself and laughed.

"You sure know how to use that thing of yours," she said.

"Fucking you inspires me," Art replied. "I'd love to do this with you every day."

"Well, I'm not going to stop you," she smiled.

Art kissed his way down her body. Along the way, he stopped to lick and suck each of her taut nipples, and then continued to her navel where he lingered a bit before continuing to the Promised Land. By then, Zoe was on fire. Art practically devoured her pussy. She was so turned on; she exploded in a series of sharp orgasms within one minute and wildly humped his tongue. He then replaced his tongue with his middle finger and teased her g-spot. Her next orgasm was huge. Zoe literally screamed with pleasure. She saw stars and rockets and began quivering uncontrollably as he continued to rub her most sensitive spot.

"Yes! Yes! Take me higher, Art! I'm all yours! For God's sake, fuck me!" she cried.

Art got between her thighs, positioned his cock against her trembling slit, and slowly penetrated her. Zoe groaned and dug her nails into his shoulders as he went in as deep as he could. Just as he thought, she had the tightest most wonderful pussy he'd ever been in. He stood still for a few seconds to savor the way her warm flesh felt around his cock, then he began a slow, in and out movement.

Zoe let him set the rhythm, and then matched him thrust-for-thrust. It was a nice, prolonged and deep fuck. To her, it was the most incredible fuck of her life. When they came, they came together.

After a short rest, he mounted her again. This time, they moved slowly so they could savor each delicious thrust. Zoe tightened her cunt muscled around his prick as she thrust back at him. After several minutes, they came again. This time, it felt even better.

"I love you!" she screamed. "I'm all yours forever and ever! I love you!"

She was in love. It was nothing like she'd ever felt before. She wanted do sing and dance and whirl around—everything. She felt light and happy and excited. Those feelings double when she was with him, too.

She wasn't just fucking him.

She was making love with him and he with her. It felt so right. So wonderfully perfect. And she was all his.

They moved faster and faster until they both came at once. It was a deep, strong, warm and exciting simultaneous orgasm that ended with them collapsing into each other's arms.

"I love you, Zoe" he said softly. "I truly love you."

No words had ever made her feel so happy.

Rita and Bart stopped to rest. They went back into the other room where he popped open the champagne and poured them each a glass. He clinked his against hers.

"To us," he said.

"To us," she replied.

Rita beamed.

She realized that she had fallen for Bart in a big way. They were definitely having an affair and she wouldn't hesitate to make it an exclusive one. Bart was funny, charming and handsome and had a touch of roguishness that appealed to her more adventurous side. In many ways, they were a near perfect match—especially in bed.

"I never expected to actually fall in love with you, Rita, but I did. I think about you every moment we're apart. If you weren't married, I'd be down on one knee putting a diamond ring on your finger right now. I'm still having trouble wrapping my mind around the fact that your husband knows about us," he said.

"I don't think he minds as long as he gets to have sex with Zoe. I'm a bit jealous of her, too, because she really wants to steal him from me and you know how good she is in bed!" Rita giggled.

"She's nowhere near as good as you, Rita. Nobody is," he said.

"Thanks. You're terrific, too," she said as they kissed again.

"Now what, Rita? Where do we go from here?" he asked.

"Wherever this takes us, Bart. Wherever you want to go," she said.

"How about we go to dinner?" he asked.

"Can we just get room service instead? I don't feel like getting dressed right now…"

After a short rest, Zoe slid Art's prick into her mouth and sucked away until it was straight and hard. She smiled at him and laid back with her legs wide apart.

"Fuck me again, Art," she said softly. "Make love to me."

He moved between her thighs. She opened her legs wide and bent her knees. Then she felt him enter her. She moaned and pulled him into her. His prick felt warm and hard.

Exciting.

He moved in and out gently. After a few strokes, she moved with him. They were fucking now. She was actually being fucked by a man for the first time in her life and she was loving it.

They moved faster and faster together. His strokes her deep, hard and steady. She was breathless now as she neared her orgasm. They fucked harder and she began to tremble as the first waves of pleasure raced through her body.

He was loving this, too.

Her cunt was good and tight and she really knew how to move with him.

Faster and faster.

"OOooh yes! Ohh fucking yes!" she cried as she came.

She dug her fingers into his arms and fucked him back as hard as she could. And she kept coming and coming.

"Fuck me! Fuck me! I love it! Fuck me!" she cried.

He didn't hear her. He was too busy filling her cunt with his cum as he, too, erupted. He came a lot, too.

So much, that his prick now made squishing sounds with each thrust and some of his cum began running out of her cunt and down between her ass cheeks.

"More! More! Fuck me!" she cried as one last, explosive orgasm took her over the edge.

He went with her.

When they came back to Earth, she looked down at the river of white oozing from her throbbing slit and smiled.

"You came a lot. You filled my entire pussy," she said. "In fact, anytime you want me, I'm yours. All yours."

That's when she realized that he had another erection. She laid back with her legs wide apart and sighed deeply when he entered her.

Since he'd already come—a lot—this fuck lasted much longer. This time, he moved slower in order to really savor the feel of her cunt as it hugged his prick. His strokes were deeper and gentler.

She thrust her hips up at him and matched him stroke for stroke. It felt so damned good. Better than the first one.

"I love it. I love it. Fuck me, Art. Fuck me good," she moaned as they moved together faster and faster until they came together in one, good, powerful orgasm.

"Yes! Yes! Yes! Yes!" she screamed as they fucked harder.

His prick pistoned in and out of her cunt, spurting cum into her with each inward thrust as he flooded her again.

"Holy shit! That was great!" she said when she caught her breath. "How does it feel to have two wives, Art? Because that's what you have right now and neither of us are going away any time soon."

"It feel great, Zoe. You are the best lover I ever had, too. You're so tight and you hold nothing back when you make love, so I don't either," he said. "Do you and Rita make love the same way?"

"Oh yes! We go all out to please each other. I'm crazy mad in love with both of you. Maybe I should move in with you to make things easier?" she said.

"I don't think I could handle having a three-way every night!" he said with a laugh as he stroked her cunt. "But I could do this with you forever."

Rita lay on her back and sighed as Bart explored the folds of her cunt with his tongue. Each pass of his tongue across her swollen clit made her quiver and moan. When he knew she was close to coming, he licked her clit faster and faster. Rita gasped and raised her hips off the bed. Then she grabbed his head and fucked his tongue as she came and came.

Bart got between her thighs. She bent her knees and smiled, then trembled as he slid his prick deep into her cunt. She closed her eyes and relaxed as he began fucking her nice and easy. It felt nice, she decided.

Very nice.

After a few good thrusts, she wrapped her legs around him and began to fuck him back. Bart increased the tempo. Rita moaned, dug her fingers into his shoulders and moved with him as he fucked her harder and harder. They immediately began moving together. This time, the rhythm was faster and a little bit harder.

"Oooh, yes! Yes! Fuck me, Bart! Fuck me good!" she moaned

They fucked faster and faster. Rita gasped, arched her back and cried out as she came. It was a good, deep orgasm, too. One that shook her entire body.

"Yes! I love it! Fuck me!" she cried

He leaned into her and fucked her as fast as he could. Rita moaned and gripped his arms as she matched him stroke for stroke. Then she came again.

Bart did, too.

He filled her cunt with every drop of cum he had. Then they kissed and caressed each other for a long time. Bart started out with another French kiss while he stroked her cunt and she pumped his prick. He kissed his way down her chest and sucked and licked each nipple. By then, Rita's body was on fire. Bart eased his middle finger into her slit and "fucked" her nice and fast. Since she was so close to the edge already, she arched her back, emitted a deep moan and came.

Hard.

As she came, she pumped his prick a little faster. As another wave of warm, intense pleasure rippled through her sweaty body, she let go of his prick. Bart moved and positioned himself between her open thighs. She opened her legs as far as she could and bent her knees. Bart slid into her all the way and ground it into her so it massaged every part of her cunt. Rita shivered and moaned at the delicious sensations.

She threw her body up at him.

"More! I love it! More!" she moaned as he kept doing it.

He did it slowly in order to give her the most pleasure. She quivered and moaned louder then Bart then began moving in and out. This, too, he did nice and slow and his thrusts were deep and strong. Rita shivered all over and fucked him back.

It was a nice, easy rhythm that sent waves of pleasure through her body and she realized she was enjoying the very best sex of her entire life. In fact, this was positively magical and she fucked him faster and faster.

Bart picked up the pace.

Rita matched it with enthusiasm.

"Oooh yes! Yes! Fuck me, Bart! Fuck me!" she cried. "Make love to me!"

Bart slid his prick all the way in and moved it in a circle each time. Rita quivered and used her inner muscles to squeeze him several times. Bart moaned. It felt exquisite. Then he began to move faster. Rita moaned on each thrust then began to fuck him back. They soon fell into a good, easy rhythm. Rita wrapped her knees around his hips and smiled up at him.

"That's it, Bart! Fuck me!" she said. "That feels so nice. So nice!" she moaned. "Fuck me harder now!"

Bart did as she asked. He thrust into her faster and faster. Rita quickly matched him thrust for thrust.

"Oooh yes! Yes! That's the way I like it! Fuck me!" she cried. "Use my pussy! Make it yours!"

They kept at it for a few more good thrusts. Then Rita came.

Hard.

As she did, she fucked him faster.

"Yes! Yes! I love it! I love it!" she screamed

Bart held off as long as he could, then rammed his prick all the way into her and erupted. He came so much and so hard that he nearly passed out. Rita kept milking his prick with her cunt muscles until she could barely move. He fell next to her and gasped for air as he came back down to Earth.

"My God! This is fantastic! I never fucked so much in my life!" he finally said. "Do you fuck Art like this?"

"Most of the time," she said with a smile. "I admit that I'm giving you a little extra because I know you're doing the same. Your dick feels so perfect to me and you make me so good."

"Do you do this with your girlfriend?" he asked.

"We do different things than this, but our lovemaking can become very exciting and intense," she said as she stroked his prick. "Do you think you can do it again?"

"Well, maybe—if you make me hard again by sucking my dick," he suggested.

She smiled then slid his prick into her mouth...

After another round of foreplay and a good, easy "69", Zoe turned over and got into an all-fours position. Art caressed her beautiful, firm behind and ran his fingertips along her crack. Zoe quivered as he massaged her rear opening.

"You have the most exquisitely sexy ass," he said.

"Do it now, Art. Fuck me in my ass—just like you always wanted," Zoe almost begged.

He got behind her and licked her asshole. She moaned as she felt his tongue move inside of her and nearly came on the spot. When he was finished licking her, he got behind her. Then he placed his hands on her behind and spread her cheeks apart.

"Do it, Art! Fuck me good!" Zoe said with a trembling voice. Art wouldn't be the first man to use her this way. She'd already been done this way by others. The last time felt rather nice, so she decided it was about time to let Art do her there. She felt his knob press against her sphincter and gritted her teeth as it slid inside.

Art's prick went in easier than the last two had. And he was gentler with her. She felt him go in all the way to his balls.

"Ahh! Yes!" she moaned as she shoved her behind back at him and squeezed his prick with her muscles.

Art groaned. She felt so deliciously tight that he almost came. Somehow, he managed to fight this off and, after a few moments, began to screw Zoe nice and easy. He wanted to take his time now, to really feel the way her rear channel caressed his prick on each in and out movement. Zoe's asshole felt exquisitely tight, wonderfully erotic. And it hugged his prick perfectly with each and every thrust.

Zoe moaned and shivered as he fucked her. His thrusts were slow and deep and he took care not to hurt her. Her ass belonged to him now. Everything of hers belonged to him and she knew that it would always be like this.

"I love you, Art! Oh God, how I love you!" she sighed as the delicious sensations rippled through her entire body.

To Zoe, Art's prick felt perfect inside her. It didn't stretch her like others had. Instead, it massaged her. It made love to her. She felt herself soaring toward what promised to be an explosive orgasm.

"Harder! Fuck me harder! Faster!" she gasped as she began to tremble.

From years of experience, Art realized she was about to come. He began moving in and out as fast as he could, trying to time it so they'd come together. He wanted this one to be perfect…memorable.

And it was. They came as one. They kept coming, too. Art came so much that his cum drizzled out of Zoe's ass and ran down the backs of her thighs. But she was oblivious to this as one good, hard orgasm after another rippled through her lean, sexy body. She fell face down on the bed with Art on top of her, his throbbing prick still deep inside her asshole. It was the perfect end to a perfect day.

Rita sat down on the edge of the bed. He walked over and dangled his prick before her. She reached up and explored it with her fingers, running them from his balls to the glistening, dark knob. She wrapped her fingers around it and gave him several easy pulls, which only made him longer and harder.

"I love you," she said as she sucked the knob.

They several delicious minutes exploring each other with their fingers and kissing. She shivered as he sucked each of her nipples then licked his way down to her hot open cunt. As he did, he shifted so he straddled her face and his cockhead touched her lips. She swirled her tongue all over his knob then grabbed the shaft and slid it halfway into her mouth while he ran his tongue all over her cunt. When she felt his tongue slide into her, she started to suck away.

They 69'd for few more minutes, and then shifted again. He got between her thighs and she opened them wide and bent her knees.

"Fuck me!" she said as she willingly accepted it into her hungry cunt.

He began fucking her with long, easy strokes. Taking his time to enjoy the way her cunt felt. She held his arms and moved with him. His prick felt good inside her. And the longer they fucked, the more Rita enjoyed it. She sighed and moaned with each thrust as her body raced towards what promised to be an incredible climax.

Rita came first. As she did, she fucked him faster and trembled all over. He kept going as hard as he could. Then, just before he came, he pulled out and fired several lines of cum on her writhing body. While she was still up in the air, he eased his prick back into her. This time, he fucked her hard and fast. The change thrilled her. She wrapped her arms and legs around him and fucked him back as hard as she could. Each deep, hard thrust caused her to shiver as one mini-orgasm after another rippled through her. She arched her back and screamed as she came. She fell with her arms akimbo and moaned happily as he continued to hammer away at her in what seemed to be the longest, most intense fuck of her entire life.

His thrusting began to grow erratic. Rita realized he was about come. She gripped his waist and fucked him with everything she had left. He groaned loudly and buried his prick as deep into her cunt as he could. Rita felt his cum gush into her and came again. They kept at it for a few more unsteady thrusts.

When she felt his cum jet into her, she screamed with pleasure and gripped his prick with her cunt muscles. He moaned as she humped him harder and faster. He felt her come again and again. She collapsed with her arms akimbo and smiled up at him.

He leaned over and gave her another long, deep kiss.

"Each time with you feels better and better," he said. "I wish we could be together forever."

"So do I, Bart. You do things to me. Wonderful things," she said. "We can't be together forever but my husband said that as long as we keep doing it, he'll keep fucking Zoe. So let's make this last a long, long time!"

Bart laughed and held her tight...